# PRAISE FOR SIMON TOLKIEN

"In epic fashion worthy of his namesake, Tolkien crafts a remarkable novel of an American boy swept up by love and circumstance and cast into the crucible of the Spanish Civil War. Intense, vivid, and moving."
—Mark Sullivan, bestselling author of *Beneath a Scarlet Sky* and *All the Glimmering Stars*

"[A] delight to read and deserves the success [he] will surely achieve."
—*The Washington Post*

"Simon Tolkien knows how to keep a story moving, and he does it well."
—NPR

"Written with great surety and absolutely compelling."
—*Booklist*

"Tolkien . . . proves himself worthy—and then some—of his literary pedigree."
—*Richmond Times-Dispatch*

# THE ROOM OF LOST STEPS

# THE ROOM OF LOST STEPS

A NOVEL

THEO STERLING: VOLUME 2

## SIMON TOLKIEN

LAKE UNION
PUBLISHING

Published by Lake Union Publishing, Seattle

www.apub.com

Amazon, the Amazon logo, and Lake Union Publishing are trademarks of Amazon.com, Inc., or its affiliates.

EU product safety contact:
Amazon Media EU S. à r.l.
38, avenue John F. Kennedy, L-1855 Luxembourg
amazonpublishing-gpsr@amazon.com

ISBN-13: 9781662528651 (hardcover)
ISBN-13: 9781662528668 (paperback)
ISBN-13: 9781662528675 (digital)

Cover design by Shasti O'Leary Soudant
Cover image: © Sueddeutsche Zeitung Photo / Alamy; © Jag_cz, © Dmitr1ch / Shutterstock
Interior image: Maps by Catherine Howley

Printed in the United States of America

First edition

*For Sadie and Roxanne, my faithful companions who helped me
with "the work" every step of the way*

# PREFACE

This novel continues the story of Theo Sterling from where it left off in Andalusia in the spring of 1936 at the end of *The Palace at the End of the Sea*. The action now moves to Barcelona and the events surrounding the July army rebellion in which Theo becomes caught up. Afterward, he goes on to participate in the Spanish Civil War, which broke out following the rebellion, and his experiences both in Barcelona and on the battlefields around Madrid in 1937 determine the course of his coming-of-age journey.

As the political and military history of Spain in the 1930s can seem complex and challenging to a reader unfamiliar with the period, I have provided a short timeline to explain the sequence of events and how the political parties and people that appear in the novel participated in them. The timeline follows this preface, and I urge readers to refer back to it for clarification if they become confused at any point by the narrative.

There are also four maps that appear in the novel. The first, at the beginning of chapter 5, illustrates the location of the streets, cafés, churches, etc. that Theo visits on July 19, 1936, the day of the army rebellion in Barcelona; the second, at the beginning of chapter 7, identifies other Barcelona locations that are significant in the story; the third, at the beginning of chapter 11, shows the dividing line between Republican and Fascist territory in January 1937 and includes towns and battlefields that feature in the novel; and the fourth, at the beginning of chapter 19, is a sketch map of the Battle of Brunete in July 1937. I hope that these maps will help my readers to understand the relevant events.

*The Room of Lost Steps* is a fiction set within real history. I have tried throughout to portray historical events in Spain as accurately as possible, so that my readers can share the experience of the men and women who lived through those extraordinary times. Sometimes this history can appear stranger than fiction. But that is how it was, and the reader should approach the text on the basis that nothing is invented other than the introduction of fictional characters into the historical narrative. In this context, real historical people appear side by side with fictional ones, and a short note on characters at the end of the book provides further biographical information about these persons.

Simon Tolkien

December 2024

שנ

# TIMELINE

The purpose of this timeline is solely to elucidate events in this novel. It does not seek to provide a history of the Spanish Civil War as a whole.

## 1931

April 14—The Second Spanish Republic is proclaimed; King Alfonso XIII goes into exile; Catalonia is granted the status of a semiautonomous province.

June—A left-wing coalition wins the general election and begins to implement a program of economic and social reform.

## 1933

November 19—A coalition of right-wing parties defeats the divided Left in the general election. Thereafter, the new government reverses many of the reforms enacted by the previous one.

December 25—Lluís Companys becomes president of Catalonia.

## 1934

October—An uprising of left-wing workers, including Anarchists, in Asturias Province, is brutally suppressed by Moroccan troops and the Spanish Foreign Legion commanded by General Franco.

# 1936

February 16—The Popular Front, a broad left-wing coalition, wins the general election. Thereafter, army leaders including General Franco begin plotting the overthrow of the new government.

July 17–20—A military rebellion begins in Spanish Morocco and spreads to mainland Spain. It's defeated following street fighting in Barcelona and Madrid, but succeeds in other cities, including Seville and Zaragoza. The rebels call themselves Nationalists, but their opponents refer to them as Fascists.[1]

July 28—German Junker airplanes begin the airlift of the Fascist Army of Africa commanded by General Franco from Morocco to Seville.

## July onward—

Germany and Italy start to provide extensive aid to the Fascists. This continues throughout the Civil War.

In Barcelona, Companys remains as president of Catalonia, but the Anarchists and other left-wing parties control the city. Revolutionary workers take control of businesses and public utilities and collectivize them.

## August—

---

1    The term *Fascists* is used instead of the term *Nationalists* throughout the timeline because *Fascists* is the term that appears in the novel, where the story is told from a Republican viewpoint. *Nationalists* would be the more historically correct designation, but the purpose of the timeline is to assist readers to understand the novel, and this consideration has therefore been given priority.

The Army of Africa begins its bloody march up from Seville to Madrid; on the fourteenth there are mass killings in Badajoz after the Fascists capture the town.

Britain, France, Germany, Italy, and the Soviet Union agree to a policy of nonintervention in Spain, but it is observed only by Britain and France.

September 29—The Soviet Union agrees to send arms to the Spanish Republic.

October—International Brigade volunteers begin to arrive in Spain to fight for the Republic; the German Condor Legion begins air operations in support of the Fascists.

November 6—The Republican government is evacuated from Madrid to Valencia.

November 7 onward—A Fascist attack on Madrid is repelled by the International Brigades and people's militias, including the Communist Fifth Regiment; the twenty-eight-month siege of Madrid begins.

November 19—The Anarchist leader Buenaventura Durruti is killed while helping to defend Madrid.

# 1937

February 6–27—The Battle of Jarama: a Fascist attempt to cut off Madrid by seizing the road linking the city to Valencia, is thwarted by the Republican army that includes the International Brigades.

February 21—France closes its border. Foreign volunteers can now enter Spain from France only by illegally crossing the Pyrenees on foot at night.

February 27—The American Lincoln Battalion of the International Brigades commanded by Captain Robert Merriman suffers more than three hundred casualties, including 136 deaths, in a futile attack on the last day of the Battle of

Jarama. Among the casualties are untrained men who arrived at the front only the previous evening.

April 26—The German Condor Legion bombs Guernica.

May 3–7—Street fighting takes place in Barcelona between the counterrevolutionary Communists (loyal to Stalin) and Catalan government forces on one side and the revolutionary Anarchists and the POUM (a dissident Marxist party opposed to Stalin) on the other. The fighting ends after Republican troops sent from Madrid and Valencia take control of the city.

June onward—Communist secret police conduct a witch hunt against the POUM and the Anarchists in Barcelona, and Communist prisons known as *checas* appear all over the city.

June—The Lincoln Battalion is withdrawn after spending four months in trenches on the Jarama front.

July 6–26—The Battle of Brunete: The Republicans launch a large-scale offensive against the Fascists west of Madrid. The Republican army that includes the International Brigades suffers twenty-five thousand casualties, and the battle ends in stalemate.

# 1938

November 15—A farewell parade of the International Brigades takes place in Barcelona before they leave Spain.

# 1939

January 26—The Fascists' capture of Barcelona leads to a mass flight of Republican refugees to the French frontier.

March 27—The Fascists occupy Madrid, and the war ends.

## 1939–1975

Franco rules Spain as dictator. Following his death on November 20, 1975, Spain transitions to a parliamentary democracy under King Juan Carlos I.

# PART ONE

## BARCELONA

## JULY 1936

It was the best of times, it was the worst of times, it was the age of wisdom, it was the age of foolishness, it was the epoch of belief, it was the epoch of incredulity, it was the season of Light, it was the season of Darkness, it was the spring of hope, it was the winter of despair.

—*Charles Dickens, A Tale of Two Cities*

# 1

## SITGES

As spring turned to summer, Theo wandered his stepfather's house in Los Olivos, alone with his memories. His mind kept returning to that never-to-be-forgotten Sunday as he retraced his steps from the church to the stone calvary at the entrance to the village, walking behind the statue of the Virgin on her golden throne. He remembered her meeting with her risen son, the sheaf of barley in his hand, and the sound of the church bells up above. The beat of the drums, the rifle shots, the wild taratantara of the trumpets celebrating a resurrection to which even an unbeliever like himself could not be indifferent. But then the murder: the invisible thrust of the blade right there amid the joy and the glory, and fat Pedrito stretched out on the ground, staring lifeless up at the sun, his crimson blood seeping out over the starched white of his shirtfront.

Theo remembered the robe and hood hanging in the tree, the sharp press of the cobblestones into the soles of his feet as he ran up through the empty streets and squares, and the beat of his heart as he stretched every sinew of his body to get to her before she left the village forever.

He'd got there in time. Enough to see the blood on Primitivo's hands as he held his horse's reins, enough to witness the ecstatic look in Maria's eyes, and to feel the touch of her finger on his face as she leaned down to him from her saddle. *"Don't forget me!"* she'd told him.

He couldn't even if he had wanted to. It had been different during the long months in England and later in the village when Maria had been immured in the convent in the North. Despite his best efforts to keep her vivid in his mind, she had faded, becoming more an idea than a living person, and the lock of her hair a relic of a past he couldn't touch.

But now everything had changed. The meeting in the lane had lasted less than a minute, but its effect on him had been like an electrical charge. He didn't even need to close his eyes to see her face, hear her voice, feel the touch of her hand. He thought of her constantly and of Primitivo, who had saved her from a foul marriage when he couldn't. The boy was vicious; if Theo hadn't known that before, he knew it now. Primitivo hadn't needed to kill Pedrito. He'd done it because he wanted to, and because he knew the effect it would have on Maria.

The murder was the ultimate expression of the Anarchists' "propaganda of the deed." Death at Easter; religious parade transformed into stampeding terror; the arrogant cacique and Alvarez, his sidekick, struck to the heart. It was an act of grand theater and showed imagination and daring that Theo hadn't credited Primitivo with possessing.

And afterward, to cap it all, the killer had run off with his victim's intended bride. Vanished into the ether without a trace. The Civil Guard had tracked them through the mountain villages, but after that the trail had gone cold. Impatient for results, Don Fadrique and Maria's father had hired their own detectives, who had searched as far as Barcelona, but the bloodhounds found no scent, even though they were convinced that the city was the fugitives' likely destination. For decades, the starving braceros had been leaving the Andalusian countryside for the Catalan capital, hoping to find work in the mills and factories. They had taken their Anarchist creed with them, and the city was now the home of the CNT, the Anarchist trade union. It provided a refuge and support system for Anarchist outlaws who could disappear into the teeming backstreet tenements.

Theo didn't need to guess at Maria's and Primitivo's whereabouts. He *knew* they were in Barcelona, because Maria had told him that that was where they were going. He reminded himself that she had trusted him, told him that he was "one of us," but that was cold comfort if he could not follow her. And how could he do that when he had no money for the enterprise and his mother had become so nervous since the murder that she started to panic if he was gone from the house for more than a few hours?

Like it or not, he was reliant on his stepfather for financial support, and he couldn't ask him for help without telling him what he intended. Unless he lied, but he couldn't bring himself to do that. Not after all that had passed between them. He lived in dread of the day when Andrew would ask about the watch that he had given to Maria.

So he stayed where he was, tortured with an aching jealousy and sense of loss, made worse by having no one to confide in. He missed Antonio and he missed Saint Gregory's. The school had given him structure and purpose, whereas now the hours stretched out interminably, offering him no distraction from his pain. Only running helped. Pounding the paths and roads in the early morning before the sun rose too high and sent him home, he could forget himself, at least for a while.

It wasn't just Theo; everyone was restless. Night and day, the villagers argued and speculated. In the cafés where frenzied radio announcers broadcast news of violent clashes breaking out on city streets all over Spain, and in the church where Elena went every day to hear Don Vincente calling down the fires of heaven to punish the godless Reds. Everywhere he went, Theo could feel the festering hatred and division, hanging like the heat in the still, stagnant early-summer air.

He felt trapped. As if he were locked up in an airless room from which he had no means of escape, until a day came when the door unexpectedly opened and everything that he wanted seemed to drop down into his outstretched hand.

Since Pedrito's murder, Andrew had remained in the village, unwilling to leave Elena, who had become more obdurate than ever in her determination to stay put. But now something had to give. Strikes and industrial unrest were jeopardizing Andrew's business interests in Barcelona, and he knew he had to go there to deal with the problems in person.

"I can't let this go any longer," he told Elena at lunch one day in June. "And I don't want to leave you here alone. Not with everything that's happening. Barcelona is a beautiful city, and it's a crying shame that you've never seen it. I didn't marry you with the intention of keeping you holed up in a remote village halfway up a mountain with Don Vincente and a group of gossiping black widows for company. Hiding your light under a bushel."

"I like my bushel," Elena said tartly.

"No, you don't," he shot back. "The atmosphere here is toxic and you know it. You need a change. It'll be good for you. And for all of us. It isn't doing Theo any good sitting here with nothing to do all day. You'd like to go to Barcelona, wouldn't you, Theo?"

"Yes. More than anything," said Theo fervently, shocked into candor by his heart's desire suddenly being offered to him on a plate.

"I don't want to go," said Elena, clenching her small hands and pushing out her chin with that look of childlike defiance that Theo knew so well.

"You're just saying that because you're nervous of trying something new," said Andrew. "But this isn't like going to London. We can come back as soon as I've finished my business, which shouldn't take much more than a week. And once you're there, you won't want to leave. Barcelona is magical at this time of year. In the mornings, you wake up to the pealing of a hundred church bells, and in the afternoons, you can go shopping in the Passeig de Gràcia, which makes Oxford Street look shabby and gray, and in the evenings we'll go to the opera on the Ramblas, and you and Theo can go to the seaside too. At Sitges, the sand is golden brown and the sea is . . ." Andrew stopped, out of breath, as he searched for the right jewel to compare in color to the Mediterranean just south of Barcelona.

And Elena laughed in spite of herself, unable to resist her husband's enthusiasm, which made Andrew laugh too. "Say yes," he pleaded, getting up from the table and going down theatrically on one knee beside his wife, just as Constanza came in with the coffee.

"I'll think about it," Elena said. "But only if you get up and stop playing the fool. I'm sorry, Constanza. What must you think of us?"

Barcelona didn't disappoint. They stayed at the Hotel Colón in palatial rooms with floor-to-ceiling windows that overlooked the great main square, Plaça de Catalunya, in which crowds of well-dressed people walked this way and that, passing amid the statues and fountains, while on the outer hub, cars and trucks stopped and started and blew their horns at each other as they came and went through the myriad of roads leading off the square in all directions: arteries running out from the city's beating heart.

The morning after their arrival, Theo stood in his room looking out, amazed by the sheer numbers of people down below. They were as anonymous to him and to each other as the flocks of pigeons that took off and wheeled and swooped and settled back down onto the marble walkways in a constant flurry of quick gray movement. He felt bewildered and energized in equal measure. The city had no connection to the slow-moving life of the village, where everyone knew everyone and nothing ever changed. It was as if he had been taken back in a time machine to the New York of his childhood.

After breakfast, he walked with his mother across the plaza and into the boulevard called the Ramblas, which sloped gently down toward the sea. Everywhere was a blur of vibrant color. In the flower market, where dahlias and tulips and white black-eyed orchids vied for the eye's attention; in the bird market, where green-and-yellow canaries sang in their tiny cages, as if yearning for a freedom they would never attain; and under the striped awnings of the cafés, where girls in pastel dresses sat with their lovers sipping ice-cold drinks through wax straws.

Waiters in tuxedos moved like dancers between the tables, silver trays balanced high on their upturned hands; sailors with their arms linked and the wide ends of their blue trousers flapping walked arm in arm up from the port; and, under the spreading canopies of the plane trees on the central walkway, performers in leotards juggled rings and clubs or swallowed fire or walked on their hands while their assistants held out their hats to passersby in hopes of reward.

The noise jangled in Theo's ears: not just the traffic but the bells of the yellow streetcars rattling under their contact lines, the barrel organs churning out popular songs, people shouting to make themselves heard. He was entranced, but the sensory overload gave Elena a headache, and she soon asked him to take her back to the hotel to rest.

Left to his own devices for the afternoon, Theo went to the concierge desk and obtained directions to Antonio's barracks from a round-faced, thick-lipped official in resplendent uniform who bore an unfortunate but remarkable resemblance to the pictures of Al Capone that used to regularly appear in Theo's father's newspaper at the time of the Saint Valentine's Day Massacre, and which had given him such terrible nightmares when he was a boy. Up close, Theo saw that the man even had a name tag above his breast pocket, giving his name as Alfonso, and he had to turn away and hold his breath hard for a moment to stop himself from laughing.

But the concierge was too polite to notice, or perhaps was just used to such reactions from American tourists, and he couldn't have been more helpful as he took out a map of the city and showed Theo how to get to the Tarragona Street barracks. At the end, Theo felt so grateful that he made the mistake of putting his hand out to thank Alfonso, only remembering when it was too late that that might not be the right etiquette for how guests were supposed to deal with employees at the Colón. However, the concierge was only too happy to shake Theo's hand and even came out from behind his desk to escort him through the revolving door of the hotel, rendering him a formal bow before he retreated back inside. Out in the plaza in the sunshine, Theo felt suddenly buoyed, having made his first friend in Barcelona.

He still managed to get lost on the way, but it didn't seem to matter, and eventually he found himself standing outside a stone gateway manned by a sentry, who stepped out in front of him and told him "No visitors!" in a commanding voice when Theo tried to walk through into the big empty courtyard beyond. At the back Theo could see the long gray wall of a building with square windows set in symmetrical rows, surmounted by a clock tower. But there was no sign of life. The place looked to him more like a prison than a barracks.

Theo told the sentry Antonio's name, said he was a friend who was just in town for a few days, and asked when it would be a good time to come back, but he soon realized he was wasting his time. "No visitors!" the sentry repeated in exactly the same peremptory tone of voice, as if these were the only words in his vocabulary, until Theo turned away disconsolately with his earlier sense of euphoria punctured like air escaping from a child's balloon.

He started to walk back down the road the way he'd come, but he stopped halfway, watching as a troop of khaki-clad soldiers appeared around the corner, led by an officer on horseback with a thin mustache and a swagger stick. He reminded Theo of Barker, even though he didn't in the least look like him. The ramrod-straight back, the sneering expression, the polished boots and buttons, took Theo back to the parade ground at Saint Gregory's and Barker shouting ridiculous commands at him and the other terrorized cadets.

The soldiers marched four abreast and Theo checked their faces as they went past, each a blank until the last row, when he caught sight of Antonio on the far side. He was gone in a moment, wheeling toward the barracks gate, but as Theo watched from behind, Antonio held out the fingers of one of his swinging hands.

Theo felt sure it was a signal of some kind. Five minutes, perhaps. And he went back and waited close to the gate, but out of view of the sentry.

Five minutes passed and then fifteen more and Theo started to wilt in the heat. He closed his eyes, wishing he'd brought water, and felt a hand on his shoulder.

"Hello, old friend," said Antonio. He hugged Theo briefly and then leaned back against the barracks wall and lit a cigarette. He looked weary, Theo thought. And not the kind of weary Theo was feeling, but a fatigue that went to the core, sucking away hope.

"You look rotten," Theo said. "Is soldiering that bad?"

"Worse than bad. And don't say 'I told you so' or I'll shoot you with my rifle, if I can get it to fire," said Antonio with a wan smile that was at least familiar.

"All right. I won't," said Theo, smiling too. "What's so terrible about it?"

"Never being alone, never getting to spend time with anyone I like, never seeing trees or grass or girls. Bad food, stupid orders that make no sense and aren't intended to . . . Do you want me to go on?"

"You make it sound like my old school."

"Except that you learned to like your school, didn't you?" said Antonio bitterly. "I'm never going to like the army."

"I'm sorry," said Theo. He didn't know what else to say, because part of him did think that Antonio had only himself to blame. He'd always acted like he had no choice about his career because he had to obey his father, but maybe he should have tried showing some backbone, like Maria. Anyone could see that he wasn't cut out to be a soldier.

Antonio looked at Theo and suddenly grinned with that look of wry amusement Theo knew so well. "I know what you're thinking and you're right. It is my fault. I should have realized what I was letting myself in for. My father was a Fascist before Mussolini came up with the idea, and he loves the army because it's run by Fascists like that captain you saw up on his horse. Darnell's his name and he calls me *Rat* and makes my life hell because he says he can smell me."

"Smell you?"

"Smell a rat, smell that I'm not one of them. And that's true, of course. I'm not. I'm no Anarchist, but I believe that the poor have rights, and that's enough to make me a Red in their book. And there's nothing worse than a Red in the army. Not even a Jew!" Antonio laughed harshly.

"How does he know what you are?" asked Theo. "He can't smell you. That's ridiculous."

"Probably heard me talking to one of the other recruits," said Antonio. "Or got to hear about my sister and Primitivo and made the connection. News like that travels fast. It's been in all the papers."

"Is she here?" asked Theo, trying to keep the excitement out of his voice.

"Maybe. I've looked. It would've been the logical place for them to go. There are more Anarchists here than in Andalusia, but if she's here, I don't think she wants me to find her. She probably thinks I'd tell our father. Which is a joke, of course, although she's not to know that. I'd like to run away, too, but unlike her, I've got nowhere to hide." Antonio laughed. A hollow, humorless laugh that was like a window opening on his despair. It frightened Theo and grieved him, too, because he felt powerless to help his friend.

"Have you heard anything?" Antonio asked.

Theo shook his head. He didn't want to lie, but he thought that revealing his conversation with Maria in the lane would make it seem like he'd been a part of what had happened with Pedrito, and he didn't want Antonio to think of him as involved.

"I have to go back," said Antonio, grinding his cigarette out under his foot—Theo noticed that he had smoked it right down to the butt so that it had almost burned his fingers. "Are you here next weekend?"

Theo nodded.

"Good. I've got a day's leave next Saturday. Come at this time and I'll show you the real Barcelona, just like I guided you in the mountains. Remember those days? Before everything went bad? Who knows? We might even find my sister."

In the evening Elena was better, and she and Andrew and Theo took a taxi to the Liceu Opera House halfway down the Ramblas. The Colón's resident hairstylist had come to her room in the afternoon and arranged her jet-black hair in an elegant chignon and, to please her husband, she was wearing a diamond necklace that had belonged to his mother. In the refracted light of the chandeliers, the jewels shimmered and sparkled above her simple black dress, drawing admiring eyes to the symmetry of her face, in which the suffering of recent years had created an ethereal look, as if she was not of this world but rather a Madonna in a painting by Murillo or another of the old Spanish masters. Theo had never seen his mother looking more beautiful, but it was a beauty so fine that he felt it could break at any moment, and he wished they had not come.

But Andrew was elated. He passed through the lobby with Elena on his arm, introducing her to his friends. Theo was surprised. His stepfather seemed to know everyone. Standing awkwardly alone with his back to a gilded pillar, Theo watched him talking animatedly to a group of men whose affluence was evident from the oversize jewels pinned or hung on their wives' haute couture gowns. He didn't need a guide to know who they were, these merchant princes of the city. They owned the factories and the mills, and Andrew was one of them.

A bell rang overhead, and the audience passed into the horseshoe-shaped theater. It was like nothing Theo had ever seen before. Immense Corinthian columns rose to support a ceiling encrusted with gold and polychrome moldings in which eight circular paintings of Renaissance nymphs in diaphanous robes surrounded a central globe of light, while below, red velvet armchairs matched the thick weave of the carpet. Theo thought it decadent: a baroque extravaganza celebrating the city's wealth. Alone in the lobby, he'd noticed a memorial tablet on the wall dedicated to twenty patrons killed by an Anarchist bomb thrown from the balcony in 1893, and it didn't surprise him in the least that the theater should have been an Anarchist target. Sitting beside his mother in Andrew's sumptuous box, he glanced uneasily upward, wondering whether tonight might see a repeat.

He knew nothing of opera. He'd never seen one or heard one, and he'd gone expecting to be bored. But, to his surprise, he was enthralled from the moment the curtain rose, transporting him back to Seville a hundred years before. The music was alive with melody, and the Romany factory girl Carmen exerted a magnetic attraction not just on the soldiers on the stage but on him too. Spellbound while the orchestra played, he believed she was Maria. There was enough resemblance in her darting eyes and her dancing movement to sustain the illusion, and just like Maria, she insisted on her right to be free. Free to fall in love with Don José and free to throw him over when she met the glamorous young bullfighter Escamillo. Free to do as she liked, regardless of its effect on others. Theo believed in her right to choose, but he also understood José's terrible pain when he learned of his rejection and, even though he was appalled, he understood why José killed her outside the bullring. He understood how love could lead to that. Death and despair.

In the darkness, he was swept away on a tide of emotion and so felt a shock when the lights came on at the end, destroying the illusion of make-believe, and the actors, stepping forward, became themselves as they joined together in a line and took their bow. The audience stood and cheered and, looking around at them, Theo felt an unexpected revulsion replacing the grief he had been experiencing a moment before. They were voyeurs, these rich theatergoers in their evening dress. Bourgeoisie watching the lawless, amoral antics of the working class through their opera glasses before they went home to their hilltop villas built on the backs of those same workers' hard labor.

The thought made Theo uneasy, a feeling that intensified when he came out of the theater and saw a man watching from the corner of a narrow street less than a hundred yards away down the Ramblas. He quickly disappeared from view when he caught Theo's eye, but the road was well lit, and the glimpse was enough to make Theo sure it was Carlos, notwithstanding the unlikelihood of meeting someone he knew in this vast city, far away from Andalusia. He couldn't mistake the daggerlike shape of the face, the pointed beard, the staring intensity in the eyes.

Instinctively, Theo moved to go after him. He had no idea what he wanted to say. "It's not what you think; this isn't me; I'm not one of them." Something like that, perhaps. But he was denied the opportunity. He'd gone only a short distance when he felt a hand on his shoulder and his stepfather called him back.

"You need to stay with us," he said. "It's not safe to go in there at night. Or even during the day, for that matter."

"In where?" asked Theo.

"The Fifth District—all this area to the south," said Andrew, pointing up and down the side of the Ramblas on which they were standing. "But particularly down here, when you get closer to the port. I'm sorry. I should have told you before."

"Why? What happens in there?"

"There are criminals, drug dealers . . ."

"Anarchists?"

"Yes," said Andrew, looking closely at his stepson, as if guessing the reason for his question. "Them too. As I've said, it's not safe."

They were back with Elena, and Theo said nothing more as they got into their taxi and sped back up the Ramblas past the cafés, which were as crowded as in the afternoon but illuminated now by thousands of tiny glittering lights.

Saturday, Theo thought. On Saturday I will see the real Barcelona.

But first he had to leave the city. Early the next morning Andrew drove Elena and Theo down the coast to Sitges. The winding road had been carved out of the cliff, with the Garraf Mountains rising precipitately above and the Mediterranean stretching away below to a distant horizon. Azure blue in the sunlight, ruffled here and there by silvery waves, it was spectacularly beautiful.

Andrew had promised golden sand, and Sitges didn't disappoint. The beach stretched brown and smooth all the way from their hotel to the picturesque church of Santa Tecla on a headland at the other end, with the clear view interrupted only by small fishing boats pulled up here and there out of the water.

Elena had felt carsick on the corniche, but now she suddenly revived. "It's perfect," she said wonderingly. "Oh, Andrew, can't you stay?"

"No," he said, smiling. "Not even for a minute. This is your holiday with Theo. I'll be back at the end of the week." And with a wave of his hand and a skid of fast-turning tires, he was gone.

Standing in front of the hotel, Theo was shocked to realize that the empty feeling that had suddenly overtaken him was in fact disappointment that his stepfather had left. For years he had blamed Andrew for taking away his mother, but no longer. Irony of ironies, he felt closer to him now than he did to her. It was the last thing he would have expected. At least superficially, they had little in common, separated as they were by age, nationality, and political outlook, but what mattered more was that they shared a willingness to at least try to see each other for who they were. At critical moments in Theo's life when he had gotten into trouble, Andrew had come to his rescue. He felt supported by his stepfather—loved, even.

Theo knew his mother loved him, too, just as he loved her, but a polarizing dichotomy in the way they each saw the world had pushed them further and further apart, creating barriers between them that he didn't seem able to overcome. Once upon a time—so long ago that he could hardly remember— they had been close. Mother and son together, speaking Spanish in an English world, gathered with the exiles in the church in Gramercy Park. But while he had grown and gone out into the world, she had stayed behind, clinging to a faith that he could not share. The faith that had given her the justification to consign her first husband to oblivion as if he'd never lived, and which she was now using to defend the terrible injustices in Spanish society that so outraged her son.

As the rift between them had widened, Theo had learned to keep important parts of his life secret from his mother. It was a process that had begun five years earlier in New York when she had practically thrown Coach Eames out of their apartment. The poor man's efforts to help her son had meant nothing to Elena once she found out he was a Communist. In the blink of an eye, he had gone from being an honored guest to becoming "a devil" and "a ravenous wolf." Her words were ridiculous. Anyone could have seen that, except Elena herself, who had never been able to get beyond the fear and hatred of the godless Reds that she had taken with her out of Mexico.

So, afterward, in England and Spain, it was little wonder that Theo never spoke to her of Esmond or Maria. How could he when he knew she would condemn them out of hand? And become sick if he argued with her. His mother's fragility cemented the separation between them, stifling the possibility of honest communication.

It might have helped if she had been able to relax her determination to look forward and not back, so as to avoid having to deal with experiences that upset her. But New York remained a closed subject because it reminded her of the disgrace, poverty, and sickness that had followed her first husband's suicide. She needed to forget to survive, and it didn't seem to matter to her that this meant she and Theo would lose access to their shared past. The good was thrown out with the bad. Spain was where they were now and as far as Elena was concerned, the past was another country that they'd had to leave behind to begin again.

None of this was what Theo wanted. Life was hard and confusing, and he would have liked nothing more than to be able to talk to his mother about the painful problems he was wrestling with, but he knew what would happen if he tried, and so he remained silent.

Elena, for her part, appeared blissfully unaware of his buttoned-up constraint. She acted as if everything was fine between them, and as long as they kept away from difficult subjects, she remained everything a loving mother should be: solicitous for her son's welfare and happiness, proud of his success at school, and excited by his achievement in getting into Oxford.

She told Theo how delighted she was that they were going to have a holiday together in such a beautiful place. Everything about Sitges pleased her: the hotel with its wide-open views of the sea, as if you could reach out of the windows and touch the water; the stone terrace of the restaurant where they ate their meals and where she forsook her usual temperance to order cocktails with names that made her giggle, and which came in strange, exotic colors and with tiny striped umbrellas that matched the parasols above their table; the palm trees with brightly colored birds singing in their fronds; the beach where she walked out into the sea and then came running back when the waves came in, hanging on to Theo's arm and splashing his legs and laughing.

It reminded her of her childhood, she said, when her parents took her to Puerto Vallarta for the holidays and she stood beside her father at the end of the pier and watched the pearl divers go out in their tiny boats to where there were dolphins in the Pacific, flying through the sea spray with such a weight of abandon. And sharks, too, lurking in the water, waiting.

Inevitably it was the church that Elena loved the most. Its setting was magical, rising up from the rocks at the end of the beach into weathered walls that glowed like pink quartz in the sunset. At high tide, the waves splashed up onto the stone steps leading to the door.

At Elena's request, the hotel organized a guide to take them around, and on their last day they spent a very long hour with an octogenarian man who appeared to know the date and provenance of every object in the church, down to and including the candlesticks. He took them through every appalling detail of Santa Tecla's martyrdom as portrayed on the altarpiece, while Elena listened intently and Theo inwardly groaned, longing to be released out into the sea air and the light.

As was often the case, the visit to the church crystallized his irritation with his mother and, walking back, he told her that the beach reminded him of his childhood, too, even though it didn't.

"When I went to Coney Island with Dad, we walked on the sand," he said, turning to look at her, as if he was challenging her with the statement.

And when she would not answer, he went on, refusing to let the subject go. "I don't care what he did. I think of him every day," he told her. "Don't you?"

"I can't," she said, shaking her head. "It hurts."

Theo looked at his mother. He could see that she'd pushed the memory of her first husband aside in the time it took to answer his question and was smiling expectantly now, just as she used to do years before when he was a boy in New York and the whole day was before them, theirs to do with as they pleased. As if nothing had happened—no factory, no suicide, no separation. But it didn't work. Those things had happened. They were a part of who he was, who he had become. Not to be denied.

She loved him. He could see it written in her luminous dark eyes. He felt their warmth, like a fire on a cold night, and he understood her extraordinary fragility and the precious ephemerality of this moment in time that they had together. He wanted to respond—to tell her that he loved her, too, and that everything was going to be all right. He longed to, but he couldn't, and there were no words to explain why. Or no words she could understand or accept.

He stopped, feeling like he'd hit something hard, something he could not get beyond. He picked up a stray black stone at his feet and threw it out into the sea, wishing it had been the plaster statue of Santa Tecla that his mother had bought at the back of the church and was carrying in her hand as she walked on in front of him, leaving tiny footprints behind her in the sand.

At night he dreamed that his mother was the saint. It was the same story that the old guide had told them in the church. She was being pursued through caves, and each time the pursuer got close, she prayed to God, who opened up the wall to another dark passageway, providing her with a temporary escape. But he could see the pursuer, too, enveloped in a black cloak, and he knew that it was death.

He woke trembling in the early light and went out into the hall and knocked on his mother's door, terrified that she would not answer. And when it finally opened, he put out his hands and hugged her close and whispered that he was sorry. She reached up and ran her fingers through his hair and he stood still, looking out over her shoulder through the open windows of her room toward the vast gray sea.

# 2

## CHINATOWN

Antonio was excited. His head bobbed from side to side as he pointed out landmarks, naming streets and squares and distant hills in a cascade of information that made Theo's head spin. His weariness of the previous weekend had been replaced by a frenetic vivacity, reflecting a determination to experience to the full every moment of his day's leave from his hated barracks.

They crossed a great square populated with baroque statues and fountains and walked down a long, wide road that Antonio said was called the Paral·lel because it ran parallel to the equator. He was the guide again just as he had been in the village two summers before, although it was not long before Theo began to realize that his friend's knowledge of the real Barcelona, as he called it, was a thin veneer, concealing the ignorance of a dyed-in-the-wool country boy.

It was Theo who was at home in this urban world. He had grown up in it. The Paral·lel was a larger version of Fourteenth Street, where he had spent his childhood. There was the same spillage of shops and cafés out onto the sidewalks and the same crazy traffic—overcrowded trams with riders on the running boards hanging on for dear life and immobilized automobile drivers incessantly blowing their horns in a vain effort to get around carts laden with vegetables or coal.

In the middle of this chaos, a policeman in a fancy blue uniform stood on a box, making elaborate signals with his white-gloved hands that everyone ignored. He was like a conductor of an orchestra that had gone rogue, and Theo was reminded in a flash of the similarly ineffectual traffic cop he'd passed on that long-gone day when his grandfather had taken him through the New York streets to meet his *bubbe*.

He remembered her so clearly even though he'd met her only once: her wide-open green eyes and her foreign voice searching for the English words; the feel of her hands on his head, pressing. Leah Stern, who was dead now, gone beyond his reach.

Theo felt that same stab of loss and missed opportunity that he always felt when he remembered his grandparents, but then it was gone in a moment, swallowed up in a more general nostalgia for his hometown. Someone had painted **BROADWAY DE BARCELONA** in big white letters on a wall, and the sign made sense. It was as if the Paral·lel was consciously aping Manhattan. The cinemas were showing American films—Clark Gable and Bette Davis stared down from gigantic posters, and jazz was playing in all the cafés. Amid all the cacophony, Theo thought for a moment that he could hear Louis Armstrong singing "St. James Infirmary Blues," but when he stopped to listen, the song was gone.

This was a different world to the Ramblas. There was no grandeur or pretension or luxury—no flower or bird markets, no hats on the women made of exotic plumage. The cafés were lit by naked bulbs, not chandeliers, and everyone wore black and white and talked in those terms. The medieval church towers rising above the Ramblas were replaced here with the roofs of smoke-belching factories. Over on the right, toward Montjuïc, the three tall chimneys of the Canadenca power station were the cathedral spires of working-class Barcelona. Coal dust settled on surfaces like a thin gray dew.

At Café Chicago, the Paral·lel opened up to the north in the La Bretxa de Sant Pau, and Antonio turned left toward the Ramblas, plunging almost immediately into a warren of narrow side streets, lined on either side with tenement buildings whose height and proximity to each other prevented the angled sunlight from ever reaching the ground. The contrast to the wide, open Paral·lel was extraordinary and induced in Theo a sudden cramping claustrophobia that he had to struggle to overcome.

Some of the buildings were doss-houses with signs outside offering beds by the hour or even something called *las cuerdas*, which allowed those who couldn't afford a bed to sleep the night hanging on to ropes. Others were brothels. Theo and Antonio stopped outside one window, looking in on a scene that left nothing to the imagination. Semiclad girls in slips and petticoats sat in a line on a wooden bench, while an old woman waited behind a glass-fronted cash desk by the door with a pile of metal disks beside her. On the back wall, a calendar from the year before hung slightly askew, and farther along, a staircase rose up into gloom.

Elsewhere, women too old to find work in the brothels called out to Theo and Antonio and cursed them as they hurried past, their harsh, angry voices echoing back off the lanes' narrow walls. They frightened Theo with their lurid faces caked with rouge and their eyes heavy with mascara. The languid kimono-clad girls on Rivington Street who had adopted him as their mascot had no relationship to these desperate women struggling against the odds to keep their deaths at bay.

"What is this place?" he asked, turning to Antonio.

"The Fifth District, but everyone calls it Chinatown. Isn't it terrible?" Antonio sounded strangely satisfied, as if he had succeeded in proving a point, although what that point was Theo had no idea.

"It's worse than terrible. It's hell on earth," he replied. "Why's it called Chinatown? I haven't seen any Chinese."

"Because it's like the Chinatowns in America—foul and full of lowlifes," said Antonio. "That's the idea."

Was that why Antonio was pleased? Theo wondered. Because it showed where America and capitalism got you? Was that the idea? No wonder the Anarchists were strong in this town, he thought. Even the most patient would end up throwing bombs if they had to endure this life.

Everywhere there was the sound of coughing. Not just from people they could see but from hordes of invisible others, filling the stale, malodorous air with a miasma of germs. Theo pulled his shirt collar over his mouth and nose while keeping his eyes fixed on the ground to stop himself from walking in the filthy open drains that overflowed out onto the cobblestones.

The main source of the poisoned air was the factories that stood side by side with the tenements, spewing smoke and toxic vapors out through vents and chimneys into the rooms where families ate and slept.

Theo and Antonio looked in through the sealed window of a workshop. As far as they could see in all directions, big mechanical looms and spinning frames were being operated by lines of textile workers. Their bodies moved like the pistons of the machines, as if both were being remotely controlled by some invisible brain.

The light from the naked bulbs hanging down from the smoke-blackened ceiling was poor and the window through which they were looking was grimy, but Theo's eyes adjusted and he began to pick out small shapes moving about on the floor on their hands and knees. He pushed his face up against the glass and saw that the shapes were children sweeping out handfuls of dust and dirt and fallen cotton fiber from under the machines to stop them from becoming clogged. It was obvious that they risked being decapitated or crushed if they raised their heads or their backs too high.

"Look!" he said, taking hold of Antonio's arm and pointing at the children. "That can't be legal."

But before Antonio could reply, a red-faced man with a big stomach held in by a dirty singlet noticed their faces at the window and started toward them, waving his arms.

Now, it was Antonio's turn to pull at Theo. "Come on," he said. "That's the foreman. Let's get out of here."

"No," said Theo, holding back. "It's wrong. We need to say something."

"It won't do any good and you know it," said Antonio harshly. "Please don't get us in a fight. Trouble is the last thing I need."

A few yards away, a door opened and the clattering, thumping noise of the machines was suddenly deafening in Theo's ears. He could smell the hot, humid air thick with fiber, and he wanted to gag. The man was coming out. He was huge and his fists were clenched. Theo hesitated and then, at the last moment, just as the man was reaching toward him, he turned and ran after Antonio, sprinting down the lanes until they had left the factory and the sound of pursuing footsteps far behind.

Antonio stopped and pushed Theo hard on the shoulders, causing him to stagger back. "You're so stupid," he said. "I should never have brought you here."

"So why did you then?" asked Theo angrily.

"Because I thought you should see it. So you wouldn't think that fancy hotels and nights at the opera are what this town is really about. Just like I showed you what was real in the mountains. Remember?"

Theo nodded, understanding now.

"And because you want to find my sister," Antonio added. "Just like I do. And this is where she is. I'm sure of it."

Theo shuffled his feet uncomfortably and then looked at Antonio and held up his hands. "You're right she's here," he said. "She told me they were going to Barcelona just before she left. I should have said so before. I'm sorry."

"So why didn't you?" asked Antonio, sounding angry again.

"I didn't want you to think I had something to do with the murder."

"Did you?"

"No, of course not!"

"What about Maria?"

"I don't know. She was happy Primitivo killed him. I could see that."

"Yes, the bastard won her with his knife because he couldn't with his words. And now she's thrown in her lot with him, it's like she's crossed over to the other side. Gone where I can't follow. Sometimes I feel like I'll never see her again." Antonio bit his lip, trying to swallow his pain.

"You will. Of course you will," said Theo passionately, not because he believed it, but because he couldn't bear for it to be true. Not just for Antonio but for himself too.

"She was my younger sister and I let her down. I should have stood up for her to my father over Pedrito like you said. Not gone away and left her with nobody except Primitivo to turn to. But it's too late now," said Antonio despairingly.

"No, it's not. She's done nothing wrong. She doesn't have to be with Primitivo. She can come back," said Theo furiously, fighting his friend's defeatism. Maria wasn't gone. He wouldn't let her be gone. "We have to try and find her," he said. "You said it yourself just a minute ago."

"I know I did," said Antonio, bowing his head. "And I've tried, and I'll carry on trying, but that doesn't mean I think we'll succeed. There are thousands of people here. It's like looking for a needle in a haystack. And if we do find her, I don't think she's going to listen. That's all."

Up and down the streets and in the tiny, dirty cafés, they asked for Maria, but at best they drew a blank and at worst were met with open hostility. People who came asking questions in Chinatown were police or connected to police, and the cops were the common enemy. Finally, in one dingy bar, a man took out a pistol and spun it on his table meaningfully, and they ran. Without hesitation this time, turning this way and that as they searched for the light, until they burst out into the Paral·lel again, a block away from the Café Chicago, where they had started, and stood gasping for breath and laughing for no reason except relief.

"Enough for one day," said Antonio. "It's time to be happy." And Theo agreed wholeheartedly.

They sat at a café, eating fish with bulging eyes and mussels and scallops with the smell of the sea still inside their shells, and drinking Andalusian wine that tasted just like it had on that first evening they had spent together in the village, when Spain was an adventure Theo was waiting to begin. Before everything became so complicated and hard to unravel.

Looking at his friend across the table, drinking hard to forget, Theo wished he could go back to that night when everything had been magical and the square had been transformed into Dracula's castle just by pulling a sheet across the trees.

Afterward, they crossed the Paral·lel to the Moulin Rouge: a squat building with an illuminated windmill with rotating red sails superimposed on its facade above the portico. They bought tickets and coffee with rum in paper cups that they had to hold on to with both hands to stop them from spilling over as they pushed inside with the crowd. Soon all the seats were taken, rising in a steep semicircle up from the curtained stage. Everyone was squashed in together, shouting and laughing and smoking, utterly alive and, like Antonio, determined to enjoy to the full every moment of escape from the drudgery of their days.

Theo thought of the Liceu and wondered at the extreme contrast between the two theaters. Only a few streets separated them, but they belonged to different worlds. Plush carpet and sawdust, evening dress and overalls, the ostentation of great wealth and the degradation of terrible poverty. Could they continue to exist so close together and yet so far apart? Or was conflict between them inevitable as each fought for its own survival?

Suddenly there was a hush as the curtain rose and Conchita stepped out. Theo knew that was her name because it said so on the blackboard that was carried across the stage before each act. Dressed in a chemise and black trunks from which rolls of fat bulged out, and an oversize cross that glittered between her almost-exposed breasts, she sang bawdy songs while making eyes at and presenting her gyrating hips to the men in the front row. They reached toward her with their hands, from which she withdrew with a look of mock outrage, only to advance again. Her voice was terrible, but that was part of the joke, and the audience roared their appreciation when she came back for an encore.

"They put her in jail in 1932 when her negligee fell off," Antonio shouted in Theo's ear, but he couldn't hear Antonio's reply when he asked him how he knew, because everyone was singing along to a popular song called "La Vaselina" about a newlywed wife displaying incredible naivete on her wedding night.

The laughter was infectious. Through the acts—a kaleidoscope of sequins and corsets and glitter, of double entendre and innuendo—hysteria grew like a wind rushing this way and that through the audience, creating a violent happiness that possessed Theo like a demon.

There was a fantastic irreverence at work. In the best-received skit of the evening, the stage was turned into a confessional in which a libidinous priest even fatter than Don Vincente and wearing similar silver-buckled shoes took advantage of a beautiful female parishioner who turned out, after the slow removal of her garments, to be a man! Theo laughed so hard that it hurt and wondered afterward at his savage glee. It was as if he hated the Church now as much as the Anarchists around him, but not just for their reasons—the hypocrisy, the lies, the investment in ignorance; it was more because religion separated him from his mother, creating a gulf between them that he could not bridge.

The Moulin saved its best for last. A Romany woman in a long green dress with an elongated face and features, as if lifted from a Gauguin painting of Tahiti, walked out onto the stage, accompanied by a guitar player with a wide-brimmed black sombrero pulled low over his forehead. He sat on a stool and began to play, picking out slow notes, while she looked on immobile and impassive, gazing into a space that only she could see.

The audience fell completely quiet. No one spoke, no one moved. The sudden switch from tumult to silence astonished Theo. It was like a conjurer's trick.

A minute passed and she remained still as a statue. Until the guitar all at once accelerated and she burst into life, jumping, twisting, contorted in a feverish swirl of cloth and castanets clicking in her upturned hands. All while singing with a voice that was like a nasal howl, descending through scales that made no sense to Theo to reach a lyrical beauty that she threw away as if it was nothing a moment later.

He couldn't make sense of the words. They were distorted by the strange rhythms of flamenco, but he understood the passion. The song and the dance and the music were an expression of ecstasy and agony. Life lived on the outer rim of possibility. Carmen stabbed, bombs thrown, fire in the night. An art that this audience could embrace deep in their souls.

She stopped as suddenly as she had begun and stood looking at the audience for a moment, accepting their applause, before walking off the stage. The show was over. The lights came up and Theo and Antonio shuffled out with the crowd into the night.

They walked slowly up the wide avenue without speaking, even when they had left the reveling crowds behind.

The song had awakened a sense of foreboding in Theo that he had been holding suppressed ever since Pedrito's murder. It was dread without the knowledge of what he was dreading. A growing pressure that felt like the hour before a storm that would not break. He tried hard, but without success, to push the anxiety back into the chamber of his unconscious mind where he usually kept it contained, and the effort constrained him, so that he could not think of what to say to Antonio, with whom conversation always came so easily. It didn't help that Antonio was silent, too, lost in his own thoughts.

As they entered the street leading to the barracks, Theo forced himself to speak: "It was a good day, even if we didn't find Maria," he said. "Thank you for showing me . . ." He stopped, unable to think of the right word to describe all that they had seen.

"It's an honor to guide you," said Antonio with a trace of his old smile as he echoed the words he'd spoken to Theo when they first met two years before in his father's office. "I hope I can get away again next Saturday afternoon and we can look for her again. Will you still be here?"

"I don't know. I hope so. If I am, I'll come like today," said Theo, stumbling over his words as he felt their inadequacy to match what he was feeling.

They were in sight of the barracks now: high and gray and imposing in the moonlight.

"Do you ever feel like something is coming?" he burst out. "Something bad which we can't stop?"

"All the time," said Antonio. "And I can't see past it. I try to but I can't. It's like a bull running. It's too big."

His voice was very quiet, and Theo knew that he was thinking about the day of the storm, when they had taken shelter in the lonely cottage at the top of the village and the old woman had refused to say what she had seen in his palm. A black fate written in the lines from which there was no escape.

"It'll be okay," said Theo, even though he didn't believe it. His feeling of separation from his friend was even stronger now, but he forced himself against its weight and reached out his arms to hug Antonio, who felt limp in his embrace.

He looked at Theo and nodded, as if communicating his understanding of what Theo was trying to do, and then turned and passed through the gate and was swallowed up in the darkness.

# 3

## BOOKER

Theo did not wait to go back to Chinatown and the Paral·lel. In the afternoons when his mother was resting, he rode the streetcar to the port and walked back up into the narrow streets, searching for Maria. Once or twice, he thought he glimpsed her in a café or rounding a corner. A flash of dark-blue eyes or brown hair falling around a girl's shoulders set him running, only to realize when he came up close how easily hope was playing tricks on him.

Everywhere was a dead end. But still he persisted, drawn magnetically not just by his longing to find Maria, but also by a deeper, confused sense that this world was a way back into his past.

He'd left New York behind as he tried to make a new life for himself in England and in Spain, but now he couldn't get the city out of his mind. Broadway de Barcelona, Café Chicago, Chinatown: the names seemed like signposts to his earlier life. Day and night, he returned in his mind to the skyscrapers and the cinemas, to the noise and bustle of Fourteenth Street, and to the baths where he'd worked on Rivington Street—the only job he'd ever held. And, yes, even to the tenements of the Lower East, where he'd made a home with his mother before Andrew arrived and took them away from everything he'd ever known. He felt the city close, just beyond his fingertips, and so it came almost as something he'd expected when he heard a loud American voice speaking English with a New York accent just beside where he was standing in Plaça de Catalunya.

He'd stopped out of curiosity at a newly erected kiosk as he was crossing the square on his way back to the Colón. There was a sign across the front in big black letters:

**OLIMPIADA POPULAR**
**SETMANA D'ESPORT i FOLKLORE**
**19 A 26 DE JULIOL**

Since his return from Sitges, he had seen posters for this Olimpiada going up around the city, but had not paid them much attention, assuming it was a local festival giving itself a grand name. But something about the kiosk drew his attention—maybe its unusual size, or the long line of people with suitcases snaking away from its window across the square.

It was the man at the front of the queue who was talking, or rather shouting. Old with a leathery complexion and a pencil-thin mustache. His face seemed familiar, but Theo couldn't place it until the **OLIMPIADA** on the sign suddenly gave him the connection. An empty athletic stadium in Harlem on an overcast autumn day, waiting to run, and Coach Eames's important friend telling him about the Black boy with the power of the Almighty in his arms and legs, who broke him on the final lap.

"Coach Booker! Do you remember me? I'm Theo Sterling. I was at Saint Peter's with Coach Eames . . ." In his excitement, Theo was talking a mile a minute and had his hand out, just as he had before at the City College, but just like then, Booker ignored it.

"Can you understand what she's saying?" he asked, pointing behind the counter at the exasperated-looking lady who had switched to French in a vain effort to make herself understood. "No one here speaks English. Not even at the hotel. I think I'm going out of my mind."

"She's asking what you want," said Theo, smiling.

"Where we register, where we practice, whether there's a timetable. That'll do for a start."

"Stadium, stadium, and no timetable yet," said Theo after a quick and productive conversation with the lady. "And don't worry, she's told me how to get to the stadium and I'm happy to take you there. We need to take the tram, or a taxi if you prefer."

Booker's mouth opened, but it took him a moment to find his voice. "Christ Almighty! Who the hell would've believed it?" he said, shaking his head in wonder. "I'm up shit creek with the lingo, just about to give up and go back to the hotel, when lo and behold! An interpreter drops out of the sky, and not just any old interpreter—one I actually know. Theo Sterling—Tom Eames's golden boy. Of course I remember you, son! I never forget a good runner."

Booker clapped Theo on the back and told him to take him to the nearest bar, because he needed a drink more than the stadium. The Olympics could wait.

"A Manhattan. That's what I want. More than eternal life," said Booker, stretching his legs out under the table of the bar at the top of the Ramblas and lighting a cigar. And when it came, following a word-by-word translation by Theo to the waiter of Booker's instructions for its ingredients, he sighed and closed his eyes in contentment.

"This is the best I've felt since we got onboard that god-awful boat in New York Harbor," he said. "The SS *Transylvania*! Seriously—can you believe that for a name? All that was missing was the Count sucking our blood. Half the team seasick, and the other half fighting with the other passengers because we've got Black athletes in our party and they thought they ought to be in the hold like the slaves. The captain even canceled the final of the Ping-Pong tournament because one of our Black boxers was in it. And then trains stopping everywhere all over France for no rhyme or reason so that no one got any sleep, let alone exercise. It's about the worst preparation for a Games that I can think of, and now it looks like they're starting in three days. I don't know whether to laugh or cry, although I'm happy I've met you and got this," he said, raising his drink and clinking it against Theo's glass of lemonade.

"What are the Games?" asked Theo, who was finding it hard to keep pace with Booker's rapid flow of information.

"The Olympics. Well, alternative Olympics, I guess you'd have to say. We've been running them for a few years in the States, and this time we wanted more. We joined up with unions in other countries, trying to get their governments to boycott the Hitler Games in Germany, but only Russia and Spain were prepared to do that. It didn't help, I suppose, that most of our athletes were determined to go to Berlin. I talked to Jesse Owens, and he told me that this is the best chance we'll ever have for African Americans to make a fool of the Nazis and their Aryan supremacy bullshit. Maybe he's right. I don't know."

The doubt in Booker's voice didn't fit with Theo's recollection. He remembered Coach Eames's awe of his colleague and the rough authority with which Booker had talked to him that day at the City College. As if he owned the place.

And he remembered, too, his father producing the word *Counter-Olympics* like a rabbit out of a hat when he'd ambushed Coach Eames in their apartment and exposed him as a Communist. Shooting him down in flames in front of his wife so that his son would never have the chance of fulfilling his talent. An old anger stirred inside Theo, mixed up with sadness and regret.

"But it doesn't matter if there isn't a boycott," said Booker, continuing his monologue. "We still have to do something." He seemed to be talking to himself as much as to Theo, trying to quell his doubts and make them go away. "We can't stand idly by while Hitler outlaws the Jews and tears up the Treaty of Versailles, and Mussolini drops poison gas on Ethiopia."

"What gas? What do you mean?" Theo knew about the invasion of Ethiopia, but he didn't remember hearing anything about gas.

"The Italian planes pumped it out like yellow rain all over the country, burning the skin from people's bodies and blinding them. Can you imagine? Italy—the country of Leonardo and Michelangelo! Didn't you read what Haile Selassie said at the League of Nations in Geneva? Look, it's here in the newspaper." Booker took a folded-up copy of *The Herald-Tribune* out of his pocket, pointed at the front-page photograph of the diminutive Ethiopian emperor standing at a rostrum, and began reading from the article: "'Are states going to set up the terrible precedent of bowing before force? . . . It is international morality at stake . . . It is us today. It will be you tomorrow.'

"He's right," said Booker, tapping the table for emphasis. "We have to hold the Fascists to account; we can't let them use the Olympics to legitimize themselves."

"No, we mustn't," said Theo in fervent agreement. He was moved by Booker's passion, and shamed by his own ignorance. It reminded him of the tireless way in which Esmond had talked to him about the world—an education just as valuable as the one he'd gotten from the monks—and his friend's insistence on the moral duty of engagement, culminating in what they'd achieved at Olympia. He realized now that he'd forgotten this lesson in Andalusia, grown small inside the confines of small-town life, and he felt grateful to Booker for waking him from his torpor.

"Good. It sounds like you're one of us," said Booker, who'd managed to use sign language to secure from the waiter another Manhattan, which he was now sipping with evident delight. "But enough of me and my politics. Tell me what you're doing here. This is a long way from home."

"My mother married again after my father died, and my stepfather has a house in Andalusia. North of Málaga. He's here on business."

"Is that how you speak the lingo?"

"No. I've always spoken it. My mother's Mexican."

"Ah, that's a wild country," said Booker, nodding. "I went there with the union in twenty-six, and we had to come running back in a week with the *federales* hot on our tail." He laughed and then suddenly grew serious again. "I read about your father in the papers. I'm sorry. That's a hell of a thing to have to go through."

"He was a capitalist. You wouldn't have been on his side," said Theo, surprising himself with the bitterness that the thought of his father's death still evoked in him all these years later.

"No, you're right. I wouldn't," said Booker, nodding in agreement. "But that doesn't mean I'd have driven him to suicide like that bastard Alvah Katz did. He destroyed your dad's business when it could have been saved, just so he could make a name for himself. He didn't give a damn about those people's jobs when they weren't going to find any others. Not in thirty-one."

"How do you know all this?" asked Theo, amazed. Alvah Katz and Coach Booker were from two entirely different parts of his life, and he knew of no connection between them.

"Curiosity, I suppose, to begin with," said Booker. "The story about your dad said he had one son, Theodore, and I connected that with you because of seeing you run and because Tom Eames would never stop singing your praises, so it stuck in my mind. And it mentioned Alvah as leading the strike, which I remembered when he swam into my corner of the fishpond a couple of years later, all puffed up with that nasty, superior-looking smile wrapped around his gills! So I went back and asked some questions because I wanted to know who I was dealing with."

"When you say *fishpond*, are you talking about the Communist Party?" Theo felt nervous asking the question, but Booker answered it without reserve.

"Sure," he said. "And the union. Alvah's a big wheel in both these days. He was one of the people we had to get to sign off on this little jaunt."

Alvah! The name conjured up vivid memories for Theo. Not only the cutter's sardonic smile, but his neatness, and his cleverness and his mockery too. He'd been a master at getting under people's skin. Theo's father had called him Lenin, and now he was a Communist like Booker and Coach Eames. Although not like them, because they wanted justice, whereas Alvah was in it for himself. *"Alvah's what Alvah cares about,"* Frank had said, and he'd been right. Communism would be a route to power—just a hat to wear like the worker's flat cap he'd put on for the strike. He was out there now, plotting. Theo sensed his presence even though they were thousands of miles apart, and felt again that strange premonition that they were headed toward each other across space and time, destined to meet at some future crossroads in their lives.

After Theo had translated the bill and Booker had paid it, they hailed a taxi at the corner of the Ramblas, which took them at terrific speed up boulevards where the driver seemed to be racing other vehicles, to corners where he threw the wheel violently to the side so that the car seemed to almost take off from the ground as it turned. All this accompanied by grinding of gears, ceaseless horn-blowing, and the sight of terrified pedestrians jumping out of the way of the oncoming juggernaut. In the back, Theo and Booker were thrown from side to side, several times landing in each other's laps, but the driver completely ignored Theo's increasingly desperate appeals for him to slow down. If anything, he seemed to speed up, and Theo spent the last minutes of the ride with his eyes closed, muttering prayers for salvation to a god he didn't believe in.

Finally, the driver braked and they came to a juddering halt, whereupon he immediately became politeness personified, opening the door for them to alight, and taking off his cap with a low, sweeping bow to the "señoritos," as he called them, before he got back in the car after receiving payment and roared away.

"Next time I'm taking the bus," said Booker, bursting into loud laughter that Theo joined in after a moment, finding it helped to release the tension.

They were standing in front of a long white wall, decorated with baroque sculptures and surmounted by a line of colorful flags, among which Theo made out the Stars and Stripes and the Union Jack.

"Looks like we're in the right place," said Booker and stepped forward purposefully through a monumental archway with Theo in tow.

Neither of them was prepared for the size and scale of the Estadi Olímpic. On all sides, tier upon tier of metal seating stretched up from the flat ground at the bottom, climbing into the sky.

"It's almost as big as Yankee Stadium," said Booker, whistling his appreciation. "If we get a full crowd, that'll really be something. Worth crossing the ocean for."

Theo nodded. The place took his breath away. A bewildering variety of sports were being catered for. Tennis courts, boxing rings, a swimming pool, and, running around the oval contour of the central athletic field, a red four-hundred-meter cinder track with white painted lines that brought Theo's skin out in goose bumps.

Crowds of people—some in athletic costumes, some not—were milling about on the field and in the vast entrance area, where more kiosks similar to those in Plaça de Catalunya had been set up. Queues snaked this way and that, crossing and recrossing each other so that it was hard to know which one was going to which kiosk. A babble of languages was being spoken, but none of them sounded like English.

Slowly and laboriously, with questions and answers being translated backward and forward by Theo, they ticked off everything on Booker's list: the American team registered, its practice times and location agreed on, and the event days explained, although the exact times of the heats had not been fixed, so there was no timetable yet. Booker was even given two navy-blue windbreakers with **OLIMPIADA POPULAR** emblazoned in white across the front.

"Do you want a job?" he asked, holding one out to Theo. "I could sure use your help with the lingo."

"I want to run," said Theo. The words came out of his mouth unbidden, leaving him shocked at his audacity. He was fit, but entirely unqualified. He hadn't run a competitive race in years.

Booker looked surprised too. It wasn't the answer he'd been expecting. And then his brow clouded: "Are you trying to bargain with me?" he demanded. "I don't take kindly to that."

"No," said Theo. "Of course not. I'm happy to interpret for you. It's just . . . I want this. I didn't know I did until just now, seeing the track out there, but it feels like it's meant—"

"Meant? What are you talking about?" interrupted Booker, looking at Theo as if he'd lost his mind.

"Meeting you in the square when I'd been thinking about New York so much these last few days, and then coming here. It feels like . . . I don't know. Like it's for a reason," said Theo, stumbling over his words. Now he wished he'd kept quiet or at least thought out what he wanted to say instead of making a fool of himself.

"When did you last do any running?" asked Booker, cutting to the chase.

"I run most days. Not competitively. I haven't done that since I left Saint Peter's, but I've been playing rugby for my school. On the wing like Eric Liddell, so I can sprint now. Coach Eames said you saw him once . . ." Theo's voice trailed away as he realized the full absurdity of what he was asking. To represent his country when he hadn't run a race in five years! Who was he kidding? "I'm sorry," he said, hanging his head. "It's stupid. I shouldn't have asked."

To his horror, he thought he was going to cry. He swallowed hard and put his hands up over his face, as if to push back his hair. He couldn't bear the humiliation of Booker seeing his tears.

When he felt safe to look back up, he was amazed to see that, far from looking thunderous, Booker was actually grinning.

"I think I prefer the stupid Sterling to the sensible one," he said. "I remember you had guts from that day at City College when you wouldn't give up, even though Ledley Clay had you beat. And Tom Eames never stopped saying you had the gift, and he was a good judge of talent. He'd want me to give you a chance. So I'll tell you what I'll do. You join the team as our interpreter and I'll give you a chance to run in the practice. It's fifty to one that you can hold your own, but if you do, then I'll put you in. You have my word on it."

"What about the organizers? You've registered your team now."

"They're not going to care. They've got thousands of runners here, and we've got four. So what do you say? Is it a deal?" he asked, holding out the second windbreaker again.

"Sprint too?" asked Theo, keeping his hands by his sides.

Booker laughed. "I see crazy Sterling's back in the driving seat. All right, sprint too," he said. And they shook hands.

Feeling ecstatic when he got back to the Colón, Theo went whistling up the steps into the lobby, but then stopped in his tracks outside the elevator. He hadn't told Booker that he needed to get his parents' permission because he didn't think he needed it. But he still had to tell his mother and Andrew what he was intending to do, and the thought of his mother's likely reaction filled him with sudden foreboding.

In New York, she'd supported his father in taking him out of school when she found out his running coach was a Communist, so what was she likely to do when she found out he was intending to work for a Communist here? Get mad, get sick? Bring the whole world tumbling down, like she did in the village because her husband insisted on paying his workers out of season? And this was way worse of a sin.

He thought of lying, but he hated to do that, and the lie seemed too big, anyhow—Andrew and his mother would find out the truth sooner or later. He had to tell them. And his mother would have to accept it, he told himself. He had a right to his own life. She'd stopped him once from fulfilling his dreams, and he wouldn't allow her to do it again.

He waved at Alfonso standing behind the concierge desk and entered the elevator.

Upstairs, he walked down the blue-carpeted corridor, past a succession of gold-numbered doors, until he got to his mother's. He thought of walking on to his own room to compose his thoughts but forced himself to stop. "Best get it over with," he muttered to himself as he dried his clammy hands on his trousers, irritated by his timidity.

He knocked harder than he intended and took a step back in surprise when his stepfather opened the door. Andrew had been out in the city every day since their return from Sitges, and Theo had anticipated dealing with his mother alone before he spoke to the two of them together.

"Come on in. We were just talking about you," said Andrew with a smile and a beckoning wave of his hand, and Theo edged past his stepfather into the living room of the suite, but then stayed near the door, realizing that it would be harder to make his announcement if he wasn't standing up. And perhaps he was also preserving an escape route if the world did come tumbling down.

Through the open door to the bedroom, Theo could see his mother taking clothes out of drawers and cupboards. Again, he was taken aback. Elena's spark of energy in Sitges had been extinguished once she returned to the city, and she had spent every afternoon since then lying in bed in the semidarkness, complaining of headaches and exhaustion. But now light was streaming in through the open windows, and she was wreathed in smiles.

"Andrew has finished his work, so we can go home tomorrow. Isn't it wonderful?" she said, and he realized now what she was doing in the bedroom: she was packing her bags.

"I'm sorry that my business here has taken longer than I expected," said Andrew. "But now I want to make up for my neglect. I thought we might make a holiday of the journey home. Go the long way round and visit my vineyards in Jerez and maybe take in Seville, too, which I think you would both find interesting after seeing *Carmen*. What do you say, Theo? Elena likes the idea."

"No! I can't, I have to stay here. I've got a job," said Theo defiantly. He was almost shouting. Ever since he'd come through the door, everything had gone in the opposite direction from what he'd anticipated, with plans for departure and holidays being bandied about, and he knew he had to assert himself if he was to avoid being swept away on the current.

"What job? What are you talking about?" Elena demanded. He'd certainly got her attention now.

"It's for the American team at the Olimpiada Popular. They want me to interpret for them, and there's a possibility I could run too."

"Who's 'they'? Who offered you this job?"

"One of the coaches I knew when I was in New York. I met him in the square," said Theo, trying to avoid saying Booker's name in case his mother remembered it.

"Coaches! They were coaching you to be a Communist until we stopped them!" said Elena, erupting with sudden rage. "Do you think I've forgotten that devil man sitting in my home in his suit and tie, telling me with his forked tongue that you could go to the Olympics when all the time he meant the *Communist* Olympics? That's what this Olimpiada is too. Communist! Everyone knows it!"

"No, it's not. Lots of organizations are involved. And even if there are Communists, I don't care because this is my chance to get back what you and Dad took away from me, and to be an American again, because you took that away too. Ever since we left, you've acted like the place doesn't exist. But it does. For me it does. It's my country. It's who I am." Theo had spoken in a rush and now he stopped, breathless and biting his lip. For the second time that day, he thought he was going to cry, and he was damned if he was going to give his mother the satisfaction of letting her see his weakness.

"Theo, please. No one's trying to stop you being an American," said Andrew, trying to reason with his stepson. He looked appalled by the sudden explosion of hostility between mother and son, which now had them squared up against each other across the room, like boxers in a ring. It had come out of nowhere, like thunder out of a blue sky.

But Theo was in no mood to be conciliatory. Not now, when there was so much at stake. "She's trying. By stopping me doing this," he shouted, pointing a finger of accusation at his mother. "And I won't let her, I tell you. I won't go back to Andalusia and be a mother's boy. It's my life and I'll lead it how I choose."

"With Communists!" screamed Elena. "Just like you did at school and in London. How could you, after what they did to your grandparents and to me? How can you be so cruel? You're doing this to punish me, aren't you? You admitted it just now."

"I'm doing it because it's good. People need to stand up to Hitler and stop him using something wonderful like the Olympics as propaganda for his hateful regime. Storm troopers and jackboots and barbed wire and Jews being beaten in the streets and sent to Dachau. That's what he's really about."

"Jews!" Elena spat out the word as if it was an obscenity. "They had a *funeral* when your father married me. They tried to take you away! I hate them too."

"Elena, please. You don't mean that," said Andrew anxiously. "You need to calm down. You know what the doctors said. And, Theo, you need to think about that too. Oxford's your opportunity, not this jamboree they're putting on here. It's not worth tearing this family apart for. Can't you see that?"

"No, I can't," said Theo, furious with his stepfather now for taking his mother's side. "You're so selfish. You get to do what you want for two weeks, strutting around Barcelona with your millionaire friends while your wife lies here with migraines. And then, as soon as you're done, you come back here and snap your fingers and I'm supposed to pack my bags and give up my dreams because if I don't, it'll upset her. You're such a hypocrite!"

"How dare you talk to me like that!" said Andrew, outraged. "I've not been strutting. I've been having business meetings. Vital ones, as you well know. Money doesn't grow on trees."

Theo had never been so rude to his stepfather before, and he felt intimidated by the force of his response, but he was determined to stay on the attack, because the alternative was to give way, and he couldn't let that happen. "Your business is with capitalists who say all the right things but then look the other way while children half my age work for a pittance in their horrible factories," he shot back. "I know, because I've seen them in Chinatown, so don't deny it."

"Chinatown! I told you not to go there," said Andrew sharply. "Why did you disobey me?"

"Because I wanted to see it for myself and because I wanted to find Maria. Yes, I know what I told you about moving on, but that doesn't matter anymore because I want to be with her."

"You mean the Anarchist girl who ran away with the murderer? *That* Maria—you want to be with her?" repeated Elena, aghast. She'd gone white in the face as if she'd received a physical blow as the full extent of the secret life her son had been leading dawned on her for the first time.

"Yes," said Theo. "That Maria! I gave her that watch you gave me to help her get away, and if I had the chance, I'd do it again. I'm on their side, not yours, and it's about time we stopped pretending. I'm not going back with you. I'm staying here. And that's the end of it."

Theo stopped, looking at his mother and stepfather as if expecting them to defy him, and when they said nothing, he walked out. His words had left him with no other option.

The tide of Theo's anger bore him down the corridor to his room, where he took less than five minutes to throw his belongings in a suitcase, and then out across Plaça de Catalunya to the Hotel Europa, where he told Booker an abridged version of what had happened and asked whether he could stay there with the American team.

Booker agreed straightaway. It made obvious sense that they should all be together if Theo was going to be translating for them, but the hotel manager was not so accommodating. They were full, he told them. Every bed in every room was taken, and the city wouldn't allow them to take more. There were inspections; the hotel would be fined thousands of pesetas. It was impossible.

The more Theo pleaded, the more adamant the manager became, emphasizing his words with extravagant hand gestures that reminded Theo of the traffic policeman on the Paral·lel. It wasn't just the Europa, he said. Everywhere was full. There had never been more visitors in Barcelona. Not even for the exhibition in 1929. He raised his hands high above his head and opened them in a rapid downward motion to demonstrate the meaning of the word *overflowing*. Theo would have thought it comical if he hadn't been so desperate.

He had only a few pesetas, and he couldn't ask Booker to pay for a room elsewhere. The Americans were on a tight budget and couldn't afford that kind of expense. He realized with a sinking heart that he'd have to return to the Colón and ask his stepfather to extend his room if it had not already been given to someone else. He began to regret his hotheadedness earlier. He'd had to stand up to his mother, but he hadn't needed to be so rude to Andrew, who'd always been generous to him. Maybe he would have given him some money if he'd waited to ask, but now Theo didn't feel he could face going back, cap in hand.

He racked his brain for alternatives and thought of the kiosk in the Plaça de Catalunya, emblazoned with black-lettered signs on white board. **OLIMPIADA POPULAR** above, and then down the sides of the front wall in Spanish and French: **ALOJAMIENTOS / ACCOMODATIONS**. He was sure that was what it had said.

Maybe the people there could help. As an interpreter, he was part of the American team, and so he should be accommodated too. He left Booker at the door of the hotel and took off running down the street, and got to the plaza just as the kiosk was closing. A woman wearing an Olimpiada blouse was locking the door and waited impatiently while Theo breathlessly explained his situation.

"Try the Olympic on Plaça d'Espanya," she told him. "They're the official hotel, so they're not taking visitors, only athletes, and if you have a note from your team, then maybe . . ." She shrugged her shoulders and walked away.

Back at the Europa, Theo found Booker in the hotel bar, drinking something reddish brown with two olives on a stick sticking up out of the glass.

"Not a Manhattan!" he said with disgust, pushing it away. "Not even close to it. Without you I'm a lost man, and that's the truth."

Theo told Booker about the note he needed, but Booker refused to write it. "You're going to need my help," he said, and took Theo outside, where they hailed a taxi that took them across town at a speed that seemed sedate compared to the death-defying journey to the stadium they'd endured earlier in the day. Five minutes later, it deposited them in front of a huge boxlike building with rows of square windows punched in its concrete facade like holes in a block of Swiss cheese. Theo recognized it from the previous weekend when Antonio had pointed it out to him on their way to Chinatown, calling it "the ugliest hotel in Barcelona."

Booker was right that his presence would help. He loudly announced that he was the head of the American team, which got the attention of the manager in the back office, who spoke excellent English and had a brother who'd immigrated to Cincinnati. He listened sympathetically to Theo's story and offered him a bed in a room with three Czech athletes. The vacancy had arisen, he said, because the fourth athlete had been run over earlier that day and was now recovering in a hospital.

"Most unfortunate!" he said. "But fortunate for you, of course, señores. Without this, there would have been nothing."

"I bet our friend the taxi driver had something to do with that," Booker whispered to Theo, tipping him a wink as he was going out. "But hey, you know what they say: 'One man's loss is another man's gain.' See you tomorrow, young man. And don't be late. You've got some more running to do."

A handwritten **NO FUNCIONA** sign was hung on the elevator, so Theo had to climb the stairs with his suitcase to the sixth floor and walk down a poorly lit corridor, peering at the numbers on the doors, until he got to the right one and opened it with his key. Inside, three of the four beds had been slept in, but one was newly made up. He lay down on it, exhausted, and went straight to sleep.

He woke up being shaken. He opened his eyes and the three Czechs were towering over him, shouting in a language—presumably Czech—that he couldn't understand. He tried talking to them in English and Spanish and in his schoolboy French, but none of it did any good until he got out his Olimpiada Popular windbreaker and made running motions with his arms, calling out: "America, America . . ."

They clapped their hands, understanding, and made boxing and throwing motions to communicate their own sports, and laughed, and shared their dinner with Theo, which included two bottles of cheap wine that sent him straight back to sleep.

He woke again in the small hours, sweating in the heat, and stood at the open window, breathing in the night air and looking out at the dark city, thinking of his mother.

He felt fearful for her, and looking down, he saw his hands were shaking when he lifted them from the sill. She was so fragile. Like a bird, like one of the orioles she'd loved, singing in the apple tree in the garden of their apartment off Union Square. And he had hurt her with his harsh words. He knew he had. But what choice had she given him, if she wouldn't allow him to fly the nest? He wanted to reach out and hold her in the same desperate way he'd clung to her when they skated on the ice in Hyde Park or on that last morning in Sitges, but instead he'd pushed her away violently with both hands.

He wished now that he'd returned to the Colón earlier in the evening to try to talk to her, but he'd been too tired and then too drunk, and now it was the middle of the night. It would have to wait till the morning.

# 4

## OLIMPIADA POPULAR

In the morning there was no time. Booker had set an early start for the practice before the sun got too hot, and Theo was still bleary with sleep when he lined up with two of the American athletes to race the 1,500 meters.

They were bigger and older than him and knew what they were doing, whereas Theo's mind was scrambled and he seemed to have forgotten everything he'd ever learned about distance running. He used up too much energy on the first two laps and was left behind as they steadily pulled away and passed the distant figure of Booker on the finish line, standing impassively with his stopwatch in his palm, recording times.

At the end, Theo stood hunched over, gasping for breath and trying to hide his bitter disappointment. He was thinking that maybe he could have done better if he'd played it differently, but he knew that he was deceiving himself. They were better than him. It was as simple as that.

But he had a second chance. There was still the sprint. Being stupid wouldn't hinder him there. Strength and speed and nerve were what mattered, and he had been practicing this kind of running for years as he stood out on the wing on the rugby field, waiting to receive the ball and take off, racing for the line as if his life depended on it. Like Eric Liddell: too fast to be caught.

There were two athletes lined up against him again. But different ones from before. One was black, the other white, and he was surprised when they both came and shook his hand at the starting line, telling him their names and wishing him luck. Frank and Harry. It made him remember the camaraderie of the team at Saint Pete's, singing "Battle Hymn of the Republic" on the bus as Coach Eames drove them bouncing down Broadway.

All at once he felt his old coach beside him as he knelt. *"Believe!"* he was saying. *"Believe!"* And Theo took off in perfect rhythm, racing for the tape. Concentrated only on himself and no one else, so that he did not even know whether he'd won or lost until Booker came over to him and clapped him on the back, and told him that he'd beaten Frank Payton and given Harry Engel, who was the Labor Sports Union track champion, a run for his money.

"You're in," he said, shaking Theo's hand. "I should never have doubted you. Tom Eames wouldn't have. I wish he could have been here to see you. But you can't have everything."

Theo was ecstatic. He'd had one chance, the chance of a lifetime, and he'd taken it. It made everything that had come before worthwhile, although Booker was right about his old coach. The moment of success didn't seem complete without him. It made it more poignant that Theo had felt his presence so vividly when he began to run, only to lose him completely when the race was over.

"Do you know where he's gone?" he asked Booker.

Booker sighed and shook his head. "No, I don't," he said sadly. "Someone pointed the finger at him and called him a Red, and Saint Pete's kicked him out. It's happening all the time back home. Land of the free is the one thing our country isn't!" He laughed harshly, and Theo sensed a well of bitterness beneath the coach's words.

"He went west, I suppose," Booker went on after a moment. "Like so many others who get blackballed out of their jobs. Rode the train until he got to some place far enough away that no one would have heard of him. But it's hard to start again when you get older, hard to find the energy . . ."

Booker stopped with a faraway look in his eyes and then shook his head again, this time to banish his unexpected attack of the blues.

But something in Theo rebelled against Booker's defeatism. Coach Eames was out there somewhere. Theo was sure he was. And one day he was going to take the train, too, and find his old coach and thank him for the gift of self-belief he'd given him when he was a boy. He'd tell him about the Olympiad and show him how a tall tree could grow from a small seed. Theo vowed he would, filing the promise away for the day when he would return to America and find Frank Vogel waiting for him on the dock at Chelsea Piers. And who knows—maybe he would have a girl on his arm as he came down the gangway, just as Frank had predicted. And maybe that girl would be Maria. At that moment, standing in the vast Olympic Stadium, filled with the innate optimism of youth, anything seemed possible.

"Come on, son," said Booker, interrupting Theo's reverie. "Practice is over. We'll go and tell them to amend that sprint list, and then I'll buy you and the team a beer. It's been a good day, and you've given us something to celebrate."

Theo escaped from the celebration as soon as he decently could and used half of his remaining pesetas to take a taxi to the Colón. He hoped that maybe Andrew and his mother hadn't left yet. It was still early in the day, and he thought that if he could talk to them calmly and get his stepfather on his side, then maybe he could get his mother to see sense. It had to make a difference that he'd now been selected for the team. Surely they could not ask him to forgo such an extraordinary opportunity? Surely she would want to see her son compete?

But he was quickly disappointed. Alfonso the concierge told him that his parents had left two hours earlier and handed him an envelope addressed to *Theodore Sterling* in his stepfather's handwriting, which Theo quickly tore open.

Inside was a bundle of twenty-five peseta banknotes and a short letter obviously written in haste:

> Dear Theo,
> We are going straight home because your mother insists upon it. She is very upset and I hope you will use this money to join us there soon. Looking after your mother is not the same as being a mother's boy, but I think you know that. I trust in your better nature.
> Your loving stepfather,
> Andrew

The words hurt Theo, causing a spasm of pain to cross his face, which the concierge noticed. He solicitously offered Theo a chair and a drink of water and even the use of the telephone, but Theo declined. He needed to be alone to think and decide what to do.

But outside, in the glare of the sun, he quickly realized that everything was simple and that there was nothing to decide. He had to run, and so he couldn't go back to Los Olivos even if he wanted to, which he didn't. Andrew and his mother should have supported him, but instead they had turned their backs. His mother cared about only herself and Andrew cared about only her. To hell with them both! Theo thought angrily as he crossed the square.

After morning practice the next day, Theo got special permission from Booker to go back into the city. A dress rehearsal for the opening ceremony had been scheduled to take place in the stadium at five o'clock, so there wasn't much time, but he needed to keep the meeting with Antonio that they had arranged the previous Saturday.

He had a natural wish to tell his friend about the extraordinary change in his life that had taken place since he saw him last—a desire made stronger by the fact that he had no one else to share the news with, now that his stepfather and mother had left Barcelona. But he realized as he hurried up the street behind his hotel to the barracks that it was more than just a need to tell. He was hoping, too, that talking to his friend about the Games would make them seem more real, because everything that had happened since he met Booker at the kiosk had felt like some fantastic dream, and he kept expecting to wake up from it with a jolt. He was like Alice gone through the looking glass and now waiting for it to shatter.

The long, gray wall of the barracks ended at the iron gate in the entrance archway, which was firmly closed just like before. But this time soldiers were drilling in the courtyard, marching with their rifles held high above their shoulders. The pounding of their feet on the cobblestones and the harsh words of command unnerved Theo, who stepped back, almost colliding with a sentry who had come up behind him.

He was a different man to the guard whom Theo had spoken to two weeks before and much more aggressive. He shouted Theo down when he tried to explain his business and told him to leave, and when Theo protested, another soldier with stripes on his arm came out of a guardroom inside the gate with a pistol in his hand, and Theo turned and ran.

Something was happening that he didn't understand, and even though he hadn't seen him, Theo sensed that Antonio was caught up inside it. But there was nothing he could do. He had to go back to the stadium. And as he passed through the somnolent siesta-time streets, he kept looking back, stricken with the sense that he was leaving his friend behind.

The stadium was transformed. The cavernous emptiness had gone, replaced by a chaos of noise and color. Theo caught sight of the Stars and Stripes in the far corner of the athletic field and found Booker stamping his feet in annoyance, surrounded by his new teammates, who looked disoriented and confused.

"It's not a Games, it's a circus," Booker said, shouting to make himself heard above the babble. "A woman told us to go out on the field with the flag, but then another one said we had to wait because they're building a castle. At least that's what the word sounded like. A castle! What the hell has that got to do with running and jumping?"

As Booker was talking, Theo could see that the area in the center of the field was being quickly cleared, until all at once there was a hush filled almost immediately by the music of flutes and drums as hundreds of barefoot men dressed in identical costumes came running out from a side entrance. They wore white trousers and green shirts with thick black sashes tied around their waists and straightaway formed themselves into a circle of lines leading out from a central hub like the spokes of a wheel.

The men on the outside began to climb, using the sashes on the backs of the men in front as footholds to hoist themselves up, before walking lightly over the mass of shoulders to create a new center and then another. Up and up in a kaleidoscope of moving color until previously invisible children emerged from the throng and climbed nimbly to the very top, six levels above the ground, where three supported one, who held out four fingers in a triumphant gesture, answered by a crescendo of music and wild cheering from all over the stadium. The achievement lasted only a moment as the children and men dropped down at incredible speed until nothing remained except the *castellers* running back the way they'd come.

"Christ Almighty! I stand corrected!" said Booker, letting out a low whistle. "I've seen some wild and wonderful things in my day, including a nutcase tightrope walker hanging upside down above the Niagara Falls, but that was something else, wasn't it?"

Theo nodded. The human castle had filled him with wonder too. It was a marvel of what could be achieved if people worked together for a common purpose. A living symbol of the Anarchist dream. But it seemed out of place in this country where everyone was pitted against each other, filled with such murderous hatred.

As the American team readied for the parade, standing in their small group behind a Black woman athlete from Harlem, holding the flag, Theo felt moved by a profound gratitude. Booker had not just given him back the opportunity he'd lost years before and restored him to his country; he had also given him the chance to join with thousands of others in making a stand against the evil that was spreading across the world. It was the lesson that Esmond had tried to teach him years before. You could not stand idly by and acquiesce while innocent people were stripped of their rights and imprisoned and attacked with mustard gas from the sky, just because they were Jewish or African or believed in freedom and justice. You had to stand up and be counted, and it seemed to Theo that this was what each athlete was pledging to do as the band struck up "The Internationale" and they began to march around the stadium, singing with their hands held over their fast-beating hearts.

"Bliss was it in that dawn to be alive, but to be young was very heaven!" The line of poetry that Esmond had once quoted to him floated into Theo's mind as he got on the bus outside the stadium after the rehearsal was over. Everything felt right, until they'd gone a mile down the road and the driver put on the brakes and brought the bus to a grinding halt. The traffic was jammed bumper to bumper in front of them, the cause of the obstruction invisible somewhere up ahead.

After several minutes of sitting motionless, Theo volunteered to go and find out what was happening. He walked up the sidewalk and turned a corner. Beside him, he was surprised to see that the cars in the road were empty, their open doors evidence of recent abandonment. A hundred yards farther on, a police car had crashed sideways into an oak tree, blocking the way. On the opposite side of the road, an open-backed truck with **CNT—FAI** white-chalked on its side had stopped, but its driver was in his seat with the engine running, and Theo could see his fingers drumming impatiently on the wheel.

Between the two vehicles, two uniformed policemen were lying on the ground in the middle of the road. Theo could not tell whether they were alive or dead. A man in a blue overall was standing over them with a rifle slung over his shoulder and another that he was holding in his hands. Suddenly he lifted it and fired toward the empty cars, and Theo ducked down behind the one next to where he had been standing. He didn't know if he had been seen.

After a moment he raised his head a little way and found that he could see through the car's rear windows to a big shop on the other side of the road. The front window had been smashed and men were moving about inside, while the terrified owner stood shaking behind the cash register on the counter.

Now they were coming out, laden with guns. Rifles, pistols, shotguns—all being thrown into the back of the truck, and then they went back inside for more. Several had strapped bandoliers across their chests, stuffed full of cartridges, and looked like Mexican bandits in the B movies that Theo had watched in New York years before.

Inside the shop a man came up beside the cowering owner and pulled open the cash register and began taking out the money, piling up wads of banknotes on the counter. Then, when he was done, he leaned down and struck a match on the sole of his shoes and set the notes alight.

Instinctively the shop owner reached forward to put out the flames, but the arsonist pulled him back by the scruff of the neck and held him immobilized until all the money was burned.

"¡*Viva la anarquía!*" he shouted at the top of his voice. "¡*Viva la CNT!*" And outside, the other men joined in the cry, brandishing several of the stolen guns above their heads. Moments later they were all in the truck, and the driver roared away down the empty street.

Theo stared at the two prone policemen, willing them to get up, and as if in response, they did. They dusted themselves off and then walked over to deal with the hysterical shopkeeper, who had come out into the street, wringing his hands and crying over the ruin of all he had in the world.

Theo turned away and went back to the bus and told Booker and the others what he'd seen.

"I don't know what it means," he said. "They're Anarchists. Maybe they just want guns."

He was trying to reassure the others, but he couldn't reassure himself. The robbery of the gun shop was linked in his mind with the way he'd been chased off from Antonio's barracks at pistol point. And his anxiety grew when he got back to his hotel.

Athletes were milling in the lobby among the potted palms and noticeboards, and he could hear French and Spanish voices talking about an army rebellion in Spanish Morocco.

"There's fighting in Seville, too, and Cádiz," someone said. "They've risen all over the country."

"Rubbish," said another. "It'd be here, too, if that was happening, and the streets are quiet."

There were general murmurs of agreement, and several said that Morocco was a long way away. Theo remembered Antonio's father, Bernardo Alvarez, holding forth about his army days there under the command of crazy General Millán-Astray, who paraded Moors' heads on his legionnaires' bayonets and told them that they were *novios de la muerte*—bridegrooms of death. The athletes were right, Theo thought. Morocco was another world, where they played by different rules. What happened over there had nothing to do with the situation in Spain.

Finally, at the turn of the hour, they persuaded the night clerk to turn on a wireless that he had behind the desk, and the newsreader on Radio Barcelona announced that the Games would definitely be going ahead, with the opening ceremony taking place as scheduled on the following day. Talk of insurrection was an unpatriotic rumor being spread by enemies of the Republic. No one should pay it any attention.

Anything else that the reader had to say was drowned out by an outburst of wild cheering in the lobby, followed by a rapid dispersal as everyone including Theo began climbing the stairs to their rooms. The elevator was still not working.

Later in the evening there were lights outside, and Theo got up from his bed and went to the window. Outside, Plaça d'Espanya was quiet and almost empty, but beyond the tall, redbrick Venetian towers on the opposite side of the square, the National Palace on Montjuïc Hill glowed gold with an aurora of lights dancing above its dome. And below, a river of constantly changing colors flowed in undulating waves down the great stone staircases toward him.

Theo stared, spellbound, unaware that one of the Czech athletes had got up, too, and was standing behind him.

"Beautiful!" the man said, pronouncing the word slowly and with great care, as if it were the one lump of gold he'd extracted from the dark mine of the incomprehensible English language.

"Yes," said Theo. "It is."

And they stood together, side by side at the window, looking out at the river of light, believing that all would be well.

# Barcelona – July 19, 1936

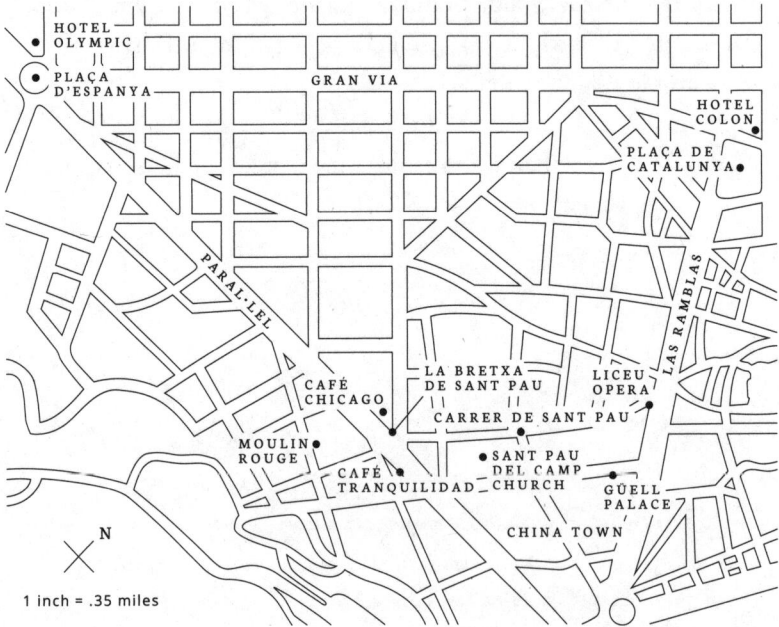

HOTEL OLYMPIC

PLAÇA D'ESPANYA

GRAN VIA

HOTEL COLON

PLAÇA DE CATALUNYA

PARAL·LEL

LAS RAMBLAS

CAFÉ CHICAGO

LA BRETXA DE SANT PAU

LICEU OPERA

CARRER DE SANT PAU

MOULIN ROUGE

CAFÉ TRANQUILIDAD

SANT PAU DEL CAMP CHURCH

GÜELL PALACE

CHINA TOWN

N

1 inch = .35 miles

# 5

## THE BARRICADE

Theo woke to the sound of fireworks, or so he thought—intermittent cracks and bangs that he assumed in his sleepy state to be related to the opening of the Games, except that there were no lights in the night sky, or at least none that he could see from his bed facing the open window.

He got up and looked out. The magic river of light had disappeared, and the palace at the top of the hill was now no more than a gray shape in the light of the half-moon. Below, the Plaça d'Espanya was lit here and there by streetlights, and Theo could see groups of men in the shadows, shooting. There were whiffs of white smoke in the darkness when they fired their guns.

They were standing or kneeling behind trees and lampposts and statues or were running between them and shouting slogans: *"¡Viva la República!" "¡Viva Cataluña!"* Flocks of birds flew up, screeching to escape the bullets, and then tried to return before they rose again, scattering in all directions.

Some of the men Theo recognized as the Assault Guard police that he had become used to seeing all over the city in their all-blue uniforms with distinctive peaked caps, but others looked like army soldiers in helmets with brown belts crossed over their khaki chests. The same uniform that Antonio had been wearing on the day Theo saw him marching back to his barracks. Was he down there in the melee? Firing and being fired at? Risking death?

Somewhere far away, Theo thought he could hear church bells, before all the noise was subsumed in the wail of sirens—first one and then many, breaking out all over the city, summoning the workers to the factories. Except that that made no sense, because it was Sunday and the sun hadn't yet risen. The sound sent a wave of fear and excitement through Theo and a flash of understanding to his brain. The sirens were calling out the workers to defend the Republic, which the soldiers down below were trying to destroy.

The radio announcer had been wrong. The army had risen in rebellion, just as it had in Morocco, and the Assault Guards were trying to stand in its way. But they were failing, outmanned and outgunned by the soldiers, who were still pouring into the square. As he looked down, Theo could see some of the guards waving white handkerchiefs, while others were running away.

Theo wanted to stop them. To call them back to continue their resistance. But he was impotent, looking down at what was left of the fighting with tears running down his face. He hated the soldiers and their guns. Hated their arrogant belief that they were entitled to impose their will on their countrymen when they should be defending them instead. Hated their willingness to take away a people's right to choose, its right to hope. Everything the athletes had marched for in the stadium, singing "The Internationale," trampled in the dust.

In the room behind Theo, one of the Czechs turned on the overhead light. Immediately bullets cracked and snapped against the surrounding wall, and Theo ducked down below the window ledge.

"Put it out, you fool!" he shouted, forgetting that his roommates spoke no English.

It didn't matter. A bullet flew through the window; everything seemed to shake, and the light went off.

Theo felt someone beside him on the floor, reaching a hand up toward the windowsill and then blindly out to pull back the wooden shutter. Theo did the same on his side and pulled the iron bar across to secure the shutters in place.

Behind the thick wood, the darkness in the room was pitch black and the sound of the gunfire was muffled. Theo felt an intense relief that the moment of danger had passed, but this was a physical reaction, quickly replaced by a sense of self-reproach that bordered on shame. Closing the shutters was the same as shutting out Spain. It was like running away. The siren was calling to him, too, to defend the Republic, and he felt that his life would have no meaning if he covered up his ears.

One of the Czechs lit a candle, and in its guttering light Theo pulled on his clothes. He left his suitcase behind, but at the last moment some instinct made him put on the windbreaker Booker had given him, even though he doubted whether he'd need it with the summer heat so stifling.

At the door he said "Goodbye" and "Good luck" to the Czechs, pronouncing the words slowly in the hope that they might understand them, but they looked at him like he'd taken leave of his senses, which perhaps he had.

He ran to the elevator, pressed the call button, and waited impatiently for a minute until he remembered it was out of order, and then took off down the stairs, jumping them two at a time. Flight after flight with his leaping footfalls echoing off the turning, whitewashed walls of the stairwell, until he burst out into the lobby and was brought to a sudden standstill by the locked front doors of the hotel. He pushed and pulled on the handles, but his efforts had no effect.

He looked around for help, but the lobby was empty and there was no one at the reception desk. Thinking that there might be keys in one of the drawers behind it, he used his hands to vault up onto the mahogany surface and jump down on the other side, where he just missed landing on the clerk from the night before, who had been cowering on the floor in terror and now backed away into a corner with his teeth chattering. Theo didn't think he had ever seen a man looking more frightened.

"I need to get out. Have you got the keys?" Theo asked, pointing back toward the door.

The clerk shook his head, but Theo wasn't sure that he had understood his question, so he repeated it more loudly this time, only to get the same result. The clerk looked like a cornered animal, scared out of his wits. Theo couldn't wait any longer. He raised his hand and smacked him hard across the face. "Give me the keys!" he shouted, holding up his hand, ready to deliver a second blow.

"Don't. Please," the clerk whimpered, and Theo was mortified to see that blood was coming from the man's nose and that he was crying.

He felt disgusted with himself, but he couldn't let up now. "Where are they?" he demanded, and the clerk pointed with a shaking finger up to a drawer above his head, which Theo immediately pulled out. The keys were at the back, behind a well-thumbed pornographic magazine that obviously belonged to the clerk, because he dropped his eyes when he saw Theo take it out.

"I'm sorry," said Theo. And he meant it. He wished he hadn't had to resort to violence, but he'd had no choice. He had to get out.

But now he was frightened himself. He'd had time to think about what he was doing and had to force his shaking hand to fit the key in the lock, and then once it turned, he stood motionless with his hand on the door handle, confounded by the enormity of the moment.

He'd never risked his life before. He looked back toward the stairs. He could go back up to his room and wait with the Czechs until the fighting was over. There was nothing stopping him. But he also knew he couldn't. His whole life had been defined by taking up challenges. It had made him who he was and he couldn't stop now, just because the stakes were higher than ever before. He opened the door.

To Theo's surprise, the previously slackening gunfire had intensified and was snapping on all sides like the cracking of a hundred whips, but this made sense when he saw in the dawn twilight that there were more people out now: not just the soldiers and the Assault Guards, but Anarchist workers in trousers and shirts. Running and falling, and some in cars that rushed by on screaming tires, with the black snouts of guns firing from the open windows.

And there were horses, too, some with riders, some without. All maddened with fear. One charged by Theo with the whites of its eyes rolled back and its sides lathered with sweat, dragging a cavalryman whose foot was caught in a stirrup. He screamed in agony as his limbs broke on the concrete sidewalk.

So many noises. Not just gunfire. Shouting and screaming, car horns and over-revved engines, someone somewhere blowing a bugle. Over to Theo's left, two horse-drawn gun carriages had entered the square and mounted the grass, headed for the monumental fountain at the center. An officer rode in front on a jet-black horse, sitting erect in the saddle and apparently impervious to the chaos and danger all around.

Theo instinctively moved around behind, making for the Paral·lel, the boulevard that he had gone down with Antonio the weekend before. But before he got to the intersection, he stopped, ducking down behind a shut-up kiosk. There was less firing here, and he felt a compulsion to see what was going to happen.

The two cannons had been quickly taken off their limbers and were now facing west down the Gran Via toward a ramshackle barricade that the workers had built, blocking part of the road. The officer on the horse was behind the guns. He had his arm raised and he was wearing a white glove.

Theo couldn't comprehend what he was seeing. He'd seen cannons in movies. They were battlefield weapons. They had nothing to do with city streets where people went shopping and sat outside cafés, drinking coffee and reading the morning newspaper. The juxtaposition of the two made no sense. It couldn't happen.

But then it did. The officer's arm dropped and the cannons exploded one after the other, violently recoiling back toward the fountain. Theo clapped his hands over his ears too late, feeling like his eardrums had burst. Up ahead, the billowing smoke cleared, and he saw a scene of carnage that nothing in his life up to that moment could have prepared him for. Plane trees growing along the sidewalks had been sliced apart, and severed arms and legs and other nameless chunks and strips of flesh were hanging in the leafy branches, mixed up with colored metal from cars that had been blown to pieces by the shells. Trolley cables hung down beside twisted lampposts and, in the middle of the dusty road, a decapitated head with braided black hair lay resting against a piece of fallen masonry, with no body parts anywhere near to which it might have belonged.

Theo bent over and was violently sick. He stepped back, away from the vomit, and felt a rush of wind that almost knocked him over as a truck raced by within feet of where he was standing, headed toward the fountain. There were men in shirtsleeves standing on the flatbed behind the cab, and at the last moment they jumped down, hurling hand grenades at the soldiers beside the cannons.

Gunfire erupted all over the square, including the unmistakable *takka takka* rattle of a machine gun. Terrified, Theo turned and ran.

Down the Paral·lel with the images of what he had seen seared across his brain and taking root in his memory, from where they would return to haunt him at unguarded moments for the rest of his life.

A man in pajamas with his hair standing on end rode past Theo on a bicycle, swaying from side to side. He was shouting over and over again at the top of his voice: "The soldiers are coming! The soldiers are coming!" The few people walking on the pavement turned and began to run like Theo toward the sea.

But the soldiers weren't coming. Not yet. And apart from the cyclist and the panicked pedestrians, the great wide road was almost deserted, in stark contrast to the hubbub of the previous weekend. The streetcars had not yet started to run, and on the sidewalks the shops and cinemas were shuttered and the outdoor chairs and tables were stacked up inside the locked cafés. It seemed like a different place, and Theo felt a jolt of surprise when he glanced up and recognized the **Broadway de Barcelona** sign that had so excited him when he'd passed it before.

Up ahead, everything *had* changed. A vast barricade stretched across the Paral·lel from the sidewalk outside the Moulin Rouge over as far as the roadway in front of the Café Chicago. As he got closer, Theo could see that its line bent away from there to run alongside the *bretxa*, or opening of the road, on the Chinatown side before it turned back across the Paral·lel to complete its irregular rectangle shape below the Moulin. It was like a stockade and Theo could immediately see its strategic importance, cutting the connection between Plaça d'Espanya and the military barracks at the port, and commanding access to the narrow routes through Chinatown to the Ramblas.

He was astounded by the size of the barricade. The builders hadn't yet finished, but they must have been working all night to have got as far as they had, which meant that they had to have known what was coming, all the while that he was parading around the Olympic Stadium and looking out of his hotel window at the river of lights flowing down from the golden palace, full of his fool's dreams. Living in his fool's paradise.

"You there! Olympic boy! What are you doing?"

It took Theo a moment to realize that the man standing on the parapet with the rifle was shouting at him, and then he couldn't think of a good answer, so he just stammered "I was running away" and felt his legs turning to jelly because he thought he might be shot.

But the man kept his rifle by his side. "Who from?" he asked.

"The soldiers. They had cannons. They fired them up the road . . ."

"Which road?"

"The big one to the west. There were people in the trees. Bits of them. It was terrible. I can't explain." He was stuttering again, and he thought he was going to break down completely until he sucked in the air and obliterated the memory.

"Bastards!" said the man, spitting out the word with venom, and Theo nodded his head, because that was exactly what they were. "But it'll take more than cannonballs to stop us this time," the man went on. "It's not going to be like two years ago when the army only needed to fire one shell at the Presidential Palace before Companys and his cronies ran up the white flag. This time we're prepared."

"Yes, I see what you mean," said Theo, looking admiringly at the barricade.

"So, are you part of that?" asked the man, pointing with his gun toward a round kiosk standing in the center of the road between them.

Theo didn't understand the question for a moment until he looked closer and saw that the kiosk was plastered with the Olimpiada Popular posters that had gone up all over the city during the previous week. The same wording as on the windbreaker he was wearing.

"Yes," he said. "I'm a runner—on the American team." It seemed unreal to say it, even though it was true.

The man whistled. "That's impressive," he said, and put out his hand. Theo went to shake it, but instead the man pulled him up over the barricade. "I'm Miguel," he said. "Maybe we'll need you to run later. But for now, it's your hands we need."


Behind the stockade, men stripped to the waist were using pickaxes and crowbars to break up the pavement with the cobblestones being passed down a human chain to the barricade, which was growing higher by the minute.

There was shingle under the stones, and other workers were packing it in sandbags to use on the parapets.

They all worked in rotation, digging until their hands bled and blistered and then exchanging positions with a carrier. Theo did both but kept his windbreaker on despite the hot sweat that the work induced. His conversation with Miguel had made him realize that it was his passport to acceptance by the Anarchist workers, who now all began to call him *Yanqui*—a name that delighted him after all the hostility he'd met with before when he was looking for Maria.

He kept expecting the soldiers to arrive, glancing over toward Miguel and the other riflemen who were keeping watch both ways through specially constructed loopholes in the barricade, but nothing happened until he was sent back to fetch water from the Tranquilidad Café, located several buildings down from the Moulin Rouge.

He was staggering back up the road, reeling under the weight of the oversize water canisters that he was carrying in both hands. He'd lost all sense of what was happening around him, focused only on completing the task he'd been given, until suddenly he lurched to his left, almost losing his balance. He looked down, wondering if he'd been hit, and saw that the container in his right hand was empty. A bullet had passed clean through it, causing all the water to gush away. He trembled at the closeness of his escape and flung himself forward into the stockade behind the line of Anarchist riflemen who were returning the soldiers' fire up the Paral·lel.

He was sitting on the ground, and there were others there too. But they weren't frightened like he was. It was just that they didn't have weapons, and the leaders like Miguel had told them to stay down until they were needed. If a man on the barricade was hurt, then one rushed forward to take his weapon and take his place, while others carried the wounded man back to the Tranquilidad, which had been transformed into a combination of field hospital and command post. On the return journey, they brought up ammunition and food and more water.

Theo helped with the carrying. He'd never fired a gun, so it was all he could do. Inside the café, neighborhood women tore up bedsheets for bandages and cursed President Companys, who was speaking on the radio to denounce the coup.

"Now he talks!" they sneered. "When he refused us guns yesterday because he fears us more than Franco. We should hang him from the flagpole outside his palace when this is over. Let him swing for what he did."

It seemed to Theo that they hated the Catalan president more even than the army rebels, but beneath their vitriol, the women took comfort in the broadcast.

Companys's speech meant the soldiers had not yet captured the radio station near Plaça de Catalunya, and that was cause for hope.

Gradually Theo got used to the crackling and spitting of the gunfire as he passed, hunched over, between the café and the stockade. He'd been frightened at the outset that the soldiers would bring up the cannons from Plaça d'Espanya, but they didn't even seem to have a machine gun or, if they did, they hadn't yet found a defensible place to set it up. Instead, they crouched in doorways and around the corners of side streets, unable to mount any concerted attack on the barricade.

In the lulls between firing, the Anarchists shouted to the soldiers, imploring them to switch sides. "Your officers are lying to you!" they bellowed. "They started this. *They're* the ones trying to seize power, not us. We're defending the Republic. Come over! You belong with the people."

It seemed to work. Two of the Assault Guards who had changed sides to join the soldiers in Plaça d'Espanya took off running and made it over the barricade with bullets whistling around their ears. Everyone cheered, and Miguel stepped back for a moment to talk to them, hoping they might have information the Anarchists could use. Immediately Theo ran forward to look through the loophole Miguel had vacated. Over to the left, across the road from Café Chicago, he could see that the soldiers had broken into a restaurant and had pushed the tables and chairs out onto the sidewalk, piling them up to create a makeshift barricade of their own. They were moving about behind it and Theo could hear their raised voices, no doubt arguing about the desertions that had just occurred. For a moment he saw a head through a gap in the furniture, and then it was gone. But there'd been enough time for him to recognize the face of the captain whom he'd seen on horseback leading Antonio and the other cadets back to the barracks two weeks before. Darnell, Antonio had said his name was. A Fascist bully who called Antonio *Rat* and took pleasure in making his life a misery, in the same way that Barker had once enjoyed persecuting Theo.

If Darnell was here, then Antonio was too. It stood to reason. And if Antonio had seen the Assault Guards get away, then he might well try to do the same. Theo knew how much Antonio hated the army, and he might think that this was his opportunity to escape. But it wasn't. It had been little short of a miracle that the two guards had got across unharmed, and Theo knew that anyone who tried it again wasn't likely to be so lucky, particularly as Darnell and his henchmen would be prepared this time.

But the Anarchists didn't see it that way, or if they did, they didn't care. They were calling out to the soldiers again, urging them to come across. "You can make it," they shouted. "If those two did, you can too. It's not far."

"Stay back! Stay down!" Theo could hear his own voice in his head, repeating the same instruction over and over again as he stared unblinking through the loophole, willing his friend not to show his face. But then, as if in direct response, Antonio did.

He was leaning forward just where Darnell had been, in the gap between the tables, and Theo knew from his body shape that he was going to run.

He had to stop him. "Don't, Antonio! You won't make it. It's too dangerous," he bellowed, standing up above the parapet to make himself heard and waving his hands before he ducked back down again just in time to avoid a flurry of bullets whistling past where his head had just been.

But his foolhardy bravery made no difference. Antonio had already set off, and Theo's voice was drowned out by the cries of the Anarchists who were yelling at him to run, not stop. "Faster! Faster!" they screamed like they were punters at a horse race, as Antonio zigzagged across the road, headed for the poster-plastered kiosk that Theo had stood beside earlier when he was challenged by Miguel from the barricade.

A moment later and Antonio had reached the kiosk and was crouching down behind it to catch his breath. Now it was only a few yards to the barricade. Nothing in comparison to the distance he'd already covered.

Perhaps he'd been wrong; perhaps Antonio would make it, Theo thought, staring at his friend through the loophole, rigid with a newborn hope that felt like a prayer. But then Antonio took off and fell almost immediately, shot through the throat so that he had to have been dead by the time he hit the ground, and the shaking movement in his body was from the impact of the second and third bullets fired by Captain Darnell, whom Theo could now see, looking out triumphantly over the barrel of his rifle on the other side of the road. Like a marksman in a shooting gallery, admiring his perfect score.

Theo's hands were on the parapet. He wanted to go out and get his friend. Bring him in and cover him. But he couldn't, because strong hands were pulling him so hard that he fell back on the ground, hitting his head. He must have blacked out for a moment, and when he opened his eyes, Miguel was standing over him with his rifle aimed at his chest.

"You knew him," he said accusingly. "You were calling his name."

"He was my friend. My best friend," said Theo, forcing out the words between hard, sobbing breaths that wrenched his chest and tore at his throat.

"He was a fucking soldier," said Miguel with his finger now curved around the trigger.

"He didn't want to be," said Theo. "He hated it. That's why he ran." He didn't give a damn in that moment if Miguel shot him. In fact, he'd have welcomed it. Anything to shut out the pain of what had just happened.

Miguel looked hard at Theo and lowered his gun.

"I'm sorry about your friend," he said. "But he has to stay out there until this is over, you hear me? I'm not having anyone risking their lives because of the dead. Their race is run."

Theo nodded. All the energy had gone out of him suddenly, like air from a punctured balloon. He didn't feel he could get back on his feet, let alone haul Antonio's body over the parapet.

The firing had almost completely stopped as the soldiers melted away into the side streets above Café Chicago. Behind the barricade, the Anarchists drank water to soothe their parched throats and used their red bandannas to wipe the sweat from their faces. They began to think they might have won until they heard screaming, followed by the appearance out of the side streets of a crowd of women and children and old people half running, half walking down the Paral·lel toward them.

Two shots rang out and the crowd stopped, strung out across the center of the road. Silent now, like their husbands and brothers and fathers and sons twenty yards away on the other side of the barricade.

And then a voice cut through the silence. Hard and even. A voice used to command. "Attention, lawbreakers. You have three minutes to leave this road. Completely leave it. If you don't, we will start shooting. You have no time to lose; look above you—you can see the clock."

It was Darnell. Theo knew it was, even though he couldn't see him. He wanted to run through the crowd and tackle him to the ground and beat his head against the cobblestones. Up and down, up and down, until there was nothing left to smash. But he didn't. He stayed rooted to the spot, staring up at the ornamental clock high on the facade of the six-story building that housed the Café Chicago. Watching time suspended: the black minute hand like an executioner's axe hanging over the defenseless people down below.

"¡Viva la anarquía! ¡Vivan los anarquistas!" cried an old, gaunt woman at the front of the crowd, raising her clenched fist in the air. But Darnell didn't respond, waiting to see if his ultimatum would succeed.

Behind the riflemen at the front of the barricade, the Anarchists were quickly withdrawing down the side streets. The clock's hand moved, and at a signal from Miguel, the riflemen turned and ran as well, and Theo was left alone as the panicked crowd broke, surging away to both sides with the soldiers advancing behind. They trampled Antonio's body as they clambered forward up onto the barricade, and now Theo was running too. Back down the Paral·lel and away into Chinatown. Behind him, the shooting had begun again and he rushed blindly through the winding streets, until he soon had no idea where he was.

He stopped to catch his breath. He was alone on a narrow road, looking through iron railings toward the long, peeling-stucco wall of a building lined with Moorish horseshoe-shaped windows. Beyond its red-tiled roof, an octagonal stone tower rose to two arches open to the sky.

It was old and beautiful and entirely out of place among the tumbledown tenements, and appeared at that moment to Theo as a magical sanctuary, offering an escape from the horrors of the morning, at least until he was ready to go on.

He pushed open a gate in the fence, which swung back on rusty hinges, and quickly crossed a patch of rough ground dotted with several untended palm trees. Dead fronds hung down like knotted gray beards beneath the living foliage.

Around the side of the building, he found a locked door honeycombed with woodworm. He bent down to look through the empty keyhole and saw dappled light and a gray stone column. Somewhere, out of sight, beneath the sound of the gunfire, he could hear water dripping, and the thought of it so close and yet so out of reach made his parched throat unbearable. He pounded his fists uselessly on the door, expending the last of his reserves of energy.

He was exposed. Alone, in full view of the deserted street with the hot July sun beating down on his weary head. The ground seemed to rise and the sky to fall, and his legs gave way beneath him as he slid down, knocking away a dustbin in an alcove by the door with his feet.

He opened his eyes after a moment and the first thing he saw was a key, lying on the ground where the dustbin had been. With trembling hands, he fitted it in the lock and stumbled through the door into another world.

He was in the ancient cloister of what had once been a monastery. The sunbeams shining through the exquisitely constructed trefoil arches were golden lines cutting across the dark shadows in the walkways, and the capital of each column was decorated with sculptures of fantastical beasts. In the center, water seeped down over a stone fountain that Theo clung to with both arms as he knelt and drank.

Once he'd slaked his thirst, he retreated back into the cool shadows, running his hands over the gray stone, trying to feel it was real, instead of a dream that he had conjured up to block out the images of the morning: the maddened horse dragging its rider, the severed limbs in the trees, and the decapitated head, Antonio running and falling—his body on the ground, jerking this way and that as Darnell's bullets found their mark.

He could still hear the gunfire. That was real and louder now than before: not just the crack of rifle shots but the telltale rattle of machine guns. He needed to escape it, leave it behind. There was another door in the far corner of the cloister. Not the one he'd come through. He pushed it open and entered the church, and when it closed shut behind him, the gunfire was muffled and far away, swallowed up in a vast silence.

Theo had never been in such a place. The immense weight of the barrel-vaulted ceilings and the absence of windows, except for small stained-glass medallions high in the thick stone walls, made the church seem subterranean, even though it was aboveground.

There was almost no decoration. Wooden pews, a stone altar and font. Nothing to distract from the sense of antiquity that was the church's essence. It had stood here when all around were fields. Before Columbus, before the world was round. Unchanged, while generations fought and toiled.

This was not his mother's church, peopled with gaudily dressed saints and bloodstained martyrs. Don Vincente would have no place here, railing from his pulpit against the godless Reds. This was the other church that Father Laurence had once shown him, and which he had forgotten: shadowy and twilit with the vespers chant of the monks rising and falling on the still air. Outside of time. Closing his eyes, Theo heard voices echoing in the corridors of his memory:

*"Why did you bring me here, Father?"*

*"So you could see that there can be beauty and peace in the world if you choose to look for it."*

Beauty and peace: Father Laurence's answer comforted Theo. He folded up his windbreaker for a pillow, lay down on a pew at the front of the church, and slept.

# 6

## ASCASO AND DURRUTI

There were men in the church. Their loud voices and heavy footfalls echoed off the thick walls. Perhaps they had come for Mass, Theo thought. It was Sunday morning after all. But he knew the thought was ridiculous even as it passed through his muddled brain. Churchgoers didn't shout and curse as these men were doing. And someone at the back was crying out in pain.

One of them was in charge. He told the others to be quiet and counted up to sixteen: the number of men he had with him. And just as he finished, he saw Theo, lying on his pew.

Immediately they laid hands on him, hauling him to his feet and standing him like a prisoner across from the leader.

They weren't soldiers. They wore trousers and shirts, stained yellow with gunpowder, like the Anarchists on the barricade, and they carried pistols. Small and dark blue like toys, except that the leader's was bigger, and he had it in his hand pointed at Theo, ready to kill.

He was shorter than the other men, and thin. He wasn't going to win any physical fights. But his strength was in his eyes. They were dark and penetrating and shrewd, redolent with a fierce intelligence. An ironic half smile played across his mouth, detached and slightly mocking, and his hand holding the gun was utterly still. Theo sensed that he would pull the trigger without hesitation or remorse, but that it would be a deliberate act. There was nothing hotheaded or emotional about the man.

"Who might you be?" he asked. Not shouting. His voice calm and even, confident in its authority.

"Theo. I'm American but I live here. Not here but in the mountains, in Andalusia. I was going to run in the Games, but now maybe they're not happening," he said, pointing to the windbreaker that one of the men had picked up and was trying on. He spoke in a rush, unable to stop the flow of contradictions and acutely conscious of his shaking hands. He was terrified.

"And so you decided to take a siesta on a pew in Sant Pau del Camp instead? Is that the idea?"

The biting sarcasm of the leader's question got Theo talking again, trying to overcome his fear to explain and justify himself.

"No, I was on the barricade in the Paral·lel with Miguel and the others," he said. "Not shooting, but helping carry the wounded back to the café and bringing water, and it was working. We were holding the soldiers off, but then they rounded up the women and children, and the army captain said they'd shoot them if we didn't get out. So everyone ran, and I don't know what happened after that."

"They took the barricade and set up machine guns that have killed half my men," said the leader. "And Miguel, too, which is no more than he deserves. He should have held his line. That's what he was told to do. The position is vital if we are to keep the troops apart, and we have to find a way to retake it."

Theo trembled as he took in the meaning of the leader's words and imagined the dead lying in heaps in the Paral·lel, riddled with bullets like Antonio. But the leader smiled, and Theo knew that he was being read like an open book.

"How many soldiers were there, do you think?" the leader asked.

"Fifty. Maybe less. They were moving all the time, so it's hard to be sure."

"Good," said the leader, nodding. "Fifty's good. Let him go," he told the two men holding Theo. "And give him his jacket and something to eat. He looks like he needs it."

Theo ate hunks of bread with olive oil and pieces of uncooked ham, washed down with water in a goatskin bag. Even before he'd finished, he felt his strength returning, and the men clapped him on the back. Friends now, when they would have shot him in cold blood at a nod from their leader five minutes before. They called the short man Ascaso, and Theo sensed that they would lay down their lives without hesitation if he gave them the word.

In a pew at the back, the wounded man had stopped crying out, and Theo wondered whether he was dead.

Ascaso was over by the main door of the church, which he had half opened to look out. He was smoking a cigarette, and the golden sunlight wreathed with the blue smoke to illuminate his diminutive figure as if he were an actor on a stage. The gunfire, muffled before, was now louder than ever.

Suddenly he shouted twice, calling out a name that sounded like Oliver, and ran out.

"Who's that?" Theo asked.

"Juan García Oliver. He leads the other group," said one of the men. "They crossed Chinatown farther up, so perhaps they didn't lose so many when they came out. If we join together, then maybe it will be enough." But he looked like he had no faith in what he was saying. A hundred men would be no match for machine guns protected by the walls of the barricade.

A couple of minutes later, Ascaso came back into the church. "Time to go," he said. "We have a plan."

He walked to the end of the church and leaned down over the man in the back pew, verifying that he'd died. He closed the man's eyes and took his pistol and handed it to Theo with an ammunition clip. "Let's hope you can shoot as well as you can run," he said.

On the way out of the church, he flicked his burning cigarette into the font and laughed when he saw Theo flinch.

"This church is beautiful, isn't it?" he said.

Theo nodded, uncertain of the right response.

"It's the oldest in Barcelona. A thirteenth-century Romanesque jewel, but tomorrow it will burn. All of them will. You'll see."

They were standing in a stone courtyard behind an iron-railing fence, similar to the one Theo had gone through at the back of the monastery compound. In front, a street called Carrer de Sant Pau led directly back to the top of the barricade that the soldiers had taken from the Anarchists on the Paral·lel. It was a hundred yards away at most, but none of them ventured through the gate in the railings and out into the roadway, as that would have exposed them to machine-gun fire from the soldiers. Everyone was smoking and shifting on their feet, with their nerves strained to the breaking point. Except Ascaso, who remained imperturbable as he gave them their instructions.

"Watch the clock!" he told them, pointing to the top of the Café Chicago building over to their left, just as Darnell had instructed the Anarchists to do earlier, when they had been the ones standing behind the barricade. "Oliver is taking a machine gun up there to fire down on the soldiers. Once he's ready, we attack."

Ascaso took homemade grenades—dynamite packed into tomato cans— out of a haversack and passed them around, one to each man, including Theo. "Light them before we run," he said.

"We got the dynamite off a boat in the harbor," one of the men told Theo proudly, but Theo had his eyes fixed on the clockface just like before, and was barely listening.

Ten minutes past eleven, eleven minutes past, twelve . . .

There was movement at the top of the building. Theo was frightened the soldiers would see, and looking over at Ascaso, he could see his eyes flicking up and down and knew that he was thinking the same thing.

"Light them!" he shouted suddenly as Oliver's machine gun opened up from above, and they were running and shouting: "¡Viva la anarquía!"

Theo threw his grenade at the barricade and stopped, watching as his and the others' exploded upon and around it. Through the clearing smoke, he could see Darnell's head above the sandbags, lifting his rifle to his eye and taking aim. Theo stood paralyzed, his pistol useless in his hand, waiting for the bullet, but it never came. Darnell crumpled and fell, and Ascaso darted away.

Over on the other side of the road, Theo could see the surviving soldiers retreating into the Moulin Rouge, where they barricaded themselves inside.

The Anarchists celebrated wildly, putting on the dead soldiers' helmets and firing their rifles in the air. "We won! We beat the army!" they shouted until they were hoarse, and Theo sensed not just their ecstasy but their incredulity too. If they could do this, then anything was possible. Anything!

He looked for Antonio's body, but he couldn't see it. The dead were everywhere, mixed up with the wounded, and people were running this way and that. Through the chaos, as if down a tunnel, he could see Ascaso beckoning to him from outside the Café Chicago.

"You saved my life," Theo said. "Thank you." The words seemed entirely inadequate, but he couldn't think what else to say. Ascaso's inscrutability rendered him tongue-tied.

"I killed the captain," said Ascaso. "Saving you had nothing to do with it."

"He deserved it," said Theo fervently, surprised by the bloodthirsty joy he took in another man's death. He would not have felt that before, but the morning had changed him.

"I need you to run. I can't spare any of my men, and it's the one thing you're good at, I reckon," he said, glancing scornfully down at the unfired pistol in Theo's hand.

Theo nodded. "Where?" he asked.

"Down there to the left," said Ascaso, pointing toward the next intersection below the Carrer de Sant Pau. "All the way through to the Ramblas and across to the other side. Durruti's in the square on the right with the trucks, and you'll tell him what happened here, but that there are soldiers still resisting. Say I sent you."

"Durruti?"

"Yes, Durruti. Even you must have heard of him. Now go!"

Theo turned and ran. Almost slipping on bloodstained cobblestones as he skipped over the dead men from Ascaso's group who had fallen in their first unsuccessful attack on the barricade while he was sleeping in the church. Charging down the road and remembering Maria talking about the Anarchist leader, Buenaventura Durruti, years before in the village. A "lion" she had called him and had shown Theo a crumpled photograph cut from a newspaper, which he still remembered, because the face was unforgettable. Big and savage: it looked as if it had been hewn out of rock. He had been imprisoned, tortured, exiled, left for dead, Maria said. But he would never give up, because Anarchism was in his soul. She would follow him to the ends of the earth, she had told Theo. If she had the chance.

Theo recognized him straightaway, listening and issuing orders as fighters and messengers ran up to him from all directions. Maria was right, Theo thought, as he waited his turn. Durruti was exactly like a lion, caged but ready to break free.

He listened intently without interrupting while Theo described what had happened on the barricade, starting from the beginning, and when Theo reached the triumphant conclusion, he unexpectedly opened his arms and folded Theo in a tight embrace.

Theo was shocked. No one had ever held him like this before, let alone a complete stranger. Through the clasp of Durruti's arms, he felt the immense, oxlike strength of his body. It made Theo feel weak, as if he might dissolve.

After a moment Durruti released him but kept his hands on Theo's shoulders, looking into his eyes. Durruti's were glittering gray and childlike, as if he saw everything with the freshness of the first time, untouched by irony or the dullness of repetition.

"What's your name?" he asked.

"Theodore," Theo replied, and afterward he often wondered why he had given Durruti the long version of his name, which he never used. It had to have been the importance he'd attached to the moment. As if it was a beginning. A kind of baptism.

"Thank you for bringing me this news. We're going to be free, Theodore. I know it," said Durruti and kissed Theo on both cheeks.

"Free!" he repeated, before he turned away to speak to the next man in line.


Theo walked up the Ramblas in a state of extreme excitement, with adrenaline coursing through his veins. The encounter with the charismatic Durruti had cemented his conviction that he was touching history. It was the same visceral emotion he had felt at Olympia, but magnified to a new level.

There was no fighting in the Ramblas, but the gunfire that he could hear, coming from all directions, was the noise of history being made. Raw and bleeding and world changing, and he had been a part of it. He had fought the enemy and carried the wounded; he had brought the victory message to the Anarchists' leader; he had made a difference.

None of this would have happened if he had chosen the safe option and stayed in the hotel with the other athletes, cowering under their beds. Instead, he had made that same courageous but reckless choice of action over inaction, deplored by his stepfather, that ran like a thread through his life. He could not stand aside from life, even if it meant risking his own. He had to embrace the agony and the ecstasy of the Romany woman's song.

But the agony was terrible, swamping the ecstasy as soon as he remembered that Antonio was dead. *Dead*: the word echoed in Theo's mind like a bell that wouldn't cease its tolling. Unreal, impossible to absorb and understand. Because Antonio had always been so alive: lying beside him on the pine needles in the dappled summer sunlight, leaning forward and laughing in the firelit cave or in the square, running through the Chinatown lanes just the weekend before . . . How could it be that he was gone, never to be again?

The image of Antonio's dead body, riddled with bullets like a sieve, flooded Theo's mind, overwhelming the forlorn attempts he had been making to keep it at bay. All he had left now to combat it was anger. He remembered just as vividly the face he'd seen as he looked up: Darnell, the cavalry captain, smugly enjoying his handiwork. Theo hated him and rejoiced that he was dead. Because Darnell was the face of the enemy—the Fascist army officers, who had destroyed the Olympiad and were trying to enslave the Spanish people.

But they wouldn't succeed. Freedom was coming, just as Maria had said it would. The Anarchists' long-awaited revolution had begun.

Theo caught sight of the Liceu Opera House on the opposite side of the road and remembered Carlos watching him from the shadows on that first evening, before he melted back into the darkness of Chinatown, where anyone could hide. Carlos was the last person Theo wanted to think about, but he couldn't rid himself of a sudden sense of foreboding. He could see him in his mind's eye, just as vivid as the figure of Durruti, whom he'd just left behind. The one so calculating and cruel; the other so generous and pure, breathing his ideals. How could it be that they shared the same faith?

Carlos was here in the city. Theo was sure of it. The thought like a sixth sense stopped him in his tracks as he tried to work out the exact street corner at which Carlos had been standing, as if half expecting him to reappear.

And if he hadn't been gazing intently across the road as he recalled that moment, he wouldn't have seen Maria, because she passed him in the blink of an eye, standing with a group of other Anarchists in the back of a flatbed truck that went roaring up the Ramblas toward the Plaça de Catalunya. At their feet, a machine gun had been set up, buttressed with mattresses. Its black snout pointed out expectantly, waiting to be fired.

She was gone in a moment, but he was sure it was her, just as he knew that the man beside her had been Primitivo. He'd shaved his beard and was thinner in the face, but he had that same expression of cruel menace that Theo remembered as he gripped the side of the truck, ready to jump down. He had a rifle over his shoulder and two bandoliers of bullets stretched in an X across his chest.

Theo immediately took off, running after the truck. It had disappeared in a cloud of black exhaust smoke, but the noise of gunfire was intensifying as he got closer to the Plaça de Catalunya, and he felt confident that it would have to stop and unload its passengers at the top of the Ramblas.

Sometimes Theo had to dart out into the road when his path was blocked by rudimentary barricades thrown up when the soldiers had tried unsuccessfully to force their way down the Ramblas earlier in the day. But he had to be lightning quick to avoid being hit by the commandeered cars that drove wildly by with their horns blaring a constantly repeated three-honk tattoo: CNT, CNT, CNT . . . The initials of the Anarchist trade union were daubed in white paint on the vehicles' sides, and rifles were pointed out of the windows, some firing up at the sky.

Several of these cars had already crashed, creating more obstacles for Theo to get around. He quickly averted his eyes from one where the dead driver had gone through his windshield and now lay on the hood staring up the road, but he couldn't look the other way when he tripped and fell over a corpse lying in the gutter. The dead man's head had smashed against the curb, and his gray brains were spilling out in a foul mess that a lean dog was sniffing at. It snarled and bared its teeth, but shied away when Theo kicked out at it with his foot, giving him enough time to get up and resume his run. His knee was bleeding through his torn trousers, but he ignored the pain as he sprinted toward the top of the street.

There he had to stop. He was standing just behind the front line in a battle, with the huge square beyond a no-man's-land in which the two sides were exchanging a constant stream of heavy gunfire, crisscrossing in all directions. It was hard for him to credit that this war zone was the same Plaça de Catalunya that he'd gazed down at so many times from his hotel window, watching well-to-do couples walking their dogs and children among the statues and fountains and flocks of fluttering pigeons with their bobbing heads.

Now the pigeons and the strollers were gone, and dead men and horses lay strewn about where they had fallen in the course of failed attacks and counterattacks that had raged across the square throughout the morning. The putrid, nauseating smell of human and animal flesh rotting in the heat made Theo retch, and he leaned forward to vomit up the food that Ascaso's men had given him in the church.

People were running and shouting all around him, and the noise combined with the incessant gunfire to create a cacophony that made his head spin. He thought he was going to faint again, and he fought hard to stay on his feet, because he was certain he would be trampled if he lost consciousness and fell.

He looked wildly around and focused on an ornate black lamppost only a few yards away from where he was standing. There were four brass water taps near the base. He'd seen them before when he'd crossed the square from the Colón to walk on the Ramblas. He pushed through the crowd and squatted down to drink and to wash the cool water over his burning face and his throbbing, bleeding knee.

He pulled himself up, still holding on to the lamppost as if it were a raft in a stormy sea. Maria! That was why he was here. He'd seen her. He knew he had, even though she'd passed him in a flash. But now she was gone. Unless . . .

Again, the sighting was momentary, and this time he couldn't be sure, but he thought he glimpsed her in a crowd of Assault Guards and Anarchists that was pouring down the concrete ramp into the dark mouth of the metro entrance over to his right. A flash of her beautiful face among the mass of unbuttoned blue tunics and sweat-stained white shirts.

He followed, but the pain in his knee prevented him from running, and the ticket station was deserted when he reached the bottom of the ramp. He stepped over the broken wooden barrier and entered a maze of vaulted tunnels, trying to track the pounding footfalls that he could hear up ahead—echoes of echoes bouncing off the white-tiled walls lined with brightly colored advertisements glowing in the fluorescent light.

He came out onto a long platform littered with cigarette butts. Beside him, rats were running between the rails, and above his head, condensation dripped down through the tangled black ceiling cables in the humid heat. He was alone, but voices were all around, garbled and intermingled.

At the end of the platform, corridors and stairways opened up in all directions and he hesitated, not knowing which way to go. In the end he took the ascending staircase, not because he thought it was right, but because he had to get out. His head was throbbing and he couldn't breathe.

At the top was another empty ticket hall and, beyond it, another staircase. He couldn't see where it ended, but he could smell the outside air, and he could hear gunfire again: the unmistakable rat-a-tat-tat chatter of machine guns that he recognized from earlier in the day when he'd stood with Ascaso's men outside the church, waiting to attack the barricade.

He thought of Maria amid the maelstrom of bullets. He saw her dead like her brother, and the image in his mind's eye propelled him forward and up the steps, one by one until he slipped, on blood perhaps, and fell back down to the bottom in a heap, lost to the world.

How long he lay there, he didn't know. He returned to consciousness briefly when someone tripped over him and swore, and he crawled away into a corner like an animal and slept, curled up on the floor, dreaming of Maria, so that when he awoke to hear her calling his name and feel her shaking his shoulders, he doubted the evidence of his senses and thought he must still be asleep. Some tresses of her long brown hair had come loose from under her cap as she bent down over him, and it was the sensation of their touch on his face that convinced him he was awake.

She was smiling in just that way he remembered that lit up her face, and she said his name and kissed him, and that was when he heard Primitivo behind her.

"What the fuck are you doing, Maria?" he demanded angrily, pulling at her shoulder. "Can't you see he's a quitter, skulking down here while we do the fighting? Yellow as horse piss. Leave him alone!"

Maria threw up her arm hard without looking around, knocking Primitivo's hand away, but she looked at Theo expectantly, as if waiting for him to answer the allegation.

"I fell," said Theo. "I must have hit my head. But this morning I was on the barricade on the Paral·lel. Before the soldiers took it. And then I was with Ascaso when we won it back, and he sent me to Durruti—"

"Durruti! You were with Durruti!" said Maria, her eyes shining. She had hold of his shoulders again, crumpling the blue windbreaker in her fingers, and he wanted her to stay like that, leaning down over him, so he just nodded.

"He's lying. Can't you see that?" Primitivo shouted, enraged by Theo's unexpected response to his cowardice gibe, which had rebounded back on him like a verbal boomerang.

"No, I'm not," said Theo quietly. "I've never lied to you, Maria. You know that."

"Yes," she said. "That's true." She stroked the side of his face, just as she had on the day of the murder before she'd ridden away. Except that this time, she wasn't going anywhere. She was here, she was real, and he wouldn't let her go.

"What's this?" she asked, running her finger across the Olimpiada logo on his windbreaker. Each time she touched him, it was like an electrical charge running through his body, and he sensed that Primitivo felt it the same way, because he could see the barrel of his rifle twitch, as if in response.

"I was going to run for the American team, but the soldiers put an end to that," said Theo, answering Maria's question.

"What a disaster!" Primitivo cut in sarcastically. "Hundreds of our people are lying out there dead and dying, and he's crying because he can't run in a fucking race."

Immediately Theo felt ashamed. "You're right," he said. "I'm not thinking straight." And then he remembered that Maria's brother was one of the dead and felt even worse. He had to tell her. He couldn't understand why he hadn't already.

"Antonio's gone," he said, hiding behind a euphemism because he couldn't bring himself to say the words *he's dead*.

"Where?" she asked, not understanding.

"On the Paral·lel. The army captain shot him when he tried to change sides. I shouted at him to stop, but he didn't hear me. And he'd already started running," he told her miserably, remembering the impotence he'd felt, watching from behind the barricade. Knowing how it was all going to end.

"Didn't try hard enough, did you?" said Primitivo contemptuously.

But he hadn't anticipated the effect his words would have on Maria, who jumped up and slapped him hard across the face. "Shut up!" she shouted furiously. "Can't you understand he's dead? My brother's dead."

Maria was crying, and Theo didn't know what to do. He wanted to comfort her, but he thought Primitivo might well shoot him if he touched her. He looked crazy. More than capable of another murder.

"Antonio was looking for you," he told Maria. "We both were, but he's been searching ever since he got here, whenever they let him out of the barracks. He said he thought he'd let you down by not standing up for you to your father. He wanted you to know that."

He wished he hadn't spoken as soon as the words were out of his mouth. He could see that they were no comfort. Their only effect seemed to be to make her cry harder.

"I know he was," she said between sobs. "People told me, but I didn't want him to find me because I thought he'd tell my father."

"Which is exactly what he would have done," said Primitivo impatiently. "He was a soldier, for Christ's sake, Maria, or maybe you've forgotten that."

Maria gave Primitivo a vitriolic look, but didn't otherwise respond as she struggled to regain her self-control. Evidently their time in hiding together had not led to true love and happiness, although Theo was not naive enough to assume that Primitivo didn't still retain some hold over her, just as she had clearly maintained her control over him.

"You said he ran?" she said, turning back to Theo.

Theo nodded. He didn't know whether it was a question.

"To get away from the Fascists, to be with us?"

"Yes, I shouted to him not to. That it was too dangerous. But he—"

"He ran, because he was brave," said Maria, interrupting. "Not like those cowards, who shoot people in the back. He ran because he'd chosen the right side. It was a good way to die, and it makes me proud of him. Proud I was his sister."

"Yes, you're right. He wasn't going to give in anymore. I thought it was all a waste, but it wasn't, because he chose hope," said Theo with sudden fervor, remembering Antonio's abject acceptance of the doom the old fortune-telling woman had seen in his palm. He'd defied her when he ran, defied fate. "Thank you for making me understand," he told Maria. "I wouldn't have without you."

Maria looked at Theo curiously but said nothing more. Instead, she stepped back and picked up the carbine that she'd propped against the wall when she saw him, and turned toward the stairs. The time for conversation was over. Antonio's death was behind her, and Theo would be, too, if he stayed where he was.

"What's happening up there?" he asked, getting gingerly to his feet. His knee was not as painful as before, but it was still sore and he put his weight on his other leg.

"We drove the rebels out of the square. They weren't expecting us to come through the tunnels, so we took them by surprise." Maria said this proudly, making it sound as if she had come up with the strategy herself. "Now they're holed up in the hotel and some of the other buildings, so we're going to have to go in and flush them out."

"We are. He isn't," said Primitivo contemptuously. "Look! He can hardly walk. What fucking use is he going to be? He hasn't even got a gun."

"Yes, I have," said Theo, taking the small pistol Ascaso had given him out of his pocket. He wondered if the safety catch was on or if there even was one, but he wasn't going to reveal his ignorance to Primitivo. It was a gun, even if it was the size of a kid's toy. That was what mattered.

Primitivo laughed, but before he could say anything, a voice was shouting down from above: "The Civil Guard are here. Hundreds of them." And everyone was on their feet, talking all at once as they converged on the stairs.

"Are they with us or against us?" someone asked.

"What a damn stupid question!" said Primitivo, pushing forward. "They're the enemy. Everyone knows that."

"Not today," said another. "They've got the hotel surrounded."

He was right. Looking out over an improvised barricade at the top of the steps, Theo could see diagonal lines of green-uniformed guardsmen positioned in a wide V shape around the grand revolving door at the entrance to the Colón, through which he had passed so many times. They stood still as statues, and their shiny tricorn hats gleamed in the noonday sun.

He felt just as surprised as Primitivo. He remembered the eagle-eyed lieutenant interrogating him in his stepfather's salon, tricorn hat in his hands, and how frightened he'd felt, picturing the tortures that the Civil Guard had inflicted on their Anarchist prisoners in Asturias. In the villages, they served the landowners and the Church, but perhaps it was different in the cities. Perhaps here they were like the Assault Guard police, loyal to the elected government and ready to resist the army rebels who were trying to overthrow it.

Up above the guardsmen, many of the hotel windows, including the one where Theo had stayed, were blocked by upturned mattresses, leaving small gaps at the sides, through which rifles were pointing out menacingly. But, for the moment, a ceasefire seemed to be holding.

The point of the V had been left open, giving people coming down the steps access to motorized wagons that were driving up as Theo watched and parking with their backs facing the hotel. Blue-uniformed Assault Guards with their rifles at the ready were stationed in a cordon along the road, separating the Anarchists from the wagons.

Theo was impressed by the precise orderliness of the guards. Somewhere out there, an officer had clearly given careful thought to the positioning of his men, and his instructions had been obeyed to the letter. Their coordination and coherence represented the antithesis of the chaotic fighting Theo had seen throughout the day, and he was surprised to realize how grateful he felt that they had arrived in time to prevent the bloodbath in the hotel corridors that Primitivo and Maria had been grimly anticipating as vengeance for their comrades lying dead all over the square.

What did it say about him that he welcomed the arrival of the forces of law and order? Theo wondered. Whose side was he on?

Now, the Civil Guard commander, carrying only a baton, was walking up the steps toward the hotel entrance. All around, there was silence and the tension was palpable. One stray shot was all that was needed, Theo thought, and the Anarchists would have their bloodbath. But the colonel didn't hesitate or hurry, displaying an extraordinary composure.

He passed through the revolving door, and the guardsmen closest by went to follow him inside, but they moved too quickly and got stuck in the door's compartments. Around and around they went, faster and faster, just like Charlie Chaplin in one of his silent films, until the doors disgorged them back out onto the steps, where they staggered about like drunks, until the other guardsmen pulled them aside. A wave of laughter passed through the crowd, releasing the tension, and Theo suddenly knew that the evacuation was going to work.

The disarmed soldiers came out of the hotel, passed through the lines, and climbed into the wagons and were driven away, and the Anarchists did no more than shout insults and catcalls. And at the end, when the soldiers were all gone, the guards threw their tricorn hats up into the air, and everyone came together and cheered.

Suddenly it seemed right to hope again, to believe that everything was going to end well. *"We're going to be free, Theodore. I know it."* Theo could hear Durruti's voice in his ear, expelling doubt, drowning it in the certainty of his conviction.

# Barcelona – July 1936

DIAGONAL

CARRER LLÚRIA

● CARMELITES

PASSEIG DE GRÀCIA

● TARRAGONA STREET
BARRACKS

GRAN VIA

PLAÇA
D'ESPANYA ◉

PARAL·LEL

PLAÇA DE ●
CATALUNYA

LAS RAMBLAS

OLYMPIC
STADIUM ●

MOULIN ●
ROUGE

COLUMBUS ◉
STATUE

MONTJUÏC ●
CASTLE

PORT

N

MEDITERRANEAN SEA

1 inch = .75 miles

# 7

## THE CARMELITES

They sat on the steps of the Colón, drinking wine from expensive bottles that someone had requisitioned from the hotel bar. Out in the square, ambulancemen and stretcher-bearers picked their way through clouds of swarming flies as they sorted the wounded from the dead. They had tied handkerchiefs over their noses and mouths to ward against the smell, so that they looked like bank robbers. Car horns and sirens and occasional gunfire seemed as if they were all coming from somewhere else, having no effect on the essential desolation of the scene.

Maria was half sitting, half lying, with her head cushioned against the side of Theo's arm, which he concentrated on keeping perfectly still so she wouldn't have reason to move. She was asking him questions, just as she used to do in the village the summer before. Then, they had been about New York and London, but now she wanted to know every detail of his encounters with Ascaso and Durruti and the full story of how he had been selected for the Olympiad, although she avoided the subject of Antonio, for which Theo was grateful. His friend's death was a raw wound that he could not bear to touch, and he imagined that Maria was feeling the same.

He answered her as best as he could, but nervously, too, because Primitivo was sitting less than a yard away, watching with a murderous expression on his face. Out of the corner of his eye, Theo was aware of his enemy fingering his rifle, and he would have feared for his life if Maria had not been there. It was as if they were back again in Jesús's father's shop, but with a singular difference. There, she had delighted in provoking Primitivo with her praise for Theo, but now it was as if her intense focus on Theo made her indifferent to Primitivo's presence, which of course only served to enrage him even further.

Theo's mind swirled, caught up in a welter of conflicting emotions. Grief for Antonio, fear of Primitivo, and, rising above everything else, his longing for Maria. Adrenaline was still coursing through his veins, and the day's extraordinary events—its agony and ecstasy—had exhilarated him into believing that finding her had not been a lucky coincidence, but instead the work of some unseen hand bringing them together. Only Primitivo stood between them now, and Theo was irrationally convinced that if their meeting had been predetermined, then so, too, would be his removal. He would leave. How, Theo had no idea. But he felt certain it would happen because this was a day like no other, and it couldn't end in anticlimax, with Primitivo applying the brakes to the runaway train on which he and Maria were riding.

So he was not surprised when a car filled with gun-toting Anarchists screeched to a halt outside the hotel and the driver, wearing a red-and-black bandanna, shouted up to Primitivo to get in because Carlos wanted him at the port. Theo watched his enemy walk slowly down the steps, half expecting him to turn around at the last moment and shoot him dead, but instead the Anarchists pulled Primitivo into the car, which roared away in a cloud of dust.

Maria watched it go and spat on the ground. "I hope Carlos puts him up against a wall and feeds him to the dogs," she said viciously. "Not that he will, of course. Primo's his blue-eyed boy."

"I thought you liked him," said Theo, surprised by her vehemence. "He saved you from Pedrito."

"Yes, so he could get me for himself. Out of the frying pan into the fire! That's where I went." Maria laughed humorlessly. "Hiding in a dingy attic from the police and my father for months on end. Only getting out at night. He had me just where he wanted me, didn't he? Until today. But now everything's changed and he knows it. That's why he's so angry—because I'm going to be free."

She looked wild-eyed out at the carnage in the square, and Theo realized that where he saw death and destruction, she saw freedom and a new beginning. Suddenly he was assailed by that same doubt he'd felt before in the village, intensified by the knowledge that he'd been right: Carlos was in Barcelona and sending out thugs like Primitivo to do his bidding. Theo remembered the Anarchist leader at the inn in the mountains, describing his vision of the road to liberation: an orgy of bloodletting that would only end when *"the last marquis has been strangled with the guts of the last priest."* For him, the deaths today would be only a beginning.

And he remembered Carlos, too, in the dingy shop in Los Olivos, telling him with a cold smile on his thin, pale face to go home. *"You're not one of us,"* he'd said, and Theo thought now just as he had then that Carlos was right. He understood the Anarchists' passion, but he didn't think that their political vision offered any lasting solution. Violence would beget violence, not liberation. But he knew, too, just like before, that by standing back he would lose Maria. And that he could not bear to do.

Perhaps, with time, he could get her to see things differently. She was conditioned by the way she'd grown up, imprisoned by a cruel father who saw her as a piece of property to be sold to the highest bidder. But she was quick and clever. And perhaps there was another vision they could follow. Durruti had not seemed to him to be a man who would kill for the sake of killing. Theo felt the revolutionary's bearlike arms around him again and felt a new hope. He was here now with the girl he loved, and the army rebels had been defeated against all the odds. Anything was possible.

"What are you thinking about?" Maria asked, running her hand across his furrowed brow. "I've never known anyone to puzzle over things as much as you do."

"I don't know. Everything. What it all means. It's as if this day has been a lifetime, as if I was another person when I woke up this morning."

"Yes, I feel that too. But whoever I am now is still hungry! Come on, let's see if we can get something to eat in there," she said, pointing back toward the Colón. "Where there's wine, there's food, and whatever there is, it's free!"

She took his hand as he got up and kissed his cheek, reaching toward him with a spontaneity that made him giddy. Truly, everything had changed.

Others had had the same idea. In the vast kitchen at the back of the hotel, disheveled fighters were frying chicken and meat, and Theo and Maria sat down beside them at a long table where the hotel servants usually ate, devouring the food and gnawing at the bones. The blood sickened Theo, reminding him of what he'd seen, but he was too hungry not to eat.

No one talked, but a radio somewhere was playing jazz, so they all sat up and took notice when the music was suddenly cut off and Companys, the Catalan president, came on the air, speaking in a solemn voice, and introduced General Goded, the captured leader of the rebellion in Barcelona, who "has an important announcement to make."

The general spoke without hesitation in a clipped, aristocratic voice: "Destiny has been averse and I have fallen prisoner, for which reason I release all those who have followed me from your obligations toward me . . ."

It took less than a minute, and when he was finished, everyone in the room remained silent for a moment, as if they could not believe what they had just heard, and then, as one, they stood up and began cheering and stamping their feet.

Theo looked at Maria and saw ecstasy in her eyes. This was what she had hoped for, dreamed of, fought for all the long years since Nicolás had first opened her eyes to the truth. It was the fulfillment of the promise, the dawn of the new day come at last. Real instead of imagined, tangible as their hands, which had somehow become entwined as they joined in the celebration.

"Let's go," she said, pulling Theo away.

Out in the lobby, he half expected to see Alfonso the concierge coming out to offer his help. But there was no one in sight and he climbed over the reception desk, just as he had done at the Olympic Hotel at the start of the day, and took the key to his old room from off its hook. Behind them, the Anarchists in the kitchen had launched into a raucous rendition of "The Internationale."


The room was empty, but it had been used in the fighting. The bed's mattress had been stood up on its end and leaned against the window, so they were in darkness until Theo pulled it away, letting in the violet evening light. It was heavier than he'd anticipated and he collapsed under the weight, falling back on the floor, and then had to push his way out from underneath, looking up sheepishly as he emerged at Maria, who was doubled up with helpless laughter.

They somehow succeeded in pulling the mattress onto the bed and fell on it, both laughing now. He plucked her cap from off her head and threw it across the room, and the waves of her amber-brown hair cascaded down over his head so that he was suddenly lost in her and she in him, sightless and sensate as their bodies came together, joined in final fulfillment of long-suppressed desire. Eden!

He was in Eden! Rising into rapture and crying her name: "Maria! Maria! I love you, Maria!" Until he fell back, spent.

She was leaning on her elbow, looking down at him, and he lay completely still under the spell of her sapphire-blue eyes. He desired to reach out and touch the roundness of her arm, the contour of her cheek, the rise of her breast, but he wouldn't, because the moment was as close to perfection as he could imagine and he did not want it to end. Ever.

She ended it. "You can't love me," she said softly. "I won't allow it."

"Why?" he asked, not understanding. What they had just shared was love. What else could it be? It was a part of him, like his breath or the beating of his heart, hard under his skin.

"Because love is possessing. And I won't be possessed," she said fiercely. "Not by you, not by Primitivo, not by anyone. Do you understand?"

She was staring at him so hard that he quailed, certain that she would leave if he argued with her, and so he told her what she wanted to hear, even though it hurt him to do so. A pain behind his eyes that made everything seem broken.

But she didn't seem to notice. Once she had his assurance, she was happy again. She threw up her hand and turned on the radio by the bed and lay back humming the tune the orchestra was softly playing. A smile suffused her face as if she had entered the realm of bliss, and she was asleep.

Theo picked up a pillow from off the floor and slid it under her head, and walked over to the high windows, noticing for the first time the bullet hole in the center of the one on the right. Around it, the glass was a myriad of tiny concentric fractures, from which long radial cracks stretched out across the rest of the pane. Like my heart, he thought bitterly—still intact but shot through the middle.

He looked back into the room. There was no impact mark on the far wall, which meant that the bullet must have embedded itself in the mattress. He found the hole almost immediately, close beside where Maria lay sleeping. Carefully, so as not to wake her, he dug down through the coils with his fingers until he felt the slug and pulled it out. Hard and cold in his hand. It had been right there underneath where they had lain together.

He opened the left-hand window and dropped the bullet out, hearing the ping as it landed on the sidewalk down below. The closed windows meant no one had been shooting from inside the room, he realized. Only sheltering, hoping to survive the whirlwind. He wondered who they were and thought of Antonio. Another nameless soldier, caught up in events he could not control.

He felt a wave of guilt, realizing he hadn't once thought of his friend since he'd entered the hotel with Maria. How easily forgotten! How selfish happiness was! The smell of death wafted up to him on a slight breeze from the square down below, and he was just about to close the window when he caught the acrid scent of something else. Burning and smoke. Looking out, he could see gray columns rising above the twilit skyline, and he knew immediately what they were. The churches were burning, just as Ascaso had told him they would. He remembered the Anarchist leader's dark eyes boring into him and the stillness of Ascaso's hand holding the gun pointed exactly at his heart, and all at once he was afraid.

Maria was already dressed when he woke up, and light was pouring into the room because he had forgotten to draw the drapes.

"Come on," she said. "Get dressed. We've got work to do." She was all business, as if the night before had never happened.

She turned on the radio. An overwrought newsreader was talking. He seemed close to hysteria. "Attention! Much attention! People of Barcelona! The army rebellion has been defeated," he announced. But it hadn't been. Not completely. Because the next moment he was warning that the military were still holding out at the port and in the Carmelite monastery on the Avenue Diagonal, where the treacherous friars had given the soldiers shelter.

"We need to go there. We need to help," said Maria, picking up her carbine and talking over the recording of General Goded's surrender announcement from the previous evening, which the radio was playing again.

"Where?" Theo asked, scrambling into his trousers.

"I don't know. Either. Both. I want to be a part of it. That's all," she said impatiently.

He wished he'd washed. Now there was only time to cup water in his hands and pour it over his head and body, drying himself on an embroidered hotel towel that had turned from white to black by the time he'd finished. At least his knee was better: it still felt sore, but a scab had formed over the wound.

"The situation is in hand; the situation is calm," the announcer was declaring breathlessly as they left the room, although it seemed anything but when they got out into the Plaça de Catalunya and heard the sound of gunfire coming from the north. Instinctively, Maria turned toward it.

They were half walking, half running up the Passeig de Gràcia, with shattered glass from the broken shop front windows crunching under their feet. A breeze blowing across the boulevard picked up a litter of pink leaflets dropped by government airplanes the previous day, telling the soldiers that they had joined an illegal rebellion and appealing to them to go home, and Anarchist-commandeered automobiles drove hell-for-leather through the eddying pink cloud with fighters squeezed in so tight that some of them were literally hanging out of the windows, shaking their fists and shouting. All headed up the street toward the gunfire.

One car, emptier than the rest and flying a red-and-black Anarchist flag, screeched to a halt beside them. Theo took an involuntary step back when he saw Primitivo in the passenger seat, staring at him intently. He felt the truth of what had happened between him and Maria written all over his face and had to force himself to follow her as she climbed into the back seat.

Primitivo said nothing. He just kept his head turned, staring at them with his dark eyes smoldering and his thin lips pursed in accusation. Theo was frightened, sensing that Primitivo could kill him as easily as snapping his fingers, and enjoy it too. He remembered Primitivo's hands pressing down on his face and arm on the night he stood lookout outside the ayuntamiento and the scarlet blood spreading out across Pedrito's chest on that never-to-be-forgotten Easter Sunday. How could he defend himself against such quick-and-easy violence?

Only Maria could keep Primitivo in check, which she accomplished now by the simple trick of laughing in his face. "Keep your dirty thoughts to yourself, Primo," she said scornfully. "Who the hell do you think I am?"

He nodded, dropping his eyes. "Your friend's dead," he said to Theo, giving him one last vicious look before he turned back to the front.

"Who?" Theo asked.

"Ascaso. The soldiers got him down at the port." Primitivo made it sound as if Theo was going to be next.

"But we captured the San Andrés barracks last night," said the driver excitedly as he veered back out into the traffic, grinding the gears and steering wildly as if he was driving a Dodgem car on a fairground. "We got in there before Companys's men could stop us and seized the rifles. Thirty thousand of them they say."

Maria's face lit up. "Now we can win," she said ecstatically. "And Companys and his bourgeois flunkies can't stop us. Our time has come. I know it has. I can feel it." She breathed in deeply, as if the morning air contained a different kind of oxygen to the day before.

"Damn right it has," shouted the driver and blew his horn in the familiar three-beep blast: *CNT, CNT.* They'd reached the top of the Passeig de Gràcia, and he threw the steering wheel violently to the right so that the car just missed colliding with an obelisk that seemed to loom up out of nowhere. Now they were on the Diagonal, and the gunfire was suddenly all around them. Theo put out his arms and pulled Maria down, just as the car screeched to a halt.

For a moment he thought the driver had been hit until he saw that the lunatic man was laughing. "Fuck!" he said. "That was close." And Maria was pushing Theo away and laughing, too, as she opened the door to get out.

"We just passed the Carmelite monastery on the other side," the driver said, pointing back up the Diagonal. "The bastards are firing from the tower, but they can't see you here. We're too far down the road."

They edged along the sidewalk, keeping under the trees, and stopped as soon as the church came into view. Tall ogival windows above the big arched doorway faced out onto the Diagonal, and a round dome surmounted by a cross emerged from the invisible monastery buildings behind. The church's east wall curved and ran north up a narrow tree-lined street, the Carrer Llúria, and ended in a tall bell tower in which the soldiers had sited their machine guns.

Nothing was moving, and the guns were quiet now after their recent flurry of fire. Anarchist fighters were densely gathered in the doorways on both sides of the Diagonal, and some had got into the houses. Theo could see them lying on the roofs and behind piled-up furniture in the open windows. White sheets hung down from under the balconies to demonstrate the occupiers' loyalty to the Republic.

The bodies of several Anarchists shot in the earlier fighting were lying out in the road and on the sidewalks around the church. They lay haphazardly here and there, as if they had fallen from the sky, with blood seeping out from under their clothes and congealing in dark pools on the ground. One of them wasn't dead. He twitched, regaining consciousness, and cried out for help and water. Two men dashed out from a nearby hiding place to rescue him, and immediately, the guns in the tower sprang back into life, sending bullets spattering across the roadway so that they had to turn back. The cries stopped, although it was impossible to know whether this was because the fallen man had been hit again or had just relapsed back into unconsciousness.

Later, a government biplane descended out of the clouds and circled the tower, firing its guns through the open arches. The machine guns responded but then fell silent, and the Anarchists cheered the pilot as he leaned out of his cockpit, shaking his gloved hand in the familiar clenched-fist salute, before he flew away. But their hope that he had knocked out the tower's defenses proved short-lived as the soldiers started shooting again immediately after a fighter had dared to venture out into the road.

The standoff continued with sporadic firing until the Civil Guard arrived, and Theo felt a sense of déjà vu as he watched the same commander as at the Colón walk up to the church alone, showing the same calm bravery he'd displayed on the evening before. He carried no weapon except his baton, with which he rapped on the door three times.

Silence. So many eyes inside and outside were focused on this one lonely man, but nothing moved except the leaves on the trees, gently rustling in the light midsummer breeze. A minute passed and the door opened slightly. In the narrow gap, Theo caught sight of an army officer wearing a cap with eight-pointed stars. He talked with the Civil Guard commander for several minutes, and then the door shut again and the waiting resumed.

Suddenly Maria grabbed Theo's arm and yelled "Look! Look!" pointing up at the bell tower, where a white flag had been run up. Everyone around them was shouting, too, surging forward out of their hiding places toward the church door, which had opened again.

Just as at the Colón, the Civil Guards had formed a cordon in front of the church buildings, running around into Carrer Llúria, but Theo was alarmed to see that there were far fewer of them than there had been at the hotel, and that there were almost no Assault Guards present this time to provide support. They were heavily outnumbered by the Anarchists, who were shaking their fists and baying for the soldiers' blood. Some began throwing stones at the church windows, lobbing them over the guards' tricorn hats, and the sound of breaking glass was added to the mayhem.

"Where are the fucking friars hiding?" someone shouted. And another voice answered: "They're down in the crypt." Looking around, Theo saw that Primitivo had disappeared, and he breathed a sigh of relief. He'd been thinking that it was quite possible Primitivo would plunge a knife in his back if the scene descended into chaos and gave him an opportunity to do the deed unseen.

With great difficulty, the guards succeeded in maneuvering one of their motorized wagons close to the door of the church, and a group of soldiers came out through the cordon, climbed inside, and were driven away. Theo began to hope that the evacuation might succeed despite the disparities in numbers, just as it had at the Colón, but the Anarchists quickly filled the space left by the departed wagon, and the next one could not get anywhere as close. Now, fatally, the military changed their tactics and began to send out their wounded, carried by soldier stretcher-bearers over to ambulances that had parked farther up the Diagonal.

Fools! Theo thought. Can't they see that there isn't time? The crowd was growing in size by the minute, and it was obvious that the guards would not be able to hold them back for much longer. The soldiers and the friars needed to make a run for it, while they still could, carrying their wounded on their shoulders if they had to. But instead, the stretchers continued to come out one by one, as if they had all the time in the world, and as each one passed, the Anarchists pressed closer, leaning through the guards to spit on the wounded and their bearers.

The breaking point came when a badly injured man, writhing in delirium, threw out his arm from under his bloodstained blanket, revealing gilt stripes on his sleeve. He was a captain! One of those who'd given the orders to kill! The Anarchists surged forward and broke the line, beating the stretcher-bearers and the captain onto the ground and kicking them where they lay.

Theo instinctively pulled back as the crowd rushed forward, and he lost contact with Maria. Some of the Anarchists were flinging lit torches through the broken windows of the church. And farther to his right, someone was running on Carrer Llúria, shouting, "We've smoked them out. They're coming out. Look!"

Theo did. Up past the bell tower, a side door had opened in the wall and friars were stumbling out, coughing and spluttering. They had taken off their habits and put on civilian clothes, but the disguise was fooling no one. An old man at the front was wearing black trousers that flapped around his ankles and a yellow shirt that couldn't fit across his chest because he was too fat. His hair stood up on end, and he looked like a clown.

"Now!" a voice shouted and a machine gun opened up. *Rat-a-tat-tat; rat-a-tat-tat.* Theo could see it set up on a tripod wedged in by sandbags, facing up the side street toward the friars, less than fifty yards from where he was now standing. Someone he didn't recognize was firing the gun, but Primitivo was the one feeding the ammunition. Without thinking, Theo took off running and threw Primitivo to the ground, and he'd raised his fist to punch him when he got hit himself. With what he didn't know, but stars exploded in his head as he fell, crashing down on the cobblestones, and it was this second cranial impact that knocked him out.

He came to, looking out across the wide expanse of the Diagonal. His vision was blurred, but he could make out the yellow-shirted priest crossing the road with a soldier beside him, holding him up. An oddly matched pair, they tottered together as if they were drunks returning from a night on the town, not fugitives from a massacre.

Theo willed them forward. The mob were fully occupied inside the church and monastery, and each stumbling step the priest and soldier took edged them closer to safety.

They had almost reached the far sidewalk when the soldier fell. Whether it was a lucky shot or a marksman's bullet, Theo had no way of knowing, but the old man was now alone. He staggered into a large doorway but was pulled back out onto the pavement by two Anarchists who had run across the road and now used the butts of their rifles to force him to walk.

The priest held his palms together as he shuffled forward under the arching branches of the poplar trees, and his lips were moving, so Theo knew he was praying. He wanted to go to the old man's rescue, but he knew at the same moment that it was too late. One of the Anarchists had raised his rifle and taken aim, and the old priest fell.

He crawled a little way farther and then collapsed beneath a fractured lamppost, whose top leaned down over him, as if in an iron sorrow. His dead face looked back toward his church, etched with a final expression of petrified terror.

Theo summoned all his strength and got unsteadily to his feet, stumbling away down the Diagonal. He was expecting a shot like the one that had killed the soldier, but nothing happened. He looked back once and saw that the white flag in the tower had been replaced by a red one and that crimson flames were licking up the church walls toward it. He couldn't escape the thick gray smoke that was billowing out from the burning church and monastery in all directions, but the cries and screams diminished in volume the farther he moved away, until at last they were no more than remembered echoes in his mind.

# 8

## THE RED CITY

He went back to the Colón, although afterward he could hardly remember how he got there. Just streets with people running and shouting and sheets hanging from windows and smoke. Everywhere smoke, choking his nose and mouth and sinking in through his pores.

He lay on the bed without even taking off his shoes and slept, and when he awoke, it was dark. He lay still, listening to his breathing and thinking it could be hers too. A synchronicity of breath. As long as he didn't stretch out his arm, she might be there, sleeping beside him.

But he knew all the time that he was alone. He had lost her when she most needed his protection, stepping back as the angry crowd surged forward into the church. Lost her when he had found her against all the odds, one face among thousands caught up in the turmoil of the rebellion.

Had he let her go? He didn't know. It was too quick. He searched back for the moment of separation in vain. But he could remember what happened afterward. He had walked away from the burning church without going back into the smoke to try to find her. Why? He'd hurt his head. He'd not been thinking straight. All that was true, but wasn't it also because he'd assumed she was safe? Because she was one of the victors and he wanted no part of what they were inflicting on the defeated? He'd seen enough, and so he'd left her to Primitivo.

He walked the room as if it were a jail cell. Backward and forward, trying in vain to calm his racing mind. Where was she? Would she come back? What had happened inside the church? Questions and questions with no answers, until he was too exhausted to walk anymore and lay down, pressing his face into the pillow where her head had lain the night before, searching for her scent.

Sleep must have come to his rescue again, because when he opened his eyes, early rays of sunlight were dancing in the windows. He got up and ran a bath and scrubbed his face and body in the hot water until his skin was red and raw.

He barely recognized himself in the mirror. His unshaved face was gaunt and drawn, and there were bruises and swelling on the side of his head, although there was no blood. His eyes were big in their sockets, staring back at him, as if intent on keeping focus so they wouldn't go slipping away.

"Seen too much. That's the trouble," he said out loud, testing the sound of his voice in the empty bathroom as if to confirm he was looking at himself and not a wraith impostor molded by the steam. It was oddly comforting to hear the words, and he thought he might try talking to himself more often.

He went downstairs, meeting nobody until he got to the lobby, where a familiar voice greeted him. Alfonso was standing behind his desk, dressed in his concierge uniform, as if it was just another Tuesday in the Colón, apart of course from there being a two-day-old battlefield outside the front door.

"Alfonso! I'm so happy to see you!" said Theo, going over to the concierge and shaking him warmly by the hand. It was an understatement. Seeing a friendly face lifted his spirits, but Alfonso's unexpected appearance also gave him a sudden hope that normality might be about to resume, like a ship righting itself after a storm.

"And I'm happy to see you too, sir," said Alfonso, making a small bow. "I didn't know you had returned to us."

"Yes, I took the key. Because there was no one here," said Theo, feeling the need to confess.

"That's perfectly in order. Will you be wanting some breakfast?" Alfonso asked and then abruptly stopped, looking embarrassed at his mistake in offering something that was no longer available. "I'm sorry," he said, opening his hands in a gesture of impotence. "These unfortunate events take a little getting used to. I hope that we will have more staff tomorrow."

"Don't worry. I understand," said Theo, resisting the temptation to laugh because the whole conversation was so surreal. But he wanted to cry too. The mention of food had made him realize how hungry he was. He hadn't eaten anything the previous day, and it was agony to remember the sumptuous hotel breakfasts he'd had in the dining room with his mother and stepfather.

Alfonso looked distressed, as if he could read what was going through Theo's mind. "I do have some sandwiches which my wife made for me this morning," he said hesitantly. "She always makes me more than I need."

"Do you?" said Theo, unable to conceal his excitement.

"Yes. And I would be honored if you would join me," said Alfonso, bringing out a well-filled bag from under his desk, accompanied by a thermos of hot coffee.

Theo ate not one sandwich but two, and the food and the coffee gave him a new energy that he would not have thought possible when he woke up. He felt moved to tears and wanted to kiss the concierge, but realized that that really would be a bridge too far in relation to hotel etiquette even in these unusual times, and so he confined himself to another wringing of the poor man's hand.

"Is there anything else I can do for you, sir?" Alfonso asked, returning to his previous formality now that the picnic had been put away.

"Yes," said Theo purposefully. "Can I use the telephone?"

Less than a minute later he was talking to Booker, who sounded just as grounded and unflustered as Alfonso. He told Theo that the Olympiad had not yet been canceled. In fact, there was going to be a parade of athletes through the streets, which he thought was a damn-fool idea because there were snipers about who'd like nothing more than to take a potshot at one of them.

"I told the team they can do what the hell they like, but I'm going to sit on my butt and drink Manhattans until someone pulls the plug on this fiasco, because after that, I'll be the one having to organize our goddamn evacuation. It sure was a long way to come for *nada*! Still, you know what they say—men plan, God laughs!" Booker said, laughing at the old Jewish joke.

"I thought you were an atheist!" said Theo, laughing too.

"That I am! That I am!" said Booker. "And proud of it too!"

It helped to laugh, just as it had helped to eat, and Theo was surprised that he didn't feel more disappointed about the Games. Three days earlier, he hadn't been able to think of anything else, but now the whole adventure felt like an experience another version of himself had had, in a different time and place.

With Alfonso's blessing, he tried to call his stepfather, too, but there was no reply and he couldn't tell if the telephone line was dead. Alfonso had told him there was fighting all over the country, and it frightened him to think of what might be happening in Andalusia. But there was nothing he could do, and he tried to put his anxiety out of his mind and concentrate on the goal he'd set for himself for the day: to locate Antonio's body and arrange his funeral. He owed that to his friend, and it was the only positive plan he could come up with amid the chaos and confusion.

He didn't acknowledge it to himself, but he was also hoping that the search for the dead Antonio might lead him to Maria, and he took the Ramblas route to the Paral·lel because that was where he'd seen her before.

The walkways were filled with people. Many not walking but gathered under trees in which radio loudspeakers had been hung from the branches. Revolutionary songs and appeals for blood, for calm, for volunteers, were interspersed with bursts of static and news announcements: Madrid was safe; Zaragoza was in enemy hands, and so was Seville; but the navy was loyal, and the air force too. *No pasarán*—they shall not pass. The Republic would prevail. The crowd cheered and groaned and cheered again, and Theo pushed his way through, taking care to keep out of the roadway where appropriated cars careered up and down, blowing their horns just like before: *CNT, CNT, CNT.* None of them contained Maria.

Once or twice the cars' engines backfired and the crowd dispersed, scurrying away into doorways like frightened birds, shouting "Sniper! Sniper!" before they realized their mistake and flocked back onto the sidewalks. The tension was like an electric charge running through the air.

There were real gunshots, too, fired into the sky by Anarchist fighters on the street corners, using the rifles they had seized from the army barracks. The guns had given them power, even though they claimed not to want it because it was contrary to their beliefs, and they were drunk on a heady concoction of victory and revolution. President Companys might still be sitting in his office giving orders, but no one was listening. The Anarchist militia controlled the city.

Farther down the Ramblas, a dead militiaman was being borne up the center of the road on the shoulders of his comrades. Theo thought it might be Ascaso and stood on a bench to see over the forest of upturned fists, but he did not recognize the dead man, who still had two sticking plasters over his lacerated cheek. As if he needed them! Theo thought bitterly, hating how death made a mockery of everything.

At the Güell Palace—Antoni Gaudí's imposing architectural masterpiece of marble and wrought iron—Theo turned right onto the side road he had run up before to bring the news of the victory on the Paral·lel to Durruti. The Anarchist leader's tight embrace and the feel of his kisses on his cheeks were among Theo's most vivid memories of the day of the rising, and he could still hear Durruti say *Theodore*, as if he was recognizing him in a way nobody ever had before.

When Durruti had told him *"We're going to be free!"* Theo had believed. Completely. And he could believe again, he told himself; he just needed to put the horror of what had happened at the Carmelite church behind him and find Maria. Then everything would be right again. Perfect, like it had been the night before.

He reached the junction with the Paral·lel where two days before he had leaped over the bodies of the dead killed in Ascaso's first failed attack on the barricade. The corpses had been removed, and now all that remained were splotches of blackened blood on the cobblestones, and flowers and handwritten names nailed here and there to tree trunks. It hurt Theo to think that Antonio didn't even have such a token memorial, making him even more determined to try to find his friend's body and give him a decent funeral before it was too late.

He turned toward the barricade, noticing how it had been repaired with an even line of sandbags running around the entire parapet. Narrow openings had also been made in the corners, where groups of armed militiamen were standing under red-and-black flags. He'd ask them. Maybe they would know something.

Theo's involvement in defending the barricade led him to assume he was among friends, so he wasn't prepared for the hostility he encountered as soon as he began to talk. Perhaps it was because he was speaking Spanish instead of Catalan, but the militiamen cut across him straightaway, demanding to see his papers, which Theo didn't have. The Olimpiada windbreaker had won him acceptance on the day of the fighting, but he had left it behind at the hotel, and all he had in his pockets was a roll of pesetas, which wasn't going to do him any good with Anarchist militiamen who thought that money was the root of all evil and had their rifles pointed at his head.

Fear made him stupid. He tried to explain himself and ended up telling them that he was looking for the body of a friend who was a soldier.

"A soldier!" one of the militiamen shouted, advancing on Theo with his weapon raised. Whether to shoot him or hit him with it, Theo didn't know, but just as he was bracing himself for the assault, a voice shouted, "Stop! He's one of us," and a man in a forage cap and a torn shirt stepped between Theo and his assailant.

His face was familiar, and after a moment Theo recognized him as one of Ascaso's men from the church. The one who'd told him before the attack that they'd got the dynamite from a boat. Theo had hardly paid attention at the time, but now this man had probably saved his life, and he didn't even know his name.

"Sergio," the man said as he led Theo over to the Café Chicago and ordered two glasses of wine that he didn't seem to have to pay for. Over at the barricade, the militiamen waved to them, all smiles now when they had been ready to blow Theo's brains out minutes earlier.

"Thank you," said Theo, raising his glass. "You saved me back there."

"Anytime," said Sergio. "I know you're a comrade, but the others don't, and you need to be careful what you say around them. And most of all you need to shut up about your soldier friend," he added, leaning close. "People get the wrong idea, and it doesn't take much . . ." He put two fingers up to the side of his head and made a popping sound with his lips as he pulled them away.

Theo's hands trembled as he drained the rest of his wine, and Sergio leaned across the table and patted him gently on the cheek. "It's okay," he said. "We've all been through a lot, so I'm not surprised you're jumpy. Come on. I'll get you a pass and you'll be fine."

They crossed the road, and to Theo's surprise Sergio led him into the Moulin Rouge. There was a queue of people in the lobby, waiting to see a bespectacled man who was sitting at a desk where the ticket office used to be. Sergio pushed his way to the front and told him what he wanted, and then watched impatiently as he laboriously wrote out Theo's name and address (*Olympic Hotel*; Theo almost made the mistake of saying Colón before he corrected himself) and occupation (*Athlete*) and stamped the pass.

"Good," said Sergio, shouldering his rifle. "You've got what you need now, but remember what I said." He put his finger to his lips, shook Theo's hand, and hurried away.

There was a noise of shouting coming from behind a half-open door at the end of the lobby—the same one that Theo had gone through with Antonio to enter the theater on the night of the burlesque show.

"What's going on in there?" Theo asked the clerk.

"Tribunal," the clerk replied, not looking up.

"Can I go in?"

"You've got the pass, haven't you?"

Theo pushed open the door and stepped inside. He was at the top of the stalls, looking down at the stage on which a big table had been set up, covered with two pieces of black and red cloth crossed over each other. Three people were sitting behind it, and the man in the center was Carlos. Whoever had been shouting was no longer present.

A burly militiaman came out onto the stage, pulling along an older man with bushy white eyebrows who looked a strange mixture of rich and poor. Half tramp, half señorito, he was wearing an expensive tailor-made suit and shirt, which were torn and stained, and his hair was sticking out at all angles. He looked terrified and had to repeat his name because it was inaudible the first time he said it.

"Where's the accuser?" asked Carlos, and a man stood up at the front of the auditorium.

"He's a Fascist," he said, pointing at the prisoner. "I've seen him in the blue shirt, going to their meetings."

"He's lying," the accused man responded, showing unexpected spirit. "He's just saying that because I fired him. He was lazy and spreading unrest among the workers and—" He obviously had more to say, but the militiaman cut him off in midsentence, cuffing him around the head.

And immediately another man stood up in the stalls, close to where Theo was standing. "I know him too," he shouted. "He paid us next to nothing and got in scabs when we went on strike. He's a dirty Fascist bastard, just like the rest of them."

Carlos conferred in a whisper with the men on either side of him and then nodded to the militiaman, who moved to take the prisoner away. But the condemned man resisted, clamping on to the stage curtain with his free hand as he begged for mercy. "Please! I've got children. I don't want to die." But his words ended with a scream when the militiaman twisted his other arm up and back until it snapped.

Theo cried out in horror. The sound was so sickening that he couldn't help it. Up to that moment the theatrical setting had allowed a part of him to hide behind the illusion that he was watching a performance that would end with the actors taking a bow, but now he could not escape the reality of what was happening in front of his eyes.

His cry had drawn Carlos's attention. Theo could see that he was looking up toward him with that same eagle-eyed malevolence he remembered from before. Carlos hated him. Why, he didn't know. But it was enough that he did, and Theo knew he had to get away from the Moulin Rouge while there was still time. He cursed his stupidity for having gone inside the theater.

He pulled open the door and pushed his way through the people in the lobby, but then stopped stock-still on the corner of the first street junction he came to on the Paral·lel. Primitivo was standing only a few yards away, next to an open-backed truck parked with its tailgate down. The driver was inside and the engine was running.

Theo ducked back behind a tree, sure that he hadn't been seen, because Primitivo's attention was focused on a line of prisoners that was coming up the side street, escorted by a militiaman with a rifle in his hands. The prisoners had their hands tied in front of them and their legs tied just above the ankles, forcing them to waddle like a group of penguins. When they got to the truck, Primitivo seized them one by one from behind and pushed them up into the flatbed, where they stood with their teeth chattering and their eyes wide with fear.

Then, just as Primitivo had got all the prisoners put away, the burly militiaman whom Theo recognized from the theater appeared, dragging along the man who had been condemned as a Fascist. Halfway up the street, the man's legs gave way and the militiaman beckoned to Primitivo to come and help. Taking an end each, they tossed the man up into the back of the truck just as if he had been a sack of potatoes and then stood back, laughing.

They secured the back of the truck and climbed into the cab with the driver, who drove away at high speed. Theo didn't know where they were going, but he had no doubt what was going to happen to the prisoners when they reached the end of their journey. He remembered Maria's description of the peasant crying out in outrage against his death in Goya's painting. The violation of life appalled him, rending something deep inside his soul, and he leaned against the tree behind which he'd been standing, feeling faint. He longed to sit down at one of the nearby cafés and recover his strength, but he knew that he had to get away before Carlos found him, and so he stumbled away up the Paral·lel.

He wandered through the streets, turning corners at random, but he must unconsciously have had a destination in mind, because hours later he found himself on the Diagonal, approaching the Carmelite church.

The door out of which the wounded had come was now a gaping hole that Theo stepped through into the charred interior. The walls were still standing, burned back to a scorched brick, but all that was left of the church's internal furnishings—its tapestries, paintings, and statues—was a mess of blackened plaster, twisted iron, and charred wood that littered the floor, coated with gray ash. Baroque turned to rubble.

In the area where the altar had once been, a group of Anarchist militiamen were sitting in a circle around a small fire from which a thin column of smoke was drifting up and out through the smashed clerestory windows. One of them got up wearily to challenge Theo but sank back onto his haunches after glancing at Theo's pass, and beckoned him over to sit with them. They were frying sausages on sticks, which tasted delicious, and drinking wine from a goatskin *bolsa* pouch, and they laughed just like Antonio had once done at Theo's failed attempts to arc the stream into his mouth.

"Were you here when all this happened?" Theo asked.

They shook their heads. They'd fought at the port for two days running, and now they were tired. Too tired to talk. So, after they'd eaten, they doused the fire and lay back on their haversacks to sleep.

Theo watched them for a while before he left. Children of the revolution—their dirty, bearded faces and ragged clothes illuminated by shafts of sunlight arcing down through the holes in the walls that had once been stained-glass windows.

Inside the ruined church, the noise from the road outside was muffled, and he felt an unexpected sense of peace, which made no sense. Here, where men had died in terror twenty-four hours earlier, he felt at peace. How could this be?

He resumed his wandering, feeling like a traveler who'd lost his bearings, lacking any frame of reference into which to fit what he was seeing. Everywhere, churches were burning or had burned. At one, firemen were present not to put out the flames but to ensure that they didn't spread to neighboring buildings. At another, disinterred, desiccated corpses were propped up against the pillars flanking the entrance doors with their skeletal legs dangling as if in a danse macabre, while a crowd laughed and jeered at this proof that eternal life was a lie peddled by the Church to keep the common people in thrall.

Death was everywhere. He couldn't escape it. The old dead dug up from tombs for public display; the new dead laid out in morgues across the city, waiting to be claimed; the soon to be dead being driven out to the hills and quarries to be shot.

Finally, he got back to the Plaça de Catalunya, stumbled through the door of the Colón, and staggered up the stairs to his room. The energy he had felt in the morning had drained away, and he collapsed on the unmade bed and fell into a thin, restless daydream, halfway between sleep and wakefulness.

He dreamed of Maria. With her arms out wide and her hands in perpetual motion as she described to him her vision of freedom, willing him to believe just like her. Her sapphire-blue eyes looking into his when he replied to her questions, making him feel that everything he said mattered. That he could be so much more than he was. Or with her eyes closed as she slept beside him in this same bed with her breath gently rising, gently falling, under his trembling hand. Such fragile contact, now broken. She breathed life into his world. How could he have let her go?

He felt her hand slipping out of his again as he stepped back from the crowd. He couldn't change the sequence of events, however hard he tried. He called out her name. A cry of distress from his conscious mind, pulling him up out of the misery of sleep. Not one to which he expected a reply, so he was befuddled and bewildered when he heard her say "Yes, what is it?" Not from far away but close at hand. And not in a dream, because he was awake now with his eyes open and she was standing over by the window, looking out. Her golden-brown hair falling around her shoulders, illuminated by the sunlight in a hundred shades of glowing amber.

"You came back," he said, sitting up. His voice was faint with astonishment.

"Yes," she said. "I did."

"Why?"

"To warn you, if nothing else. Stay away from the Paral·lel. I know you went there today. Primitivo said that Carlos saw you in the Moulin Rouge."

"I was looking for you."

"In there?"

"No, of course not. I was getting a pass and got curious. That's all."

"Curiosity killed the cat!" She laughed harshly. "Carlos doesn't like you, and you need to stay out of his way. He has a lot of power now."

"I saw that," said Theo, thinking of the condemned men in Primitivo's truck. "Why does he hate me so much?"

"Because you're a rich man's son. Staying in the fucking Colón." Maria threw her arms out in a sweeping gesture, encompassing the room and its expensive furnishings.

"He doesn't know that, does he?" said Theo, alarmed.

"No, but he knows your stepfather does business in Barcelona. He's got his name on one of his most-wanted lists. And he knows you're clever. He doesn't like people who answer back."

"Which is why he likes Primitivo so much. Someone vicious and stupid to do his bidding."

"Primo's not as stupid as you think. He got me out of Los Olivos, remember?"

"Does he know about us?"

"No, but he still hates you. He's jealous of anybody I even say hello to. And he knows you threw him over outside the church. Why the hell did you do that?"

"Because he was going to machine-gun those friars. I'd do the same again if I had the chance," he said defiantly.

"They'd been sheltering the Fascists," she shot back angrily. "The priests are our enemies too. They've kept the people in ignorance and poverty and told them they'll inherit the earth when they know it's a lie. For hundreds of years, they've been doing it. The rich persecute us, but the priests are worse. They justify the oppression. You don't understand because you're not Spanish."

"Maybe you're right," said Theo, shrugging. He understood the reasons for the Anarchists' anger, but he felt repelled by the burning churches and obscene displays he'd seen in the afternoon. He hadn't suffered like the poor and so he couldn't feel their rage. And nothing in his mind could condone the cold-blooded murder of defenseless friars.

Maria stamped her foot with irritation. "Why do you have to make everything so damned difficult?" she said. "It drives me crazy."

"I do what I think is right," he said quietly. "It's who I am. It's not because I want to annoy you."

"Even if it means trying to stop a machine gun with your bare hands?"

"I guess so."

"I guess so!" she repeated the phrase incredulously. "Is that all you've got to say? No one in their right mind does a thing like that."

Theo shrugged his shoulders again, and Maria ran her hands through her hair and let out a half-stifled scream of frustration, all the while looking down at him where he sat on the bed with his back to the wall, tousle-haired from sleep.

And then all at once she seemed to make up her mind. She crossed the room and took his head in her hands and kissed him. Hard, so that he had no capacity to respond before she pulled back, staring into his eyes. "You're not the person I'm supposed to feel like this about," she said accusingly. "You question everything; you don't believe like I do; you refuse. But you've got more courage in your little finger than all of them put together. Where does it come from?"

She took hold of his hand and traced the fingers with the tips of her own, as if in search of an answer to her question.

"I don't see any bravery," he said, looking at his hand, too, and shaking his head. "I let you go with those fingers. I don't know why."

"Because you wanted to save those friars. And I could see what you were thinking before, when the soldiers were coming out. You wanted them to get away, too, didn't you? It didn't matter what they'd done."

Theo nodded sadly. He'd always told her the truth.

She let go of his hand and buried her head in his shoulder, so that he had to listen hard to understand what she was saying:

"I stayed away last night because I didn't want to come back. Because Carlos is right: you're not one of us. But then I couldn't do it anymore. I needed to see you, to know you were all right. I told myself that it was to warn you, but it wasn't just that. It hurt not to know. Here!" She put her hand over her heart. "Can you understand that?"

"Yes. I looked for you all day. And tomorrow I would have done the same, whatever the danger. Every day until I found you. I have no choice."

"Oh, why do I have to feel like this? Why?" Maria cried as she bent to kiss him again, and this time he responded, drawing her down toward him and feeling her body enclosing his.

He knew that one day, soon, she would have to choose, but for now they were together, and this bed, this room, was a world of their own, and they needed nothing more.

# 9

## PARTINGS

"We're going tomorrow," Booker announced, smacking his lips with satisfaction after his first taste of the Manhattan with an extra shot of bourbon that the waiter had just set in front of him.

He looked far more at home in the hotel bar than he had been a week earlier and had clearly found a way to communicate his liquor needs to the management. Perhaps it helped that the hotel had now been collectivized, like so many other businesses in the city. A sign over the front door read RUN BY THE WORKERS FOR THE BENEFIT OF THE WORKERS.

"The boat's taking us to Marseille," Booker said, "and from there we take the train up through France to Cherbourg, and then next stop New York City. Do you want to come? I can wangle you a ticket."

"I can't," Theo said, taken by surprise by this unexpected question. "I have to stay here." He was thinking of Maria, and of his mother and stepfather, from whom he'd still heard nothing. He was living from day to day, clinging to the roller coaster his life had become. Leaving was impossible, even though a small part of him was tempted. Every time he went out, he took with him the fear of being dragged away to the Moulin Rouge for an appearance before Carlos's tribunal. And he knew firsthand what that would lead to. But he couldn't leave Maria, whatever the danger. She intoxicated him, the nights in the Colón an ecstasy that he would never have dreamed possible before he found her so miraculously on the day of the rebellion.

But he was touched by Booker's offer. It made America seem like a real country he could return to one day. He felt American, and perhaps this new sense of identity was the most important legacy of his strange Olympic adventure that had come and gone in three short days, destroyed like the dreams of so many others by the military uprising.

"Thank you for asking," he said. "It means a lot. One day I'll come home."

"Of course you will, and we'll drink the town dry," said Booker. He turned his glass ruminatively in his hand. "I guess I'm a bit envious, if I'm being honest with you," he said ruefully. "Going now feels like leaving the theater after the first act. Just when everything's about to get interesting. I'd like to see how it all—"

He stopped in midsentence, looking toward the door, where a well-dressed man had just come in, taking off his hat.

"Come and join us, Lawrence," Booker called out, waving his hand.

The man looked like a dandy from another era. He wore a pale-blue bow tie, a pince-nez, a double-breasted pinstripe suit with a pale-blue pocket square handkerchief to match the tie, and patent leather shoes that gleamed in the light of the chandelier. His face was a contradiction: his carefully groomed white hair put his age at forty plus, but he had a boyish look, with a puckered mouth and round cheeks. His hazel eyes conveyed both irony and engagement.

"Good evening, Charles," he said when he got to the table, bowing slightly. He spoke English with an upper-class American accent.

"Sit down, sit down! Have a drink," said Booker, waving at the waiter. "You're just the man I want to see. If anyone knows what's coming down the track, it's you."

"Aren't you going to introduce me to your young friend?"

"Sure, I was just about to. Theo, this is Lawrence Fernsworth of *The New York Times*. I met him in here two nights ago and we stayed up until three talking, and I've never known five hours to go by so quickly. He knows everything there is to know about this crazy country."

"You exaggerate, Charles. One of our national failings, I'm afraid," said Fernsworth, giving Theo a wry smile as he shook his hand. "I do my best to avoid the pitfalls of hyperbole, but it's not easy, particularly in these eventful times."

"Eventful times!" repeated Booker, laughing. "A hyperbole of understatement: that's what that is. It's a goddamn revolution out there and you know it. I'm surprised the Anarchists haven't lynched you, looking like that!"

"My tie, you mean," said Fernsworth, straightening the bow.

"Sure I do. And your collar and hat. You're the only one dressed up in the whole of Barcelona. How the hell do you get away with it?"

"I suppose they know me," said Fernsworth. "And I'm certainly not going to pretend to be someone I'm not. How can my readers rely on me to tell them the truth if I imitate the bourgeois who are putting on their servants' clothes to go out? Keeping a low profile, hoping it's all going to blow over?"

"Do you think it is going to blow over?" asked Booker, serious now.

"No, I don't. As you rightly say, it's a revolution. But it's also one that's happened by accident. We have the generals to thank for that. Our Anarchist friends have been talking about this day for seventy years, but that doesn't mean that they know what to do with it now that it's landed in their laps. I think they're just beginning to realize that you can't have a revolution without telling people what to do, but the problem is that that's what they're most against. Which creates something of a dilemma for them, going forward. It's why they haven't overthrown President Companys, even though they've got Barcelona at their mercy."

"They're fools," said Booker scathingly. "They need a Lenin. Someone prepared to seize power and make things happen. Someone who knows what they're doing and isn't going to worry about their principles while they're getting it done."

"A dictator, you mean?" said Fernsworth, raising his eyebrows. "They certainly don't want that."

"It's a damn sight better than chaos," said Booker. "Half the town is on fire and they've let all the criminals out of the jails, in case you haven't noticed."

"They don't believe in jails either," said Fernsworth, smiling.

"But they sure as hell believe in killing people," said Booker, warming to his theme. "Every night they're taking their enemies out for rides. Isn't that what they call it? Like it's all some kind of Hollywood movie."

"They're angry. Understandably so, after how they've been treated. This country's been run under a medieval system of injustice and repression for centuries," said Fernsworth. "But yes, you're right: they're settling old scores too. The Catalans have memories like elephants when it comes to that. What do you make of it all?" he asked, turning to Theo.

"I don't like what they're doing. In fact, I hate it. It makes me sick," said Theo, groping for words to describe his reaction to what he had seen at the Carmelite church and inside and outside the Moulin Rouge. "But I don't think it's all of them who are like that. And what they achieved against the soldiers was amazing. Their courage . . . I've never seen anything like it."

"Nor has anyone," said Fernsworth. "It's a unique moment in history that we've been privileged to see. Something to tell our grandchildren. But you talk as if you were with them. Were you?" he asked, looking at Theo with a new interest.

Theo nodded but stayed silent. He didn't want to talk about what he'd seen. It was too raw and confused. Talking would be an attempt to make sense of his experience, and he wasn't ready for that.

Fernsworth waited a moment and then nodded, too, and Theo had the sense that he understood his reasons for staying silent. He liked Fernsworth, he realized, and he was glad that their paths had crossed.

"So what do you think is going to happen, Lawrence?" asked Booker. "Tell us what you see in your crystal ball."

"I'd say a lot turns on whether General Franco can get his Army of Africa across the strait from Morocco," said Fernsworth thoughtfully. "The navy's stayed loyal to the government, which is good, but they won't be able to stop the rebels if Hitler or Mussolini give Franco planes. His troops are the best in the Spanish army: they're a ruthless fighting machine. We saw that in Asturias two years ago. The Anarchists defeated the soldiers here, but I think it would be very different if they were up against the Foreign Legion and the Moors." Fernsworth shuddered at the word *Moors* and closed his eyes, as if he was remembering some past horror.

"Have you met Franco?" Theo asked curiously, remembering the photograph on the wall of Maria's father's office.

"Yes. He's not what you'd expect: short and soft, with a high-pitched, squeaky voice, and he won't look you in the eye, even though he's watching you all the time. He's shrewd and soulless, and cruel too. It's an ugly combination. He'll be the rebels' leader, now that General Sanjurjo's gone."

"What happened to him?" asked Booker.

"He was too fat for his own good," said Fernsworth, smiling. "He took a flight from Portugal on Monday in a two-seater De Havilland and insisted on bringing all his dress uniforms and medals, which meant the plane couldn't get above the trees." Fernsworth arced his hand slowly across the table with his outstretched fingers and then brought it down on the surface with a small thud.

Booker roared with laughter and ordered another round of drinks, and Fernsworth told them about a famous Mexican singer at a collectivized theater on the Paral·lel who was refusing to sing if she was paid the same as the man who took the tickets at the door. "I will clean the toilets, and the toilet cleaner will sing in my place," said Fernsworth, breaking into a perfect imitation of the high-strung *vedette*'s imperious response. "It didn't take the theater committee long to change their tune after that."

They all laughed even more, and Theo was filled with a sense of euphoria and camaraderie, fueled by alcohol, that was his body's way of escaping from the fear and tension that had held him in an iron grip ever since the fighting began.

When he got up to go, Fernsworth rose to his feet too.

"You seem a most unusual young man. I am very pleased to have made your acquaintance," he told Theo as he shook his hand.

"And me you," said Theo awkwardly.

"Let me give you my card," said Fernsworth, extracting one from a silver case that he'd removed from an inside pocket of his suit and handing it to Theo. "Don't worry if you lose it. My telephone number is easy to remember—the first five prime numbers in sequence: 235 711. I'm often away with my work, but if you find me at home, it will be my pleasure to buy you dinner. We can talk some more about this 'crazy country,' as Charles insists on calling it."

"I'd like that," said Theo, smiling.

Maria was just as exuberant when she came back to the Colón later in the evening.

"I have a job," she burst out as soon as she was through the door. "The best job in all the world!" She took Theo's hand and danced him around the room, singing the words as if they were the chorus to a popular song, and almost colliding with a standard lamp from which he saved them with a last-moment lurch out of the way.

"Working for who?" he asked breathlessly.

"Women—the free women of Barcelona," she said enigmatically, and then laughed at his look of puzzlement before she relented and explained: "I'm going to help them find the work they want to do. In schools, in hospitals, in factories. No one is going to hold us back anymore. We can be whatever we want to be. It's a new world."

And she took his hands and wanted to start dancing again before he stopped her with more questions.

"Where is it? When do you begin?"

"In the Anarchist women's building over there on the other side of the square. The one with the sign in front: *Mujeres libres*," she said, pointing through the window. "I get my own office and a telephone. Starting tomorrow. Aren't you going to congratulate me?"

"Of course. I'm happy for you. Really, I am."

He meant it, but he felt anxious too. How could he be part of her new life when he could not show his face on the Paral·lel for fear of being arrested—or worse, if Primitivo found him? And what about elsewhere? How long would his luck hold?

"Come on," she said, seemingly unaware of his inner turmoil. "There's something I want to show you."

They walked out of the hotel into the hot night and were swallowed up in the eddying crowd on the Passeig de Gràcia. Everyone seemed to have their fists raised and clenched, caught up in the contagious revolutionary excitement. Spontaneous orators climbed up on the tops of cars to make speeches that could hardly be heard above the noise, strangers talked passionately to each other as if they had known each other all their lives, and the radio loudspeakers in the trees belted out the new Anarchist anthem, "A las Barricadas."

Anarchist posters aflame with bright primary colors had gone up on all the walls. Muscled arms holding rifles aloft and rugged faces shouting in exultation beneath huge, billowing banners with black-lettered slogans: *¡Libertad! ¡Victoria! ¡No pasarán!* They had been put up in a hurry, pasted over other posters among which Theo recognized the familiar flag-wielding advertisement for the Olimpiada Popular. It hadn't taken long for the Games to become yesterday's news.

Booker had been right: everyone was wearing working-class clothes, and there was not a hat or tie in sight. Men and women were dressed alike in blue mono overalls or trousers and shirts, and walked with their arms around each other in a way they would never have dreamed of doing before the revolution.

Theo cautiously put his hand on Maria's shoulder and she responded by putting hers around his waist, and he felt an overwhelming happiness that hurt because it was more than his body could contain.

The Ritz Hotel was on the next corner. Big and palatial, with a facade that looked like the prow of an ocean liner, it had long been the emblem of unashamed wealth and opulence in the city, a bastion of privilege where the rich and famous came to see and be seen. But now it was transformed: a large rectangular sign advertising **HOTEL GASTRONÓMICO No. 1** was hung over the restaurant entrance, and inside, the tables had been pushed together into long rows where working-class men and women sat on plush seats, eating dinner off monogrammed porcelain plates, served by an army of enthusiastic waiters who had been dancing attendance on aristocrats and captains of industry just a week before.

As they queued up outside, Theo gazed, spellbound, through the tall windows open wide all the way along the Gran Via into this new world brightly lit by sparkling chandeliers. It couldn't be, and yet it was: the meek *had* inherited the earth.

Maria handed two vouchers to the union official at the door, and they found a pair of seats wedged between an old woman in black who ate with tears coursing down her cheeks and an Anarchist militiaman whose rifle was leaning against the back of his chair, pointing at a golden cherub holding up a corner of the rococo ceiling.

"See!" Maria said, her eyes shining as she opened her arms, as if to embrace everything around her. "The revolution is succeeding. People are eating, the lights are on, the trams are running, and it isn't the owners who are making it all happen—they've run away—it's the workers. Now do you believe?"

"I'm beginning to," said Theo, smiling. The happiness and enthusiasm all around him were infectious, banishing doubt. Perhaps the Anarchists could achieve the impossible and make their human castles last.

"Because this is what you get when no one makes a profit out of anyone else," Maria went on, warming to her theme. "There's literally nothing we can't achieve when we work together and not against each other. We'll beat the army just like we did here, and we'll take back Zaragoza. Durruti is leading a column there tomorrow."

"He's leaving Barcelona?" Theo asked. The unexpected news upset him, puncturing his brittle sense of well-being.

"Yes," she said. "What's wrong with that?"

"I wish he wasn't. That's all. Not all the Anarchists here are like him."

"Carlos, you mean?"

Theo didn't answer, worried that the militiaman beside him might be listening to their conversation.

But afterward, outside, he couldn't stay silent. "Don't you know that Carlos is running a kangaroo court which is executing innocent people, using thugs like Primitivo to carry out his orders?" he demanded.

"There are Fascists in the city. Enemies of the people who have to be rooted out."

"Not like that."

"You hate Carlos and Primitivo because they hate you," said Maria. "I can understand that."

"I hate them because of what they're doing."

They walked on silently, the bond between them broken. Theo wished he hadn't spoken, but the words had escaped him, almost against his will.

"I don't like Primitivo either," she said, taking his hand. "I like you. Isn't that enough?"

"Yes," he said. But however hard he tried, he couldn't shake the sense of unease that seemed to dog him wherever he went, clinging to him like the smoke from the church fires that continued to burn all over Barcelona, mixed up now with the sulfurous stench of burning hair and flesh rising from the horse carcasses that had been dragged into the center of the Plaça de Catalunya and set on fire.

In the morning, Maria left to start her new job and Theo went to say goodbye to Booker. He approached this final meeting with a heavy heart. It had been little more than a week since their chance encounter at the kiosk in the Plaça de Catalunya, but the intensity of their shared experience since then had led Theo to develop a strong affection for the old man that he sensed was reciprocated, even though it would have been against Booker's prickly nature to admit to such feelings.

He liked to remember the coach he'd been so intimidated by when they'd first crossed paths in New York seven long years before. Booker had refused to shake his hand and had shocked him with the quick-fire blasphemies that rolled off his tongue every time he spoke. A cantankerous old man—that was how Theo had thought of him back then. But closer acquaintance had made Theo realize that the quick, abrasive humor and straight-talking refusal to suffer fools only touched the surface of Booker's character.

He was the best kind of Communist: one whose political faith was grounded in a passionate concern for human justice and dignity—his searing description of the rape of Ethiopia remained etched on Theo's memory. And he possessed a natural generosity that expressed itself in unexpected ways. Theo remembered with gratitude Booker's sympathy for his capitalist father and his willingness to give Theo the chance to fulfill his talent and represent his country, which still astonished him whenever he thought of it. Even though the rebels had taken that opportunity away, Theo still felt that Booker had given him his country back.

Now that Booker was leaving, Theo realized how much of a sense of security he had derived from knowing he was close by. Booker had filled the hole that Theo's mother and stepfather had left when they abandoned him in Barcelona, but he was also a friend to whom Theo could talk openly in a way he couldn't with them. It didn't matter that he hadn't seen much of Booker in recent days; what was important was that he could. And now he was going to lose that support. The thought intensified the restless anxiety that Theo suffered from now all the time and that he couldn't find a way to shake off.

Booker was waiting for him in the lobby of his hotel with the rest of the American team. Their luggage was piled up near the door, and they were all wearing their navy-blue Olimpiada Popular windbreakers, notwithstanding the heat.

"There's a farewell parade," said Booker. "And we're going to be part of it."

"We?"

"Yes, you too. You're one of the team, in case you've forgotten," Booker said, handing Theo another windbreaker that he had ready in his hand.

"I thought you didn't like parades," said Theo as they walked out.

"This one's different," said Booker shortly. "It's to say goodbye."

A Scottish bagpiper led the procession, walking behind a slow-moving car, and Theo wondered whether the crowds on the sidewalks had ever heard this strange northern instrument before. The volume of the music was extraordinary, drowning out their cheers, and the insistent, penetrating notes seemed to Theo to combine defiance and lament in equal measure.

The athletes marched four abreast, just as they had in the stadium, each team behind its national flag. They circled the Plaça de Catalunya, marching slowly past the stone buildings furrowed with bullet holes and hung now with red-and-black Anarchist flags, and then stopped in the Ramblas, where they split into two groups, waiting on the sidewalks for Durruti's column to pass through on its way to Zaragoza.

Durruti came first, sitting in the passenger seat of an open-topped Hispano-Suiza motorcar, staring straight ahead. Theo wanted to call to him just to see the Anarchist leader's wide gray eyes turn in his direction and perhaps recognize him for a moment, but he knew that Durruti wouldn't hear him above the delirious cheering of the crowd, and that even if he did, he would pay no attention, because it was as if he had already left Barcelona, switching his attention to Zaragoza and the task ahead.

A moment later and he was gone, leaving Theo with that first aching sense of loss that doubled and redoubled with each parting that this day and the next would bring.

Behind Durruti came his column. Theo was struck by its incongruity: it was like a slow-moving oriental caravan filling a stately Western boulevard. Militiamen were inside, outside, or clinging to a motley collection of cars and trucks and even buses. Some were in shirts, some naked to the waist with red-and-black handkerchiefs tied around their heads to ward off the sun. Some had guns, but many were armed only with knives or hatchets hanging from their belts. Some looked serious, with their eyes far away, as if imagining the fighting to come, while others waved their fists in the air and sang. Some even stopped to pose for photographs.

The crowd reserved their loudest cheers for the trucks that the CNT autoworkers had been laboring day and night to convert to armored cars. Iron sheets had been welded onto their frames so that they looked like boxes on wheels, and they rattled and bounced as they drove over potholes where the road had been pried up to make barricades.

"Madness!" said Booker with a deep sigh, as the last of the column disappeared from view down the Ramblas.

"What do you mean?" Theo asked.

"They're sending untrained men without proper arms up against soldiers. Knives against Mausers, iron boxes against tanks and planes. They're marching to their deaths. Lambs to the slaughter. Look!" he said, pointing over at a group of left-behind wives and girlfriends in the center of the Ramblas, who were crying and wringing their hands. "They know!"

"Durruti beat the soldiers here," said Theo. "So why can't he do it again?" He was echoing what Maria had told him the night before, but he sensed that Booker might be right. He just needed him to be wrong.

"It won't be the same next time," said Booker, shaking his head. "The generals will be better prepared. I tell you, these people's only hope is to start building their own army with proper training and discipline, the same way the Bolsheviks did in Russia. Like I said before, they need a Lenin."

"You're saying that because you're a Communist."

"And because I'm a realist," said Booker. "Just like you will be when you get to my age."

They walked back to the Europa in silence. There was so much to say and no way to say it. A pickup truck was parked outside with its engine running, and one by one the Americans threw their bags into the flatbed at the back and then climbed in themselves, until only Booker was left on the ground.

"Are you sure you won't change your mind?" he asked, pointing at the truck.

"I can't," said Theo, swallowing hard. He didn't want Booker to see him cry.

"No, I get that," said Booker quietly. "But if you won't come, then maybe you'll listen to some advice?"

It was a question, and Booker waited for Theo to nod his head in response.

"Don't let your heart rule your head. You're strong in both. Stronger than I ever was. But if you don't think things through in this crazy country, you'll end up dead. Like those poor fools we just saw. Think before you act! Can you promise me that much?"

"Yes," said Theo with a wan smile. "I can do that."

To Theo's surprise, Booker reached out and put his arms around him, hugging him close before he let him go.

"See you in New York," he said and, turning, climbed up into the truck. Straightaway, hands pulled up the tailgate behind him, and with a wave of their hands, the Americans drove away.

Theo wandered back across the Plaça de Catalunya toward the Colón. Not because he needed to, but because he had nowhere else more purposeful to go. All around him, people were hurrying toward destinations, busy with the work of the revolution, but he was adrift. Lonely and invisible among the crowds.

Less than a week before, he had fought side by side with the Anarchists, but now it was as if they had moved on, leaving him behind. He sensed the process beginning with Maria, too, however much he clung to her. He had too many doubts, and it was their world, not his. And even if he wanted to join them, he knew he wouldn't be able to. He had become more relaxed in his movements in recent days, lulled into a fragile sense of security simply because nothing had happened, but he was sure that his name had been added to Carlos's most-wanted list that Maria had told him about when she came back to the Colón after they were separated at the Carmelite church. Theo Sterling had been labeled an enemy of the people and nothing was going to change that, no matter the injustice of the accusation. All he could hope for now was that Primitivo had assumed he'd left Barcelona and so was no longer looking for him.

He had become lost in his thoughts, unaware of the people around him, so it came as a shock when he felt a hand on his shoulder, stopping him just as he was about to climb the steps to the hotel entrance.

He looked around and found himself face-to-face with Alfonso, the hotel concierge, dressed in his green-and-gold uniform.

"Señor Sterling, please," Alfonso said, taking hold of Theo's arm and guiding him toward a nearby statue of a nude goddess on a wide plinth, which he crouched down behind, pulling Theo in close beside him. He was breathless and shaking, and he took out a handkerchief to mop his brow.

"What's going on?" Theo asked, looking at Alfonso with astonishment. The concierge was a model of formality, and the only possible explanation Theo could see for his extraordinary behavior was that he had lost his mind. Perhaps the revolution was starting to do that to people.

Theo didn't know whether it was best in these circumstances to humor the poor man or run away. The concierge's agitation made him look even more like Al Capone than usual, and Theo was just about to vote with his feet when Alfonso recovered himself sufficiently to start talking, and everything changed.

"I'm sorry, sir. But I had to stop you going inside. There are three men waiting to arrest you. They say they have instructions from the tribunal. They were calling you a Fascist."

"Who are they? Did they say their names?" Theo asked, breathless himself now.

"No, sir. But one of them is up there, outside the front door. I hope he can't see us."

Theo peered around the statue, looking up toward the hotel. Primitivo had moved to the top of the steps and was scanning the crowd with his hand over his eyes to block out the sun. Theo ducked back, almost knocking Alfonso over.

"How long have they been here?" he asked.

"They were already in the lobby when I arrived for work," said Alfonso. "The man you can see—he went up to your room, and when he came down, he was very angry, waving his gun. Fortunately he didn't shoot, even though I thought he might. I waited a few minutes, and then I said I had an errand to run and went outside. He didn't stop me. I was hoping I'd see you when you came back."

"You risked your life to help me!" said Theo, looking at the concierge with wonder.

"It was the least I could do, sir," said Alfonso, shrugging his shoulders.

"No, it wasn't. It was the most. And here I was, thinking I had no friends left in this town, when all the time I had you. You were the first friend I made here and the best." Theo felt so moved that he put his arms around the concierge and hugged him close.

Alfonso turned red as a beet, either with pleasure or embarrassment or both. "Thank you for your kind words," he said, making a slight bow with his head only as they were crouching on the ground, and then he reached in his pocket and handed Theo a folded telegram. "This came today," he said.

"Thank you," said Theo. "Should I pay you or something? For my stay, I mean?"

"No, sir. Accounts will send your stepfather the bill when things get back to normal." Alfonso hesitated and then went on: "I don't mean to be rude, sir, but I think you would be wise to leave now. It isn't safe here."

"Yes, you're right," said Theo, getting reluctantly to his feet. Despite the danger, he didn't want to go. As he'd said, Alfonso was his friend. Without him, he'd be on his own. "Thank you," he said, gripping the concierge's hand. "I won't forget."

He waited for a group of women to walk close by where he was standing and then slipped around behind them and joined the throng of people on the sidewalk. He turned down the first street he came to and hid inside a doorway behind two huge iron trash cans filled to overflowing. Maria was wrong: not everything was working in Barcelona.

He counted the seconds by the pulsing beats of his heart. A minute passed and then two more and he breathed easier. Primitivo hadn't seen him. He was safe for now. He took out the telegram and spread it out across his knees.

### ARRIVED GIBRALTAR. BOARDING SHIP, HMS LONDON. STOPS BARCELONA EN ROUTE MARSEILLE. YOUR MOTHER VERY SICK. WISHES TO SEE YOU. ANDREW X

It was dated the twenty-second—two days earlier—but there was no time given. Had the *London* come and gone? Theo had no clear idea how long it would take for a ship to go from Gibraltar to Barcelona, but he thought it possible that it could have done the trip in two days or less. But perhaps the ship hadn't left on the twenty-second. Boarding didn't necessarily mean an immediate departure. He'd have to go to the port and ask. But then he realized he couldn't. Not when the Anarchist militia was out looking for him.

He felt a rising panic as his mind raced from thought to thought. What to do? What to do? He felt like a climber on a high ledge, testing handholds and distrusting them all.

The noise of an emergency siren brought him to his senses. He was being hunted. He couldn't stay where he was. He needed to make choices now, for better or worse.

He thought hard. Only two things felt certain: he had to go to the port to try to find his mother, and he had to see Maria before he went, in case he couldn't come back.

*Couldn't come back, couldn't come back*—the words reverberated in his mind, and each time he felt the pain of separation like a wave breaking hard on his chest. It was more than he could bear, so he stopped thinking and ran instead. Down the street to the end, where he doubled back on Carrer de Pelai to the junction with Plaça de Catalunya and the Ramblas.

He couldn't miss the building. Outside, there was a huge sign with **MUJERES LIBRES** painted in white letters on a red-and-black background, and Anarchist flags hung down from the fretted iron balconies on each floor. He went straight in and asked for Maria, and she must have heard his voice because she came out almost immediately and led him through to her office at the back. It was tiny—more a cubicle than a room, with plywood partition walls and a sliver of a window looking out at a sad-looking olive tree wilting in a dingy courtyard—but she did have a telephone.

He started telling her about what had happened at the Colón, but kept repeating himself and tripping over his words, which made him realize how nervous he was. He couldn't stop thinking about the prisoners in the truck outside the Moulin Rouge, waiting to die. He didn't want to be one of them. He wanted to live. But he couldn't bear to let Maria go. Not now that they were together. If Primitivo was coming after them both, then they would both have to flee. What was there to stop them from starting a new life somewhere else? Oxford, perhaps?

"I came to warn you," he said. "Before Primitivo gets here."

"He won't come here," she said flatly, looking him in the eye, and he had the sense that she saw through his words and knew what he was trying to engineer.

"Why not, if he knows about us?" he asked, sticking to his guns.

"Because he intends to keep me out of it. He wants me for himself. Alive, not dead. That's why he'll have waited last night. He must have followed me to the Colón and seen us together, and then gone back to get the arrest warrant from Carlos. He thinks that if it's done that way, I won't blame him for carrying out the tribunal's orders. I told you before, he's not stupid."

"So you're safe but I'm not. Is that what you're saying?" Theo asked bitterly.

"Yes. Now that he knows about us, he won't rest until he's found you. And it's not just him. He's Carlos's right-hand man, and that gives him the power to set the whole militia after you. You've got to get out of Barcelona."

Maria sounded frightened herself now, which scared Theo even more, but also gave him hope. If she cared enough about him, perhaps she wouldn't be able to let him go.

"I know that," he said. "My stepfather's coming in a ship from Gibraltar. I hope I haven't missed him."

"Of course you haven't," she said, smiling with relief now that an exit strategy had presented itself. "You should go now. When all this has blown over, you can come back. I'll work on Carlos to make it happen." She put her hand on his shoulder as if to push him out of the door.

"I don't want to go without you," he said, taking hold of her hands.

"You must."

"You could come too."

"No!" She shouted the word so loud that he took a step back. "Everything I dreamed of all my life is here. Now. In this city. Can't you see that? I like you, Theo. More than like you, you know that, but you can't ask me this. You can't!"

She was right. He couldn't. How could he claim to love her if he was trying to take her away from the revolution? He had to love her for who she was, not what she was to him.

She saw the understanding in his eyes and leaned forward and took him in her arms, kissing his lips and then his forehead in farewell.

"This is not the end," she said.

At the door, he turned and looked at her one last time through his tears, enraptured by her loveliness, and then he walked quickly away.

# 10

## THE PORT

Outside, Theo set off running, feeling his fear like breath on the back of his neck. He ran down the Ramblas, past the flower market and the Liceu, dodging between pedestrians and hawkers and militiamen, and didn't stop to draw breath until he reached the end of the road. Sixty yards above his head, Christopher Columbus, atop his pedestal, looked out to sea.

*"Guess where he's pointing. Go on. Try!"*—Theo could hear Antonio's voice in his head, see in his mind's eye his friend pointing up at the explorer in the sky, digging Theo in the ribs as he demanded he guess. *"America,"* Theo had said, falling effortlessly into the trap. And Antonio had laughed and told him: *"No, Africa. I think it's the architect's secret joke. He's saying: 'That's all Spain's got left, now we've lost everything else.' Lost glory: that's what's got the Fascists so revved up, isn't it? Remember old Millán-Astray."* Antonio had put a hand over his right eye, hung his left arm down limp, and contorted his face into a maniacal expression, just like the crazy general's in the photograph in his father's office.

Antonio! Humorous and curious, credulous and cynical, and above all mercurial. Laughing one moment and serious the next. Theo ached with grief when he thought of his friend. But he was frightened too. By death, *of* death . . . Antonio had been so alive, and yet now he was gone. Vanished from the world in the time it took to run across a road, and without even a gravestone to remember him by.

Like Ascaso. So powerful a leader—small, and yet so effortlessly dominant of all those around him. But he, too, had been snuffed out in a moment by a ball of lead. Shot down just a few yards away from where Theo was standing now as the Anarchists attacked the Drassanes army barracks on Monday morning. He'd been able to predict the churches burning all over Barcelona, but he hadn't seen his own death hurtling toward him.

So quick, this crossing from the infinite complexity of life to the utter void of death. Was that what his mother was facing now? Was that why she wanted to see him? To say goodbye?

And was that what he was facing too? He was friendless and defenseless, and he knew that if the Anarchist militia found him, he'd be dead within hours, left to rot on one of the hillsides that he could see rising above Barcelona behind him.

He looked around, surveying the port, which he was seeing up close for the first time. On both sides of the wharf at the end of the plaza, huge concrete quays jutted out into the sea, covered with cranes and prefabricated storage sheds. An immense variety of boats were anchored alongside them—freighters low to the water, forlorn yachts whose owners had fled, fishing craft of all sizes— but the only one resembling a passenger ship was a rusting black hulk with the name *Uruguay* painted in fading letters on its stern, and Theo knew what that boat was. Maria had told him that that was where the Anarchist militia was holding General Goded and the high-profile rebel prisoners. Locked up with the rats until they were ready to be taken out and shot. Theo shivered and looked away, scanning the harbor again, but in vain. Nowhere was there any sign of the *London*.

He walked out onto the quay on the left, going almost to the end, and sat down with his back against an upturned boat covered by a tarpaulin that sheltered him from the sun. All around him, stevedores were loading and unloading cargo, but none of them paid him any attention.

He must have slept, because the sun was much lower in the sky. Close by, he'd thought he heard someone talking in English, but he was only half awake, and he wasn't sure it hadn't been the end of some now-forgotten dream. Stiff from lying on the hard ground, he got unsteadily to his feet and looked around. Work on the docks seemed to have finished for the day, and the only people in sight were a man and woman farther down the quay, walking back toward the town.

He called out, "Please, can you help me?" His voice sounded strange and hoarse in his ears, and the couple looked back nervously and quickened their pace.

He hesitated and then ran after them. He was frightened they would call for help and bring the militia down on him, but if they were English, then they were the only hope he could see of finding out about the ship.

He shouted "Friend!" over and over again as he ran, because he couldn't think of anything else that might allay their fears, and it must have worked, because they stopped and turned around.

"I'm sorry. I didn't mean to frighten you," he said breathlessly when he caught up to them, and was encouraged when the man asked him what he wanted. He'd been right: they were English.

"Do you know about the *London*? The ship? Is it coming?" he asked, stuttering over his questions because he was so terrified of what their answer would be.

"Tomorrow early. That's what they told us in there," said the man, pointing back toward the customhouse behind where he was standing. "They're quite helpful if you've got questions."

"No, I'm fine. Thank you," said Theo, stuttering again as he backed away. The customhouse, big and imposing with its long line of ornate stone windows surmounted by eagles, terrified him, and he turned and ran back down the quay, leaving the couple looking after him, scratching their heads.

He got back to the upturned boat, feeling ecstatic. The ship hadn't sailed! He still had a chance! But as the sun sank toward the horizon, his mood darkened. The ship wouldn't save him if he couldn't get on it, and how could he do that without papers?

He had the pass he'd got at the Moulin Rouge but he knew he couldn't use it. He took it out of his pocket and stared at the inscription: *Theodore Sterling, Olympic Hotel, Athlete*. Two days earlier, he'd thought it guaranteed his safety; now it might as well be a death warrant. How quickly everything had changed!

His hand shook as if the document was burning his fingers, and all at once he scrunched it up into a ball and threw it in the sea. But it wasn't enough. The Olimpiada windbreaker that he'd been using as an improvised pillow was incriminating too. He picked it up, intending to get rid of it the same way, but stopped his hand at the last moment. Even though the windbreaker was a replacement, it mattered that Booker had given it to him and that it was now the only physical evidence he had of what he'd been through.

He looked back at the city. Menacing and hostile, it seemed like a vast creature ready to swallow him up. He had fled from it as far as he could and now he could go no farther, standing stranded and exposed on its outermost shore.

He turned away toward the south, where the last rays of the sun lit the square stone tower of Montjuïc Castle, for so long the sinister seat of power and repression in Barcelona. Gulls circled it and then flew out to sea, where the still water stretched away like a gigantic sheet of dark, opaque glass. Somewhere out there, in the gathering gloom, an invisible ship moved its searchlight beam across the port, and a foghorn blared out its mournful wail.

He lay down but sleep was impossible. The heat of the day had disappeared with the sun, replaced by a harsh cold that his windbreaker couldn't keep out. He tried the doors of the nearest sheds, but they were all locked. He was hungry, too, not having eaten all day, and he bitterly regretted not having stopped to buy something on the Ramblas, instead of running like a crazed hare from hounds that had not yet been set on his trail.

As the hours passed, he changed his mind about going to sleep. Now he was frightened he wouldn't wake up early enough in the morning. He had no idea when the ship would arrive or where it would dock. Perhaps it wouldn't come into the harbor at all and the passengers would be taken out to it on smaller boats, passing by him unnoticed as he slept.

His mind raced in the darkness, alert to every sound: the creaking of boards and chains, the lap of the sea against the quay, the scurrying of rodent feet, all set against the dull background noise of nighttime traffic in the city. He imagined he heard voices and footsteps, and then he did. Militiamen were coming up the quay, shining flashlights into its corners and recesses. He counted the lights. There were two of them, perhaps three. He felt in his pocket for the pistol Ascaso had given him, but realized he had left it in his room at the hotel.

Trembling with fear, he rolled under the tarpaulin, stretching himself tight against the side of the upturned boat. But it was not a complete hiding place. The canvas did not quite reach the ground, and his attempt to pull it down over his body had no effect because the material was too heavy.

He lay completely still as the footsteps approached and prayed like the most fervent believer. And at the last moment, just as he was certain of discovery, a man's voice broke out, uttering a string of obscene curses.

"Fucking bat!" he shouted. "I think it touched me." And the next moment a shot rang out, fired into the sky.

There was the sound of laughter, and then someone was squawking, making an excellent imitation of a distressed chicken, followed by more laughter.

"Fuck you, Felipe!" the first voice shouted furiously. "I've had enough of this. There's no one here. Let's go back."

"All right. Keep your pants on," said a second voice, still laughing.

The voices receded, but Theo stayed where he was, pressed rigid against the wood, even after he could not hear them anymore.

He needn't have worried about missing the passengers' departure. Soon after dawn, a destroyer flying the Union Jack and bristling with guns sailed into the harbor and anchored against the wharf at the foot of the Columbus statue, and immediately afterward a noisy crowd began to gather outside the customhouse. Theo edged back down the quay, stopping when he was close enough to hear what was being said.

The people in the queue were mostly talking English, although there were other languages being spoken, too, and each person, even children, was carrying one suitcase—obviously the limit imposed for luggage.

After about half an hour, a door opened and the emigrants filed in, and then emerged one by one about five minutes later through another door farther down the facade, loudly complaining about being searched for money. Several were protesting that they had had excess amounts confiscated.

From the customhouse, the passengers passed down a roped-off walkway to where a swinging gangway had been set up to enable them to board the destroyer. There was no sign of the *London*, but Theo assumed that it must be anchored out at sea, with the destroyer being used as a ferry between it and the port.

He stood uncertainly outside the customhouse, watching as the last passengers went inside. He hesitated, walking toward the door and then backing away. It was his only route of escape, but he knew that he would never get through without papers and that trying to do so would lead to him being questioned and arrested, even if he gave a false name. And from there it would only be a matter of time before he was identified and sent to his death.

He looked over toward the walkway, trying to see if he could slip in among the passengers unnoticed. But it was impossible: militiamen were standing alongside the ropes, and they were also checking everyone's papers just before they embarked, no doubt comparing them to the list of names they'd been given by the tribunal.

It was hopeless. Something gave way inside him and his head dropped. It was as close as he'd ever come in his life to giving up, but just at that final moment of unraveling despair, he heard a voice calling his name.

It was coming from the destroyer. There was someone tall running on the deck and pushing past the last passengers coming up the gangway, who cursed him loudly as one of their suitcases fell in the water. Theo could see him now beside the militiamen at the bottom, wild-eyed and agitated with his suit crumpled and his tie askew and his silver hair standing up on end, shouting "Theo!" at the top of his voice and waving. It was his stepfather like he'd never seen him before, but it was him.

Theo ran over to the gangway, and Andrew reached across a militiaman and clutched his arm.

"Papers!" demanded the militiaman, pushing Andrew back.

"He's my son," said Andrew, waving his passport in front of the man's face.

"I need papers. Not yours, his," insisted the militiaman, becoming angry.

Andrew looked around wildly and then, without warning, grabbed hold of Theo again and pulled him past the militiaman and up the gangway. "Run!" he shouted.

Theo ran and slipped, but instead of falling, he felt arms around his shoulders, lifting him up and over the top of the gangplanks, and depositing him in a heap on the iron deck of the destroyer.

"Stay down!" said an authoritative English voice belonging to an officer in a white uniform with gold braids, towering above his head.

Outside, out of sight, other voices, including Andrew's, were shouting, and Theo braced himself for the sound of shots, but none came. Instead, Andrew appeared after a couple of minutes at the top of the gangway, which was immediately hauled up behind him.

He walked over to Theo and sat down beside him, wearily leaning his head back against the side of the boat.

"It's all right," he said. "You're safe. Thank God!"

"How did you do it?"

"Money: some Anarchists aren't averse to its charms. And fear: they don't want to pick a fight with a British destroyer. Not when it has its guns pointing at the port."

Beneath them, the destroyer's engines burst into life, and sailors pulled in ropes as the boat began to move away from the quay.

"Where's my mother?" Theo asked.

Andrew said nothing, looking up at the control tower, but Theo could see that there were tears glistening in his eyes.

"Tell me!" Theo demanded.

Andrew nodded and took a deep breath. "She's gone," he said. "I'm so sorry."

Theo looked at his stepfather, absorbing the blow as he took it down through his consciousness into his body, and then got up and walked away, crossing to the other side of the deck, where he stood, looking back toward the shimmering city as it receded from view. The destroyer was plowing fast through the water and the sea spray came up and soaked his face, mixing with the tears that were streaming down his cheeks.

He felt like the world had come to an end, but was aware at the same moment of a seasick passenger a few yards away, vomiting over a gun platform, and a dog in a cage uselessly barking. Life continuing just as it always did.

Andrew was beside him again, talking, and his words came as if from far away: "It happened in Gibraltar, just an hour or two after I sent you the telegram. The final thing she said was for me to find you. She made me promise, so you were the last person she was thinking of when she . . ." He stopped, unable to say the unsayable word, but then went on: "And I keep thinking that that's why she stopped struggling. She knew I wouldn't leave her and that she was too sick to go on the ship, and so giving up was the only way to get me to go. She thought you were in danger, and you were, weren't you?"

Theo nodded, not trusting himself to speak. He felt a surge of anger toward his stepfather for looking for consolation amid the ruin. It didn't matter at that moment that Andrew had saved him. What mattered was that he hadn't saved Elena.

"It's my fault," said Andrew sadly. "I shouldn't have let her come back to Spain after her breakdown, but she insisted and I could never say no to her. And after that, she wouldn't leave. It's Spain that's killed her: this black, cruel country."

What she saw in the village was more than she could bear, and I couldn't protect her from it."

"What did she see?"

"Horrors. The first day, they took everything out of the church—the holy cross, the statues, the canopies and vestments she helped sew—and burnt them in the square, and then they hung Don Vincente from the bell in the tower. You could see him from our house, swinging. They'd cut off his ears like he was a bull."

Theo was utterly unprepared for the grotesque immediacy of the image Andrew's words had summoned up, and he took an involuntary step backward, grabbing hold of the guardrail for support. But Andrew didn't seem to notice: his eyes were open wide, as if he couldn't believe the truth of what he was describing.

"Why didn't you leave?"

"I couldn't. Right at the start, they arrested all the landowners, except Don Fadrique—he must have known what was coming and slipped away, the wily old fox. They called themselves a people's court and put each of us on trial one after the other, even though they were drunk on Communion wine and cared nothing about the law. I was the only one they let go. Two of my workers were there and said I'd treated them well, paying them out of season, and I think that made all the difference, so I've got you to thank for that, making me see what was right two years ago," he said with a wan smile. "And then they took the condemned men out one by one and shot them against the wall of the ayuntamiento, and propped up their bodies in a line with cardboard signs hung around their necks: **FASCISTA, FASCISTA, FASCISTA** . . . Bernardo Alvarez, the café owner, got special treatment: they cut off his head and put it on a pole and paraded it around the town. They must have really hated him."

Andrew talked without intonation, as if he was describing distant events, and Theo's anger cooled as he began to understand the trauma his stepfather had suffered. The thought of the village square being turned into an obscene killing ground appalled him.

"Once I got out, we left," Andrew went on. "I know now that that was a mistake. Elena was too sick to travel. But I wasn't thinking properly, and I didn't know what might happen. I was scared they might come for her because she'd been close to Don Vincente. She got worse in the car, and by the time we got to the hospital in Gibraltar, it was too late. She was always so fragile."

Fragile! Yes, that was it. Like a wounded bird. The word broke through Theo's emotional defenses, and he saw his mother as clearly as if she were standing beside him on the deck: small and defiant, burning up her body's strength with her ceaseless determination to make the world fit to her vision, until she was so brittle that the slightest pressure would make her break.

He remembered how he had hugged her in the early morning in Sitges when he had gone to her room, frightened by dreams of her death, and she had seemed so insubstantial in his arms, with the great gray sea outside the window. And now, as he looked out over the gunwale, it was as if it had swallowed her up, leaving nothing behind.

"You're wrong about Spain," he said in a broken voice, turning back to his stepfather. "She loved this country. After all her years of wandering, she felt as if she had come home. You gave that to her, so you have nothing to reproach yourself for."

"And she gave me you," said Andrew, reaching out to take Theo's hand. "The son I'd never had."

Theo nodded, moved by Andrew's words. He was alone in the world now. All his family and friends were dead or lost, but at least he had Andrew. They were linked not by blood but by something more than friendship. His stepfather was his lifeboat amid the wreckage.

The destroyer's engines slowed as the *London* came into view. The great ship ready to take them to Marseille, from where they would travel first class to England and begin the next chapter of their lives, leaving Spain behind. Theo understood that that was what Andrew intended, but he knew that for him it would not be so easy. He looked back at the hazy outline of the Spanish coast and felt as if there were an invisible wire stretched out across the sea, connecting him to the country and to the girl he loved.

# PART TWO

## MADRID PROVINCE

### 1936–1937

For the first time in history, for the first time since Fascism began systematically throttling and rending all we hold dear—we are getting the opportunity to fight back—to make a determined struggle against Fascism . . . Here finally the oppressed of the Earth are united, here finally we have weapons, here we can fight back. Here, even if we lose, which is a possibility we will not admit, in the fight itself, in the weakening of Fascism, we will have won.

*—Eugene Wolman, Lincoln Battalion volunteer, in a letter to his family written one month before he was killed in action at the Battle of Brunete on July 23, 1937*

# Spain – January 1937

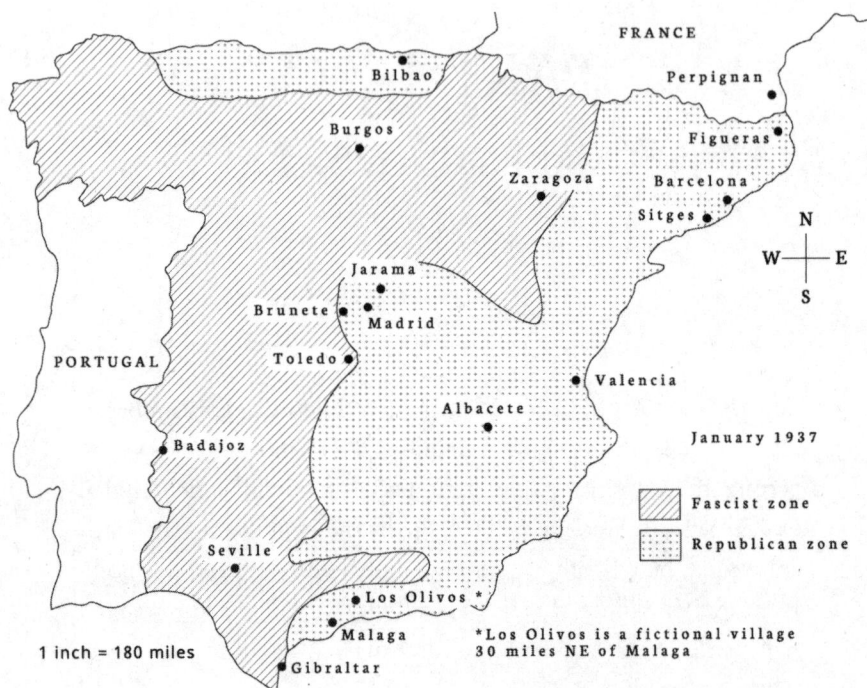

FRANCE

Bilbao

Perpignan

Burgos

Figueras

Zaragoza

Barcelona

Sitges

N
W —|— E
S

Jarama

Brunete ● ● Madrid

PORTUGAL

Toledo ●

Valencia

Albacete

January 1937

Badajoz

Fascist zone

Republican zone

Seville

Los Olivos *

1 inch = 180 miles

Malaga

*Los Olivos is a fictional village
30 miles NE of Malaga

Gibraltar

# 11

## OXFORD

The city was beautiful, bathed in golden, late-summer light. Everywhere Theo went, he passed carefully tended lawns and gardens and silvery-gray buildings that were unimaginably old, with their stone stairs worn smooth by generations of scholarly feet passing back and forth, as if in time with the slow wash of the river lapping gently against its banks in Christ Church Meadow or under Magdalen Bridge, where red-cheeked boys in straw hats and striped jackets stretched out their hands to girls in white muslin, tottering as they boarded the long punts, before they settled in their low seats like hens to their nests.

White wine and picnic hampers of latticed wood with calf-leather buckles, and hands trailing in the cool dark water under weeping willow trees as the boats glided by, and everyone laughing because life was sweet and places like Spain and Germany and Ethiopia were far, far away. The stuff of newspaper stories that they might talk about over beer in crowded pubs in the long evenings after essays were written and handed in, exchanging honestly held opinions that filled them with a pleasant sense of their own importance. Until they headed back through the echoing twilit streets to their colleges, where mellifluent bells marked unchanging time in quadrangles and cloisters, and lamps glowed welcoming in the dusk.

For years, Theo had toiled to reach this earthly paradise, a world away from where he'd begun amid the jangling mayhem of New York, and he wanted nothing more now than to immerse himself in all it had to offer. But he couldn't.

However hard he tried, he remained on the outside looking in, filled with a dull irritation that poisoned his days.

He had felt this same sense of disconnection when he had arrived at school in England four years earlier, fresh from the experience of his father's suicide and the poverty and despair that had followed in its wake. He hadn't belonged there either. But he had persevered and made friends and had ended by making a success of his time at Saint Gregory's.

But this time it was different. It was as if he had done what Father Laurence had counseled him not to do and had gotten ahead of his life, and couldn't now turn back the clock, leaving him marooned in a no-man's-land between youth and manhood. He had experienced too much, too soon. The violent death of his friend yards away from where he stood, helpless to save him; the loss of his lover, who had rejected him in favor of a revolution from which he'd been lucky to escape with his life; the wanton destruction of a country that he had come to love, which was continuing every day as he sat in lecture halls and tutorials, trying unsuccessfully to block out the images that kept springing into his mind unbidden. The decapitated head lying in the road after the cannon fired; the fat priest hurrying across the road to escape the death that was awaiting him on the other side; the trembling bound men in the back of Primitivo's truck, waiting to begin their last journey across the blood-soaked city; Don Vincente hanging from the bell rope above his church, swinging slowly from side to side. His mother dead, broken by the destruction of all she had held dear.

The visions pursued him into his sleep, from which he would wake, sweating and crying out in the dawn light. And then the only escape was to get up and run down the empty, leafy roads, forgetting his pain in the rhythm of his pounding feet. In the evenings, he relied on alcohol to blot out his thoughts, but it just made him angry. Alone in the corner of smoke-filled pubs, he listened to his fellow students holding forth about Fascism and Communism and Anarchism until his irritation boiled over and he got unsteadily to his feet, spilling his drink.

"How can you talk about changing the world when you know nothing about it?" he shouted at them one evening.

"And you do?" one of them shot back, the first to get over his shock at being attacked out of the blue by a wild-eyed stranger with an American accent.

"Yes," Theo yelled. "I've seen things that you people can't even imagine. Blood and fire and hunger and you—all you're going to do when you're done here is move your fathers' money around, so why don't you stick to that instead of pretending . . ."

He stopped, conscious of the complete silence in the room and the open-mouthed bewilderment of the faces looking up at him from all sides like he was a lunatic escaped from the asylum.

"I'm sorry," he muttered, and staggered out, feeling a rush of choking shame as he heard the laughter starting up behind him, just as it had when he had lost his temper in the Lamb and Flag the previous weekend.

He was getting a name for himself: "that gawky boy in the checked shirt and running shoes, who sits in pubs, saying nothing, until *boom*—he explodes like he's some kind of ticking time bomb, shouting stuff about Spain and knocking over people's drinks. There's something wrong with him. He needs locking up before he does something really nuts . . ."

Theo played out these and other imaginary conversations in his head as he walked up the narrow lane from the pub, and it was only when he reached the road that he heard the quick footsteps behind him and someone calling out for him to stop.

He turned with his fists clenched, expecting to see one of the boys he'd insulted, looking to continue the argument outside, but instead it was a girl with thick glasses and a mass of tangled-up black hair that seemed to grow out from her head instead of down her shoulders.

"What have you seen?" she asked, staring up at him. "I want to know."

And because he was lonely and hadn't spoken to anyone about anything that mattered to him in over a month, he told her what she wanted to know. About the Anarchists who wanted to kill him and the Fascists who almost had. About bullets in the air and dynamite exploding and what the dead looked like when they'd been left to rot for a day in the summer heat.

He talked and she listened and they walked up one street and down the next, until they arrived as if by magic at the door of his room, where he drew her toward him and kissed her. He could feel the eagerness of her response and put his hand in his pocket to find his key, and it was the momentary pause that this required that gave him the time to remember looking down at Maria lying asleep in the bed they'd shared in the Colón on that last morning in Barcelona before everything went to hell.

"I can't," he said, stepping back.

"Why not?"

"Because . . ." He couldn't explain. Not without talking about Maria, and he wasn't going to do that. The night was already enough of a betrayal.

"Because I know nothing either. Is that it?" she demanded.

"I didn't say that."

"But you meant it, didn't you?"

And when he didn't reply, she slapped him hard across the cheek. It stung, and he put up his hand to the hurt.

"You didn't even ask me my name," she said through her tears. And he was about to do so, but she'd already turned away and was going back down the wooden staircase with the banging of her heels on each tread sounding like nails being hammered into a coffin, while he stood at the top with the key in his hand, hating who he'd become.

He was faithful to a chimera. Since his return to England, he had written at least ten letters to Maria at the *Mujeres Libres* office building off Plaça de Catalunya, where he'd seen her last, but had received no reply.

He knew that it was more than possible that she hadn't received the letters. Barcelona was chaotic, and she might be working elsewhere or have gone to join Durruti's militia, whose advance had stalled outside Zaragoza. This last possibility kept Theo awake at night, worrying that she could be dead without him knowing, killed in some meaningless exchange of rifle fire across the ravines.

But then at other times he felt sure he would know through some sixth sense if she was gone from the world, and he blamed her for her silence. Even if she had not received his letters, she could have written to him. He had told her the name of his college.

He felt hurt but not surprised. He knew Maria lived within her own experience. It was not in her nature to reach beyond it. He would remain outside her life until he came back, when their relationship would resume or not, depending on how she felt at the time.

But Theo's insight into Maria's essential character didn't stop him yearning for her, and in his dreams, he still searched for her through the narrow Chinatown lanes. Chasing shadows.

Sometimes the ache of separation was so intense that neither running nor drink could dull it and he cried alone in his room, convulsed by his own misery. And at such times the barriers he'd built in his mind to shut out the deaths of Antonio and his mother would crumble and he would be back on the Paral·lel impotently shouting or on the beach at Sitges, unable to tell his mother what was in his heart. He'd loved her and she'd loved him, but it hadn't been enough, and they had parted with an acrimony that could never now be undone.

The pain of loss was unbearable. One after another, dead or alive, those he'd loved had disappeared from his life, swallowed up by that wild and tormented country far across the sea. Spain, always Spain, filling his mind with visions from which he couldn't escape.

Every day, he went to the library and devoured all the newspaper accounts of the war that he could lay his hands on, and in the evenings he listened to the news on the radio that his stepfather had given him as a going-away present when he went up to Oxford. But he liked little of what he heard, and after the announcements were over, he turned the dial to Radio Luxembourg, which played the American jazz music that reminded him of Esmond and of the New York childhood he'd almost forgotten.

It was hard to discover the truth of what was happening. All the European powers had signed a Non-Intervention Agreement in August, and the official line, followed slavishly by most newspapers and the BBC, was that there was no foreign involvement in Spain.

But Theo soon came to the conclusion that this was a bald-faced lie. It had to be, because the Army of Africa could not be advancing on Madrid—as it was—if it had not been transported across the strait from Morocco in German and Italian airplanes as was reported in the *News Chronicle* and the Communist *Daily Worker* newspapers. The Spanish Navy had stayed loyal to the Republic and so this was the only way Franco could have done it. Logic told its own story.

And if the press and the British government was concealing the truth about German and Italian intervention, then he thought it just as probable that it was behind the lack of coverage of the White Terror that Franco's Moors and legionnaires had unleashed on the Republican towns that they'd captured on their march north.

The few accounts he had found fitted exactly with all Theo had heard about Millán-Astray's infamous *novios de la muerte* when he was in Spain. In August, thousands of Republicans had been herded into the bullring at Badajoz and machine-gunned, some still holding the filthy white towels and shirts they'd used to surrender. Their blood had soaked into the yellow sand, turning it to viscous orange. And in Toledo the following month, the Moors had gone through a hospital, flinging grenades into the wards. They returned when the smoke had cleared to hack out the gold from the dead men's teeth with their rifle butts and piled up their loot at the city gates from where it was shipped back to their families in Morocco. To encourage recruiting, the article suggested.

They were simply repeating the atrocities that they had inflicted on the Asturian rebel towns in 1934. But most newspapers acted as if this wasn't happening, concentrating instead on the Red Terror in Barcelona, which they exaggerated beyond the bounds of anything Theo had witnessed in July. He had certainly seen horrors, but not on the bloodbath scale that was being reported. He found several articles by Lawrence Fernsworth in the London *Times* that provided a more balanced picture, but this was drowned out by the *Daily Mail*'s banner headlines that the Reds were feeding their prisoners to the animals in the zoo!

Everyone was lying and Theo thought he knew why. Red Terror could be used to justify the British government's refusal to help the democratic Republic against the rebels, whereas White Terror would discredit Franco, whom the British wanted to win the war, and so needed to be suppressed.

British policy was to pretend that everyone was observing nonintervention when Prime Minister Baldwin and Foreign Secretary Eden knew full well that Franco was receiving massive support from Mussolini and Hitler. It was the worst kind of hypocrisy: pretending to be fair while at the same time conspiring to destroy a democracy and hand it over to the Fascists whom the British thought were a better bet to preserve their extensive trading investments.

Theo's anger toward his adopted country intensified as the Fascists got closer to Madrid. Nothing seemed able to stop their deadly advance, and he assumed that the city would quickly fall when the attack began at the beginning of November. But against all the odds, it survived. Durruti's Anarchists and the newly formed International Brigades arrived to support the ragtag Republican army and their line held, as if by a miracle.

On November 22, a Sunday, Theo read that Durruti had been shot and killed while leading a counterattack. He sat quite still at the library table, unconscious of the tears running down his face and of the readers all around him, scratching and sniffing and turning the pages of their books and magazines. He was back in Barcelona, feeling the touch of Durruti's hands on his shoulders and hearing Durruti's voice in his ear, assuring him with such utter certainty that they would be free.

In a few moments, on a busy street with a battle going on all around them, Durruti had made Theo believe, and now his death made Theo ashamed. Durruti hadn't hesitated to go to Madrid and sacrifice his life for the cause of freedom, but Theo remained shut up in his ivory tower, reading dusty books and attending lectures. His life made no sense to him. How could he be content studying history when he had touched it in the making? How could he be satisfied writing essays about Spain when the country was being destroyed by Hitler and Mussolini and a gang of Fascist army officers? How could he live with himself in the decades to come if he sat on his hands and did nothing? Conducting his own personal campaign of nonintervention.

Only the Communists seemed prepared to do anything. Sometimes Theo went to their meetings and listened as they earnestly discussed mounting collections for medical aid to Spain and organizing demonstrations and petitions against the arms embargo. But he resisted their invitations to join the party. It seemed too much of a talking shop, a home for lost and lonely people who wanted to feel important. He knew that he was just as lost and lonely as the rest of them, but he didn't think that selling the *Daily Worker* on street corners and passing motions in committee rooms would make any real difference to the world.

And he distrusted the Communists' slavish deference to Stalin. Every time he saw the familiar pockmarked, mustachioed face with the wily, hooded eyes on the posters that the Communists hung so ubiquitously on their walls, he remembered Father Laurence's cool exposition of how Stalin had caused the death of millions of peasants with his program of forced collectivization and had then lied about the famine while he sold grain to pay for his Five-Year Plan.

*"The more colossal the lie, the more likely it is to be believed."* That was what Father Laurence had said and he was right, because Stalin was doing it again. In the library, Theo read about the show trials in Moscow of the old 1917 revolutionaries, charged with conspiring against the party to assassinate Stalin and restore capitalism. Absurd accusations and ludicrous confessions were an

insult to the truth, but the Communists in the meetings he attended didn't want to talk about that, any more than the British establishment wanted to talk about what was really happening in Spain.

As the end of the term approached, Theo felt paralyzed. As if he were trapped in a gilded cage that was starving him of oxygen but from which he couldn't escape. He drank more at night and ran farther and faster in the mornings until, coming back to his staircase one wintry morning, soaked in sweat, he heard a familiar voice calling his name. And when he turned around and saw it was Esmond, walking toward him across the grass, he was surprised at his own lack of surprise. It was as if he'd been in suspense ever since he'd got to Oxford, waiting for a moment like this to arrive.

Esmond looked the same and yet different. He was as handsome as before, with the same delicately carved features and penetrating blue eyes that Theo remembered so well. But he was no longer scruffy. His hair was cut and groomed, and his jacket and trousers were clean and pressed. He looked like he'd grown up.

What was most familiar was the smile that lit up Esmond's face as he approached. It lit Theo, too, and filled him with an unexpected happiness that he hadn't felt since Barcelona. It was as if he had gotten so used to his internal darkness that he had forgotten the possibility of light, and the burst of it in his mind made all his surroundings seem suddenly different. The college's gray buildings turned to silver, and the twisting branches of the old cedar trees casting patterned shadows over the great lawn in the front quadrangle appeared beautiful now instead of gloomy.

He put out his hand, but Esmond ignored it and hugged him instead, and the physical sensation made Theo tremble, making him realize how much he'd missed his friend.

"I've been running," he said, feeling as if he should apologize for the sweat and dirt covering his body.

"Well, some things don't change," said Esmond, pushing Theo back but still keeping hold of his shoulders as he looked him up and down. "Are you playing rugby too?"

Theo shook his head.

"Why not?"

"I don't know. I suppose I lost my enthusiasm. I'm sure you approve."

"Why would you say that?"

"Come on, Esmond. Don't you remember the lectures you used to give me about schools using games to get inside your head. You told me I was becoming a cog in the bourgeois machine!"

"I said that?" said Esmond, sounding surprised.

"Yes. You should be delighted I've quit. One less cog."

"Well, I'm not," said Esmond, looking pained. "I think people should carry on doing things they're good at as long as they've got the chance. That's how we keep our enthusiasm. I must have been a real killjoy back then. I'm sorry."

Theo didn't know whether he was more taken aback by Esmond's forgetfulness or his newfound flexibility. Both seemed out of character, but he wasn't going to argue. A tolerant, even-tempered Esmond had to be an improvement on the doctrinaire dogmatist he'd been at school.

"Aren't you going to show me your room?" asked Esmond, pointing to the staircase Theo had been about to climb when he called to him.

"It's a mess," said Theo. "Like me."

"It can't be a worse mess than my room used to be," said Esmond, laughing.

"That's true," said Theo, laughing, too, as he remembered Esmond down on his hands and knees, searching for tea and sugar among the chaos of books and magazines. But as they climbed the stairs, he couldn't help wishing that Esmond had given him some warning that he was coming, so that he could have prepared himself for their reunion. He was happy to see his old friend, but he also felt pushed onto the back foot, whereas Esmond seemed completely in control of the situation. That much hadn't changed.

While he made tea, Esmond wandered about the room, inspecting. "You kept it!" he called out suddenly with obvious pleasure.

When Theo turned around, Esmond was holding up the postcard that he'd sent Theo to congratulate him on getting into Oxford. It had been on the mantelpiece.

"Of course I did," said Theo. "It meant a lot to me. I didn't know where you were . . ." He swallowed, choking back a sudden onrush of emotion.

"But that was the deal we had. Remember?" said Esmond quietly. "I didn't want to get you into trouble."

"I know. It was good to hear from you, that's all." Theo took the postcard from Esmond and looked at the picture of the Kremlin on the front—the same one that had hung in Esmond's room at Saint Gregory's.

"Did you go to Russia?" he asked.

"Yes," said Esmond. "It was my version of college. Only shorter and more intense."

"So you're still a Communist?"

"Of course. Just a more thoughtful one, which is no bad thing."

"Thoughtful—what do you mean?" Theo asked. It hadn't been the word he was expecting.

"The party's evolved. We're still Marxists, of course, but we've learned to look at problems based on the evidence and not jump to preset conclusions. We have to be prepared to admit mistakes when we make them, and learn from them too."

"What kind of mistakes?"

"Well, treating all other left-wing parties like they're enemies, for example. All that did was make it easier for the Fascists to gain power. It certainly helped Hitler that we fought the Social Democrats in Germany. But now we've learned from the mistake and changed the policy, so that we're committed to working in a popular front against Fascism."

Theo nodded, even though he was not convinced. He'd noticed how Esmond framed his answer in terms of what the party thought rather than what Esmond thought himself. Theo distrusted the Communists, but he wasn't going to spoil the day with an argument about politics.

He poured Esmond his cup of tea and sat down on his unmade bed, stirring his own. But instead of drinking, Esmond reached inside his jacket and produced as if by a sleight of hand the silver hip flask that he'd had at Saint Gregory's. "No need for the hollowed-out Bible anymore," he said, laughing again, as he poured a generous measure of brandy into Theo's tea and then his own, before raising his cup in a toast. "To friendship!" he said. And Theo echoed him with enthusiasm, elated that his friend had returned.

"I went to Russia and you went to Spain," said Esmond after a moment, looking at Theo with that same expression on his face that Theo remembered from school. Watchful after he spoke, as if trying to gauge a reaction.

"How do you know that?" Theo asked, surprised by Esmond's knowledge of his whereabouts.

"Because I was there too. And when I heard about this American boy called Theo who was going to be a runner in the Barcelona Olympiad and fought on the barricades before the Anarchists chased him out because his rich stepfather was on their wanted list, I knew it had to be you. Famous in your own time." Esmond grinned.

"Were you in Barcelona?"

"No, Madrid. I got there after you left or I'd have come to find you."

"What were you doing there?"

"Organizing."

"Organizing what?"

"People, supplies. It's what I do: I move stuff around."

"During the Fascist attack? You were there for that?" asked Theo eagerly. For weeks, he had followed the battle for Madrid in all the newspapers, and he felt a sudden breathless excitement that he was sitting opposite an eyewitness to what had actually happened.

"Yes, I was," said Esmond, smiling at Theo's enthusiasm. "It was 'the nearest run thing you ever saw in your life,' as that old Fascist, the Duke of Wellington, said about Waterloo. I'll tell you about it if you like, but not here. It's lunchtime and we're going to the pub with the best cheese and ale in Oxford. Come on— you won't be disappointed, I promise."

"You know this town?" asked Theo, feeling surprised again. Conversation with this new Esmond seemed to be constantly punctuated with these lurches into the unexpected.

"I've been here a couple of times," said Esmond, as if it was a matter of no importance.

"Why?"

"Just to look around."

"Why would you do that?" Theo pressed. *Looking around* was not something Esmond did, or at least not the Esmond Theo remembered. His actions had always had purpose, even if Theo had sometimes had difficulty working out what that purpose was. He felt sure that his friend was holding out on him, and he was curious to know why.

Esmond hesitated, as if deciding how to answer, and then he smiled and there was a wistful expression on his face. "I like it here," he said. "I chose the road I took and I have no regrets, but maybe in another life I would have enjoyed it here."

"But you called it an ivory tower. Don't you remember saying that?"

"I said a lot of things," said Esmond. "But Oxford is more than that. It's an amazing opportunity. You're lucky to be here."

It wasn't the answer Theo had been expecting, and for the second time that morning he was left scratching his head, remembering Esmond's previous contempt for climbing the academic ladder. But he decided not to press the point any further, and busied himself instead with changing his clothes and getting ready to go out, while Esmond read a copy of the *Times* from two days before that was lying on the table. The entire front page was covered with news of the abdication crisis, and there was not a single mention of the war in Spain.

"They're saying that the wily Mrs. Simpson has got some bizarre sexual hold over the king, using practices she learned in a Chinese brothel," said Esmond, laughing. "Do you think he'll abdicate?"

"I neither know nor care," said Theo irritably. "It shows how morally bankrupt this country has become that that's all anyone talks about anymore."

"Strong words!" said Esmond, raising his eyebrows.

"Not really. You're the one who taught me about the British ruling class, remember? And I'm grateful—everything you told me turned out to be true. All they care about is money, and morality be damned! Nonintervention's a joke. They know perfectly well that Hitler and Mussolini are helping Franco win the war, which is what they want because it'll be good for their pocketbooks. They're just too hypocritical to admit it," said Theo bitterly.

"Napoleon hit the nail on the head when he called them 'a nation of shopkeepers,'" said Esmond, smiling. "I'm glad you think I taught you something. That's the greatest compliment I could hope for. Thank you."

Theo was ready now, and they went out into the Broad Street, from where Esmond led them through a warren of twisting medieval streets, before ducking down through a low doorway into a small, half-subterranean, timber-beamed room with a bright fire burning in a grate below a reproduction of Van Dyck's famous triptych portrait of Charles the First, who had kept his court in Oxford during the Civil War.

"I don't think they share your politics," said Theo.

"Damn politics," said Esmond. "It's the beer I'm here for."

And Theo had to admit it was good, served in huge dimpled mugs with round handles, accompanied by slabs of extremely blue Stilton cheese and hunks of bread and butter and pickles. Harsh tastes alternating with one another in a thick, hot fug of tobacco and fire smoke that made Theo's eyes water as he sat across from Esmond in an inglenook—a real seventeenth-century inglenook with diamond-paned windows—looking out on only the lower extremities of passing pedestrians in the street outside, because the pub's foundations had sunk a foot with every century that had passed since its construction. Or so Esmond said.

Theo looked across the table at the familiar but long-absent face of his friend and was suddenly ridiculously happy. Esmond returned him to his past, or at least the only part of his past that he could now reach: the boy in the armchair brushing the mass of blond hair out of his eyes, the arm wrapped around Theo's shoulder when he confessed his father's suicide, the gramophone needle rising and falling as it traveled across the jazz records that they got to know by heart—Satchmo and Duke and sad Bessie Smith, providing a soundtrack to their days. And laughter, so much laughter, the like of which Theo had never experienced before or since. Antonio had been funny, but not like Esmond.

"Remember the pub in Carborough?" Theo said. "Under the billiards table . . ."

Immediately Esmond was transformed. He sucked in his cheeks, pursed his lips, and rubbed his hands together, and became Sergeant Raikes as he leaned across the rickety table and intoned in a horribly knowing voice: "T'aint the agony, Sterling, yer know that, don't yer? It's the disgrace."

Theo laughed so hard that he knocked the table half over, spilling their beer, and the landlord arrived with a cloth and a severe expression. "I'll have no rowdiness in here, you 'ear me," he told them and pointed a stubby finger up at a notice on the wall beside the door, prohibiting disorderly behavior on pain of ejection.

Esmond mollified the landlord with an elaborate apology delivered in a cut-glass, upper-class voice that made him sound as if he were being strangled with their old school tie, and then hissed "Fascist" to Theo as soon as the man's back was turned, making Theo laugh even more, so that he upset the table again, completely this time, whereupon they fled out into the cold December afternoon.

Two minutes later they emerged into the bustling High Street, full of cars and buses and the sound of horns and the smell of exhaust, making Theo feel, as he often did in Oxford, that he had crossed in a moment from one century into another.

They walked down to Magdalen College and in through the echoing quadrangles until they came to the water meadow, where they sat side by side on a bench, looking out across the river, empty of boats now that winter had come.

White fluff clouds scurried across the pale sky, blown on the breeze that was sending the last red leaves fluttering down from the branches of the elm trees into the eddying water, and a lark circled high overhead, singing its liquid song. They were quite alone.

"I love that you can go just a short distance here and leave the city behind," said Theo meditatively. "It's not like that in London."

"Or Madrid," said Esmond. "Although that's not what the architects intended when they built the new university there a few years ago. They planned a haven of tranquility looking out toward the Casa de Campo Park, but instead they got themselves a war zone. Not fair, really, is it?"

"What happened?" said Theo, turning to look intently at his friend. "You said you'd tell me."

It was as if the pub and the walk had just been an interlude in a conversation between the talk that mattered. About Spain: the land that was calling Theo back. Louder and louder, in a voice that would not be denied.

But Esmond didn't seem to notice Theo's excitement as he looked out across the river, composing his thoughts before he began to speak.

"The Fascists got there at the start of November, and the government fled to Valencia, cowards that they are. But we Communists stayed. *No pasarán* meant something to us, you see. Not just a slogan to chalk up on the wall. No one gave us a chance: the journalists were writing that we had hours, not days, and Franco's right-hand man, General Mola, told one of them that he'd buy him a coffee on the Gran Via the next day. Since then, Alberto at the Café Molinero keeps a table reserved for Mola and pours him a fresh cup every day, but he hasn't been by to drink it yet. And if we have our way, he never will."

"We?"

"The Communist Party. We saved Madrid. The Fifth Regiment and the International Brigades—men from all over Europe and this country, too, volunteering not for money but because they hate Fascism and are prepared to sacrifice all they have to defeat it. The Spanish people know they're the heroes. That's why they're joining the party in droves, inspired by their example. They understand that the Republic's army officers are corrupt and self-seeking—they'd change sides in a moment if they thought it was to their advantage—and that the Anarchists are unreliable, which is putting it mildly."

"Durruti wasn't," said Theo angrily, and Esmond looked over at him in surprise.

"Why do you say that?" he asked.

"I met him in Barcelona. It wasn't for long, but it was enough for me to know the kind of person he was. And I fought with the Anarchists. They were brave. They saved Barcelona, just as much as you say the Communists saved Madrid."

"And then they tried to shoot you, didn't they?" said Esmond, raising his eyebrows.

It made Theo even angrier that he couldn't think of a good response. He got up from the bench and paced up and down with his hands thrust deep inside his pockets, while Esmond watched him carefully from the bench with an absorbed expression on his face, as if he was making calculations in his mind.

"I didn't say that the Anarchists aren't brave," Esmond said quietly. "I said they were unreliable. They won't accept orders or hierarchy, and you need both to fight the Fascists. In Aragon, they require a show of hands to agree on an attack, and they go home at the weekends if they feel like it. No wonder they've failed to take Zaragoza."

"Maybe, but Durruti was a great man, and the men who followed him were true believers, willing to give their lives for a new Spain. I saw them leave for Zaragoza, and I know what was in their hearts," said Theo passionately. "The executioners were the ones who stayed behind. I saw that too."

"Yes, that's what happens," said Esmond, nodding. "But it doesn't change what I'm saying. You need discipline to fight the Fascists. The Anarchists broke and fled when they came up against the Moors and their machine guns outside Madrid last month. And it was after that that the Fascists crossed the river and entered the University City."

"And Durruti died."

"Yes. And I don't mean that he wasn't a hero, too, just that his Anarchists couldn't fight like we could. They weren't organized or prepared; they didn't have the discipline. And the Moors and the legionnaires were terrible. They fought like tigers. Through every building—lecture halls, libraries, dormitories. Those were the front lines, and we defended every room on every floor, only falling back when no one was left."

"You fought? You were there?" asked Theo with his eyes wide.

"No, I helped to organize. I told you that. Someone has to do it, but I felt part of what the party was doing. It made me proud to be a Communist. And I saw the battle. It was a short subway ride away from where I was staying, and I went out there most days. I needed to know what was happening."

"You took the subway to the battle?"

"Yes." Esmond smiled. "It was crazy. Everything was crazy. Our soldiers sheltered behind parapets constructed out of encyclopedias. Three hundred and fifty pages of text is what you need to stop a bullet, apparently. And behind them the blackboards were still covered with the professors' teaching.

"There were times our soldiers occupied half a building and the Moors the other half, and they'd pull the pins on their grenades and send them up in the elevators so that they'd explode on the bastards when the doors opened. And one time the Moors were stuck in the basement of the science faculty without anything to eat, and they ate the lab animals that had been infected for experiments and died terrible deaths, screaming out their agony in Arabic or Berber or whatever it is they speak. I heard them. It went on for hours." Esmond winced at the memory.

"So what happened?" asked Theo, enthralled by Esmond's account of the fighting.

"We held them, and after a few days they realized they couldn't break through, so they started the bombing. German and Italian planes, taking it in turns, going over day and night. I went down in the subway when it started and almost got trampled and suffocated in the panic, so I took my chances aboveground after that, watching the bombs come down like silver bowling pins out of the blue sky. Making a noise like cloth ripping. Louder and louder, until the bang, and then the dust and rubble rising and everyone turned to white, running this way and that like pieces of paper blown about in a wind. And afterward, everything would be pulled apart so it didn't make sense anymore.

Telephone poles and streetlights twisted and drooping and bundles of sparking wires hanging down like streamers and body parts in the trees—a head, a foot, some piece I couldn't tell what it was. Fires starting, lighting up houses from the inside like pumpkin lamps before their roofs collapsed, and the bells of fire engines—arriving when it was already too late. Once, a girl came over to me from a doorway and put her head in my arms and cried and I held her. I remember that."

Esmond stopped with a faraway look in his eye and then swallowed and took a deep breath, as if to reassert control over his memory that had risen up and taken him over when that was the last thing he'd intended.

But Theo felt a wave of affection for his friend, sensing that they had shared two parts of the same experience, which bound them together again after their long separation.

"Why did you come back?" he asked.

"To see you," said Esmond, smiling.

And Theo smiled, too, sharing the joke, as the bell in the clock tower behind them tolled the hour. The wind had dropped, and the utter peace of the afternoon felt unreal when he thought of Spain. Like a dream from which he was about to awake.

They parted company outside Magdalen with Esmond promising he'd be back the following weekend, and as the days passed, Theo thought constantly about all his friend had told him, turning every facet of their conversation over in his mind.

Esmond's disparagement of the Anarchists had annoyed him, but it didn't surprise him either. He remembered that Booker had said much the same when they'd watched Durruti's column leave Barcelona. Booker had thought the people's only hope of beating the Fascists was to build an army with proper training and discipline, and that was exactly what the Communists were doing.

Theo had always doubted Marx. History seemed to him far too accidental and fluid to be marching toward an inevitable Communist conclusion, and he shared the Anarchists' distrust of state power as a means to bring about a just world. "Power tends to corrupt, and absolute power corrupts absolutely"—the old adage had become a cliché, but that didn't make it any less true, and Theo's suspicion of Stalin had grown since the days when he first talked politics with Esmond at Saint Gregory's. He felt sure that the dictatorship of the proletariat in Russia was just another name for a dictatorship of Stalin.

But none of this changed the fact that the Communists were the only ones outside Spain trying to help the Republic. They acted, while others talked. It had been the same two years before when Mosley was busy turning his Blackshirts into a national party, just like Hitler had done with the Nazis. The Communists had exposed their violence at Olympia, allowing the country to see them for what they really were, and now they were just a splinter party with a few thousand members, whipping up antisemitic hatred in the East End of London. Theo had been a part of that success. He'd seen how the Communists made a difference.

And now they were doing it again. Organizing the International Brigades to fight the Fascists in Spain, while the British Labour Party sat on its hands and supported nonintervention. Esmond had said that the brigades were the ones who'd made the difference in Madrid and turned the tide. They'd done what no one else had been able to do: they'd stopped the Army of Africa in its tracks.

*International Brigades*—Theo turned the words over in his mind and felt their romance kindling a fire in his heart. Men from different countries and different walks of life coming together to defeat Fascism. The simplicity of the idea was glorious and inspired him in the same way that the Olympiad had when Booker offered him the chance to take part, but more now because these volunteers were prepared to sacrifice everything for their common ideal, asking nothing in return except the chance to fight for what they believed in.

You didn't have to be a Communist. Theo remembered Esmond's enthusiasm for the new policy of working with all parties of the left. He felt sure that anyone would be welcome who wanted to defend the Republic.

The more he thought about the brigades, the more his excitement grew. Ever since he'd left Barcelona, he'd wanted to go back. He hadn't chosen Oxford over Spain. He'd wanted to fight the Fascists more after they killed Antonio, not less, but Carlos and Primitivo had made that impossible. Now he had a way to circumvent them and perhaps to find Maria too. In his heart, he believed that returning to fight would take him back to her. How, he didn't know. It was enough that he felt the connection.

Theo could hardly sleep on the night before Esmond's return. In the intervening days, he had convinced himself that his friend wasn't joking and that he had come back from Spain to get him, so that they could return to Madrid together and fight the good fight, just as they'd done at Olympia two years before.

He started firing questions at Esmond about how to join the International Brigades almost as soon as he got through the door, and was completely taken aback when Esmond reacted to the idea with obvious dismay.

In fact, he looked just as surprised as Theo, putting up both hands as if he were trying to stop a runaway horse at a rodeo. "You need to calm down!" he said. "You don't want to take a huge step like this without thinking it through. Surely you can see that?"

"I have thought it through," said Theo stubbornly.

"Not enough," said Esmond harshly, and Theo could see he was angry. It was the first time since their reunion that he had seen that hard, domineering side of Esmond that wouldn't brook disagreement, and it felt perversely reassuring to Theo to know that his friend hadn't really changed.

But the mask slipped for only a moment before Esmond regained his composure. "Look, let's sit down and discuss this," he said reasonably. "There can't be any harm in that, can there?"

Theo shook his head and sat. He was happy to talk if that was going to make Esmond feel better, but it wasn't going to change his mind. He'd already decided to join the brigades, with or without Esmond's help.

"Have you considered what you'll be giving up if you go?" Esmond asked.

"This place, you mean," said Theo, waving his hand dismissively around the room. "I'm not happy here and it's not doing me any good. I'm a fish out of water."

"It's too early for you to know that. You thought the same at Saint Gregory's, and you ended up making a success of it there."

"Which you condemned me for!" said Theo pointedly. "You called me a collaborator. Remember?"

"Maybe I did, but Oxford's different. This is the best university in the world. A lot of people—me included—would give their eyeteeth to have the opportunity you've got now. You shouldn't treat it as if it's worthless when you know full well it isn't."

"But I can't stand it here," said Theo, his passion getting the better of him. "Every day I wake up thinking of Spain, wishing I was there and not here. That day in Barcelona when it all began, the workers set off the sirens in the factories, calling everyone to arms, and I know it sounds crazy, but I feel I can still hear them in my head." Theo pressed his hands on his temples as if he could actually hear the sound. "I've got to answer them or I'll go mad."

"No, you don't. You have to get a grip and think. That's what you need to do," said Esmond forcefully. "You can't be ruled by your emotions. This decision is way too important for that."

"I want to make a difference in the world. Like we did before. Like you're doing now. Can't you understand that?" Theo was half crying now as the distress that he'd kept bottled up for months came pouring out.

"Yes, of course I can," said Esmond. "But this isn't the way to do it. Getting a good degree and using it to get ahead in the world will put you in a position where you can make a real difference. Not shooting a gun at Fascists. Anyone can do that, and probably a lot better than you."

"That's not how you talked about the brigades before," said Theo, getting angry himself now. "You called them heroes."

"And I still do. But that doesn't mean they can go to the places you can. In a few years, if you work hard, you could be helping decide British foreign policy. Stopping nonintervention."

"The war will be over long before I could get to that kind of position."

"Perhaps, but the fight against Fascism isn't just happening in Spain. It's a global struggle that'll take years to resolve: the Japanese in China, the Italians in Africa, Hitler in the East. We are coming to the final battle between darkness and light. Don't you want to have a part to play in that?"

"The battle between capitalism and Communism. That's what you're talking about, isn't it?"

"In the end, yes."

"And you want me to help the Communists win. But the trouble with that logic is I'm not a Communist. I hope you haven't forgotten that," said Theo, looking searchingly at Esmond.

"Of course I haven't," said Esmond. "If you were a Communist, you couldn't climb the ladder."

"So you want me to work for you in secret. Become a spy? Is that the idea?"

"I didn't say that."

"But you meant it. And you need to get it through your head that I'm not going to do it, even though I hate this self-satisfied, hypocritical country just as much as you do; maybe even more. It's Spain that I care about now, and I need you to get me there so that I can fight with the brigades. And then, if I make it back, maybe I'll do what you want. But if you don't, I won't. I promise you that. So what's it to be?"

Theo sat staring at Esmond, waiting anxiously to see how he'd respond to his challenge. It had dawned on him as they talked that Esmond might well have the power to stop him from joining the brigades, and he hoped that his tactic of offering the possibility of future cooperation might be enough to keep Esmond on his side.

He knew he wasn't making the offer in good faith. Spying struck him as an ugly, demeaning business, regardless of how much he disliked Britain for letting down the Republic. And he had no qualms about deceiving Esmond, now that he'd realized that his friend had come to Oxford with an agenda. He'd been puzzled before about the oddity of Esmond knowing the city so well, and he wondered if there had been other promising undergraduates that Esmond had recruited to the cause.

Theo understood that he and Esmond were playing a game in which they both wanted things from each other, and that meant he had to be watchful and play his cards to the best of his ability. Esmond was right: he couldn't be ruled by his emotions.

He knew, too, that Esmond had to be making similar calculations, but his face remained inscrutable. And when he eventually spoke, it was to ask a question of his own:

"How would you get back into Oxford when you return?"

"My stepfather will oil the wheels," Theo replied easily. "Trinity's his alma mater, and money talks. You know that."

"Why would he do that?"

"Because he loves me. Even more, since my mother died. We're the only family we each have now."

Esmond looked surprised: this was information he clearly hadn't had at his disposal. "I'm sorry for your loss," he said, laying his hand on Theo's arm just as he had years before at Saint Gregory's. "You've had rotten luck, my friend."

Theo nodded. "It makes it worse that we parted on bad terms," he said bitterly. "I would give anything to take back what I said to her, but life's not like that, is it? There are no second chances."

"Not with the dead," said Esmond. "Why did you fall out?"

"I told her I was going to run in the Olympiad and she lost her temper, just like she did in New York when she found out my coach was a Communist."

"Yes, I remember you telling me about that," said Esmond, nodding. "Communists have certainly given you opportunities in your life, but they've got you into trouble too. I can see that."

"They've been my friends. They still are," said Theo, looking Esmond in the eye in a way intended to leave him in no doubt that he was included in their number. He was sure that Esmond's sympathy was genuine, just as it had been when he comforted him for the loss of his father and, later, his grandparents at Saint Gregory's. The fact that Esmond had an agenda made no difference to that.

"Will you help me?" he asked. "I need to go back."

"It's a fool's errand," said Esmond, shaking his head. "But if you promise to help me when you come back, then I'll back you now. What do you say?"

Theo hesitated and then took the hand that Esmond was holding out to him. Esmond had turned the tables, but it didn't matter. He just wanted to get to Spain and fight. The future was for another day.

# 12

## ANDREW

Theo went home for Christmas.

It was strange to think of the house in Grosvenor Square as home, because he had spent so little time there during the four years and more since he left New York, other than that first summer of 1933, which seemed a distant memory now, after all that had happened since.

Perhaps he called it home because it was the only place left in his life that could qualify for the word. But it was more, Theo thought, because Andrew was there. Grosvenor Square was Andrew's home, and so it was his home too. He felt that the bond between them had become stronger since Elena's death, even though they had seen each other for only a couple of shell-shocked weeks after their return to England before Theo went up to Oxford, and for several evenings since when Andrew came to visit, putting up at the Randolph Hotel in Beaumont Street, which seemed to Theo like a stodgy English version of the Colón, but without the view.

In an obvious sense, they were both now alone in the world, so that all they had left as family was each other, but the depth of their relationship was built on the hard times they had experienced together through Elena's bouts of illness and on Andrew's support of Theo through his various troubles. They had become allies, the link between them enhanced by its own improbability. It was strange indeed for Theo to remember that he had once thought of himself as unwanted baggage that Andrew had taken on with his marriage and to contrast that with his stepfather's heartfelt embrace of him as his son on the boat leaving Barcelona.

He'd told Esmond that his stepfather loved him, and he knew this to be true not just because Andrew had told him he did, but because he had been there for him in a way in which nobody else had in his life. He had become the rock on whom Theo had come to rely, and so it was hard for him to admit that Andrew was changing. He was not the same man whom Theo had seen in Barcelona in July. It was as if he had been keeping his age at bay, only for the accumulated years to suddenly catch up with him when Elena died. His silver hair had turned white, and the sharp creases in his weather-beaten face had turned to wrinkles. Most strikingly, his old air of relaxed confidence had been replaced by a look of creeping anxiety, which sometimes bordered on bewilderment. He talked of the world as if it had left him behind, which in Spain it obviously had, and he spoke about God in the same way.

"I think I made the mistake of relating to him through your mother. She made faith so real. I'd never experienced it in that way before I met her. It seemed eternal, but then when she died, it was as if all that glittering light was suddenly snuffed out, leaving me in darkness. She took God with her, and now I don't know how to find him again. I've forgotten how to pray," he told Theo on their first night together, piecing his words together, as if he was seeking answers to his questions as he spoke.

"I don't think I ever learned," said Theo. "But that was because I had a different experience from you."

"With God, or with your mother?"

"With her religion. You're right that it glittered, but it was that finished, diamond-like quality that cut her off from life outside of it, and from me, too, once I learned to think for myself. She loved the Mexican me who went with her to the church in Gramercy Park and sang the Spanish hymns, but the American me was outside the grasp of her imagination. My father had the same tunnel vision, but his religion was his business. Nothing else mattered. I think they were both limited by what had happened in their childhoods. Deaths and rejections: they couldn't get beyond them. I'm trying to be different. With your help."

Theo smiled hopefully at his stepfather, but Andrew did not respond, because he was thinking too hard about what Theo had said. "Yes, you're right," he said eventually. "Elena was childlike, and I loved her for it, but I can see that that was difficult for you."

"It's why we grew apart. I had to, to grow up," said Theo, warming to his theme. "I don't know if I picked my friends because they were Communists and Anarchists, but the fact that they were meant I had to keep them secret. I'd learned my lesson with my running coach in New York. He was a good man who cared about me, but she called him a devil. *A devil*—can you imagine?" Theo shook his head in disbelief at the memory. "And then in Barcelona it happened again. It meant nothing to her that I had been given that extraordinary opportunity to run for my country; all that she cared about was that the Communists had organized the Games. And you supported her, called it a jamboree. You told me to give it up!" Theo expostulated, turning on his stepfather with a sudden unexpected bitterness.

They hadn't talked about Elena in any way that mattered since their conversation onboard the ship, and Theo realized now that this had been a deliberate policy on his part, designed to protect himself, even as it condemned Andrew to suffer his grief alone. Now the memory of that last meeting with his mother in the Hotel Colón summoned up a deep, raw hurt in Theo that took him unawares, carrying him away on a tide of hitherto-suppressed emotion.

But Andrew seemed to understand. "I'm sorry," he said straightaway. "I felt I had to take her side. The quarrel between you happened so quickly, and I wasn't prepared for it. But I was wrong. I see that now. And if we'd stayed in Barcelona, we wouldn't have gone back to the village and she wouldn't have seen those things that were more than she could bear. It was my mission in life to protect her and keep her alive. And I failed. I . . . ." He broke off, and Theo was horrified to see that his stepfather had taken out his handkerchief from his breast pocket and was dabbing it at his face in an unsuccessful attempt to conceal the fact that he had started to cry.

Theo wanted to go to him and give comfort, but a force stronger than his will kept him in his chair. "It's not your fault," he said, because words were all he could offer. "You tried your best to help her, but she was burning up from the inside and there was nothing any of us could do to stop it. I realized that a long time ago. I knew what was coming."

Theo remembered the moment he'd entered the salon in Los Olivos and had thought his mother might be dead, and so had hung back in the doorway to preserve the possibility that she might be alive, because he could not bear the desolation if she was not. Stopped there, frozen in time. And now the worst *had* happened, and he refused to be overturned by it, determined to avoid the dismembering pain he had felt when his father died.

"I used to resent you for taking my place with my mother," he told Andrew. "But then I realized it wasn't true. There was no place to take, because I had already moved on. So I'm glad that you were there for her. I'm glad I ran after you in New York."

"And I'm glad I didn't shoot you when you did," said Andrew, smiling at the memory.

"Do you remember what you said?" Theo asked, looking narrowly at his stepfather.

"No. Tell me."

"That you'd had quite a few surprises in your time, but that that one just about took the biscuit."

"'Took the biscuit'!" repeated Andrew, looking appalled. "I can't have said that. You're making it up!"

"No, I'm not. They were your exact words. I'd swear to them in a court of law," said Theo, holding up his hand as if to take the oath.

"What must you have thought of me?" Andrew asked, shaking his head.

"That you were one crazy Englishman!" said Theo, laughing.

"Which I suppose is exactly what I am," said Andrew, laughing too.

And for a moment they were happy together, forgetting their troubles.


They did not talk of Elena again. Theo kept his mother's death in the same dark room in his mind where he stored the deaths of all the others that he had loved and lost in his short life, and when he felt the door creaking on its hinges, he put on his running shoes and ran down Upper Brook Street to Hyde Park and lost himself among the trees and hedgerows, with his exhaled breath rising silver in the cold winter air.

It helped that he did not associate London with his mother. He had been away at school when she had been living there, and he did not feel her presence in the corridors in the way that his stepfather did. Andrew said nothing, but Theo knew what he was thinking when he sat silent at mealtimes, eating nothing and staring away into the middle distance. Once, in the library, he got out his will and began telling Theo about the properties he would inherit, until Theo stopped him.

"You're not going to die," he said. "So please stop talking about it."

"There's no harm in putting one's affairs in order," said Andrew gloomily. "And you're my heir, so I want you to know what's coming to you."

Theo couldn't stand to hear any more and insisted Andrew put on his Russian beaver hat and accompany him out into the cold sunlight.

From that day forth, they went out together every day. They walked in the parks, drinking hot chocolate bought from sidewalk refreshment stands to keep themselves warm, and visited the National Gallery, where Andrew told him stories of the austere Spanish kings and cardinals painted by Velázquez and Goya.

"It breaks my heart to think of what is happening over there," he said. "All that was so beautiful, burnt and trampled underfoot. I wonder whether I will ever see Spain again."

Theo realized that his stepfather had unwittingly provided him with the perfect opening to reveal his own intention to go back. He had been dreading telling Andrew, putting it off from day to day because he knew how the news would upset him, and he wanted nothing more at that moment than to lay his cards on the table and get the announcement over with. All the more so because the Goya pictures had reminded him of Maria and the painting of the execution that she had so vividly described to him in the ayuntamiento in Los Olivos that first summer they had been together. She felt near to him suddenly, and the intensity of his longing to see her again gripped him, making it hard to breathe.

He opened his mouth to speak, but the words didn't come. He saw his stepfather's worn, kindly face, staring up at the paintings on the wall like they were old friends, and he couldn't bring himself to spoil their outing. Andrew had been looking and sounding better with every day that they spent together, and Theo reasoned that a short delay in his departure wouldn't make any difference to the fate of the Republic or his chances of finding Maria.

The unseasonably sunny weather held into the New Year, and Andrew and Theo built on the success of their visits to the National Gallery to go on other day trips farther afield. Causier, the chauffeur, drove them, with white wine and sandwiches packed in a large picnic hamper sitting beside him on the front passenger seat of the same polished Rolls-Royce Silver Ghost that had taken Theo to Saint Gregory's four years before.

Then, he had fiercely resented his stepfather and been ashamed of his wealth. Now, he was happy that he could put a smile on his face. Theo had never seen the great London sights, and Andrew enjoyed showing them to him and bringing them to life with his unexpectedly intimate knowledge of their history.

Their best day was at Hampton Court, where Andrew enthralled Theo with the story of Henry the Eighth's six wives, of whom one had died in childbirth and one had been arrested for treason in the palace.

"Poor Catherine Howard! She was the same age as you when that brute had her beheaded in the Tower," said Andrew, looking back behind them as if he might catch a glimpse of the cruel, fat king riding out to hunt.

Back at the house in Grosvenor Square, Theo gazed out over the rooftops toward Buckingham Palace, where a new, reluctant king was starting his reign following his brother's abdication, and marveled at the long, grand sweep of British history through its larger-than-life kings and queens, until he remembered that he was about to give up everything to join a Communist-led organization fighting to save a left-wing republic. Whatever he was, he wasn't a royalist!

Theo's state of limbo continued until the second week in January, when Andrew surprised him at breakfast by asking if he was packed for the start of the new term due to begin the following Wednesday, and offered him the services of Causier to take him down to Oxford with his luggage.

"So much easier than the train when you've got bags to carry. Railway porters can be very elusive when you need them, as I've found several times to my cost," said Andrew, smiling.

Theo swallowed hard, spluttering on the hot coffee in his mouth as he tried to think of how to respond.

The time for prevarication was over. He had to tell Andrew he was going to Spain. Their relationship had achieved such strength from unlikely beginnings because they had tried to tell each other the truth about themselves, insofar as they knew it, and had supported each other through the hard times they had both experienced. It was one thing to delay telling his stepfather; to lie to him about something so important was unthinkable.

But how to tell him? Theo had seen how Andrew's mood and demeanor had improved over the previous month. He was engaged now instead of withdrawn; cheerful instead of wretched—his empty plate was testimony to how he had recovered his appetite. And now Theo was faced with having to push him back down the slope into the slough of despond from where he'd started. Unless he could make Andrew understand. He had to try.

"I'm not going back to Oxford. At least not this year," he said, wishing that he had prepared a speech beforehand instead of jumping in like this without any idea of what to say. He'd known this day was coming.

"What do you mean? Why not?" Andrew asked, not understanding.

"Because I'm going to Spain to fight. I have to."

"To fight for who?" Andrew's mouth was hanging open, and he looked as if he'd been hit with a blunt object.

"The International Brigades."

"The Communists?"

"The Communists organize them, but anyone can join. I'll be fighting for the Republic. The brigades are the only way I can get back there and do something. I have to."

"You already said that," said Andrew, getting up from the table and going over to a cocktail cabinet in the corner of the room, where he poured himself a generous measure of whiskey that he drank off straightaway before refilling his glass, even though it was nine in the morning.

When he turned around, Theo was relieved to see that he seemed to have regained his self-possession, although his face looked pale and haggard, as if he'd sustained a serious shock.

"How long have you known this?" he asked.

"Since I came home. I'm sorry I didn't tell you, but you seemed so low. It worried me."

"So you thought you'd wait until I was better to break the news?"

"Yes. I wanted to spend time together, too, which was selfish, I know."

"No, it wasn't," said Andrew nodding. "It was kind. You are kind, Theo, and I love you for it. But you're damned reckless too. It's not the first time I've told you that."

"No, it isn't," said Theo, bowing his head.

"You think you have to do things, dangerous things, because you'll be judged a coward if you don't. But sometimes it's braver to hold back and be sensible. Have you ever thought of that?"

"Yes," said Theo, remembering the parting advice Booker had given him in Barcelona to not let his heart rule his head.

"Think about it then," Andrew pressed. "What good are you going to do, providing target practice for one of Franco's snipers? When you could have a real effect on the world if you keep your head down and do well at Oxford. You could stand for Parliament, get into government. Be a Labour man if you want. I don't care. I'd still back you."

"I know you would."

"Stop humoring me," Andrew demanded, annoyed that his words were having no effect. "Someone's put you up to this. Is it that Esmond character—the Communist who almost got you kicked out of school? Has he been to see you?"

"Yes, he came—"

"Ah, now we're getting there," interrupted Andrew triumphantly. "I knew he'd come crawling back out of the woodwork as soon as he got the chance."

"It's not what you think," said Theo, making an effort to stay calm in the face of his stepfather's anger. "Esmond wants me to stay at Oxford, just like you. He spent hours trying to persuade me."

Andrew stared at Theo and saw he was telling the truth. "Then who is it? Is it that girl in Spain? Maria Alvarez, who ran off with the murderer, and turned your head? Is she the one behind all this?"

"I haven't heard from her since we left," said Theo. "But yes, in a way, you're right. I won't feel worthy of her if I stay here and do nothing. I love her because she fights for what she believes in, and I have to do that too."

"You don't know what fighting means," said Andrew, shaking his head. "It's just a word to you to be thrown around in conversation."

"I fought in Barcelona," said Theo, beginning to get riled up now in spite of himself.

"You played the hero for a few hours!" said Andrew contemptuously. "But there are no heroes anymore. That's what you don't understand! There's no glory, just mechanized slaughter. It's not the brave that win; it's the side with the strongest weapons. Bombs, shells, gas, guns. Men are just cannon fodder in that kind of warfare. Courage means nothing. I know this, so you should listen to me. Not nod your head like you've heard it all before."

Theo was cowed. He had never seen his stepfather so incensed and impassioned, but then, all of a sudden, Andrew broke off and stopped his invective. He went over to the cabinet and refilled his glass, but he didn't drink. Instead, he kept it in his hand as he stood at the window, looking out, as if he could see in his garden down below not trees and carefully swept gravel walks, but scenes of horror from another time and place. And when he began to talk again without turning around, it was in a different, low voice with little intonation that Theo had to strain to follow. A voice from far away, fitted to the hell that he was describing:

"I was on the Somme in 1916 and at Passchendaele the year after, when men drowned in mud. God knows how I survived, but I did. And I have hardly spoken of it since because I wanted to forget. But I was wasting my time. The war is as vivid to me now as it was then. I carry it with me like an X-ray burned onto the surface of my mind.

"I can *see* it. And hear it too: drumfire before an attack—an end-of-the-world noise that doesn't end. On and on, as we waited to go over, shaking like children while the enemy machine guns sliced open the sandbags all along the parapet so that the sand was falling in our eyes when we went up the ladders and the bullets were like a scythe through the grass. And through us too. A man lay next to me on the ground with his face and hands marble white and his lungs working like a bellows, even though he was already gone, because the body doesn't know when to stop. Fool that it is!

"And then later, at night, the maggots crawling in the guts of the dead. You can hear them. They make a sound like rustling silk. Like my mother's gown when she came to say good night when I was a child in this house.

"Nothing made any sense. Nothing at all. It went on for months. Shells coming over and throwing the corpses in no-man's-land high up into the air. Tumbling up and tumbling down, and we laughed, because what else could we do? We weren't made for such sights. And when we went forward, we had to step on the dead, and our hobnail boots sank down into their poor rotting faces. Picking up your feet, putting them down again—can you imagine?

"Some shells were gas. They hissed as they came over, and we thought they were just duds until we caught the smell. Chlorine like pineapple, mustard like soap, phosgene like some kind of dead fish gone rotten. We grappled for our masks, but for some poor bastards it was too late, because the gas was already burning their lungs. Thrusting like needles up into their eyes as we tottered back to the dressing station in a half-blind crocodile, each hanging on to the shoulders of the man in front. Vomiting on him. How could this be? But it was.

"Dead trees, dead earth, dead water, dead men. We lived in a charnel house, and at the end we didn't care whether we'd won or lost. Just that it was over and that it would not happen again, to us or to our children. But we were wrong. Because it's starting again. The beast has awoken from its slumber and is even more hungry than before, ready to swallow up another generation of foolish young men like you, dreaming of justice and glory. Give it up, Theo. Not for my sake but for yours. Before it's too late."

Andrew breathed deeply and turned back from the window, looking over at Theo, who was sitting at the table with his head in his hands. He rested his own hand on Theo's shoulder for a moment, gazing down at him with a look of deep sadness and affection, and then walked out of the room.

Andrew's words had a strong effect on Theo, but they did not change his mind. They couldn't, because he felt he had no choice about going. He had come to define his identity through courage. Regardless of the outcome, he saw each challenge he had faced up to in his life as another rung successfully climbed on his ladder of self-discovery. To back away now from the greatest challenge of all would be to slip back down to the bottom, and that was less tolerable to him than the risk of death on a foreign field. Better a charnel house than to lose himself, or so he thought.

Andrew took one look at Theo's face when he entered the library in the evening, dressed for dinner, and seemed to understand that the decision had gone against him. He sighed but didn't seem surprised, and held up his hand to forestall Theo when Theo launched into the explanation that he had prepared while walking in the park in the afternoon.

"It's your life, Theo, and I cannot stop you from living it," he told him. "It's in your nature never to back down, and so you must learn your own lessons. I just hope you will survive the experience and not be changed by it into something you are not. I shall find a way to pray again and ask God for your safe return, just as my father did for me. Here, take this," he said, holding out a thin beaded chain that he had been keeping in the closed palm of his hand. "It was his. It helped me when I was gone, and I believe it will help you too. Keep it close and don't show it to your Communist friends. They might not understand," he added wryly as Theo took the chain.

It was the rosary that he had seen in Andrew's hand on the day after Theo came back from Olympia. The only other time that Andrew had ever spoken of the war. He'd said it had saved his life.

"Thank you," said Theo. "But if I don't believe . . ."

"It doesn't matter. I do, and that's enough," said Andrew, and holding out his arms, he hugged Theo close for a moment before letting him go.

"That's the Spanish side of me coming out," he said, smiling. "From my grandmother with the rose in her hair. Remember her face on the sherry bottle? We must drink a glass of vintage Campion amontillado in her honor tonight."

Theo smiled too, uncertainly. "Will you be all right?" he asked. "When I'm gone."

"Oh yes, I'm made of sterner stuff than you think," said Andrew. "Don't worry about me."

"I can't help it. You knew I was going, didn't you, even before I came back? That's why you had the rosary in your hand."

"I thought it likely," said Andrew. "I know you. Remember?"

Now that he had told his stepfather, Theo shook off his inertia and went to the address Esmond had given him, on the corner of King Street in Covent Garden Market. He had no idea that the shabby, nondescript office building in urgent need of repainting was the headquarters of the Communist Party of Great Britain.

A man in shirtsleeves asked him a few questions not including his age, and Theo sensed that he was going through the motions, because Esmond had already cleared the way for his application, as he'd said he would when they reached their agreement in Oxford a month earlier.

At the end of the interview, the man gave him an address in Paris to go to on his arrival there and wished him luck. "No need to pack much luggage," he said. "They'll give you what you need when you get there. And you won't need a passport if you get a two-day return ticket on the boat train. 'Dirty weekender' is what they call 'em, I believe." The man laughed: a harsh, humorless cackle that Theo was glad to escape when he got back outside.

He had an American passport that his stepfather had obtained for him when he left New York, but it had expired and he would have gone down the dirty weekender route if he hadn't received a telephone call from Esmond the next morning.

"You've taken your time," said Esmond.

"Is that a problem?"

But Esmond couldn't seem to hear him because the line was bad at his end, and so Theo had to shout the question several times before Esmond answered. "Not at all," he said, and his familiar drawling voice was clear as a bell. "I'd just hoped that you might be having second thoughts. That's all."

"Well, I'm not," Theo yelled.

"Have you got a passport?"

"It's expired. They said I could go without."

"Don't. Get it renewed and don't give it to them in Paris when they ask for it. Keep it hidden with money. Pounds sterling, not pesetas. You'll need them to get out."

"I don't want to get out."

"You will." Esmond laughed. "I'll be there in the spring. Until then you're on your own, so take care of yourself. You hear me?"

"Yes. Where are you now?"

But Theo couldn't hear a response. The line had gone dead, and Esmond didn't call back.

The American embassy was only a mile and a half from the house in Grosvenor Gardens, but that didn't make it any quicker to renew Theo's passport, and it was another three weeks before he could leave.

Andrew had given him fifty pounds and five hundred pesetas in banknotes, which he'd folded up small and secreted with his passport and the rosary in a cotton pouch hanging from a string tied around his neck. And at the last moment he added the lock of hair that Maria had sent him eighteen months before with the note telling him not to forget her. As if he ever could!

Downstairs, he hugged his stepfather on the doorstep and told him he'd be back.

"Yes, you will," said Andrew. "I believe that." And he looked hard at Theo, as if memorizing every feature of his face, before he let him go.

As the car drove away, gathering speed past the black wrought iron railings of the square gardens, Theo looked back through the rear window toward his stepfather, standing now out on the sidewalk and gazing after him down the street. And in the months that followed, he often thought of that moment—of Andrew focused so entirely on him. A rock among the moving sands of his life, awaiting his return.

# 13

## THE PYRENEES

In Paris he took a taxi from the Gare du Nord to the address he'd been given—the Bureau des Syndicats in Montmartre. The driver looked back at Theo over his shoulder and smiled, displaying a mouthful of gold teeth.

"You're going to Spain, to the war?" he asked.

*"Oui,"* said Theo, nodding vigorously to compensate for his inability to muster a longer reply in his schoolboy French. Classes at Saint Gregory's had given him a basic understanding of the language, enhanced by its similarity to Spanish, but he had had very little opportunity to practice speaking it.

"Good for you. The ride's on me," said the driver and accelerated away through a maze of side streets and boulevards at a breakneck speed that soon had Theo doubled over with a motion sickness that was far worse than anything he'd felt on the Channel ferry, when huge, rolling waves had had many of the other passengers vomiting over the side of the ship.

But the driver didn't seem to notice, whistling the "Marseillaise" as he executed seemingly impossible turns until they came to a screeching halt in front of the bureau.

*"Tue les fascistes!"* Kill the Fascists! the driver shouted to Theo by way of parting instruction as he got out, and then held his fist up out of the window in the Anarchist salute as he roared away down the road in a cloud of exhaust smoke.

The bureau was full of people rushing in every direction across the main hallway and speaking a babble of languages that reminded Theo of the Olympic Stadium in Barcelona, except that here no one was talking Spanish. He tried to explain himself to a severe-looking woman who was sitting behind a desk furiously banging the keys of a typewriter, but her only response was to write down his name and point impatiently toward a long bench lining the far wall, where a few other young men were sitting, nervously turning their caps in their hands. When Theo tried to talk to them, they replied in an incomprehensible German-sounding language that left him wondering nervously if he had come to the right place.

An hour passed and nothing happened. He felt tired and disoriented and hungry and was just about to try his luck with the typist again when a door opened in the wall opposite and a woman with a pointed nose and luminous dark eyes called his name.

She told him to call her Charlotte, but that was the only information she gave him about herself before she launched into a detailed interrogation in English that bore no relation to the perfunctory interview Theo had gone through in London. Clearly Esmond had not prepared the ground for him here in the same way he had before.

She watched Theo carefully as he answered, as if to test his veracity, and then wrote down his responses in a large book.

He answered the first questions about his name and background and reasons for joining the brigades easily enough, but then he did as Esmond had told him to and lied about his passport and money, which were secreted in the pouch hanging from his neck.

He hated the deceit, feeling that it was a terrible way to start his brigade career, and he thought that he must've made it obvious what he was doing, too, staring fixedly up at a portrait of Lenin hanging behind Charlotte's head to avoid meeting her eyes as he spoke. He half expected that she would summon a Communist underling to search him, before sending him packing as soon as his mendacity had been exposed, but instead she launched into a lecture about the dangers of venereal disease, which included producing several explicit and disgusting photographs that had Theo fastened on Vladimir Ilyich again as a way of avoiding looking at where she was pointing. He wondered whether it was her way of punishing him for not telling the truth.

Finally, she offered him a ticket home. "It's not too late," she said. "War is ugly and you may well not come back. All we can promise you is a chance to fight."

"That's all I want," said Theo. He shook her hand and fled the room, leaving her to her photographs.

Outside, he waited as several others on the bench took their turns in the interview room and then, just as the sun was setting outside, a stocky Frenchman came in through the main door of the bureau and gathered the volunteers in a circle around him.

He was at least fifty but could have been much older, and he was wearing a zip-up jacket and a woolen cap pulled low over his narrow eyes.

"I am Jean," he said. "You will be coming with me to a hotel, where we will wait until it is time for you to take the train to the border."

He spoke slowly in French and then in English, like a man who was used to dealing with foreigners, even though he didn't like it much. Theo sensed that he was one of those taciturn men who would have preferred to say nothing at all.

"You will not draw attention to yourselves," he went on. "You will not get drunk or visit prostitutes. You will do as I say. Do I make myself clear?"

It took several repetitions, including one in German, before Jean was satisfied that all the volunteers had understood, and then they followed him obediently in a crocodile line out of the door and down a series of narrow overhanging side streets in the dusk, until they reached a tall building squeezed between its neighbors with an illuminated sign saying **HÔTE** above the front entrance. Closer scrutiny showed that the bulb in the final **L** had blown out.

This was to be Theo's home for the next week. He spent his nights and most of his days in a tiny room high in the eaves, with a small window looking out on a matching one on the other side of the street in which the drapes were permanently drawn, leaving Theo to speculate uselessly on what was going on behind them.

Waiting turned out to mean staying inside, because the order to depart could come at a moment's notice, and Theo was grateful for his copy of *The Count of Monte Cristo* that he had borrowed at the last moment from his stepfather's library. Dumas helped to keep his boredom and anxiety at bay most of the time, although there were moments when he wanted to bang his head against the wall and scream.

Outside his tiny room, he had access to a primitive bathroom shared among six, and ate his lunch and dinner with the other volunteers in a worker's cooperative restaurant at the end of the road under the watchful eye of Jean, who frowned whenever any of his charges tried to start up a conversation. The food was basic, bearing no relation whatsoever to haute cuisine, and no alcohol was permitted.

The only variation to this routine occurred when the volunteers returned to the bureau for a medical checkup carried out by a bored doctor with a stethoscope. Everyone passed, but as they were getting ready to leave, a tall young Englishman in crumpled, dirty clothes who had just come in from outside blocked the door. He had a tangled beard and wore a black, lopsided eyepatch over his left eye, making him look like a down-at-heel pantomime pirate, and he swayed slightly from side to side where he stood, clearly the worse for drink.

"Suckers!" he shouted at Theo and the other volunteers. "You're all going to die, you know that. And if you don't, you'll damn well wish you had, once the Moors have finished with you. Do you know what they do? Did Charlotte the Harlot in there tell you that?" He pointed up at his eyepatch and Theo recoiled, sensing he was about to pull it down and reveal whatever horrible mutilation had been inflicted on the eye underneath.

But Jean distracted his attention. He'd crossed the hall in a flash and now stood toe-to-toe with the Englishman, even though he only came up to his shoulder.

"Shut up and get out!" he told him, pointing past him toward the door.

"Why the fuck should I? They've got a right to know. They'll—"

The Englishman got no further because Jean drew back his fist and punched him expertly on the chin, knocking him out cold. Straightaway, he turned back to the recruits and beckoned to them to follow him, which they did, stepping over the prone body one after the other, before they went out the door.

It was Theo's last experience of Paris. Late the next afternoon, the volunteers left on the train for the South. Jean remained behind, uncharacteristically warm at the last, when he took each of them by the shoulders on the Gare de Lyon platform and kissed them on both cheeks, wishing them *"bonne chance et bon voyage."* On the train, they scrambled with several other groups of volunteers for seats on the hard wooden benches of the third-class carriages. One climbed up into the luggage rack above Theo's head and promptly went to sleep, apparently oblivious to the raucous singing and shouting down below.

Theo recognized the tune of "The Internationale" but none of the words. The volunteers were singing the song in different languages, but none were

English or Spanish. He felt suddenly lonely, afflicted by an isolation that was all the more intense because he was in a crowd. Nobody seemed aware of him, still and silent in their midst. A ghost at the feast—it made him doubt his own existence.

He wondered if they might be singing in English in the next carriage, but he was wedged in too tight to move, and so he sat where he was, remembering how he and Booker had watched Durruti's militiamen leaving for Aragon on the Ramblas the previous summer. *"Lambs to the slaughter,"* Booker had called them, and he wondered whether he and the other volunteers were just more of the same. Naive fools intoxicated by slogans and songs and without a clue of what they had let themselves in for. He shuddered, thinking of his stepfather's description of the Somme, and unconsciously fingered the pouch around his neck, feeling for the rosary chain inside.

Darkness fell and gradually the volunteers settled down to sleep, their stomachs replete with the thick baguette sandwiches they'd bought at the station kiosks before departure, and their brains dulled by cheap wine and the endless clickety-clack rhythm of the train wheels. But Theo remained wide awake, staring out of the window at the moonlit olive groves and vineyards. France was passing them by in the night: empty fields dotted with small farmhouses, hillsides terraced with ancient dry stone walls, twisting rivers and roads, and here and there a church spire reaching up above sleeping villages toward the star-spangled sky.

The train was no express, stopping at stations all along the line. Sometimes they remained motionless alongside a dark, deserted platform for so long that Theo thought they had stopped for good, only for a whistle and a shout from invisible stationmaster to invisible guard to set them on their way again. Meandering toward Spain.

"Trains are a marvel, are they not?"

Theo twisted his neck in every direction, but everyone around him seemed to be asleep, and it was only when the boy in the luggage rack above his head lit a cigarette that he realized where the disembodied American voice was coming from. The flame of the match revealed a round, unshaven face in a halo of black, curly hair and a pair of dark eyes looking down at him, bright with intelligence.

"Yes, I suppose they are," said Theo. "Although I haven't thought about them much, to be honest. I suppose because I haven't been on many. I've been *in* places in my life, but not *between* them, if you know what I mean."

The boy smiled, amused by Theo's unexpectedly thoughtful reply. "I've had the opposite experience," he said. "A lot of between time. My family moved around when I was a kid and afterward, I hopped freights and jumped down when the mood took me. Ohio, Kentucky, Tennessee—it didn't matter. I liked that feeling, that each town could be a new beginning. The start of a whole new life. Or not."

"And were they? A new beginning?"

"Sometimes they seemed like it, but then I'd end up getting arrested and run out of town, so I guess not," said the boy, laughing. "Most places aren't that different when you get down into them. In the US of A at least. They've all got employers paying dimes for dollars and their fair share of dirty cops and bad beer. I'm hoping for better over here. Paris was a good start. What a city! Great wine, swell girls. Notre Dame, the Louvre. I even went up the Eiffel Tower, although I wished I hadn't when I got up high. I get vertigo, but I guess I'd forgotten about that in all the excitement."

"You don't get it in luggage racks?"

"No, they're the lap of luxury for a hobo like me."

"How did you get out in Paris?" asked Theo enviously. "Our group leader told us we had to stay in the hotel."

"So did mine, but that didn't mean I listened. I came back late instead, so he had to leave without me! I wasn't going to miss out on Paris just because some killjoy Communist told me to. I've seen enough of their kind in New York. Boring each other stupid at their committee meetings, mimeographing leaflets that no one wants to read, standing on orange crates shouting at people who don't want to listen. No, thanks!"

"You're not a Communist?"

"No way. I've stood on picket lines in five states and I'm proud of it. But I've never been tempted to join the party. Not once. Communists want power and I'm no fan of dictatorships. Proletarian or Fascist. What about you?"

"I don't like that about them either," said Theo. "But the Communists get things done. The International Brigades saved Madrid. You can't argue with that."

"I'm here because I'm a Jew," said the boy, making it sound like that trumped everything. "And Spain's the only place I can get to right now to fight that bastard Adolf. Oh, and I think Spanish señoritas are the best-looking girls in the world, so that helps too," he added, laughing again. Serious and funny all mixed up together. Coming forward and shying away. Theo soon came to realize it was how he always talked.

"My father was Jewish," Theo said. "He didn't want to be, but he was. By birth, at least." He stopped, surprised at himself for confiding something so personal to a stranger whom he'd known for less than five minutes. Perhaps it was the way the boy talked, without boundaries, that invited such reciprocal disclosure. He reminded Theo of Antonio on that day they first met when they drank wine together out in the village square.

"Why didn't he want to be Jewish?" the boy asked, looking down at Theo curiously from his elevated position on the luggage rack. "I've felt a lot of things, but never that, I'm happy to say."

"It was because he married my mother. She was Catholic. A señorita." Theo smiled.

"And a goy!" said the boy, shaking his head. "That never ends well."

"It didn't. My grandparents disowned him for it. Treated him like he didn't exist. They even had a funeral."

"They sat shiva?" said the boy, looking horrified. "Ai! Ai!"

Theo nodded. *"Ai! Ai!"* was right. "My father was so angry he changed his name," he went on. "Said we were Americans now and that's what mattered. But years later I met my grandfather and he told me that you can't change who you are. You have to be true to that, because without it you are nothing. I was too young to understand what he meant at the time, but I think I do now. So I guess this is all just a way of saying that I'm here because I feel I'm Jewish, too, even though I'm not. The opposite way around to my father. There's a lot of other reasons I'm going, but that's one of them."

"What's your Jewish name?" the boy asked.

"Stern. I don't have a Jewish first name, just the family one."

"*Star*—I like it," said the boy. "I'm Manny Mandelbaum. Not so pretty."

"And I'm Theo."

Theo stood up, raising his arm above his head to shake hands, and smiled, thinking how strange it was that his new friend should have known his never-used Jewish name before he knew he was called Theo.

Back in his seat, he felt a sudden unexpected joy that overrode his fear of what lay ahead. He was happy he'd told Manny his story. It was as if some instinct had told him to reveal himself when it was the last thing he'd have expected to do.

*Star!* As Manny had said the word, he'd remembered his grandfather saying it too: *"It's a beautiful name,"* he'd said. *"For the star that guides us. I am Yossif—Joseph Stern."* Theo could hear the old man's voice. It was as if he had reached back through time and at last made the connection to the heritage that his grandfather had held out to him across the table in that hot, overcrowded tenement apartment all those years ago. Something fitted now where it hadn't before.

Outside the window beside where he was sitting, the first rays of dawn touched the inland lagoons that stretched flatly away to an invisible horizon, while through the opposite window, he could see across the marshes to the sea in the distance, so that it felt in that moment as if the train had magically changed elements in the night and was now skimming across water.

The volunteers stirred and woke in the morning light, and soon the carriage was filled with the same babble of jumbled talk as the evening before, and Theo was astonished to see Manny joining in. He came down from his luggage rack and chatted to several of the volunteers in what sounded like German, until Theo realized from a few stray words that it had to be Yiddish they were speaking. And even though he couldn't understand a word of what they were saying, he was happy because he no longer felt alone.

Soon the carriage was a fug of cigarette smoke behind the steamed-up windows, which Manny kept cleaning with his sleeve to call out the names of the towns they passed. Béziers, Narbonne, and finally Perpignan, where they were met by a man wearing a yellow jersey under a blue jacket, the distinctive clothing that they had been told to look for when they left Paris. The jersey was the only sunny thing about the man, whose face was fixed in a rictus of fearful apprehension as he led the volunteers into a goods yard behind the station and counted them with his finger, arriving at a different number each time until Theo corrected him in Spanish, which he seemed to understand.

He instructed the volunteers to follow him in pairs at twenty-yard intervals, and led them on a fast trek through the cobbled backstreets of the town. If his intention had been to render them inconspicuous, then he achieved the exact opposite, as passersby stopped to stare at the procession of disheveled young men hurrying past in flapping overcoats with cardboard suitcases in their hands. The volunteers had been given blue berets in Paris, but they didn't fit with the rest of their outfits and just made them look like foreigners pretending to be Frenchmen. Perhaps the man in the yellow jersey realized all this as he kept looking back and beckoning them to pick up the pace, until he almost ran into two gendarmes at a crossroads and stopped to feverishly smoke a cigarette, leaning against a lamppost, until they had passed by.

"Our yellow friend's a bag of nerves, isn't he? He'll swallow that cigarette in a minute, the way he's smoking it," said Manny wryly as he and Theo observed their jittery guide from the prescribed twenty paces back. "I wonder what he's so damn nervous about. The French aren't our enemies, are they? They've got a socialist government the last I heard."

"I don't know," said Theo uneasily. "I'll ask him when I get a chance."

A few minutes later the guide stopped in front of a shabby terraced house halfway down an equally shabby street. The only difference between the house and its neighbors was that thick curtains were pulled tight across all the windows, keeping the interior hidden from prying eyes. He opened the door and waited outside, counting heads again as the volunteers went past him into the house. All the time, he was shifting his weight from one foot to the other and looking nervously up and down the street, as if expecting the gendarmes to reappear, and he breathed an immense sigh of relief when everyone was inside and he could shut the door, locking and bolting it, so that the volunteers felt as if they were inside a bank vault instead of a front room cluttered with stuffed armchairs and occasional tables.

A fire was burning in a potbellied stove, and the volunteers were suddenly hot when they had just been cold. There was so little room to move that they had to push their elbows into each other as they took off their overcoats.

"I am Henri. You'll be staying here until you leave," said the man in the yellow jersey, speaking French. "There is food in the kitchen and some beds upstairs if you take it in turns. You must not go outside." Then he repeated his instructions in slow English, stumbling over the words.

"Why the hell can't we go out?" Manny demanded angrily. "I'm not going to be locked up here any more than I was in Paris."

But Henri looked blank, clearly not understanding, so Theo repeated the question in Spanish, and Henri responded in the same language, leaving Theo to translate into English for the benefit of Manny.

"The police will arrest you if they see you, and me too," Henri said, his anxiety returning. "The government closed the frontier yesterday, and they will know why you are here."

"Why? Why did they close it?" asked Theo, shocked to the core by this unexpected news.

"Nonintervention," said Henri, bowing his head. "I am ashamed of my country."

Theo nodded, swallowing his bile. He hated the French at that moment, even more than he hated the English for their own nonintervention hypocrisy. How could they stop people from trying to help the Republic when they knew full well what Hitler and Mussolini were doing? And they called themselves socialists! It beggared belief.

"How can we get across?" he asked.

"You will have to go over the mountains. There is a guide who will take you tomorrow night. He is a smuggler and he knows the paths. It will be hard, but it is possible. You should ask your friends if they are prepared to go."

No one changed their mind, but the volunteers were not singing anymore as they waited out the day, and few of them slept that night. Standing at a bedroom window in the small hours, Theo watched as piercing white searchlight beams swept across the sides of the mountains that towered up above the town, and he shivered, thinking of the ordeal that lay ahead in the high passes. All the previous week, he had been worrying about how he would respond to the test that awaited him in Spain; now he wondered whether he would get to Spain at all. But then a stubborn determination not to be defeated took over and he vowed not to let the noninterventionists stop him from going back, however hard they tried. He couldn't let them win. Not when he had come this far.

The volunteers left the next afternoon, riding in the flatbed of a truck under a green tarpaulin. They had had to abandon their suitcases into the care of Henri, who promised to keep them until their return, and now all they carried were brown paper parcels tucked inside the pockets of their overcoats. He had also provided them with rations consisting of a loaf of bread, slab of cheese, and bottle of water for each man and a pair of rope-soled alpargatas that reminded Theo of Antonio with a stab of unexpected memory that brought tears to his eyes. Several of the volunteers, including Manny, had feet too big to fit into the single-size sandals and so had to continue in their leather wingtip walking shoes, which turned out to be the worst kind of footwear for mountain climbing.

As the truck turned the corner of the street, Theo caught a last glimpse of Henri pushing his hand back through his hair several times before he went inside. His relief at their departure was palpable even from far away, and Theo wondered how many more times he would be putting on his yellow jersey to help the brigades.

The truck took the volunteers out of town and down roads that grew ever narrower as they drew closer to the mountains over which the sun had now set in a haze of rose-pink glory.

In the dusk, they bounced along a track serrated with potholes that sent them falling from side to side into each other's laps, until the truck came to a sudden juddering halt, which left them wondering whether the engine had failed or they had reached their destination.

The truck driver made no move to get out, and after a minute or two the volunteers jumped down, looking around until they noticed an old man sitting on a tree stump at the edge of the clearing in which they were standing. He was dressed in a dark-green jacket and pair of short trousers, with his legs below encased in rolled-up wool puttees of the same color, so that he was perfectly camouflaged against the surrounding pine trees. He beckoned them over and began counting them, just like Henri had done at the station, although he was as calm as Henri had been flustered, and needed no help from Theo to arrive at the correct number. Behind them, the truck driver turned and drove away. He had not spoken one word to them from beginning to end.

"No talking! No smoking! No lights! You understand?" said the old man in French and then in Spanish, which Theo translated to Manny, who translated it on to the other volunteers, who all nodded their agreement.

"Very good!" said the old man, picking up his pack from behind the tree stump and hauling it over his shoulders. "Let's go!"

"First Henri and now Methuselah!" muttered Manny as they set off behind the old man on a path through the trees. "This whole show's being run by amateurs. We'll be lucky if we make it over these goddamn mountains."

Theo looked up at the full moon glistening frosty white above the snowcapped peaks and silently agreed, but his fears for their chances were based on the unfitness of the volunteers and not their guide, who had set off at a brisk pace that his city-bred charges, in their flapping overcoats, were already finding hard to keep up with.

Manny wasn't the only one complaining. As they stumbled along, he and the other volunteers took it in turns to curse the committee in Paris whose delay in sending them south had deprived them of the chance to be making the crossing in the back of a bus instead of on foot in the dark, and the old man had to stop several times and order them to be quiet.

Half an hour later, they knew to take him seriously. The path had just met another and widened out to become a road when he stopped still, cupping his hand to his ear to listen. The volunteers could hear nothing beyond the sigh of the evening breeze through the pines and the croaking of bullfrogs in some nearby marsh, but the old man clearly had much sharper hearing and ordered them all down into a ditch on the side of the road.

"Cover your faces and don't make a sound!" he told them in a fierce whisper.

A few seconds later, they heard footsteps approaching and voices speaking in French. They stopped just where the volunteers had been standing a minute before.

Ten yards away, Theo lay in the dirt with his face cushioned on his folded arms, and the mustiness of the soil under his nose made him want to sneeze. He couldn't move, so he sucked in his breath and counted the beats of his heart, which felt like a hammer in his chest.

"It's an ibex! Look!" said one of the voices excitedly.

"Rubbish!" said another. "You're seeing things, as usual. There aren't any ibexes round here and you know it. They're extinct."

A rifle shot rang out and echoed back, and Theo used the noise to take a breath and bite his lip. He still needed to sneeze, and he didn't know how much longer he could contain the urge.

"Well, they are now," said the first man, laughing uproariously. And a moment later the sound of the footsteps began again, moving away, and Theo clasped both hands over his face and let go of the sneeze.

The old man kept the volunteers in the ditch for another five minutes before he allowed them back up onto the road, which they immediately left to join another path snaking upward.

"You are lucky there were no dogs," he said. "Next time maybe. Now you shut up, yes?"

Again they nodded their agreement, but meaning it this time, and the old man set off at a faster pace than before, intent on making up for lost time.

Now the slight drizzle that had been in the air before turned to rain, driven toward them by a cold wind blowing down from above. The trees became sporadic and then disappeared, leaving only scrub and gorse covering the rocky ground on which melting snow formed rivulets of freezing slush that soaked their blistered, swollen feet. Each sharp stone on which they trod felt like the point of a knife turning in their raw skin.

It was worse for those wearing shoes instead of alpargatas. The rubber soles gave them no hold on the slippery ground, and the stiff vamps provided no support for their ankles. Manny was constantly stopping to retie his laces until they broke and he had to limp on as best he could.

As the slope of the path grew steeper, the backs of the climbers bent toward the ground. All except their guide's, who remained ever vertical and sure-footed as he loped relentlessly on with the same rhythmic, measured stride.

"He's like some kind of mountain goat," said Manny between gasps. "That's what he is." But Theo kept close to the old man and tried to imitate his movement, pointing his feet sideways as if he was climbing a tree. It seemed to help. He was in pain like the rest of the volunteers, but his years of distance running had left him with greater reserves to call on in this time of need.

They weren't alone. Down below, lights were bobbing in the darkness and they could hear the noise of hounds barking. The old man pointed up at the moon. "We can see, but they can too," he said. "They're coming up the road. We must go faster."

Theo sent the message back down the line of volunteers, but all he heard in response were cries of pain as they grasped clumps of scrub and frozen grass in their bleeding hands to help pull themselves up the narrow path. It was a tightrope now between ravines that had opened up on both sides, and they all knew that one slip could be fatal.

Soon the inevitable happened. There was a scream in the dark behind them and then silence. Just the wind and the rain. The old man went back with the volunteers, retracing their steps. He'd gotten a small flashlight out of his pack—the first time he'd risked producing it—and was shining it down the cliff face, but they could see nothing and there was no response to their shouts.

"He's gone," said the old man. "We must go on. There's no time to waste." His face was impassive.

Several of the volunteers looked like they wanted to argue, until Manny unexpectedly intervened: "The old man's right," he told them. "We can't stop now or they'll find us. We're here to fight the Fascists. That's why we came."

They went on, struggling up the slope in single file, each one with his hand on the shoulder of the man in front, measuring every step over the frozen ground as if it could be their last. The rain had turned to snow that half blinded them as the howling wind blew the flakes into their faces, stinging their cheeks with icy needles, and drowned out their voices—not that they had any energy left to speak, except to plead with their guide to slow down. But he ignored them, pressing on relentlessly, ever upward.

They lost all sense of time and place. All that was left were the mechanics of motion and the will to continue, sapped by the pain in their bodies, growing more unbearable with every passing minute.

Finally, the old man allowed them to rest. A stone shepherd's hut loomed up out of the blizzard, and they almost fell over each other, trying to get inside, before they collapsed in a collective heap on the floor. The hut was empty except for a bale of straw left there the previous summer, but it felt like a palace after what they had been experiencing outside.

The volunteers pulled out their soggy rations from their coat pockets and ate and drank, and the old man took out a flask of cognac from his pack and measured precise tots for each of them in the cap. The brandy fired in their stomachs, giving them hope. The night was almost over and surely the summit could not be too far away, but the old man was noncommittal, resting now with his eyes closed, as if in a trance.

Theo thought about their lost companion. Most likely he was dead, smashed to pieces by his fall, but what if he had somehow survived his injuries and was just now recovering consciousness to find himself alone and abandoned, crying out for help with only the echo of his voice, bouncing back off the rocks, for answer?

Theo hated that he couldn't even remember what the man looked like. All the volunteers except Manny had seemed similar on the train and in Perpignan, just as they had in Paris: blond-haired and blue-eyed, unshaven and earnest, talking Yiddish or German—he couldn't tell the difference. The language barrier had separated him from them, but he shouldn't have allowed it to when he knew that he shared with them something so vital—a willingness to sacrifice all they had to fight Fascism. He looked at them now, shadowy figures stretched out against the walls, wreathed in the smoke from their cigarettes, and he loved them like they were his brothers.

"What was his name?" Theo asked Manny.

"Whose?"

"The man who fell?"

"Hans."

"Hans what?"

"Schneider," said Manny after consulting with one of the other volunteers. "He was from Germany, like most of them are. They got out by skiing across the frontier. The Nazis weren't expecting that."

"Hans Schneider. I'm sorry," said Theo sadly. It wasn't much, but repeating his name felt like something, and the others seemed to agree, because they bowed their heads and folded their hands for a moment, as if in prayer, or whatever was the Communist alternative to it.

"It's time," said the old man, getting to his feet, and when nobody moved in response, he opened the door, letting in the wind and the snow.

"You didn't need to do that," said Manny angrily as they scrambled to get up, but the old man was already outside, ready to go on.

Now the volunteers were bent almost double as they climbed the path. Theo felt a steel band inside his chest, crushing his lungs, so that each breath came out like a gasping sob. He gave all he had to reach each crest, telling himself it was the last, and despaired when another peak emerged behind, higher than the one before. Starved of oxygen, he could not think straight and imagined shapes of snow as white devils reaching out to pull him down.

It made it harder that the pain in his feet was giving way to numbness, so that he could not feel to walk. He could see that this was happening to the others, too, because several of them began to stumble and fall, only to be pulled back from the edge by their comrades—but Manny was not so lucky. He had been worse off from the beginning because of wearing shoes that had no grip, and at a turn in the path Theo looked back and realized he was no longer there. He hadn't screamed like Hans, unless his cries had been drowned out by the noise of the gale, and so Theo had no way of knowing how long he had been missing.

He pushed past the volunteers in front of him until he reached the old man, and yelled at him to explain what had happened.

They all went back, shouting Manny's name while the old man shined his flashlight over the cliff, but just like before, there was no response. Only the cruel shriek of the wind, whipping through the ravine down below.

The old man held out his hands palms up to indicate the hopelessness of the search and turned to go, but Theo wouldn't let him. He grabbed at the old man's jacket, pulling him around, but he had not counted on the old man's wiry strength. In the blink of an eye, he had hold of Theo's hand, twisting it in his, and had forced Theo to the ground.

But Theo wouldn't give in. He turned his head in the snow and bellowed Manny's name again at the top of his lungs, and from somewhere behind, he thought he heard an answer. Perhaps it was a distorted echo of his voice or a change in the cry of the wind as it switched direction, but perhaps, too, it was Manny calling back.

He looked up at the old man in mute appeal, but he was no longer there. Instead, he was moving back down the path, shouting himself and shining the flashlight, until he came to a sudden stop, craning over the edge. Straightaway, he pulled his pack down off his shoulders and removed a short coil of rope, which he hung around his neck before lowering himself over the side. He had the flashlight in his mouth, pointing down.

Up above, Theo peered over the edge. Beyond the old man, he could see in the flashlight beam a pair of stretched-out hands hanging on to a piece of gorse that was bent over so far that its roots were showing. It was a miracle that it hadn't come away from the rock and that Manny had hung on for so long. He was going to fall. Theo didn't see what the old man could do to stop it.

But he had not reckoned on the old man's mountaineering skills. Lithe as a cat, he somehow found footholds in the side of the cliff to enable him to get down below Manny's hands, where he disappeared from view.

Now Theo could see nothing. He stared down into the void, praying aloud to a God he didn't believe in, but with only the howling wind for answer. He counted the seconds, willing the old man to return, and then suddenly there was light coming up out of the darkness and the old man was clambering back up onto the path, gripping one end of the rope in his fist.

Immediately he handed it to the strongest looking of the volunteers and ordered him to pull, and a moment later Manny came up over the side of the cliff with the other end of the rope tied securely around his waist. How the old man had done it, Theo couldn't imagine. But he had, and now he knelt down beside Manny, tipped back his head, and poured a capful of cognac into his mouth, forcing him to swallow. Manny spluttered and the old man kept hold of his chin, beckoning Theo to come close to interpret.

"We have to go," he said, pointing up at the gray light in the sky, the harbinger of dawn. "We are close, but there is no time to lose."

As he struggled to his feet, Manny nodded in agreement and stammered out his thanks to the old man for saving his life, only to immediately collapse again, but it was a cramp and not an injury that was stopping him from moving. The old man pulled up Manny's trousers and massaged snow into his calves, and when Manny got up again, he could walk.

They struggled on over one crest and another, and suddenly they were on flat land—the roof of the world. Everything was white—even a cairn of stones beside the path that the old man walked up to and patted gently with his hand. *"España,"* he said, looking back at them. *"España!"* And for the first and only time, he smiled.

The volunteers hugged each other and cried, and one of them began spontaneously to sing "The Internationale" in an exquisite tenor voice. And as if in response, the wind died away, leaving only the gently falling snow, and they took hold of each other's hands and joined in the song, singing in their own languages but in a united voice, expressing all the hope in their young hearts as they gazed down into Spain, lit now by the light of the rising sun.

# 14

## ALBACETE

It was extraordinary how quickly they forgot the terrors of the night as they half walked, half ran down the hills in the morning sunshine, until they reached a road where a truck was waiting for them, driven by a militiaman who vigorously shook their hands, displaying all the enthusiasm that had been so conspicuously missing on the other side of the border.

As they climbed inside, they turned back to thank the old man who had guided them to the summit and found that he had slipped away unseen. This added to Theo's sense that he had awoken from a nightmare set in an imaginary land that bore no relation to the real world of wildflowers and almond trees laden with pink blossoms that covered the verdant hillsides all around them. In the sunlight, the mountain peaks seemed to belong on the cover of a picture postcard.

The truck descended down into the valley at breakneck speed and climbed again, grinding gears, as it entered the town of Figueres. Looking out of the back, Theo could see the same dirty, narrow streets oozing mud that he remembered from Los Olivos; the same barefoot children in filthy smocks, screaming for alms as they chased the wheels; the same wretched poverty that he had almost forgotten—until, in an instant, it was all behind them as the truck drew clear of the town and approached a castle on top of the hill. It was immense, fortified with towers and battlements and even a drawbridge over a moat that they bounced across uncomfortably before coming to a halt in front of a huge, nail-studded door over which the red, yellow, and purple flag of the Republic drooped down. In contrast to the night before, there was not a breath of wind in the air.

Inside, they passed through a reception area where a clerk wearing a green eyeshade laboriously wrote down their personal details—name, date of birth, weight, height, and nationality—in a ledger, and asked for their passports. Theo lied again, fingering the pouch around his neck, which had come unscathed through the mountain crossing, and the clerk handed them each a packet of prophylactics from a pile on the side of his desk and waved them through.

They came out into a courtyard, where hundreds of volunteers were trying and failing to perform a marching drill in response to orders in German shouted by an officer in uniform and high boots, standing on an elevated platform constructed out of ammunition boxes. The problem was that each command had to be translated by acolytes standing at the German's side, and the consequent delay in communication meant that the volunteers were all moving in different directions and even sometimes colliding with one another. It was like watching a live version of a silent comedy film, and Theo and the others had to turn away, so as not to be seen laughing.

They ate lunch and dinner in a mess hall with whitewashed walls on which ridiculously bad pictures of Marx, Stalin, and the president of the Republic had been painted under slogans written in five languages, enjoining the workers of the world to unite, and between meals they attended an introductory lecture given by the same German commander, who promised them that they would be receiving thorough military training while at the castle, so that they would be ready for battle when they went to the front.

"Nothing will be left to chance," he assured them, rapping his desk for emphasis. "Nothing!"

But Manny didn't believe it. "He's talking out of his ass!" he told Theo in a whisper. "Whoever's running this show is making it up as they go along. You mark my words."

Theo said nothing. He wanted to believe that the brigade leadership knew what it was doing, but his faith had been seriously dented by his experience in the mountains. Surely the people in Paris must have known there was a risk that the border would be closed, but still they had delayed and delayed until it was too late, and Hans had died. And Manny almost too . . .

Night fell suddenly, and after the distraction of dinner, the castle was a cold, dreary place, poorly lit by naked bulbs and noxious-smelling kerosene lamps. Melancholy wrapped itself around the volunteers as if it was a physical presence in the recreation hall, wreathed from the clouds of stale cigarette smoke hanging in the still, fetid air. Their hearts weren't in their card games, and they stared moodily into their tin cups of wine, waiting for the electric bell that would send them to their beds.

For those who had crossed the mountains, the memories of their ordeal, forgotten during the day, crowded back into their minds and made them shiver, as if they could once more feel the icy wind on their skin and experience the terrors of the empty darkness on each side of the narrow, impossibly steep paths they'd had to climb.

"I wish I'd thanked him," said Manny, looking up, and, as if by telepathy, Theo knew immediately who his friend was talking about. He'd been thinking of their guide too.

"You did when he saved you," he said. "I heard you."

"I mean properly, afterward. It feels like bad luck that I didn't."

"I know. I feel the same."

"It seems so strange that we didn't even ask his name."

"Methuselah," said Theo with a smile, trying to lighten the conversation. He didn't want to think about bad luck. Not when the future was so uncertain.

"No, I'm serious. I can't understand why we didn't. Unless it was because we knew subconsciously that he didn't have one. That he was a part of the mountain, a spirit creature of the snow, which is why he vanished back into it at the end."

"No, he wasn't like that at all," said Theo, shaking his head to emphasize his complete disagreement with Manny's mystical take on their adventure. "He was hardheaded and practical. He made us keep going because he knew that was the only way to get across. You don't know this, but he didn't want to keep searching for you. He thought you were gone, like Hans. It was only when he heard you after I shouted that he changed his mind."

Manny looked hard at Theo, clearly surprised, and then put out his hand for a moment, covering Theo's. "At least I can thank *you* then," he said quietly. "You saved my life."

"I thought you were still there," said Theo. "I don't know why. There was no reason for it."

"Maybe you just don't like to give up," said Manny, smiling. "My mother is like that. Won't take no for an answer. I remember we had this crazy cat when I was small, back in Brooklyn. Black with white markings both sides of his nose, like a mustache. We called him Dixie, after Abe Lincoln's cat, because he was so damned smart. Except with cars. When he got out on the road, he got scared and used to hide down in the areaways outside the basement apartments, and then my mother would wait until nighttime when the traffic had died down and go up and down the street, calling him: 'Dixie! Dixie!' Screeching out his name and then listening with her hand to her ear like an eavesdropper, until she heard him squeak. He always did. And up on that mountain, hanging there, I kept thinking about her doing that, because I needed someone not to give up on me and keep calling my name. And you did. I won't forget."

A few minutes later, the bell rang and the volunteers walked down a wide descending passageway into the airless underground cellars of the castle, where they slept or tried to sleep on straw mattresses laid on top of hard plank beds. Row upon row under vaulted stone ceilings, green with damp.

On the walls behind the beds, those who had passed through the castle before them had carved their names and sometimes their hometowns with a date. German names, French names, Italian . . . Where were they now? Dead, perhaps, and soon forgotten. Was that the fate that awaited him, too, when he left this place? Theo shuddered, pulling his overcoat around him in a vain effort to keep out the creeping cold.

Next morning the volunteers left Figueres on a special train. Hundreds of them, filling the carriages to overflowing. Manny had been right. The German commandant *had* been talking out of his ass. The group who had crossed the mountains departed the castle without having received any military training at all, mixed up with others who had. The new arrivals hadn't even handled a gun, let alone fired one. Perhaps there would be training further up the line, perhaps not. Everything *had* been left to chance.

The train took them down the coast. Here and there, cannons faced out to sea, but otherwise there was little to show that this was a country at war. The Mediterranean stretched away in a calm cobalt-blue sheet to the eastern horizon, with a tiny line of breaking waves along its edge, forming a border of pretty white lace. And on the other side, the land was populated with a seemingly never-ending succession of orange groves.

The train meandered along the narrow track so slowly that there was time for the volunteers to jump down, pick a few of the fruit, and climb back onto the last carriage. They ate with abandon, and the juice ran down into their beards and formed a sticky layer on their clothes and fingers and on the floor, attracting clouds of flies that flew in through the broken windows of the carriages. Later, the oranges gave the volunteers gastric problems, and they fought for access to appalling toilets, which were no more than holes over the tracks, located between the carriages.

At stations along the way, crowds threw in more oranges, and the volunteers threw back cigarettes, not realizing how valuable these would be later, when they came to look back on their profligacy with bitter regret. They put their arms through the windows, greedy to embrace this utterly foreign country that they had come to fight for, and the Spanish peasants cheered, and even the babies in their mothers' arms had their fists clenched in the Anarchist salute. "*¡No pasarán!*" the volunteers shouted, and "*¡Viva la República!*" because that was all the Spanish they knew, but it didn't matter because they were all on the same side and they were going to win. "*¡Abajo Franco!*" screamed the crowd in response. "*¡Muerte a los fascistas!*"

Throughout all this commotion, Theo sat wrapped in thought. He knew enough geography to work out that the coastal route meant that the train was headed to Barcelona, and everyone seemed to agree that after that it would go on to the International Brigade headquarters at Albacete, four hundred miles to the southwest, because that was where all the troop trains from Figueres ended up.

But no one knew if it would stop in Barcelona for any length of time. And if it did, what would he do? He longed to see Maria. No, it was more need than longing. She hadn't answered his letters and this would be his only opportunity to try to find out what had happened to her. It had been hard enough to cope when he had no means of knowing whether she was alive or dead; life would be unbearable if he'd had the chance to find out and let it slip through his fingers.

Theo knew how dangerous it would be to go to the *Mujeres Libres* office. He'd fled Barcelona in July because the Anarchist militia were looking for him, and he had no reason to think that he wasn't still on their most-wanted list. Where Maria was, Primitivo was usually nearby, and Primitivo would have him arrested the minute he saw him, and from there his fate would be sealed. Theo recalled the blanched, despairing faces of the condemned prisoners as they'd been driven off in the back of the truck down the Paral·lel. The thought of sharing the same fate terrified him, but not enough to stop him going to Plaça de Catalunya. He had to try to find Maria.

If there was enough time. If he got back to the station too late and the train had left without him, he would be a deserter. A coward who'd broken his word. He would lose his honor and his self-respect, and without them he was nothing.

How long would it stop for? How long? Theo couldn't stand not knowing. He got up and stumbled down the aisle, narrowly avoiding tripping over outstretched legs and slipping on orange peels and congealed juice as he passed through the carriages, searching for the guard. There was a locked door at the end of the train, but no one answered his knock, so he had no option but to return to his seat and wait, gnawing his nails to the quick, while all around him, Manny and the other volunteers talked and laughed, oblivious to his suffering. For them, life was simple. The waiting was over, and they were finally on their way to fight the Fascists.

At the França station in Barcelona, Theo jumped down onto the platform and ran the length of the train to intercept the driver as he was climbing out of his cab, clutching a thermos. Theo had been cursing him for the previous hour for his snaillike speed, but now he painted a supplicatory expression on his face as he asked how long the stop would be.

"*Mañana,*" said the driver, shrugging his shoulders. "First lunch"—he patted his capacious stomach—"then siesta, then train. Don't worry. The Fascists will still be there, *compañero.*" He smiled and clapped Theo on the shoulder and walked away, oblivious to Theo's requests for greater precision.

The black minute hand of the clock hanging down from the glass canopy over the platform ticked on to precisely two o'clock, and Theo decided to take his chances. He figured that lunch and a siesta had to be at least an hour and a half, maybe more. The driver didn't look like a man who'd allow himself to be hurried.

In the station's gleaming marble concourse, the volunteers were being formed into a disorganized column, and the din of their chatter in multiple languages echoed off the domes and walls. Theo saw Manny at the back.

"What's happening?" Theo asked.

"Walking tour of the city, apparently. Courtesy of the high command. I'm hoping it includes lunch but no word on—"

"I need your help," said Theo, cutting him off. "I have to go somewhere, and I need you to cover for me if they do a roll call. I'll be back before the train leaves."

"Are you chickening out?" Manny asked, looking at Theo closely. "You don't have to bullshit me. Tell me straight."

"No, I'm not," said Theo. "I don't chicken. You should know that after the mountains. I wouldn't do this unless I had to."

"Okay. I'm sorry I asked. Of course I'll cover."

"Thank you." Theo touched Manny's arm in acknowledgment, stepped behind a pillar, and then walked quickly outside into the roadway.

He looked about him and nothing was familiar. He had no idea how far he was from the center of the city. Running wasn't an option. He had to take a taxi.

There was a queue at the stand, and he glanced nervously back toward the station entrance, expecting the column of volunteers to start coming out. He'd have been safer waiting in the station until they were gone, but he knew he couldn't afford to lose the time. Now, if he was seen, he would be arrested as a deserter. The thought of the public humiliation in front of all the other volunteers was so appalling that it made him feel physically sick, and he tried to push to the front of the queue, citing an emergency, but the people in line shoved him back.

"For all of us, it is an emergency," the man in front of him said. "Why else would we be taking a taxi?"

Theo apologized and stayed still as a statue when he saw a policeman looking in his direction from the other side of the road.

Then, just as he was giving up hope, a flurry of taxis arrived at the stand, and he scrambled inside the last one.

"Where to?" the driver asked, and Theo had to give instructions, lying flat on the back seat because the volunteers *had* now come out and were crossing the road toward him.

He thought it a good sign that the driver recognized Mujeres Libres as an address, because it implied that the organization was still operating in Plaça de Catalunya, although that didn't mean that Maria was there, of course. Less good was the slowness of the taxi. How he wished he had the maniac driver who had delivered him and Booker to the Olympic Stadium in record time the previous summer or the Communist sympathizer who had hurtled across Paris, whistling the "Marseillaise"! They wouldn't have been content to sit in crawling traffic on the Via Laietana, as Theo was doing now, but would have raced through the side streets instead, sending terrified pedestrians jumping out of the way.

But Theo's attempts to persuade his driver to take a shortcut fell on deaf ears, and it was close to half past two by the time he got to Plaça de Catalunya.

There was the same **MUJERES LIBRES** sign outside the building on the corner of Carrer de Pelai and the same red-and-black flags hanging down from its balconies. But they were crumpled and tattered, and the office that had looked so businesslike the previous summer had a run-down appearance now. The windows were dirty, and bags of uncollected trash were piled up outside the front door.

Despite the shortage of time, Theo hesitated beside them before going inside. Would she be there? Would she not? Uncertainty for a moment seemed preferable to the finality of knowledge. But then, when he went inside, it was just like before, on that last day in the summer. She heard his voice in the front office and came running out.

She was dressed in a one-piece dark-blue mono with her hair tied up under a forage cap. The Anarchist uniform wrapped her, concealing the person underneath.

It was hard to tell with the baggy mono, but Theo thought she was thinner. Her cheekbones seemed more prominent, and there was a fire in her eyes that reminded him of his mother, as if she was burning up from within.

Perhaps some of it was agitation. She didn't kiss him or even say hello. Just took him by the arm and led him outside and pointed to the same bar that he had gone to with Booker on the day they met in the square outside the Olimpiada kiosk.

"I'll be there in five minutes. Sit inside!" she told him, and went back to the office before he had time to tell her that every minute was precious and that they shouldn't sacrifice five of them to him sitting alone in a bar.

But he had no choice. It was siesta time and the café wasn't crowded. He took the same table he'd sat at with Booker and drank a glass of wine to calm his nerves. Maria was here, she was alive! Relief flowed through him followed by a euphoric happiness that then gave way to an inner turbulence in which his eyes kept going to his watch and his mind kept jumping from thought to thought, careening like a bagatelle in a pinball machine.

Why sit inside? Because it was dangerous, of course. He'd known that before he came. But not as dangerous as when he'd stood outside in the July heat as gunfire raked the square and he'd swayed from side to side, trying not to faint because he knew that if he fell, he'd be trampled by the eddying crowd all around him. He looked out of the window of the bar at the Fuente de Canaletas—the ornate lamppost at the top of the Ramblas with the brass water taps at the base that had saved his life that day. He could feel the water in his parched throat and the iron in his gripping hands, smell the dead flesh rotting in the heat, and glimpse Maria in the crowd pouring down the ramp into the metro.

He saw her then and he saw her now as she came through the door of the café, pulling the cap off her head and shaking her hair free.

She was so beautiful. It wasn't just the perfect symmetry of her features and the exotic blue of her eyes; it was the spirit within that animated them with such free energy. He loved her.

And she him, or so it seemed by the way she threw her arms around his neck and kissed him.

"You came back!" she said. "To see me?"

"Yes. I had—"

"Even though it's dangerous," she said, not letting him finish. "Just as dangerous as before. It's why I had to get you out of the office. But you know that, don't you?"

"Yes."

"Primo hates you. He won't stop talking about you even now, six months later. He'd kill us both if he saw us. I'm sure of it. But you don't care. With your fool courage. Like when you attacked him in Jesús's shop, or at the church when he had the machine gun. A machine gun! How could you be so crazy brave?"

She kissed Theo again, and the effect on him was so intoxicating that it drove words out of his head. Thought, even. All he could think of was that he wanted her to do it again. And again . . .

But for Maria, it was different. She couldn't stop talking.

"He won't leave me alone. Every time I turn round, he's watching me. I hate him for trying to control me, just like I hate President Companys and the Communists who are trying to control the people. They want to take away everything we've built. And it's so beautiful, Theo. You can't imagine . . . the workers work for themselves. They receive the fruits of their labor now, not the capitalists. Women can choose what to do with their lives, and there are schools for everyone. I teach in an athenaeum in the evening after work. It's a magical place. We talk and share ideas and read and have lectures and classes and recite poetry and . . . oh, I wish you could see it."

She stopped, realizing the impossibility of that happening.

"What have the Communists got to do with it? They're not the government," Theo asked, worried now about what Maria was going to think when he told her, as he was going to have to, that he'd joined the Communist International Brigades.

"They want power and they're using Companys to get it. He's a tool in their hands. We should have got rid of him in July when we had the chance. That was our big mistake, and now they're pushing him to take over the militias and nationalize industry, while our leaders do nothing. No, worse than that—they collaborate. There are Anarchist ministers in the government of the Republic. Can you believe that?" Maria grimaced—an expression mixing pain, anger, and incredulity. "Have they forgotten that government is the enemy? It's what we've always fought against. Until now."

"But you need government to fight the war and a proper army too," said Theo, remembering what Esmond had told him about the defense of Madrid. "If Franco wins, then you lose everything."

"That's exactly what the Communists say," said Maria furiously. "'First the war, then the revolution' is their slogan. But it's a lie. They mean to destroy the revolution forever. And if they succeed, we will lose the war. Because it's the revolution that makes people want to fight. Without it, what's the point? A Communist dictatorship is no better than a Fascist one."

He had to tell her. He couldn't not. He'd always told her the truth, because without it, their relationship had no meaning.

"I joined the brigades," he said bluntly. "That's why I'm here. To help win the war. And I have to go in a minute so I don't miss the train. I'm going to Albacete."

She looked at him, wide-eyed, and then reached across the table and slapped him hard across the face. And immediately got up and left the bar.

He ran out after her and caught her by the arm outside, and she whirled around and he thought she was going to hit him again, but instead she was pointing across the Plaça de Catalunya to the long facade of the Hotel Colón.

"Look!" she said. "Can you see them?"

He did. Under the PSUC's—the Communist Party of Catalonia's—long banner hung two huge photographs of Stalin and Lenin. Stalin, on the right, half covered the window of the room where he and Maria had slept the previous summer.

"They take everything," she said. "Even you." And she reached up and stroked the red welt on his cheek where she had hit him. It was as if she was saying goodbye.

He wouldn't allow it. He couldn't. "No," he said fiercely. "I'm not a Communist, and I never will be one. I joined the brigades because it's the only way I can help win the war. Because I'm like you and I can't bear for the people to lose their chance to be free, and because that's how we can be together. When the war is won, there will be justice. I believe that. I have to. So, yes, I did come back for you, Maria. It's why I'm here. Because I love you."

She looked at him wonderingly, moved by his passion, just as he was always moved by hers.

"Yes, you do love me. I see that. And when you're here, you make everything seem possible, but then when you're not, there's times when I can't see a way through. Past Primo and Companys and Franco and the Communists." She glanced over at the Colón again. "It's why I didn't answer your letters. Because it seemed so hopeless for us. But I'll try."

"That's all I ask," said Theo. He pulled the cotton pouch over his neck and took out the faded note that she'd sent him via her brother eighteen months before. *Please don't forget me*, folded over the lock of her hair, which he kept back and returned to the pouch with Andrew's rosary and his passport and money. He put the note in her hand and folded her fingers over it and looked into her eyes, asking the question.

"I won't. I promise," she said, putting her closed-up hand over her heart.

It was all he could hope for. There was no more time. He had to go. He reached out and took her in his arms and kissed her and then turned and walked away without looking back. Because he couldn't bear to. One minute more and he could never have let her go.

She loved him. He believed that now, but echoing his footsteps, he heard the old fortune teller's harsh voice whispering in his inner ear: *"You will be lucky in love, and you will be unlucky in love,"* repeated over and over, until he found a taxi that drove him out of the square past the blown-up photograph of Stalin, whose hooded eyes seemed to Theo to be following him as the car turned the corner.

The traffic was just as bad as before, but Theo didn't care anymore. If he missed the train, he missed the train. He was burned out and left it to fate to decide what would happen.

There were no volunteers outside the station or in the concourse or on the platform. The train had gone. He had nothing left, so he lay down on a bench and closed his eyes. And dreamed that Maria was bending down over him, touching his cheek with the tips of her fingers, but then her hand was rougher, shaking him by the shoulder, forcing him to open his eyes.

"You goddamn putz!" said Manny, laughing as he pulled Theo to his feet. "I looked everywhere. I thought you'd flown the coop, and all the time you're lying here, asleep on a fucking bench. Did you cross the mountains to fight this war or sleep through it? That's what I want to know."

"Where's the train?"

"Over there. They moved it," said Manny, pointing across the tracks. "Come on. It's leaving in a minute."

They ran up the stairs and through the overpass and down the other side and hauled themselves up into the last carriage, just as it began to move.

"Now it's me who's saved your life," said Manny. "Which makes us even!"

The rest of the journey was a blur. The train reached Valencia in the dark and then turned inland, climbing slowly westward through the high sierras toward the arid tableland of La Mancha. Theo sat bolt upright and completely asleep, sandwiched in place between two equally comatose Hungarian volunteers, and woke up only when the train stopped periodically like a tired animal, gasping for breath, and sent them toppling forward like bottles in a basket. And then, as soon as it started moving again, the three of them resumed their positions and went straight back to sleep, careless of the cold air that was blowing in through the broken windows. He had never in his life been so exhausted.

Finally, the train stopped for the last time. "Albacete! Everyone out!" shouted the guard, going up and down the platform, blowing his whistle.

It was morning but there was no sun. Just a cold, gray light and a slow drizzle falling from a leaden sky. The volunteers shivered on the platform, watching the decrepit train puffing away from them down the line, as if it were an old friend leaving them behind in a desolate land, far from home.

A welcome delegation consisting of five ancient men in threadbare suits and beaten-up sombreros stood in a line outside the ticket office and blew a series of tubercular blasts on rusty brass instruments in the direction of the new arrivals, before turning on their heels and trundling away, leaving the volunteers feeling even bleaker than they had before, if that was possible.

"Where's the señoritas?" complained Manny miserably. "I thought they were part of the deal."

"I don't think they're getting up for the likes of us. Would you?" Theo asked, pointing at their companions, who'd formed a ramshackle line and were now shuffling their way out of the station and out onto a dilapidated road leading into the town. "We look like a bunch of down-and-out vagrants headed for the neighborhood soup kitchen. Not exactly heroic, are we?"

Manny nodded in mute agreement, too dejected to muster a response, or even a protest when the wheels of passing trucks and staff cars sprayed them with mud as they drove by.

They passed through a square with a few ragged palm trees and several sad cafés where the customers sat hunched over their drinks as if they were poker hands, and entered the cavernous parade ground of an army barracks through a wide iron gate set in a long gray wall.

It reminded Theo of the barracks in Barcelona. So intensely that he stopped in the gateway, looking to the side, as if he thought he might see Antonio there, leaning back against the wall with a cigarette in his hand and that same world-weary look on his face that Theo remembered so well.

Antonio had hated the army and here Theo was, volunteering to become a soldier himself. He felt for a moment as if he had missed some important lesson, but then dismissed the thought. He was on the right side, fighting Fascism, not supporting it as Antonio had been forced into doing. The two prisonlike barracks might look the same, but they served entirely different purposes.

The volunteers turned to the left and were waved into a large guardroom in which uniformed soldiers sat at a row of desks, each with small national flags standing in holders on the corners. Some flags were grouped together, but the Stars and Stripes was on its own on a desk on the other side of the room, and Theo walked across to it through the crowd, uplifted by a sudden sense of elation that took him by surprise. It was the same feeling he'd had marching behind the American flag in the Olympic Stadium with his hand on his heart, singing "The Internationale" on that long-ago Saturday in July. Belonging, coming home, pride—all that, and something more.

Barcelona again! All day, he had felt these visceral connections to the city he'd left behind. Bad and good, bridging past and present, as he stumbled forward into an uncertain future.

Theo answered the same questions he'd already answered in Paris and Figueres, but this time there was a difference: there was a Spaniard with a flash camera, taking photographs.

"Now we know who you are," said the soldier behind the desk with a thin smile when the cameraman was finished. The comment unsettled Theo. It made him feel owned, and his hand went involuntarily to the pouch around his neck, seeking reassurance.

As if on an assembly line, the volunteers passed through an archway into another room, where unrelated items of military uniform had been thrown together in a gigantic heap. Long pants and breeches and puttees, tunics and overcoats, caps with earflaps and ones without, and even a Scotsman's tam-o'-shanter with a red pom-pom on the top. All in different sizes and colors—green, gray, olive, and khaki. The surplus stock of a dozen armies.

The volunteers went to work like crazed shoppers at a church rummage sale, trying clothes on and casting them off and even swapping them with each other in a vain effort to assemble an outfit that wasn't either squeezing their waists or falling off their shoulders.

Boots were in a different pile. Some still tied together, some not matching, some spattered with blood. And here the competition was even worse, as several of the volunteers literally fought to get the pair they wanted, while a couple of smartly dressed guards in the corner smoked and laughed, enjoying the entertainment.

Theo and Manny scrapped well and ended up looking something like soldiers, albeit belonging to different armies, but a fat American volunteer nicknamed Tiny ended up with nothing that fit him at all except an enormous pair of long johns, until the others took pity on his misery and dug deeper into the pile to find him something to wear.

At the exit door, the volunteers were each issued with a thin, flimsy blanket and a haversack containing canteen, plate, and spoon, and went back out onto the parade ground, where they gingerly walked about, pulling faces as they tried to get used to their new boots.

"Look! Bullet holes," said Manny, calling Theo over to where he was standing by one of the walls. "I bet this is where the government soldiers shot the rebels after they liberated the town. Bang, bang, bang!" He simulated firing a gun with outstretched fingers, pausing for emphasis between each exclamation.

"You don't know that," said Theo doubtfully.

"Why are the holes so close together then, when there are no others anywhere else? And look—there are bloodstains near the bottom. It's got to be that!" said Manny, pointing insistently to where the wall met the ground.

He was right. There were stains there, dark and congealed, where the anonymous prisoners had bled out after they fell, before they were hauled away to some pit somewhere and covered in quicklime. Looking down, Theo could see that the color matched the spots of old blood on his boots. Death was everywhere. Stalking them, inescapable.

He shivered, imagining the fear of the condemned men in that last moment when the sun shone and everything blazed in the July light. Before the pain and the darkness. He hoped they had died quickly.

The sound of trumpets pulled him from his reverie. The band from the station was back and had begun another tuneless blowing that stopped abruptly when a huge fat man with a black walrus mustache walked out onto the wide wrought iron balcony of a building across from where Theo and Manny were standing. He was wearing the biggest navy-blue beret that Theo had ever seen, drooping down over his right shoulder, and he spoke with a voice that sounded like a foghorn. There was no need for a microphone.

A line of his lieutenants stood behind him, dressed in polished boots and smart uniforms with Sam Browne belts and automatic pistols tucked into leather holsters at their hips. They looked like they belonged in another world to the ragtag crowd of men down below.

The fat man talked in French, but Theo was able to understand most of what he was saying, because he repeated every important sentence two or three times, raising his voice ten decibels with each repetition, and accompanying it with an angry shaking of his right fist.

He told them that this was do or die. The fate of the war hung in the balance. The Fascists had failed with a frontal assault on Madrid, so now they were trying to surround the city and cut off its supply lines. They had already crossed the Jarama River and were attacking through the valley toward the road connecting Madrid to Valencia. If they took it, Madrid would fall and the sacrifice of thousands would have been in vain. The road must be protected at all costs.

"At all costs!" he bellowed again, reaching his highest volume yet, and the exertion took a toll, because he had to stop to catch his breath, leaning heavily on the balcony rail in front of him.

"Who is he?" Theo asked Manny in an awed whisper. The force of the fat man's oratory had literally pushed him backward against the wall behind him. He felt shaken and inspired by it in equal measure.

"André Marty," said Manny. "He's the king round here. He fought in the Russian Revolution. Led a mutiny of sailors on the Black Sea."

The information excited Theo, giving him that same sense of connection to the pulse of history that he had felt in Barcelona. This was what he had volunteered for.

But now Marty was talking again, and he'd changed to a new tack. The enemy wasn't just on the other side of no-man's-land, he told them. He was in their midst. A fifth column of Trotskyites and political deviants, trying to destroy the Republic from within.

"You must be vigilant," he told them. "The man standing next to you might be one of them. Trust no one. Report anything suspicious to your commissars. They will know what to do."

He glared down at them, as if searching their faces for deviancy, and then raised his right fist one last time. *"¡No pasarán!"* he shouted, and the volunteers yelled the slogan back again and again, even after Marty had turned around and gone back inside.

"I bet old Walrus Face is having a better breakfast than us," said Manny, pointing up at the closed French windows of the balcony from which André Marty had given his speech. Through the glass, they could see waiters in white coats and black trousers, moving about, carrying plates.

"This meat's tougher than a goddamn car tire," he complained. "It snaps back like elastic every time I try to take a bite out of it."

"It's mule, I expect," said Theo morosely. "That's what the poor eat in this country."

"Horse? No fucking way!" Manny spat out his food in disgust and got to his feet. "Come on!" he said, pulling Theo by the shoulder. "We'll die of starvation if we carry on like this."

They went out through the barracks gate and bought baked potatoes from a peddler who was carrying on a brisk business from behind a small brazier set up on the opposite sidewalk, catering to a queue of similarly starved volunteers. Seasoned with salt and oil, the potatoes were delicious, and Theo and Manny carried on eating until they felt sick and then went back inside and lay down to sleep.

They were awoken after what seemed like a minute, but was in fact an hour, by someone tapping their legs with a stick. It was an officer dressed like one of André Marty's henchmen, and his thin mustache and pursed lips made Theo think for a moment, as he looked up groggily, rubbing his eyes, that he was having a nightmare encounter with the ghost of Antonio's nemesis, Captain Darnell.

"*Américains?*" the officer asked, pronouncing the word as if it was a term of abuse, and when Theo nodded blearily, he pointed his stick over toward the gate where a large truck had parked. "*Allez là-bas!*" he ordered them and then clapped his hands twice to hurry them onto their feet, before moving on to continue rounding up any other American strays.

There were about fifty men gathered around the back of the truck. Theo recognized only a handful of them from the train journey, so the rest had to have arrived in Albacete before. What they had in common was that they were all speaking English—American English—and he stopped for a second to listen, drinking in the sound of their voices. He knew that he'd reached a milestone on his journey: he was leaving the Tower of Babel behind and joining the Lincolns, a battalion of all-American volunteers united in their dedication to freedom, and he wanted to commit the moment to memory.

As he got closer, Theo saw that the Americans were unloading coffin-shaped boxes from the cargo bed of the truck and prying them open on the ground. Inside, there were rifles wrapped in Mexican newspapers and covered in Cosmoline to keep them from corroding. The Americans used their shirttails to clean off the grease and waved the rifles above their heads. It didn't matter that most of them had no idea how to load or sight or fire their weapon. Having a rifle in their hands empowered them. This was what they had come to Spain for: the chance to fight.

Theo felt the same delight but expressed it in a different way, weighing his rifle in his hands as if it was made of precious metal and running his eye over the stock and barrel. He could see tiny letters there, but it was hard to read them in the gray overcast light.

"Made in Connecticut. Just like me," said Manny, speaking over Theo's shoulder.

"I thought you said you were from Brooklyn," said Theo absently.

"New Haven first. Then New York. I told you I moved around. Peripatetic, you might call it."

Theo smiled at the unexpected word, but his focus was still on his rifle, and he ran his thumb over the Connecticut stamp, as if he couldn't believe his eyes. "Can't you see what this means?" he said, trembling with excitement. "If Roosevelt's giving the Republic rifles, then the British and the French will stop nonintervention too. They've got to. And with the right arms—"

"Roosevelt's giving them nothing," said Manny, interrupting.

"What do you mean? Look!" said Theo, pointing at the stamp.

"Look yourself!" Manny shot back, pointing instead at the newspapers in the empty boxes. "These rifles came from Mexico. The Mexicans are the only ones apart from Joe Stalin who are selling the Republic arms. And that isn't changing anytime soon. Roosevelt needs the Catholic vote, and the British want Franco to win, because they think he's going to look after their precious investments, and the French do what the British tell them to do because they're scared of Hitler. And none of them like the Communists. Not that I can blame them for that," he added, glancing up at André Marty's balcony behind them.

"I don't understand," said Theo, unwilling to give up on his hopes. "The rifles are American. Maybe they're sending them through Mexico."

"You don't give up easily, do you, buddy? I should have remembered that," said Manny, laughing. "I know a bit about rifles, and these are thirty years old at least, forty maybe. Uncle Sam sold them to the tsar, and then the Soviets got hold of them after the revolution and sent them to the Mexicans for theirs, and now they've sent them over here for ours. Revolutionary rifles. That's what these are, even if they're from before the flood." Manny smiled and patted his rifle affectionately, pleased with the name he'd given it.

"How the hell do you know all this?"

"I know where to look," said Manny, turning Theo's rifle around and showing him more faded markings on the other side of the barrel. "See there—the hammer and sickle, and under it, the imperial double eagle. I'm not a magician, even though I do a pretty good impression of one, I must admit."

Theo was surprised by the breadth of Manny's esoteric knowledge, but he was reluctant to acknowledge how impressed he was, because he also felt irritated by Manny's chutzpah and ashamed of his own naivete. His ignorance felt somehow more humiliating because he'd been an Oxford undergraduate, while Manny had been riding the rails in Appalachia, learning how to be a hobo. Add in his disappointment at finding out that nonintervention was alive and well, and he was tied up with so many conflicting thoughts that he didn't know what to say, so he was grateful for the distraction when they were called over to the truck to be issued with ammunition pouches and thin tin helmets, which Manny pronounced to be completely useless.

"Might as well wear a bucket on your head," he said bitterly, forgetting the pleasure he'd gotten from the rifles.

*"Montez dans le camion!"* A peremptory voice behind them cut into their conversation. It was the same French officer who'd woken them up from their siesta, and when the volunteers didn't rush to obey, he drew himself up to his full height and shouted the command again, reinforcing his meaning with an indicative wave of his swagger stick.

Then, having got the volunteers' attention, he stepped back and watched with amused contempt as they made a spectacular mess of trying to climb inside the cargo bed. They tripped over each other's rifles and fell back under the weight of their equipment and had to be hoisted up by their comrades, until half of them were packed in so tight they couldn't move, at which point he waved them off, and a second truck drove in through the gate to take those who were left, which included Theo and Manny, who had insisted on getting on last. "So at least we'll get some air," Manny said, spitting on the ground to show his disgust at what they were being subjected to.

"Where are we going?" he shouted down to the officer as the truck's engine sputtered into life.

"Jarama," said the officer, pronouncing the word with obvious relish.

"But what about our training?" Manny demanded. "No one's taught us a damn thing!"

The officer didn't reply. Instead, he just shrugged his shoulders, whether because he didn't understand or he didn't care or both, and banged the side of the truck with his stick—a signal to the driver to move out.

Straightaway, the truck made a sweeping, 180-degree turn through the parade ground, throwing the men in the back around like ninepins, and passed out through the gate with their shouts of pain flying uselessly out from under the canvas.

Manny had been right about the better air at the back of the truck, even if it was colder there too. The men were packed in so tight that those farther inside half suffocated and the ones behind the cab spent the journey hammering on the partition, begging the driver to stop. But he took no notice, keeping on up the straight road that cut across the plateau of La Mancha.

The wheels of the big supply trucks going back and forth between Madrid and Valencia had broken up the road surface, and each pothole they bumped through was agony for the sufferers inside, because they couldn't stop their rifles from jabbing into each other. They longed to sit down, but there was no room to even turn around or get a handkerchief out of their pockets, and they looked back on the hard wooden train benches they'd complained about the night before, as if they'd been first-class Pullman seats compared to what they were now enduring. They had no choice but to urinate where they stood, and the sweet, ugly smell seeped through the truck, adding to their misery.

The plain was flat and changeless, and its emptiness was relieved only by solitary umbrella pines sticking up above the skyline like green barrage balloons and the black sails of omnipresent white windmills turning slowly in the breeze. This was Don Quixote's country, and Theo thought miserably that he and his companions were worthy successors of the old knight, clutching their ancient Connecticut rifles like lances as they rode west to make fools of themselves and probably die in the process. He remembered what Manny had said about the brigade in Figueres: *"Whoever's running this show is making it up as they go along."* At the time, he'd not wanted to believe it was true, but now he didn't need any convincing. He shivered in the cold, wondering what the hell he'd gotten himself into.

Beyond Tarancón, the landscape changed. The flatlands gave way to hills and valleys where white farmhouses nestled prettily among the oak and cypress trees. Peasants worked in the olive groves, thrashing the silvery trees with long poles to bring down the fruit, and there was a scent of marjoram and sage in the air, redolent of the coming of spring. But there were signs of war too. Charred wrecks of bombed-out trucks had been pushed into the drainage ditches that ran alongside the road, and Theo felt his legs giving way beneath him when he heard the drone of airplanes overhead. Looking up, he could see a squadron of green biplanes flying directly toward them.

He wanted to jump out before the bombs hit. The thought of burning and not being able to move was more than he could bear. He tried to climb up onto the tailgate, but someone pulled him back. Not Manny, who seemed to be in a kind of trance, displaying that same ability to tune out his surroundings that he had shown as he crossed France lying in a luggage rack, but instead, Theo's neighbor on the other side, who hadn't said a word since they left Albacete.

"Steady there, fella," he said, patting Theo gently on the back, now that he'd hauled him to safety. "There's no need for the high jump. Those planes up there are ours."

"How do you know?" Theo asked, still nervous, even though the planes had passed out of view and the noise of their engines was fading into the distance.

"I've seen them before."

"Where?"

"Back at the barracks. The Fascists bombed the town a week ago, and those were the planes that drove them off. They've got snub noses—*chatos*, they call them."

"That's what the word means. In Spanish, I mean. Flat nose," said Theo, stumbling over his words as soon as he started speaking, because he thought the man might think he was showing off, boasting that he could speak the language and acting like a know-it-all. He felt awkward, too, because the man was Black, and he didn't want him to think he was talking down to him when he terribly wanted to do the opposite. It moved him almost to tears that he was going to fight for freedom alongside a Black man, but he couldn't think of a way of saying that without referring to the man's color, which he was desperate not to do. And it also didn't help that he'd thought he was going to die less than a minute before. Looking down, he saw that his hands were shaking.

But he needn't have worried. The man was impressed by his language skills, not insulted. "I wish I could speak the lingo," he said ruefully. "It's the only thing I got missing from this whole experience, I reckon. I love these people—well, the good ones, I mean—and I'd like to tell them how I feel."

"I'll translate for you if you like," said Theo, even though it seemed to him very unlikely that they would be meeting anyone Spanish in the foreseeable future—unless they were taken prisoner, of course, and that didn't bear thinking of. He remembered the Englishman with the eyepatch in Paris and all that he'd read about how the Moors treated their captives.

"Would you? I'd sure like that," said the man, sounding extravagantly pleased, and then he relapsed back into silence, going back to gazing out at the passing landscape as if it was the Elysian Fields, apparently unaware of the misery of everyone around him.

"Aren't you scared?" Theo asked. He liked his new friend, but he couldn't make sense of him. How could he be happy in such horrible circumstances?

"A little, I guess. But tomorrow will take care of that. Now, I'm just enjoying breathing the free air and looking forward to joining the battalion. I just missed them by a day, and they're the reason I came across the water."

"What do you mean?"

"They're my chance to fight back against the slavers, against Jim Crow. I can't do that back home. I tried, but it didn't work."

"Isn't it different here?"

"No Black men, you mean?"

Theo nodded, worried again that he'd said the wrong thing.

"Yeah, I thought that to begin with. It's why I wanted to go to Ethiopia. Because they were my people Mussolini was killing. But then I realized I was wrong. It doesn't matter if you're black or white; it matters that you're oppressed. And these poor people here are sorely oppressed. That's the truth."

"Yes, it is," said Theo fervently. He felt wide awake suddenly, remembering the starving man who'd accosted him in Los Olivos and the others bent double under their loads like animals as they came down off the mountains. Oppressed for centuries but somehow, against all the odds, keeping that glimmer of hope alive in their hearts that the Fascists now wanted to extinguish forever. He, too, was here for them. For justice.

It was as if he'd begun to forget why he'd come, wandering in a mist of doubt and uncertainty, and this stranger's simple words had returned him to himself. "I'm Theo," he said. He wanted to put out his hand, but there was no room.

"Joseph," said the man, smiling.

"Like my grandfather," said Theo involuntarily, remembering the old man telling him his name in the sweatshop apartment all those years ago.

"Well, I'm honored to share his name," said Joseph, bowing his head slightly.

And Theo remembered how his grandfather had told him that one day he might be another Joseph, helping his brothers out of slavery.

They drove through the village of Morata de Tajuña in the dusk and knew that they had at last reached the war.

Many of the buildings had been bombed, and in one house the entire outer wall had been sheared off, leaving the interior exposed, with beds and chairs and tables perched on the edge of broken floors, as if it was a stage set, ghostly in the dying light.

In the main square, the wreck of a Russian tank resembled a prehistoric, toad-like creature, sitting across from the sandbagged doors of the ayuntamiento with its blacked-out windows crisscrossed with sticky tape. A dog barked furiously, but there was no one else on the street to mark their passing.

Beyond the village, they joined a queue of vehicles picking their way at a snail's pace up the winding road with the aid of faint blue headlights. Potholes were everywhere, but the men were silent now as they jolted along, listening intently to the dull roar up ahead. Like distant thunder that didn't stop, it just kept on and on, growing louder as they got closer.

Later, those of them that survived the battle grew accustomed to the sound, so that sometimes they didn't even notice it anymore even though it was there, but now, hearing it for the first time, it filled their minds and bodies, driving out all other thoughts and sensations as they fought to control their fear.

Perhaps it made it worse that they couldn't see what was making the noise because the front line was hidden behind the black hilltops, silhouetted in the moonlight. All that was visible now were the beams of the turning searchlights, reaching their pale fingers high into the darkening sky, and the flares and tracer bullets arcing through high parabolas of colored light before they fell invisibly to the ground.

The men knew that terror was waiting for them over the ridge, even though they couldn't see it. And they knew, too, that anyone in their right mind would run away as fast as they could, instead of trundling up the road toward it like lemmings headed for the cliff.

Finally, they stopped, and by the time they'd clambered out of the truck, stretching the blood back into their aching, stiffened limbs, the driver had slipped away into the night, escaping the punishment that they had sworn to mete out on him as soon as they got the chance.

They'd reached the Lincoln Battalion's field headquarters: a series of dugouts and a cookhouse built into the lee of a hill. The front line was less than a kilometer away.

They ate lukewarm stew and drank hot coffee, cupping their hands around the tin mugs to keep out the intensifying rain driving down at them from the hill above, and grumbled with their comrades from the first truck that had arrived five minutes before them about the crushing horrors of the drive, while all the time glancing nervously upward, wondering what lay ahead.

And then, all at once, they were quiet. A big man was forcing his way along the far edge of the crowd toward the front, pushing people out of the way. He was tall, towering over everyone around him, and Theo could see from his position at the back that the man had no hat and that his head was bald, shaped like a cannonball. The rain was beating a tattoo on it, but he didn't seem to care, and it bobbed up and down and a bit to the side as if he was walking with a limp.

And there was somebody behind him whom Theo couldn't see, but knew was there because there was the top of an umbrella following in the big man's wake.

They reached the truck—the same one in which Theo had come from Albacete—and the big man must have put down a box because the man behind was able to step up easily upon it into the cargo bed, where he shook out the umbrella, gave it to the tall man, and turned to face the new arrivals, standing just where Theo had been minutes before. He cleared his throat and began to speak.

# 15

## JARAMA

Theo already knew it was Alvah before he saw him, because he'd recognized Easey Goldstein as Easey had pushed his way through the crowd, but the moment of realization had brought with it no sense of shock. For as long as he could remember, he had carried within him the conviction that Alvah had only temporarily disappeared from his life. He'd felt him coming closer when Coach Booker had unexpectedly mentioned his name in the bar on the Ramblas back in July, and now, finally, he had returned.

Five years older but essentially unchanged. Alvah had exchanged his cutter's waistcoat and rolled-up shirtsleeves for a shiny leather jacket zipped to the throat, his flat worker's cap for a navy-blue beret smaller than André Marty's but worn at the same angle, and his tape measure for an officer's swagger stick and a Colt .45. But he'd kept the clipped black mustache and goatee and had the same thin, sardonic smile on his face that Theo remembered from those painful meetings in his father's office, when Alvah had taken such pleasure in tormenting his employer, running verbal rings around him in the same way a picador jabs at an enraged bull before the final kill.

Alvah liked the sound of his own voice just as much as before, too, raising and lowering it for effect as he spoke, and he didn't need a loudspeaker anymore, even though he was talking over the noise of a war. Like Marty, he had mastered the art of making his voice carry. He had always been clever, and years of public speaking in smoky halls as he climbed his way up through the ranks of the New York Communist Party had no doubt made him an accomplished orator, but

Theo had the impression that Alvah was really speaking to himself, enjoying the setting of the rainy night on the edge of the battlefield and his own centrality within it. The weary faces of the volunteers looking up at him from below were like the strikers at the garment factory. He felt no sense of responsibility toward them, because they didn't exist for him as separate human beings. They were just tools for him to manipulate for his own benefit and discard without a backward glance if and when their usefulness expired.

"Welcome to the Jarama Valley, men," he began. "I'm your commissar, Alvah Katz, and I'm here to tell you what I know you all want to hear. You've arrived just in the nick of time, because tomorrow morning we attack. Not defend, as we have up to now, valiantly with our backs against the wall. Attack! Because that is always the best form of defense.

"As long as the Fascists remain on the hilltops"—Alvah pointed over the heads of the volunteers toward the invisible battlefield behind them—"they threaten the road. You have traveled on it today. You have seen the trucks bringing supplies to Madrid. Without the road, the capital will fall. We know that. The Fascists know that. And that is why we must drive them off the hills and back across the river, so that they can never return."

"How are we going to do that?" asked a voice in the crowd that Theo recognized as Manny's, and others immediately backed him up, echoing his question.

But if Alvah was disconcerted, he didn't show it. "We're going to do it with artillery, airplanes, and tanks—and you too, of course, at the end, with other battalions attacking beside you," he said, smiling. "The barrage and the bombing will destroy the Fascists' defenses, and then our tanks will roll over them. All you have to do is follow behind. Everything has been planned to the last detail by General Gal and his staff."

"Like bringing us up here without any training?" Manny demanded. "Was that part of the plan?"

"What you lack in training, you'll make up for in enthusiasm and anti-Fascist conviction. The enemy can't match that. They're exhausted; they're there for the taking."

"We're exhausted too. We haven't slept in days," a plaintive voice called out.

"We haven't even fired our rifles yet," said another.

"You'll have a chance to do that on the way up to the line," Alvah replied impatiently. "It's not difficult."

"It's a fucking joke. That's what this is." It was Manny again, even louder this time.

"Who is that man? Step forward," demanded Alvah. And at the same time, Easey was wading into the crowd, shining a flashlight. It didn't take him long to locate Manny, whom he grabbed by the arm. But the men around Manny pushed Easey off, and Alvah beckoned his sidekick back, sensing that the mood of the volunteers was turning against him.

"Listen, men, I understand you're nervous," he said, adopting a gentler, more sympathetic tone. "It's understandable. I wish just as much as you that there had been more time for training and preparation. But what you have to ask yourself is whether you would have wanted to miss the day when the tide of the war finally turned in our favor. Isn't this what you joined the Lincoln Battalion to be a part of? Wouldn't you have blamed us if we'd left you behind in Albacete to shine your boots?"

Alvah paused, but there were no words of protest this time. He'd been clever—stopping their complaints with an appeal to their politics.

"Success is certain because history is on our side," he proclaimed in a ringing tone. "Tomorrow we will achieve a great victory."

He raised his right fist and most of the volunteers responded, albeit with a great deal less energy, as Alvah got down from the truck and walked back to the command dugout with Easey, deep in conversation. They passed close to Theo without seeing him, and Theo heard Easey say the name *Manny Mandelbaum*, although he couldn't hear Alvah's response because another officer with stripes on his sleeve had stepped up and was ordering the volunteers to shoulder their packs and move out. The trucks had come as far as they could, and the volunteers were going to have to cover the remaining half kilometer to the front line on their own two feet.

They left the path after about five minutes and formed a line, looking down into a cement quarry dimly lit by the moon that was struggling now to emerge from behind banks of scurrying, rain-filled clouds.

The officer went down the line, instructing those who had never handled a rifle before on how to load a clip of cartridges, and then they took it in turns to fire five rounds down at the broken limestone walls below. Their hands shook as they listened to the crackling echoes reverberating through the canyon like machine-gun fire.

Theo's rifle kicked like a mule the first time he pulled the trigger, and he was saved from falling over backward only by Manny applying a steadying hand. "Keep the stock tight to your shoulder! Hold your breath! And don't pull the trigger; squeeze!" Manny instructed, and it worked. Better, at least.

But other volunteers who didn't have anyone to help them were still trying to load their rifles, jamming the bolt as they tried to push it into position, or firing wildly into the air, by the time that the officer called them back up onto the path to resume their march.

"We're damn lucky we didn't lose a few back there! No one knows a butt from a barrel!" said Manny furiously. "The crazy bastards running this show are doing the Fascists' job for them. And that smug phony with the umbrella's the worst of the lot so far, if you ask me. It's a crime, sending us into battle untrained, and he knows it, but does he care? The fuck he does!"

"No, you're right. He doesn't," said Theo quietly.

"You sound like you know," said Manny, breaking off his rant to look at Theo sharply. He'd picked up on something more than mere agreement in his friend's response.

"I do. We've crossed paths before," said Theo reluctantly. He'd have preferred to keep his history with Alvah to himself. He didn't want to think about the past, and he felt that Alvah's appearance at this critical moment in his life was a bad omen. Talking about it felt like letting the evil out to spread its contagion. But his slip of the tongue had left him with no choice, and so he told Manny about the strike and his father's suicide in as few words as he could muster. "Alvah's what Alvah cares about," he finished, remembering Frank Vogel's pithy aphorism from years before. "So you're right about him, yes."

"What are the odds? A million to one!" Manny whistled, amazed, unlike Theo, by the coincidence that his friend and the battalion commissar should have known each other before, on the other side of the world.

"A lot less than that," said Theo sourly. "Alvah's been climbing the party ladder for years, and Spain's just the next rung up. He'll strut around here for a few months and then come back a hero, all ready to step in as the next leader when Browder gets his walking papers."

"Not if we have anything to do with it," said Manny angrily. "You want payback for your dad, don't you?"

"Right now, I just want us to survive," said Theo grimly. "And the odds on that don't seem that great either, do they?"

Manny grunted, for once not having an answer.

They'd reached the crest of the hill and left the path to enter a communication trench with crumbling dirt walls, running forward to the front line. They walked in single file, picking their way slowly over duckboards that had come loose in the rain. Once or twice, a man slipped and fell and had to be pulled to his feet, coughing out mud and filth, because the weight of his equipment made it impossible for him to get up unaided.

Theo was completely unprepared for the assault on his senses that he was now experiencing. In his ears the whine and shriek of shells rushing through the air and exploding on impact; in his nose the mixed-up, rotten smell of excrement, urine, cordite, and putrefaction; in his mouth the taste of his own bile rising from the gagging gorge of his throat. Only his eyes were immune as he stumbled through the dark, using all the strength he had left to just keep placing one foot in front of the other.

They turned to the right, stopping here and there while volunteers were detached from the main group to join different companies along the line, until only Manny, Theo, Joseph, and a few others were left at the end to become part of 2 Company, which was occupying the trenches flanking the black macadam road running straight from the village of Morata that they'd just passed through in the truck onto San Martín de la Vega behind the Fascist lines.

Theo took off his rifle and pack and sank down against the back wall of the trench. The rain and the mud and the guns meant nothing to him. All that mattered was that he could close his eyes and rest. He slept where he sat.

It was still dark when Theo opened his eyes, but the trench was lit by the moon and the pale-green glow of star shells arcing overhead. The rain had turned to a steady-falling snow, and the mud floor was covered by a thin layer of frosty white: a stark contrast to the black walls hemming him in. Snow had settled, too, on his head and clothes, and his hands were icy wet when he brushed it away. He wished he had gloves like Joseph, who was lying asleep beside him, using his pack for a pillow.

A big man in a ragged uniform was sitting opposite Theo, so close in the narrow space that their boots were almost touching. He was older than the volunteers Theo had met up to now, although how old it was hard to say, because his face was covered in a gray beard that reached down over his throat, and he had a black New York Yankees baseball cap pulled forward over his forehead to keep the snow out of his eyes.

He was combing the blond hair of a younger soldier of Theo's age, whose head was lying in his lap, and now he held the comb up close to his eyes and popped the lice on it with the tip of his cigarette, making a noise like a pistol shot with his lips as each one of the translucent yellow vermin exploded.

"It's a losing battle. Bit like the war, I suppose. But that doesn't mean we don't have to fight the bastards, does it?" he said with a smile, glancing over at Theo, who nodded, not knowing how to respond. Fascists and lice, defeat: it was more than he could get his head around when he had just woken up on the front line of a battlefield.

An artillery shell screeched as it passed overhead, and he instinctively put his head down between his knees, but the man in the cap paid it no mind. Just went on with his combing.

"You don't need to be scared," he said, and Theo was touched to hear the note of sympathy in his voice. "The whizbang's traveling faster than sound. It's gone already when you hear it. It's the ones you don't hear that might have your name on it, but I don't see that happening tonight. It'd spoil the fun for tomorrow, wouldn't it?"

Theo nodded and swallowed hard, trying to control his fear, but his teeth kept chattering, whether from terror or the cold or both he couldn't tell.

"Alvah—Commissar Katz—he said it's going to be a big attack," Theo said hesitantly. "Shells, planes, tanks. He said all we have to do is follow up behind." He was looking for corroboration and reassurance, but what he got back was the opposite.

"I'll believe it when I see it," said the man in the cap. "We attacked them up the hill three days ago, and it was a total A1 disaster. We lost twenty men and we didn't get anywhere near them. Not even close enough to throw a grenade. We had one tank, which exploded, our machine guns didn't work, and the Fascists mowed us down from above like it was a goddamn turkey shoot. The truth is we can't drive 'em off from where they are. They're too well positioned, too well dug in, and we haven't got the firepower, but General Gal over at Division HQ doesn't want to hear that. He's got André Marty breathing down his neck, and he wants the glory."

"Hey, Uncle," said the boy with the blond hair, suddenly sitting up, "I heard he's got a picture of himself now in his office. Life-size, bigger than him. One of the runners said you have to salute that as well as him when you go in. Must get pretty confusing." He laughed.

"Yeah, he sure likes his saluting, does our general," said Uncle, laughing too. "All of them do. Makes them feel all military, when most of them don't have a clue about soldiering."

"What do you mean?" asked Theo. "He's a general, isn't he?"

"No, he's a Communist and a Russian. That's what puts stars on your cap round here. It's got jack shit to do with experience. He's flying by the seat of his pants. They all are. Gal, Copic, Katz, Merriman, the whole damned lot of them. The day we came up here, two of our trucks took a wrong turn and were never seen again. Twenty of America's best, gone to Jesus because the guys in charge didn't have a map!" Uncle snapped his fingers for effect. "Commissar—we call him Comic Star—Katz blamed it on Trotskyite saboteurs, but that's their excuse every time anything goes wrong. Trotsky this, Trotsky that . . . and then, a few nights later, Harris, the battalion commander, decides to take us on a walk round no-man's-land. 'Follow the polestar,' he says, like we're a bunch of Boy Scouts. Damn good thing there wasn't a moon or we'd all be dead. When we got back, they put him in an ambulance. 'Psychotic'—that's what the doc called him."

"You're kidding," Theo said, gasping in disbelief.

"No, he's not. It's what I've been telling you ever since we got to this crazy country," said Manny, who was sitting only a few yards down the trench but whom Theo hadn't been aware of until now because his attention had been focused on Uncle. "They're throwing us into battle untrained. Doesn't that tell you something? You need to wake up and start listening, Theo!"

"Maybe, but isn't it a bit late for that?" said Theo gloomily. "We're here now, aren't we? We can't run away."

"Yeah, it sucks, doesn't it?" said Uncle, shaking his head. "You decide to go when you don't know what you're getting yourself into, and then when you do know, it's too late to change your mind. It's a one-way ticket they're selling you to this place. They just don't tell you that at the station."

"I knew," said Theo. "My stepfather was at the Somme, and he told me what it was like."

"And you didn't listen?"

"No, I listened all right. But it didn't make a difference. I felt I had to go. I think I still would, even now."

"Well, you're an idiot then," said Manny, spitting on the ground to express his disgust.

"No, he's not," said Joseph, who'd woken up now too. "I know what Theo means. I wouldn't swap being here for Georgia. Not for love or money. This is the only place in the world where my people can fight back and stand up for themselves. Where I'm me and not some Black man waiting to be kicked around like an animal. If I die tomorrow, it'll have been worth it because I'll die a free man."

Uncle looked at Joseph long and hard, and then leaned across and shook his hand. "Yeah, that's why I'm here too," he said. "Thanks for reminding me, buddy."

"I don't mind dying," said the blond-haired boy thoughtfully. "I just don't want to get mangled. Or taken prisoner by those fucking Moors. They'll cut you up into a hundred pieces and feed you to the crows. Sometimes at night, when they start up with their weird chanting, it scares the bejesus out of me, I'm telling you."

"But not tonight, Bobby," said Uncle. "This night we got all to ourselves, so let's make the most of it. Treat it like it's Christmas, which it sure looks like with all this snow lying about, deep and crisp and even."

Uncle launched into a surprisingly tuneful rendition of "Good King Wenceslas," until Bobby interrupted him.

"Who the fuck was he? This Wenceslas dude?"

"He was an old king with a young servant who got caught in a blizzard. The servant couldn't keep up until Wenceslas showed him where to step in his footprints. Then they were okay."

"Like you and me?"

Uncle smiled. "Yeah, Bobby, something like that."

"Do you know 'In the Bleak Midwinter'?" Theo asked, remembering the house in London and his mother singing beside the piano.

"Frosty wind made moan / Earth stood hard as iron / Water like a stone / Snow had fallen / Snow on snow on snow / In the bleak midwinter / Long, long ago . . ."

Uncle was singing lustily again and Theo joined in at the end, and was happy but sad, too, because his mother was dead, under the iron earth, and they'd shared so little in the time they had.

"No Christmas where I come from!" said Manny cheerfully. "We had Hanukkah, which was way more fun. Went on for longer and a lot better chow. My grandmother made the best brisket in Brooklyn. I'm not exaggerating. If there'd been a competition of *bubbes*, she'd have won the gold medal. By a mile. Oh, the smell of it, the taste of it . . . ai, ai! And afterward, she'd take me on her knee between her big, billowing breasts and sing to me and tell me stories about the old country. She had a wig for holy days, and one time I pulled it off. She gave me a smack and I peed my pants."

"Is that your favorite memory?" asked Uncle, laughing.

"It's a good one," said Manny. "What's yours?"

"Oh, that's hard," said Uncle, scratching his beard. "Yankee Stadium, maybe, with the Babe in the ninth inning of the World Series, raising his bat and everyone knowing what was coming . . ." He stopped. "No, that's my second favorite. The best has got to be dancing. In the Savoy Ballroom on Lenox Avenue on a Saturday night with my girl in my arms and Benny Goodman playing his clarinet and that big crystal ball up above turning us round and round through all the colors of the rainbow." He sighed, remembering.

"Yeah, I get that," said Manny. "What about you, Theo?"

Theo hesitated, even though he knew his answer without having to think about it. Confidences didn't come easy to him, particularly with people he didn't know, but then he told them, because the night seemed to demand it, and his words came in a rush: "Walking in Barcelona in the night last summer with the girl I love and everyone out on the streets singing because we'd defeated the army and it felt like a new world had just begun and everything was possible. It wasn't, but we didn't know that then. We thought it was forever."

Simon Tolkien

"Nothing is," said Uncle, sighing. "What about you, buddy?" he asked, looking over at Joseph. "You got a memory you want to share?"

"Not about girls," said Joseph with a chuckle. "Me and them never seen eye to eye, for some reason, or maybe I just didn't have time for loving with all the iniquity and injustice I was knocking my head up against every day. But I remember when I was low in spirit, I'd walk out into the fields, by a slow-moving river, maybe, and lie there in the high grass under the firmament and feel the rays of the sun on my face and know I had everything I could want. I was rich as Croesus, with nothing in my hands."

"And wise as Solomon," said Uncle with a smile, looking down at Bobby, who'd closed his eyes and gone back to sleep.

Slowly a gray light crept into the trench, and the snow died away. Theo felt his clothes crackle with the frost as he struggled to stand. He tried to climb a step to an empty firing aperture in the trench wall opposite, but fell back on the ground in a heap because he had no feeling in his feet, and was only able to get up the step after he had spent a whole minute stamping the blood back into his toes. His hands felt like they were made of swollen rubber.

Looking out at no-man's-land through the wisps of mist, Theo could see the black road to the right and in front, lines of ghostly olive trees with their trunks and branches broken and blackened by bullets and shellfire, running forward to where the barren hillside rose steeply to the high ridge on which the Fascists were entrenched. The shelling had tailed off and there was no sign of life except for periodic puffs of smoke, but he knew they had to be up there, waiting patiently behind their guns. Moors who liked to cut their victims into small pieces and feed them to the crows.

Theo quailed at the sight of the bare, stony slope. It had to be at least two hundred yards long, without a fold or a tree for cover, and he didn't need military training to know what it would mean to run up it under fire. His knees trembled and he stumbled back down into the trench, where jars of cold coffee and loaves of bread and jam had been brought up from the cookhouse behind the line with news that the attack had been postponed for three hours until ten o'clock.

The sun broke through the clouds, but Theo continued to shiver, thinking of what lay ahead. He wanted to talk to Uncle about the slope, but was ashamed to show his fear. The impetus toward conversation that they had all felt the night before had evaporated in the morning light, and they sat tense and silent, gripping their rifles and waiting for what was to come.

At half past nine, the lieutenant commanding 2 Company appeared in their section of the trench. He was older than the other soldiers—in his forties, perhaps. His brow was wrinkled and he had an air of patient weariness, as if he had seen too much of the world. He spoke with a quiet authority and without any trace of Alvah's self-important narcissism. Beside him, a soldier of Theo's age or younger was holding a thick bundle of white material, while another, red-faced and out of breath, was standing a couple of paces behind. Neither of them was carrying a rifle.

"Captain Merriman wants us to put out a T signal for our planes, so they know where to attack," said the lieutenant, pointing to the material. "White, because the road's black," he added, as if feeling the need to explain.

"You're kidding!" said Uncle angrily. "All that'll do is give the Fascists a heads-up on where we're coming from. Do you want to make this worse than it already is?"

"No, of course I don't. I know it's stupid, but it's an order, so we haven't got any choice, do we? I need another volunteer to help Howie here spread the damn thing. Anyone willing?"

"What about him?" asked Uncle, pointing to the second boy.

"No, he's Merriman's runner. He's got to report back."

The lieutenant stood waiting, and time seemed to stand still. Everyone was quiet, and Theo could feel his heart beating hard against his ribs. He wanted to say yes. He really did, but he couldn't open his mouth, and he couldn't put up his hand. He was mute, frozen with fear.

"I'll do it," said Bobby, stepping forward.

And immediately Theo felt the blood moving through his limbs again, and with it an overwhelming sense of relief that turned his legs to jelly and flushed his cheeks with shame.

But no one was looking at him. Uncle had his hands on Bobby, pulling him back. "No, you fucking won't," he was shouting.

But Bobby shrugged him off, and Uncle turned his rage on the lieutenant. "You go," he shouted, seizing his arm. "Leave my guys alone."

"That's not the way it works, Pete, and you know it," said the lieutenant, looking Uncle in the eye and making no effort to remove Uncle's hand from his arm.

Uncle kept hold for a moment or two longer and then stood back, looking at Bobby, who was paying him no attention. Theo could see that there were tears in Uncle's eyes.

"Okay," said the lieutenant, straightening his sleeve. "Let's get this over with."

Howie and Bobby clambered over the end of the trench and up onto the road. They had hold of the signal at both ends, and, opened out, it looked like laundry ready to be hung out on a washing line—white towels and shirts pinned loosely together.

Now they had it stretched across the black tarmac, and Bobby was pulling out the leg of the T and dragging it down the middle of the road, so that the signal would face west, up toward the enemy. He bent—to weigh it down perhaps, but it wasn't that. He'd been shot in the chest. He was holding himself and now he was falling back, shot again, and his blood was pooling out across the white cloth.

Uncle screamed and launched himself forward but was held back by the lieutenant and Manny, so it was Howie instead who ran over to Bobby, intending to drag him back off the road. But he hadn't got to him before he, too, was shot down, and the fire, concentrated and incessant now, ricocheted off the road like hail and cut the two bodies to pieces where they lay.

"No one else goes out there. You hear me?" said the lieutenant, pulling Uncle close to make sure he understood, before he let him go.

But Uncle was in no state to be going anywhere, as he slid down the side of the trench and sat, collapsed on the ground, trembling with shock and grief. He bore no resemblance to the self-possessed man of the night before.

Several hundred yards behind them, two soot-colored armored cars had appeared, trundling slowly up the road. They weren't tanks—they looked nothing like the wrecked leviathan in the Morata village square that Theo,

Manny, and Joseph had driven past the day before. Instead, they reminded Theo of the iron boxes on wheels that he'd seen in Barcelona the previous July, although these had heavy-caliber guns mounted in turrets on their roofs.

Farther back still, a mass of Republican soldiers had begun to advance on the other side of the road.

"Tell the captain we've got two armored cars and that the Spanish troops are moving and the signal's out," said the lieutenant, turning back to the runner, who had stood ramrod straight, waiting for orders, while the two men died out on the road. He saluted and ran away down the trench, dodging expertly from side to side to avoid the men standing in his way.

The Fascist fire had not slackened since the fusillade they'd unleashed when the signal was put out. If anything, it seemed to have intensified, and Theo could hear the bullets clanging against the armored cars, which had stopped in their tracks, firing back up the hill with their guns. Shells were exploding, too, on both sides of the road.

Now the cars abruptly about-turned and retreated back down the road, leaving the advancing troops behind them exposed. They were still at least four hundred yards to the rear of the Lincoln trenches.

"Holy Christ. The bastards are going back too," said the lieutenant, who had his field glasses clamped to his face, gazing at the scene unfolding behind him. "We can't go without them. It'd be suicide."

He dropped the glasses and turned around. "We have to tell Merriman what's happened. I need another runner. Someone faster than the wind." He walked back down the trench, yelling "Runner! Runner!" at the top of his voice, trying to make himself heard above the noise of the gunfire.

It was the opposite of before. Then, Theo had wanted to volunteer, but had said nothing. Now, he heard himself shouting, even though he wasn't conscious of having made a decision to open his mouth.

"I can do it, sir!" he called out after the lieutenant. "I'm a runner. I was going to run at the Olympics but it got canceled. The one in Barcelona . . ."

The lieutenant stopped and turned, looking Theo up and down as he tried to make a decision.

"Are you bullshitting me?"

"No, it's the truth. I swear it."

The lieutenant hesitated a moment more and then nodded. "All right," he said. "Find Captain Merriman and tell him that the Spanish troops have retreated, and the armored cars too. Tell him I said it would be suicide for us to attack now. And if you get there before that other guy, make sure he knows you're the one with the up-to-date message. Now run like it is the goddamn Olympics, you hear me?"

"Yes, sir," said Theo, saluting fiercely, before he took off down the trench, almost knocking over Manny and Joseph, who were staring at him open-mouthed.

It was hard going. Everywhere, there were men and equipment he had to get past, and the duckboards kept slipping under his feet so that he was constantly falling over and hurting his knees. But he was up again immediately, immune to the pain. Nothing mattered except getting there before the other runner so that the captain wouldn't give the order to attack.

He ran, dodging from side to side like he used to do on the rugby field at Saint Gregory's, filled with the same exultation he'd felt back then, as he approached the try line, except that this was different. The fate of all the men he was passing depended on his speed and skill. Life and death—he was touching history, just as he had in Barcelona.

But there was doubt, too, growing now with each step. Because he didn't know what the captain looked like. He could run past him and all his effort would be wasted. Perhaps he already had. The lieutenant had obviously assumed he knew. Why wouldn't he? It had been Theo's responsibility to ask for a description, and he hadn't because he was so full of himself and eager to start his race. Idiot! He'd have smacked his head against the trench wall in self-disgust if he could have done so without stopping running. Instead, he did the only thing he could, which was to keep shouting "Captain Merriman? Captain Merriman?" at every soldier he went past, leaving behind their looks of bewilderment as he kept hurtling on down the trench.

And in the end he was only saved from running past the captain through the sheer luck of colliding with the first runner just as he'd finished making his report to a tall, broad-shouldered, bespectacled officer in a peaked cap, who was standing to the side at the intersection of the trench and another, wider communication trench that descended back behind the plateau. It was the same place where Theo had entered the front line the night before. He had given the other runner a three-minute start and had almost beaten him to the captain.

"What the hell do you think you're doing?" Merriman demanded, looking angrily at Theo as he picked himself up off the ground. It clearly hadn't occurred to the captain that he might be another runner.

Theo was so out of breath that, at first, he couldn't speak, and this made Merriman even more annoyed. "Who are you?" he demanded. "I haven't seen you before."

"He was at the road when they put the signal out," said the first runner, who'd now gotten back on his feet too.

"Oh," said Merriman, understanding now. "Have you got something for me?" he asked, friendlier now, though still impatient.

"The lieutenant sent me. He says it's suicide to attack. The armored cars retreated. And then the Spanish troops too," said Theo, gasping between each sentence. "It was after he left," he said, pointing to the first runner.

Merriman recoiled as if from a blow. "Why did they go back?" he asked. "Did you see?"

"The gunfire was too much. The Fascists started it when we put out the signal on the road. And there were shells, too, exploding all around."

"I told the colonel that would happen, but he wouldn't listen," said Merriman. It seemed like he was talking to himself, drumming with his fingers on the leather binocular case that was hanging from his neck.

"Get him on the line again," he ordered, wheeling around to instruct a soldier who was squatting down at the entrance to a small dugout hollowed out of the back wall of the trench. He had a field telephone beside him, housed in an open oak-wood box.

The operator cranked the handle, but there was no connection, just crackling. Merriman stamped his foot and shouted in frustration, but snapped out of it when an imperious Slavic-sounding voice broke through the static. The operator handed the receiver to Merriman as if it were a live coal.

Merriman started to explain what Theo had told him, but Theo could see that he was being constantly cut off by the voice at the other end of the line.

"There are no tanks, no barrage, no planes—"

He stopped and then began again: "The Spanish have gone back—"

Now Merriman was holding the telephone away from his ear because the voice at the other end was shouting so loud that Theo and the others nearby could hear him as well.

"They are ahead of you. Seven hundred yards ahead. They are being killed because of your failure to support—"

"No, they're not," Merriman protested, shouting himself now. "They've gone back to their trenches. It'll be a massacre if I send my men out—"

"Don't you dare contradict me!" The voice was enraged, rising to a bellow: "Attack now! That's an order. You have ten minutes to make up the ground. I have sent officers. If you will not lead your men, they will. I will have you shot. You hear me, Merriman?"

"I hear you," said the captain, dully now.

"Good. Do it!"

The line went dead, and the captain put his hands over his face, squeezing his temples, as if to control an unbearable pain inside his head.

Up above, three planes came into view, flying toward the Fascist lines. The Republican colors—red, yellow, purple—were painted on their tails. They dropped a short flurry of bombs and then flew back toward Morata and weren't seen again. Artillery shells were also going over, but most of them were landing short of the Fascist line, and it was nothing like the sustained barrage that had been promised. Nothing had any effect on the enemy fire, which was as strong as ever, exploding the sandbags along the parapet. It sounded, Theo thought, like the riveting machines in his father's factory in New York—an endless, inhuman beat.

He watched Merriman, who was pacing up and down, wrestling with his conscience. He seemed different from the other soldiers Theo had encountered up to now, because he looked like an officer rather than a civilian pretending to be one. Tall, physically strong, wearing an immaculate tailor-made uniform. And yet he had a schoolmasterly look, too, with his horn-rimmed glasses and educated voice. A face that would have fitted in at Oxford, walking across a quadrangle in cap and gown, on his way to give a lecture to his students.

Theo sensed that he was seeing him now at the crisis of his life. A lucky man who couldn't quite believe that his luck had just run out as he stood at a fork in the road where each turn led to death. Out in no-man's-land, riddled with Fascist bullets, or behind the line, riddled by Republican ones when he faced Colonel Copic's firing squad for disobeying orders.

Two men—Copic's enforcers no doubt—were running toward them down the communication trench. One of them had a pistol in his hand. But it didn't matter. Merriman had made up his mind. He smiled at the newcomers and took off his glasses, folding them carefully away in a chest pocket.

"It's murder, but it's got to be done," he said.

The order to fix bayonets went down the line, and the Lincolns gathered at the foot of the attack ladders, waiting for the whistles that would send them over the top.

The trench around Theo was suddenly far more crowded than before. Men were all around him, men he didn't know. He'd burst his lungs running from the road for no purpose. The attack was still going to happen, even though it was hopeless, even though it was murder. All he'd achieved with his stupid volunteering was to leave his friends behind and put himself in the company of strangers, here at the end of everything.

"*Ave Maria, gratia plena . . . ora pro nobis peccatoribus nunc et in hora mortis nostrae . . .*" (Hail Mary, full of grace . . . pray for us sinners now and at the hour of our death . . .) Theo could hear his mother's voice whispering her Latin prayers inside his head. He reached for the rosary in the pouch around his neck and thought of his stepfather, who had been in this place, too, shaking like a child as he waited to go over. But Andrew had survived. The rosary had saved him, and perhaps it would save Theo too. That was what Andrew had said.

Hope flickered in Theo's mind for a moment, but he couldn't sustain its guttering flame against the steel wind of the gunfire up above. He'd thought it like a riveting machine before, but it was faster than that now—a hail so intense that it had become a continuous beat, pulverizing the sandbags. No man could live through that.

Theo looked back at the telephone operator in his dugout. He hated him because he didn't have to go, just as much as he'd loved Bobby when he'd volunteered to take out the signal in the morning. Death: dodging it or meeting it. That was all that mattered. How had he not understood that before, with all his talk of love and changing the world? Why hadn't he listened when Andrew told him what war was really about? *"No glory, just mechanized slaughter"*: that was what he'd said, and that was exactly what it was.

There were holes in the side of the trench. A honeycomb of holes that he hadn't noticed until now. A pair of tiny pink eyes was watching him. Rat's eyes. This is your place, not ours, Theo thought. The belly of the beast.

It was as if time had slowed and he was a camera, recording everything around him down to its last detail. His brain working in overdrive now that it was faced with its own extinction. Men were wiping their clammy hands, fingering lucky charms, inhaling the smoke from a last cigarette down to the very bottom of their lungs. To feel it, not to be numb. Faces of strangers imprinted on his mind. Jaws set, eyes staring, lips moving. Digging down for courage into the marrow of their bones. *"Courage means nothing,"* Andrew had said. But that couldn't be true. In the end, it was everything.

And at the last moment, just as he heard the whistle sounding in Captain Merriman's mouth, someone squeezed Theo's hand. He didn't even see his face, but he felt the quick embrace of fingers in his own, and he didn't feel alone anymore, because these were his comrades, fighting like him for what they believed in. He had to hang on to that. It was all he had left.

A man was going up the ladder in front of Theo. He had dirty white sneakers on his feet. Theo could see the brand name, **KEDS**, stamped on the side. He remembered having sneakers like that too once. In New York, a long time ago. Was that going to be the last thought he ever had?

The man got to the top and then slipped down the rungs as if he'd lost his footing. Theo pulled his arm and the man, who was no more than a boy, turned with a look of wonder etched on his face. There was a stream of blood pouring out from under his helmet and filling his collar. He stood and then he fell, and someone was pushing Theo hard from behind.

He began to climb the ladder and the exploding sandbags were spilling dirt down into his eyes, just as they'd done to Andrew twenty years before, but he could still make out the tall figure of Captain Merriman up above, standing astride the parapet like a hero in a Hollywood movie. He had a pistol in his hand and he was waving it toward the men coming up, beckoning them forward, until he keeled over just as Theo reached the top, so that Theo had to jump over his writhing body as he took off, running into the inferno.

He was running through the trees, and men were falling all around him. Falling in all kinds of ways—onto their knees, onto their backs, twirling and twisting in death-dance pirouettes as the machine-gun bullets spun them around like hanging targets at a shooting range.

There was a noise in his ears that sounded like the cracking of a thousand whips mixed up with shouts and screams, but he was separated from it. He ran and that was all. With his head still and upright and his knees pushed up high to lengthen his stride just as he'd been taught, and with his boots slipping on the wet ground, and the air sharp and acrid in his lungs. Running with the same power he'd always had, propelling him forward from inside, until he fell.

He scrambled to his feet and crashed over again almost immediately, this time tumbling head over heels. He must have passed out because the next he knew, he was on his back, looking up, and the sky was rushing past, and it stopped, swinging back into place, only when he bent to the side and was violently sick. Everything hurt, especially his head, but it felt like hard bruising—a sensation he knew well from past falls on cinder tracks and rugby fields—and not the weakness and burning pain he imagined he'd feel if he was shot. Looking down, he could see no blood turning his muddy uniform from gray to red.

What had happened, then? What had sent him sprawling if it wasn't a bullet? He looked around and saw the culprits on all sides—gnarled, knotted vines protruding from the earth like the agonized, clawing hands of men buried alive underneath. He was lying on the edge of a vineyard planted in a hollow of the land that had been invisible from the trench behind him. Two hundred yards ahead, the ground rose steeply up the bare slope to the Fascist line.

Bare because none of the Lincolns had got that far. Without the support they'd been promised, they hadn't stood a chance of success. Not even one in a million. The sheer monstrous stupidity of the attack took Theo's breath away.

The noonday sun had burned off the morning mist, and he could see the snouts of guns poking out from the sandbag parapets along the ridge, with clouds of firing smoke rising above them into the still air, but there were no faces. The enemy he'd come to fight was completely invisible. He aimed his rifle at them anyway and fired, but the bolt jammed when he tried to pull it back and a volley of bullets arrived in immediate response, spattering the earth close to where he was kneeling. He threw himself flat on the ground, not moving a muscle, and his prayers were answered when no more bullets followed.

For now, he'd deceived the sniper up on the ridge into thinking he was dead, but he knew he wouldn't be so lucky if the sniper realized his mistake. He trembled, picturing the man with his merciless eye glued to the telescopic sight of his rifle and his finger ready to squeeze the trigger as soon as he detected even the slightest movement down below. The bullets traveling with such awful speed and precision through the air. Tears filled Theo's eyes as he realized he'd evacuated his bowels.

He needed cover to survive. The pruned-down vines were useless, and the splintered olive trees behind him were now just thin sticks of blackened wood. Digging was impossible: even if he could raise enough earth with his hands and bayonet, he knew he'd attract the sniper's attention long before he had a barrier high enough to hide behind. But without protection, it would be only a matter of time before he was hit by one of the enemy machine guns that continued to methodically traverse no-man's-land, cutting down everyone and everything in their path.

Very slowly, he turned his head, searching the blasted landscape all around. Men dying, men dead, but he could see nothing that would provide a meaningful shield, until he took the risk of rolling onto his side to look directly behind him into the olive grove and saw a soldier sprawled face up with a bulging pack under his body, keeping him off the ground. Theo recognized him. It was Tiny, the fat boy in the long johns, who'd become so distressed when he couldn't find a uniform to fit him in the clothes room at Albacete the day before. And now here he was again, looking exactly like an upended tortoise. But one whose crawling days were over. Tiny's splayed-out limbs didn't move when the gunfire plowed up the earth around where he was lying. He had to be dead.

How could he have gone over the top like that? Bent over like a railway porter under all that useless equipment. It beggared belief. Couldn't someone have told him to leave his pack behind?

Theo dismissed the thought. Tiny the person wasn't his concern. All that mattered was that Tiny's body and pack made a good-size mound he could hide behind. If he could reach him without getting shot. He put his hand up to the pouch around his neck, feeling the rosary beads through the thin cotton as he measured the distance. Twenty yards, maybe less, ten strides on a cinder track, but this was a different terrain, and he couldn't afford to fall.

He breathed in deeply once, twice, three times, and then pushed himself violently up off the ground and ran, leaving his rifle behind. He leaped over Tiny's body and landed on the other side with his heart hammering inside his chest. To his surprise, there were no bullets this time. Perhaps the sniper had moved or gone to the latrine or done something else entirely arbitrary that determined which of the Lincolns down below would live or die that day.

Theo was panting and Tiny was looking at him. Or rather through him. Tiny wasn't dead, because his big, hazel-colored eyes blinked slowly every few seconds, but they were indifferent, lost in a limbo world somewhere between life and death. Halfway across the Styx. Theo reached up to hold Tiny's hand, but there was no answering pressure, and as he watched, the eyes glazed over and whatever had been behind them went away. To where? Theo had no idea. Probably nowhere. That was what made the most sense, whatever the believers had to say. He'd never been this close to death before. It was so mysterious and yet so simple and matter-of-fact. It terrified him, how it just happened.

He pushed Tiny's body over on its side so that his head was facing the enemy. He couldn't stand to look into his empty eyes anymore. But as he did so, he caught sight of a folded-over piece of paper on the ground that must have fallen out of Tiny's pack or his open breast pocket. He opened it up and read it.

It was a scrawled letter, written clearly in haste and probably unfinished, because there was no name at the end:

Sweetheart,
We're going into battle soon and I just want you to know that I love you a hell of a lot. It would've been swell to be with you always, but I think maybe it's not going to work out that way

now. And if that's what happens, I don't want you to wither away like a flower without rain. I want you to love and be loved. That's what you deserve.

I'm not sorry I came. You have to understand that. We have to fight back. We have to

Theo cried. It was just so damned unfair. That this boy should have left everything behind, including his girl, to cross the world for an ideal, only to be shoved inside a cattle truck and sent over the top with no training. Not even enough to know to take his pack off before he went up the ladder. Into a hail of bullets. Did no one care? Would no one be held responsible?

Two machine-gun bullets thudded into Tiny's side, as if in response, and his body absorbed them like a sandbag. *More full of lead than a drainpipe!* The phrase floated into Theo's exhausted brain from somewhere he couldn't remember and repeated itself like a stone rattling around in an empty oil drum. Its absurdity made him want to laugh as well as cry. He was fast reaching the end of his tether.

He looked up and saw a soldier walking close to him through the olive trees. Slowly, as if he was taking the air on a Sunday in the country. He had no helmet and no rifle, and his tousled, wheat-blond hair was the color of his uniform. Theo thought of Galahad in the book Andrew had given him long ago. Inviolate. A vision. And then a mortar shell landed, sending up a momentary geyser of black earth and dust, as if it was another tree. When the dust cleared, the soldier was gone.

The firing had slackened now that the attackers had all gone to ground, and Theo could hear wounded men on all sides, crying out in pain and calling for help or water or their mothers. Someone was begging to be killed. "Shoot me, Captain Merriman! Shoot me!" But Captain Merriman was shot himself, and gradually the voice faded away as its owner drifted off into unconsciousness or death.

Now there was another, louder voice that Theo recognized, coming directly from behind where he was lying. It was Alvah, barking out orders to the men who had remained behind in the frontline trench, waiting to go out in the second wave of attack.

"Get up there, damn you! I'll have no cowards in this battalion. One, two; one, two. Show the Fascists that you mean business. One more push and we'll have them off that ridge!"

Theo was incredulous. Alvah must know that the attack had failed. He'd have needed to take only a quick look through one of the firing apertures to see that no one had gotten anywhere near the enemy line. And yet he was sending more men out to get killed for no reason. Why? Maybe those were his orders from crazy Colonel Copic, but if so, he was carrying them out with enthusiasm. Not like Captain Merriman earlier.

Theo was sure that Alvah had no intention of going over the top himself and sharing Merriman's fate. His hypocrisy was breathtaking, just as it had been in New York when he'd led the strikers into penury, just to raise his profile in the union.

But whoever was in the trench wasn't going quietly. Someone shouted "No!" and another voice yelled "You've got no right!" And then there was suddenly the sound of a pistol shot, and the Fascist guns opened up again, and Theo lay behind Tiny with his face in the dirt, trembling.

His head ached and he couldn't think straight anymore. He was too tired even to be frightened. The cries and the shouts and the gunfire coalesced into a single drumbeat reverberating in his brain. Fainter now as he closed his eyes, feeling his exhaustion pouring over him and carrying him away.

He slept. For how long, he didn't know. Only that when he woke, the sun had disappeared and rain was pouring down on him, soaking him to the skin. Just like in the morning, the weather had changed on a dime, replacing warmth with cold and sunny visibility with a creeping mist. The firing had died away again, and Theo sensed the chance to get back to the trench.

He'd had enough. He couldn't stand to lie out in the rain and mud anymore in his sodden clothes, waiting for a mortar shell to find him. His feet were numb and he had to lean on Tiny's body to get upright, swaying from side to side like a drunk, before he began to stagger back through the shattered olive trees. Each passing moment he expected a bullet, but none came, and soon he was standing again on the sandbag parapet and dropping back down the earth wall to safety.

He'd been to hell and survived the journey, but at what cost?

# 16

## COURT-MARTIAL

A voice was calling Theo's name and a hand was tugging at his arm where he lay, curled up like a fetus in the telephone operator's dugout into which he'd crawled when he got back to the trench. Perhaps it wasn't that dugout, but just looked like it. He didn't know, or care. He just wanted to sleep again so he wouldn't have to think about the dead soldier who was lying a yard or two outside, floating in the mud with the pouring rain pattering a tattoo on his upturned face.

"Go away!" Theo mumbled, closing his eyes again, but the voice was more insistent now, and there were two hands pulling him up and out of the dugout.

He thought for a moment it was Alvah, come to force him back out into no-man's-land, but the voice asked "Theo, are you hurt?" and he knew it was Manny. But Manny like he'd never heard him before—shouting like a madman and digging his hands hard into Theo's shoulders where he had him pinned against the wall of the trench.

"No, I'm not hurt. But I will be in a minute," said Theo, pushing Manny away. He looked like a demented swamp creature, caked in mud from head to toe.

"You've got to help," said Manny, pointing to where Joseph was kneeling beside a canvas stretcher on which Uncle was lying. Uncle's chest was covered in dark blood, and his breath was coming in ragged, gurgling gasps. "We got him this far, but he's heavy and the ground's a fucking quagmire and it's getting worse. We need you, Theo, you hear me?"

Manny's voice rose dangerously, and Theo put his hands up to defend himself in case Manny started trying to manhandle him again. "I hear you," he said. "Okay?"

"Okay," said Manny, exhaling hard.

Theo silently hugged Joseph, and then the three of them picked up the stretcher and set off down the winding communication trench, taking it in turns to be the one on point, carrying the double weight. It was hard going. There was little light left in the band of gray, cloud-filled sky above their heads, and the trench was crowded with other stretcher-bearers and walking wounded, all striving to stay upright as the cold rain poured incessantly down, turning the ground into a slippery bog. Theo felt the shape of something sinking under the pressure of his boot. He stopped, reaching down, and touched the limp arm of a soldier who must have drowned in the mud. He let go because there was nothing to be done. They had to go on.

All around, men were crying and coughing and falling. But Uncle still lived. Each time his chest fell, Theo thought it couldn't rise again. But miraculously it did, and he and Joseph and Manny redoubled their efforts, pushing their way forward, even if it meant shoving other men out of the way.

Near the end, they met an unusually tall soldier standing stock-still in the middle of the trench. Young and strong and not wounded, but with his eyes bulging and unblinking, fastened on some imaginary object that they couldn't see. He had the name **HAL** daubed in muddy capital letters on the front of his helmet.

Manny was at the front and asked him to help with the stretcher, but Hal didn't seem to understand the question, instead seizing hold of Manny's hand and repeating "Iwannagohome, Iwannagohome" over and over again, until Manny gave up on his attempts to free his hand and used his other one to punch the man on the side of the head.

Hal let go then but otherwise it made no difference, and they could hear him continuing his pleading monologue behind them as they resumed their journey: "Iwannagohome, Iwannagohome . . ."

A minute or two later, the crumbling trench walls beside them disappeared, and they emerged out onto a goat path that led precipitously down to the battalion first aid post at the bottom of the slope.

Theo had never seen such a place. It was a tent without walls, garishly illuminated by flickering kerosene lamps. Rain gushed down the sides of its sloping canvas roof and cascaded onto the muddy ground below. Theo looked in through it, as if into a cave through a waterfall. Two surgeons in black rubber aprons were operating at tables set up on the dirt. They had pocket flashlights strapped to their foreheads to help them see, and their exposed arms were bloody up past their elbows. One had an orderly beside him, putting a cigarette in his mouth for short puffs while his fingers continued to work, as if independently of his brain.

All at once, the man he was operating on regained consciousness and bellowed out his pain like an animal. The surgeon stepped back and closed his eyes, swaying from side to side, while orderlies held the man down and injected him with morphine, and when he was quiet again, the surgeon went back to work.

It was a butcher's shop. Beyond the tables, amputated arms and legs were piled inside a dirty white plastic barrel, while lengths of what looked like slimy pink sausages slopped over the side of another. It took Theo a moment to realize that they were intestines, and when he did, he retched and turned away.

Over to the side, the wounded lay on blankets, awaiting triage sorting. Some were crying out in pain or raving, but most, like Uncle, appeared to be unconscious, hovering on the gray hinterland of death. Clouds of cold vapor rose from their wounds. Between operations, the other doctor came over to briefly examine them, pointing an orderly to where they were to be taken. Either over near the piled-up dead because they had no chance of survival, or in a line behind the tables, ready for surgery, or placed straight into one of the waiting mud-spattered ambulance trucks that drove off toward Morata as soon as they had received their full quotient of wounded men to bounce up and down in agony over the potholed roads.

When Uncle's turn came, Manny started shouting at the doctor before he'd even had time to examine the wound.

"He's not going over there with the dead. Not after we brought him all this way. He can't, you hear me?"

That same *"you hear me?"* Manny had shouted at Theo in the trench, as if he still doubted his sensory connection to a world gone mad.

Theo thought that the doctor would have Manny arrested, but instead he smiled. "Hold this," he said, beckoning an orderly to hand Manny a blood bottle as he pulled back Uncle's sleeve and searched for a vein.

The effect of the transfusion was extraordinary. Color flowed back into Uncle's pale face, and he opened his eyes. "Bobby?" he whispered, and then was quiet again as the morphine he'd also been given took hold.

"Put him in the ambulance. There's nothing more I can do for him here," said the doctor after he'd finished cleaning and bandaging the wound. "Maybe he'll make it. Who knows? It's up to them, really, if they want to live. Or die. There's something to be said for both, I suppose," he said quietly, as if to himself, looking around at the horrors with which he was surrounded.

Later, after Uncle had gone, Theo, Manny, and Joseph helped carry the dead out under an overhanging rock where a fire had been made from empty ammunition boxes fed by petrol siphoned from the fuel tank of one of the ambulances.

They watched their comrades burn, and Theo felt himself burning up inside, too, consumed by rage against the men who had done this to them.

He was thinking of the morning when the trench had been crowded instead of empty, when these young men had been alive and he'd had to dodge between them as he ran to deliver the message that would stop the attack, if he could just get it to Captain Merriman in time. It hadn't even occurred to him to doubt that Merriman would give the order to stand down once he knew what had happened on the road. There was no support. The lieutenant had said it would be suicide to go. All he had to do was get to Merriman in time. And he had.

But then the madness had taken over. Copic had refused to listen, and Merriman had given the order to go over the top. *"It's murder, but it's got to be done,"* he'd said. Why? Why had it got to be done? Why did these young men— the best of their generation, who'd given up everything for what they believed in—have to die like this? So uselessly? Burning on the rocks . . .

"Because those were his orders," said Joseph wearily when Theo had finished explaining to them what had happened. "It's the way it works in armies. You have to do what you're told. You can't fight a war otherwise."

"You can't fight a war by committing suicide," said Manny furiously. "Merriman knew those orders were crazy. He knew they were murder and he still went ahead, which makes him a murderer too. The same as Copic and Katz and General fucking Gal."

"Alvah—Katz, I mean. You heard him too?" Theo asked. He'd told his friends about his experience in the morning, but said nothing yet about the afternoon.

"Yeah," said Joseph. "He was forcing people out of the trench when he knew what had happened to the first wave. We heard him from where we were, sending them out. He must have gone all the way down the trench doing it."

"Someone was trying to stop him, and then I heard a shot," said Theo.

"Murderer!" Manny spat out the word with even greater bitterness than before. "We need to do something."

"Do what?" asked Joseph.

"Hold the bastards to account. Make them pay for what they've done."

"Pay! Don't be stupid! Bosses don't pay. But you will, if you carry on. Inciting a mutiny—that's what it's called. You can get shot for that."

"I don't care. It's not right. It's not just. Isn't that what we're here for. Justice?"

Joseph didn't reply, because Manny wasn't looking at him anymore. He was shouting over at the other soldiers standing nearby, their haggard faces illuminated by the firelight. The stench from the burning bodies made them gag, but they wouldn't turn away. As if watching was bearing witness. A matter of honor.

"They didn't need to die, Comrades," Manny told them. "Not one of them. Katz lied. About the planes and the tanks. About the Fascists. They weren't exhausted; they weren't there for the taking. You saw what happened: we couldn't get near them. We never had a chance, and they mowed us down like Iowa corn on harvest day.

"Copic and his buddies knew it was murder, but still they sent us out. Untrained, like lambs to the slaughter. And they'll do it again if we don't stop them. Because they don't care. They've got no sense of responsibility. We're just Yankee trash to them to burn in the yard with the rest of their garbage. Will you accept that? I know I fucking won't."

Manny raised his clenched right fist above his head and began to walk away toward the road, and the others by the fire followed.

Theo would have gone, too, but Joseph took hold of his arm to stop him.

"Don't be a fool," he said. "The Fascists are our enemy, not Copic. No good will come of this. Manny's got a devil inside of him."

"So have I," said Theo angrily. "Let me go!" He knew Joseph was right, but he was enraged just like Manny, and he wanted payback for Uncle and Bobby and Tiny and the young men on the funeral pyre. He needed it. Blood was thumping in his temples, and he couldn't think straight.

He pulled away from Joseph but had gone only a few steps when he heard arguing up ahead.

It was the 2 Company lieutenant ordering the soldiers back to the line. "There's almost no one left in the trench," he said. "If the Fascists counterattack, they'll go straight through to Morata. They'll take the road."

"No they won't. Not in the dark," said Manny defiantly. "It's just a trick. Don't listen to him, boys," he called to the others, and they resumed their march to the rear.

But without Theo. It was the lieutenant's last words that had stopped him. Protecting the road was why they were here. Madrid's survival depended on it. He thought of the great city holding out against all the odds twenty miles to the west. The Lincolns were the heirs of the Internationals who'd fought the Moors through the classrooms of the University City in November and saved the capital. *¡No pasarán!* That was why he had volunteered. To hold the line, not to mount a mutiny.

He nodded to Joseph, and together they followed the lieutenant and the few men he'd gathered back into the communication trench, where the mud had risen even higher than before. Like Passchendaele, Theo thought, remembering his stepfather, who'd fought in mud twenty years before. His hand crept to the rosary in the pouch around his neck, and he felt for a moment as if Andrew was walking by his side.

The trench was a desolate place now, with no more than seventy or eighty soldiers left to defend the line when there had been four hundred in the morning. The Lincolns would have been powerless to resist a counterattack, but none materialized, and after midnight the firing died down to a point where the battlefield was almost quiet.

Theo and Joseph discovered a dry foxhole and took it in turns to sleep, while the other stood sentry on the adjacent fire step. Shadowy figures were moving among the spectral olive trees out in no-man's-land, but it was not the enemy. Men from a Belgian labor battalion were bringing in the dead. They cursed in Flemish as they stumbled with their stretchers in the mud.

They stopped at dawn with their work unfinished, and Theo and Joseph, looking out through the firing aperture, could see more bodies strewn about on the churned-up ground like flotsam left on an exposed beach by an ebbing tide.

"'On the wing of abominations will come one who makes desolate. Even to the full end that is decreed, wrath will be poured out on the desolate,'" said Joseph, murmuring the words as if to himself.

"Who said that?" asked Theo.

"The prophet Daniel. I have seen things in America. Terrible things: fiery crosses and a man of my race hanging from a tree, trussed and turning in the wind, but this . . . I have never seen anything like this before."

"No," said Theo, putting his hand on his friend's shoulder. "Nor I."

Breakfast arrived. Goat chops in gunnysacks and coffee miraculously still hot, and the carriers brought news, too, that Manny and the others who had left the line had been arrested by a French cavalry squadron outside Morata the night before, and were to be court-martialed for desertion in the afternoon.

"Copic wants the death penalty," one of the carriers said grimly, shaking his head. "To set an example."

"You don't know that," Theo burst out angrily. "You're just making it up so it'll sound worse."

"The hell I am," said the carrier, angry now too. "One of our boys overheard him talking about it with the commissar first thing this morning."

"Jesus!" said Theo, stepping back as if he'd received a blow. After all he'd been through, it didn't seem possible that things could get worse, that there could be more killing. But that was what was going to happen unless Copic changed his mind.

"I'm sorry. I shouldn't have said that," he told the carrier, feeling ashamed of his rudeness. "It's just one of the men on trial is my friend. I'm scared for him."

"So you should be," said the carrier, refusing to be mollified. "The colonel's one crazy son of a bitch if you cross him."

And so is Manny, Theo thought. He'll run his mouth off just like he always does, and then Copic will be guaranteed to have him shot.

"I'm going to ask the lieutenant permission to go back and talk to Manny, try and get him to show some remorse. And maybe I can speak for him, too, at the trial if they'll let me," he told Joseph.

"It won't do any good," said Joseph gloomily. "Manny's his own worst enemy. I told him not to go last night, but he wouldn't listen, and I doubt he'll heed you either. He's a born martyr."

"I know, but I still have to try."

"Yes, I can see that. Do you want me to come? I will, if you like."

"No, but thanks for offering. It helps."

The lieutenant was unexpectedly sympathetic. "I'd go myself if I wasn't the only officer left," he said. "Copic should be the one on trial. We've lost close to three hundred men and maybe half of them dead because of what he did. I don't like it that Mandelbaum disobeyed my order, but the court should have the whole picture. Get your friend to eat humble pie and explain what you all went through out there"—the lieutenant pointed out toward no-man's-land—"and maybe Copic will listen. He needs to, or otherwise he'll have a real mutiny on his hands. It's not just the deserters who are angry. The battalion or what's left of it have had enough of his stupidity."

Theo took heart from the lieutenant's words and felt hopeful of success as he retraced his journey of the night before. A labor squad was working to clear and repair the communication trench, and the pyre of the dead beside the casualty clearing station was now a smoking heap of ash onto which boulders were being rolled to form a limestone cairn. Inside the hospital tent, the surgeon who'd treated Uncle lay asleep on his operating table, covered in an old greatcoat.

From the cookhouse, Theo was directed down the road to a cave cut into the hillside where the court-martial was due to take place, but when he got there, he found to his dismay that it had already begun.

Guards had been posted on either side of the jagged stone entrance, and they barred the way when he tried to go inside. Looking past them into the lamplit shadows, Theo could see over a row of heads a man who had to be Colonel Copic sitting alone at an elevated table covered with a green cloth on which he was drumming his fingers. He was in full uniform with a peaked cap, tie, and Sam Browne belt and was staring straight ahead with his lips pursed above his cleft chin, giving him an expression of concentrated venom as he listened to the prosecutor outlining the charges. The defendants, with Manny at the front, were corralled in a tight group on the left side of the cave, surrounded by more guards.

The prosecutor named Manny as the defendants' ringleader and said that he had resisted arrest and had had to be forcibly disarmed. "Mandelbaum stated that he needed his rifle because he intended to teach Colonel Copic a lesson because he was a murderer—"

"He is," interrupted Manny, shouting at the top of his voice, "and so is Commissar Katz and Captain Murderman. You bastards are the ones who should be on trial, not us."

"Silence in court! Silence!" Copic was hammering his table with the butt of his pistol, and one of the guards enforced the colonel's command by punching Manny hard in the stomach. Manny was winded, but as soon as he'd caught his breath, he started yelling again, jabbing his outstretched finger toward Copic: "You lied about the tanks, you lied about the planes! You sent those boys out to die when you knew they had no chance. Half of them untrained, bunched up, not even knowing how to fire their goddamn rifles. You killed them. You're worse than the fucking Fascists!"

Manny's courage was extraordinary. It took Theo's breath away and inspired the other defendants, quiet up until now, to begin stamping their feet in support, until the same guard punched Manny again, in the head this time, cutting off his outburst and knocking him to the ground. When Manny got back up, he was being held by guards on either side and had some kind of gag in his mouth, stopping him from speaking. He was convulsed and struggling for breath.

Terrified that Manny was going to choke on the gag and die, Theo tried to force his way past the guards at the cave entrance to get to his friend, but they threw him back and he landed headfirst on the rocky ground and blacked out.

It was the second time in twenty-four hours that he'd been knocked unconscious, and the pain was even worse than before when he came around. The sky was spinning again, and he was seeing visions. Or so it seemed, because someone who looked like Esmond was leaning down over him, calling his name. He looked like Esmond, but he was dressed like Alvah Katz, in a zipped-up leather jacket with a blue beret on his head and a pistol on his hip. And boots, polished boots, shining in the sunlight . . .

Theo closed his eyes and his stomach lurched, so he opened them again and the Esmond-Alvah person was closer now, splashing cold water on his face, and he was spluttering as he was pulled up into a seated position.

Slowly everything settled into a blurred focus, including Esmond, who clearly wasn't a figment of his imagination. The same bright-blue eyes were staring into his, the same sculpted features, the same ironic smile . . .

"What are you doing here?" Theo asked, and the words came out in a jumble, so he had to repeat them twice before Esmond understood.

"Looking for you," Esmond said. "I returned to Madrid earlier than I expected, and when I heard about the battle, I came out to find you. But then you found me, courtesy of those goons over there." He pointed to the guards over by the cave entrance.

"They're trying my friend. They want to shoot him. You've got to stop it," said Theo, struggling to his feet.

He swayed and would have fallen over if he hadn't caught hold of Esmond's arm. He pulled him close. Esmond was his only hope: he had to make him understand what was happening.

"Manny, my friend," he began, stumbling over his words again, "he's shouting back at them in there and making it worse, because he's angry. We're all angry. They sent us out to die, and half of us did. We didn't stand a chance. No training, no support, no nothing. Your Communists, who you said were so organized, so disciplined—either they don't know what they're doing, or if they do, they're murderers. And now they want to kill—"

"I *said*!" Esmond broke in incredulously. "Have you forgotten that I told you to stay in Oxford? You're the one who insisted on coming out here to play the hero! Don't you dare blame me, Theo!"

Theo swallowed, trying to get control of himself. He needed Esmond, so he shouldn't be accusing him of things. That would just antagonize him, which was stupid. He let go of Esmond's coat and took a step back. "You're right," he said. "I'm sorry. It's just you don't know what we've been through. If you did—"

"But I do know. I've had a full report, and it makes me angry too," said Esmond. "Copic is a disgrace to the party. He's got no military qualifications, and he should never have been appointed. But that doesn't change the fact that he's the colonel of this brigade, which means he's a law to himself out here, and if he wants to shoot deserters, there's nothing I can do about it. Unless—"

Esmond stopped in midsentence, looking not at Theo anymore but over toward the other side of the road, where a tall man in a leather jacket similar to the one he was wearing was barking orders in a harsh-sounding foreign language at an officer in uniform who was standing rigidly to attention in front of him.

Unlike Esmond, the tall man wore no hat over his bald head, and Theo could sense his intimidating power even from fifty yards away. "Who is he?" he asked.

"A general. A Russian one. Calls himself Pablo over here, but better known as 'Tank.' For three reasons—he's built like one, he commands them, and he acts like one if he's crossed. And I'm betting that even someone as militarily ignorant as you probably knows that a general outranks a colonel," said Esmond, talking in that show-off tone Theo remembered him using at Saint Gregory's when something had caused him to be more than ordinarily pleased with his own cleverness.

Theo went rigid, electrified by a sudden surge of hope replacing his previous despair. "Will he help us?" he asked.

"Out of the goodness of his heart? Not a chance. He *likes* executions. But he'll wring Copic's neck if the mood takes him. He just needs a reason . . ." Esmond paused, thinking. "How many men are on trial in there?" he asked, pointing at the cave.

"Ten, maybe. I'm not sure."

"It's enough. Wait here."

Theo watched as Esmond went up to the general and entered into an animated conversation, while the other officer stayed where he was, still not moving a muscle. But whatever Esmond was saying was obviously having an effect on the general, because his hands clenched into fists and his puffy white cheeks flushed, until all at once, he broke away from Esmond and strode across the road to the cave, where the guards saluted and stood aside.

Theo had followed behind the general, and through the entrance opening he could see him advancing on Copic and throwing over his table. Copic got up, holding his pistol, but the general was too quick for him, knocking it out of his hands. Straightaway, he grabbed the colonel by the lapels of his tunic and lifted him bodily off the ground, shaking him like a rag doll. He was obviously strong as an ox because he was able to keep him suspended in the air, and Copic's shifty eyes looked like they were going to burst out of his head.

"*Von! Von!*" the general was shouting in Russian, and everyone in the cave rushed to the exit, pushing Theo back and blocking his view. He called to Manny when he saw him come out, but Manny didn't hear him and ran off down the road with his fellow deserters, waving their fists in the air. This time, however, Theo was relieved to see that Manny was headed toward, not away from, the line. He wanted to follow him, but instead he went back to Esmond, who'd remained on the other side of the road.

"Thank you," he said. "Whatever you said to that general worked like magic. He had Copic up in the air, shaking him. I've never seen anything like it." He started to laugh, picturing the colonel's face. He remembered his martinet voice on the telephone to Merriman. If anyone deserved a five-star humiliation, it was him.

Esmond looked pleased, his expression like that of a circus magician acknowledging the audience's applause for pulling off a spectacular trick in the ring. "I told him two of the defendants had fathers who came from Russia," he said. "Copic is a Yugoslav, so there was no way General Tank was going to put up with that. National pride can be a wonderful thing if deployed in the right way."

Theo felt a surge of gratitude for his friend. "Thank you," he said. "Thank you for saving Manny."

"I'd like to save you too," said Esmond. "Have you still got your passport?"

Theo nodded as his hand went involuntarily to the pouch around his neck. It seemed incredible that it had, like his body, survived all that he had been through unscathed.

"Good," said Esmond. "If you come with me now, I can get you on a boat in two days. You can be back in Oxford before the end of term with everything forgiven."

Theo gasped. The offer threw him into confusion. For a moment the thought of Oxford captivated him. He longed for the quiet cloisters, the slow-flowing rivers, the old books open under green reading lamps in wood-paneled libraries—all the polar opposite of the filth and the horror and the dreadful danger of the battlefield. But he couldn't go. He knew that as soon as he started thinking about it. He couldn't abandon his comrades and he couldn't turn his back on Spain. Or on Maria, however much she might dislike the Internationals. He was fighting to prove himself to her and to himself, and he'd fail if he turned back now.

"Thanks for offering, but I can't," he told Esmond. "I have to see this through."

"Why?" Esmond demanded angrily. It wasn't the answer he'd been expecting. "Your battalion's been destroyed by its incompetent commanders and Madrid's safe, however much Copic wants to pretend it isn't. There's nothing left for you to do here."

"So I can safely go back to Oxford and train to be your spy. Is that what you're saying?"

"We have an agreement, remember?" said Esmond coldly. All his earlier friendliness had disappeared.

"Yes, I remember, but that's about what happens when I go back, and I'm not ready to do that yet. It's my choice and I'm staying here, whether you like it or not."

"Well, then you're on your own. I'm not going to be here next time this happens. And it will. Believe me. You're a fool, Theo."

"Maybe, but I'm my own fool. Do you remember that day in Carborough when we came out of the cinema after watching those newsreels of Germany, and you told me that my blood will tell me that I can't stand aside and do nothing? Well, that's what it's telling me now."

"It's not your blood you should listen to. It's your brain."

"It's you who taught me," said Theo. "That's what I'm trying to say. Too well, maybe. To go to Olympia, to try to make a difference in the world. Your words. You can't change the lesson now."

Esmond stared at Theo and then unexpectedly smiled. "Checkmate!" he said softly, and put out his hand both to acknowledge defeat and to say goodbye. "Chess is an excellent game," he said. "Very Russian. We must start playing it together. I'll have the pieces ready next time we meet."

Theo took his friend's hand and pulled him close before letting him go. "I wish . . ." he began and then stopped, because everything had been said that they could say. The die was cast.

Esmond walked away, but then stopped after he'd taken only a few paces, pointing toward the cave entrance where Alvah Katz was standing on his own, looking at them intently. He must have been somewhere out of sight during the court-martial, because Theo hadn't seen him in the cave.

"Who's that?" Esmond asked.

"Alvah Katz. Our commissar."

"He looks like he knows you from somewhere."

"He does. He led the strike at my father's factory that forced him out of business. I told you about what happened years ago."

"I know you did. I remember everything you said. Did he know you were here? Before now, I mean?"

"I don't think so. But I knew about him. He gave us a speech when we got here, and then I heard him forcing men out of the trench after the first attack, when I was out in no-man's-land. What he did was worse than Copic. He was there, not at the end of a telephone."

Esmond looked over toward Alvah and then back at Theo, as if weighing a decision. "Stay there!" he said, and walked over to the cave entrance and began talking to Alvah. Neither of them raised their voices, so Theo couldn't hear what they were saying, and their conversation didn't go on for very long before Esmond came back.

"What did he say?" Theo asked.

"I told him to leave you alone. I think he will, but you should still be careful. Don't draw attention to yourself, like your friend. And watch your back. The Fascists are not your only enemies in this place."

He hugged Theo briefly again and walked away down the road, and when Theo looked back toward the cave, Alvah was gone too.

# 17

## MANNY AND ALVAH

It rained in March and in April too. Endless rain, driven by cold winds off the Guadarrama Mountains, filling the crumbling trenches with mud that the Lincolns could never finish bailing out. It got into everything: their boots, their blankets, their food, spreading a viscous misery.

Even without the contamination of filth, the cookhouse stews would have poisoned them. Galvanized washtubs were sent up every day, filled with a cold gray fluid in which shriveled potatoes, dried beans, and bits of rubbery mule meat floated on a slick of rancid olive oil. Often there were maggots too. Only copious amounts of wine and anis enabled the soldiers to force the food down their unwilling throats. Alcohol was the only commodity that was never in short supply, and they tortured themselves late into the night with drunken fantasies about rib eye steaks and chicken à la king being served to them on gigantic dinner plates in warm New York diners far away from the Jarama Valley.

Dysentery and malnutrition quickly reduced them to stick figures on which their ragged uniforms hung like scarecrow clothes, infested with lice that bit them mercilessly, raising itchy red welts on their dirty skin. Every so often an unlucky one among them caught a bullet from a Fascist sniper as he staggered to the foul, overflowing latrines and was cremated behind the lines, accompanied by a desultory rendition of "The Internationale." Death had become matter-of-fact after the massacre at the end of February.

Wretchedness drove some of them to despair. One soldier's suicide attempt was foiled when the olive tree branch that he was trying to hang himself from snapped in two. Another shot off his foot instead of his toe in an attempt to be invalided out and ended up having his leg amputated.

The Lincolns had begun to receive letters from those of their comrades who had survived their wounds. Uncle, miraculously, was one of them. In April, all the American sick were moved to a new hospital at Villa Paz, fifty miles to the southeast. Before the war, it had been the summer palace of the last king's aunt, the Infanta María de la Paz de Bourbon, and was surrounded, according to Uncle, by romantic overgrown gardens in which nightingales sang in the trees and streams flowed, filled with exotic fish. There was a tiled swimming pool screened by dark-green cypresses, and pretty American nurses in starched white uniforms attended to their patients' every need.

Villa Paz soon became a Shangri-La in the minds of the soldiers at the front, who conveniently forgot about the appalling injuries that were keeping their comrades there. The fate of the first soldier to try shooting off his toe didn't deter several others from attempting the same trick.

Once in a while the Lincolns experienced a rare interlude of happiness when the sound truck drove up from Morata and they danced, swaying in the moonlight, to recordings of "Night and Day" and "Stardust." But the truck's usual function was to broadcast surrender harangues across no-man's-land at deafening volume, to which the Fascists responded with even louder shellfire that pulverized the already crumbling trenches. The soldiers lay on the ground during these exchanges with their hands clamped over their ears, praying for the truck to be hit, which, of course, it never was.

Behind the frontline trenches, the ground dipped below the line of fire and the soldiers built ramshackle shelters with planks and corrugated iron, just like the Hoovervilles that Theo remembered from New York. They called the lanes between them names like *Broadway* and *Union Square*, and a sign to the cookhouse read **HELL'S KITCHEN** above a pointing arrow.

Farther back, there were Ping-Pong tables and a football field where they played brutal matches in the mud. Games were a distraction from the squalor and boredom of their days. In the shacks, they gambled astronomical amounts on blackjack and poker, and came to blows when they lost, forgetting in the intensity of the moment that their money wasn't real.

Theo learned chess. He remembered some of the moves from the afternoons he'd spent with his father watching the hustlers in Washington Square when he was a boy, and Manny taught him the rest. Soon he was winning, much to Manny's fury. He played a waiting game and profited from Manny's impetuous mistakes as he rushed his pieces forward in all-out attacks that were doomed to fail.

Theo wanted to be ready for the game that Esmond had promised to play with him at their next meeting, but he heard nothing from his friend and wondered if Esmond was carrying through on his threat to wash his hands of him after Theo's refusal to return to Oxford and fulfill their bargain. He thought often of that moment outside the cave when he'd decided to stay at the front. It wasn't that he regretted his decision, just that he wished he still had the choice.

He felt paradoxically that he'd left Spain behind, even though he was sitting square in the center of the country. He met no Spaniards, and the Fascists he'd come to fight remained invisible behind their rusting wire at the top of the hill. It was as if he had reached a dead end: his world had shrunk to a square mile of mud and filth inhabited by a few hundred demoralized Americans, and out in the open among the Hoovervilles he was gripped by a suffocating claustrophobia. He needed to run, but there was nowhere to run to.

The Lincolns were prisoners in all but name. No leave was granted, and all requests to return home were denied. Rumors were rife that André Marty's men were watching the American consulates in Valencia and Barcelona and that arrested deserters were being sent to Camp Lukács, a new, brutally run prison on a windswept plain outside Albacete from which inmates regularly disappeared, never to be heard of again. Uncle had been right: no one had seen fit to tell the volunteers before they embarked that it was a one-way ticket they were being offered, and that what they had freely given they would not be allowed to take back. Now that it was too late, the soldiers bitterly regretted handing over their passports, and Theo was grateful that he had kept his, never taking the pouch from off his neck, which also contained Maria's lock of hair, his money, and the rosary that he credited with keeping him alive.

Manny knew why they were being kept at the front, and he made sure to tell everyone the reason. It was simple: Gal and Copic and Katz didn't want anyone to find out what they had done. And especially not the new American volunteers who were arriving every day in Albacete after following the now-well-trodden goat paths over the Pyrenees. They had been formed into a separate George Washington Battalion and told that the Battle of Jarama had been a glorious victory that had saved Madrid from the Fascists. Months passed, and the well-fed Washingtons remained at their training base, kept apart from the ragged, half-starved Lincolns, shivering in their waterlogged trenches with their stories left untold.

Many among the Lincolns would have liked to forget the horrors of the February battle, but Manny would not allow them to. He had appointed himself the conscience of the battalion, and every passing day increased his sense of outrage. The Fascists still fired their guns, and their snipers picked off soldiers foolish enough to show their heads above the trench parapet, but they made no attempt to attack, and Manny took this as proof that there had never been a threat to the Madrid–Valencia road. According to him, the Lincolns' commanders had known this perfectly well, but they'd needed the threat as a justification for the insane plan of attack that they had devised to impress the party bosses in Albacete. They had the blood of the dead on their hands, and it was the responsibility of the living to make them pay for it.

It was hard to make Colonel Copic or General Gal pay, because they remained judiciously out of sight at their headquarters behind the line, but Commissar Katz didn't have that luxury and wouldn't have taken advantage of it even if he had. He took his duties as battalion commissar seriously and didn't appear to believe he had done anything wrong.

Theo found Alvah to be just as inflexible and pedantic as he had been in New York, perhaps even more so. He insisted on saluting and roll calls and rifle inspections and punished infractions with menial labor details that the men bitterly resented, and he required everyone to attend the political meetings that he held on a weekly basis for each company in the battalion. These were an opportunity for him to hold forth to a captive audience about the unstoppable advance of world Communism and the need to maintain the high standards that the party demanded of its members, emphasizing his points with jabs of his pipe—a new affectation that Manny said he had adopted as a homage to the chief pipe smoker of them all in the Kremlin.

"But you seem to forget that we're not all Communists," Manny told Alvah, interrupting one of these harangues. "There's a few of us here that can still think for ourselves and know when we're being lied to. Because that's what's happening when Colonel Copic says our buddies died with their right fists clenched like good Communists, and that we were throwing grenades at the Fascist trenches like professional baseball pitchers when nobody got anywhere near them. Here, you can read it for yourself. It's one bullshit lie after another!"

Manny held up *Our Fight*, the brigade newspaper, jabbing at the offending article with his finger, but Alvah refused to look at it.

"The colonel is trying to keep up morale," Alvah insisted. "And you're trying to lower it, Mandelbaum. That's what's happening here. And it won't be tolerated, I can promise you that," he added acidly.

"So what are you going to do? Murder me, like you did those poor saps you sent over the top when you knew the attack had failed? I tell you one thing you lot have got right: this outfit's name. We've been assassinated, just like poor old Abe Lincoln."

Everyone laughed except Alvah, who put Manny on a charge and stalked away, enraged that his authority had been so easily undermined.

Next day, Alvah sent Easey Goldstein to summon Theo to battalion headquarters for a talk. Since the battle, this had been moved back to a more permanent location in a requisitioned house on the outskirts of Morata from which the Fascist-sympathizing owners had fled at the start of the war. Liking privacy, Alvah had taken over a summerhouse at the end of the house's long, narrow garden to use as his office.

Theo followed Easey as he limped down the communication trench and experienced that same disturbing combination of repulsion and fascination that he always felt in his presence. He couldn't take his eyes away from Easey's oversize left boot as it cumbersomely rose and fell. It was ridiculous that he'd been passed fit for service. Alvah must have leaned heavily on the brigade doctors to let him through.

"What does the commissar want to talk to me about?" Theo asked, but Easey didn't respond until Theo tapped him on the shoulder, feeling immediately that same repugnance that physical contact with Easey always inspired in him.

"How the fuck should I know?" said Easey, wheeling suddenly around, so that they were standing face-to-face, and Theo was inches away from Easey's mean little eyes in the big moon of his face.

Easey stared at Theo, as if sizing him up, and then leaned close, put two stubby fingers up to Theo's temple, and pulled an imaginary trigger while squeezing his twisted lips together to simulate a popping sound.

Theo recoiled in shock, letting out a sharp breath. His hands were shaking, and Easey was looking down at them and laughing his high-pitched, hyena-like laugh. "Bye, bye, Daddy!" he squeaked triumphantly. "Bye, bye!"

"Fuck you, Easey," Theo shouted. The words were utterly inadequate to the hatred he felt at that moment. He'd liked to have killed Easey, but he knew he was no match for him, so he pushed past him instead and took off running down the road to Morata, which they'd now reached. There was something sick and rotten inside Easey that Theo was sure would infect him, too, if he didn't get away from him that instant.

Alvah was more friendly. He told Theo to sit down in a chair opposite his, and poured him a glass of water from a decanter on his desk, which Theo drank down greedily.

"You want some more?" asked Alvah, amused.

"Sure," said Theo, holding out his glass.

"Have you been running? Is that why you're so thirsty?"

"It just tastes good. The water we get comes up in petrol cans," said Theo, anxious to avoid any reference to his encounter with Easey. He'd need a gallon of fresh spring water to wash the taste of that experience out of his mouth.

"I do know about your running prowess, in case you were wondering," said Alvah with the self-satisfied air of a man who thinks he knows everything.

"How?" asked Theo, surprised. Perhaps the 2 Company lieutenant had mentioned it in his report on the battle, but it didn't seem likely.

"I was one of the organizers of the team that the party sent to the Barcelona Olympiad. So, naturally, I received a report when the athletes returned home. Coach Booker must have thought highly of your talent to add you to the squad."

"I guess so," said Theo, remembering the extremely low opinion Booker had had of Alvah. *"Puffed up with that nasty, superior-looking smile wrapped around his gills"* was the phrase he'd used, and Theo thought it a perfect description of Alvah now as he sat puffing on his pipe and looking pleased with himself.

"Was it in Barcelona that you met Esmond de Lisle?" Alvah asked. His pale eyes were fixed on Theo, belying the casual manner in which he'd asked the question.

"No, we were at school together in England."

"I see. And you were close friends?"

"Friends. Yes," said Theo, keeping his answers as short as possible. He felt that Alvah already knew quite enough about his life without adding unnecessarily to his stockpile of information.

"Well, he clearly thinks you're close. I hardly think he would have warned me not to harm a hair on your head if you were just acquaintances," said Alvah, showing his first signs of impatience.

"Why would you want to harm me?" Theo asked, turning the question around. He felt a sudden rush of gratitude to Esmond for his protection, superseding the doubts he'd been harboring about his friend in recent weeks.

"I don't," said Alvah. "But I think you may be bearing a grudge against me because of what happened to your father, and that would be mistaken. You may not believe me, but I grieved when he died. He had been like a father to me, too, but then the Depression came, and I had to stand up for the other workers in the factory. There was no one else to help them. He was paying them starvation wages."

Theo was aware of Alvah watching him as he talked, trying to gauge his reaction to what he was saying. But Theo was determined not to respond, keeping his eyes fixed on a photograph of Stalin hanging on the wall behind Alvah's chair. It was hard to do because each sentence Alvah spoke dredged up the past like the wreck of a ship rising slowly from the deep, causing him an exquisite pain.

It made it worse that Alvah had cleverly dressed up his argument in partial truths. Theo remembered Frank telling him how his father had loved Alvah because Alvah allowed him to dream, and he remembered, too, the shame he'd felt in the factory when the impoverished workers looked at him with hatred because they identified him with their skinflint employer. But it was also true that Theo's father had paid them starvation wages because he couldn't afford any more, and that Alvah knew this and had exploited their rage for his own selfish ends.

Theo no longer thought that Alvah had killed his father. He had certainly played a part in driving him to despair, but Theo had come to believe that his father had to take responsibility for his suicide. It was Michael Sterling, not Alvah Katz, who had put the gun in his mouth and pulled the trigger. He had had a choice, and he had opted to abandon his wife and son and leave them in penury. The wound to Theo's psyche was profound, and he could feel the hurt as Alvah's reminders pressed down on the protective cyst he had grown around it. But he wasn't going to give Alvah the satisfaction—or the advantage—of showing him what he really felt. Out of sight in his pockets, he balled his hands into tight fists and dug his nails into the flesh of his palms, using the pain to keep control of his emotions.

"It was a long time ago," he said in as neutral a tone as he could muster. "Grudges help nobody."

Alvah waited, anticipating that Theo might say more, but then nodded, as if accepting that this part of their conversation had gone as far as it could. "I'm glad to hear you say that," he said. "Glad that we've been able to clear the air. But it wasn't just on your account that I asked you here. I need your help. You are friends with Mandelbaum, are you not?"

"Yes."

"Close friends? Like you are with Esmond de Lisle?" he asked with a smile.

Theo nodded. Alvah knew the answer, so there was no point in denying it.

"He does bear a grudge against me. More hate than grudge, in fact. He is whipping up resentment against me among the men and making it difficult for me to do my job. For obvious reasons, I can't allow that to continue. I'm sure you can see that?"

"I don't know. It's not my business," said Theo guardedly.

"But I want you to make it your business. I want you to get him to stop."

"I can't. Manny does what he wants. That's who he is. He won't let anyone tell him what to do."

"Which is the root of the problem, isn't it? You can't run an army if you can't give orders. We might as well surrender tomorrow. Surely you can see that?"

"I guess so." Theo felt outmaneuvered. Alvah was right, but Manny was too. Alvah shouldn't be the battalion commissar. He'd as good as murdered those men he'd sent out into no-man's-land. But unlike Manny, Theo didn't want to fight him over it, just as he didn't want to fight him over his father. What was done was done. The men were dead, and Theo was finding life on the front line hard enough already without making it worse for himself.

"Just try and get him to see reason," said Alvah. "That's all I'm asking."

"How?"

"Tell him it won't do him any good to carry on the way he is. Tell him that my bite is worse than my bark. Your friend, Lisle, says I can't touch a hair on your head, but I can cut all Mandelbaum's hair off if the mood takes me. And more besides. All with the colonel's backing. He has no time for American troublemakers, especially Mandelbaum."

"So why don't you then?" Theo asked. He'd often wondered why Copic had left Manny alone since the court-martial debacle.

"We don't want to turn him into a martyr," said Alvah, solving the mystery. "That's the last thing any of us need when we're trying to hold the line with a depleted, demoralized battalion. I'll leave him alone if he leaves me alone. That isn't much to ask, is it?"

"I guess not," said Theo. He felt uneasy, as if he was compromising himself in some way. Following logic to a place he didn't want to go.

"So you'll talk to him? For his own good?"

"I'll try."

"Excellent," said Alvah, getting up from his chair and putting out his hand.

Theo felt he had no choice but to shake it, but as soon as he'd done so, he was seized with regret, feeling like he'd walked into a trap from which he could not now escape.

At the door, Alvah called him back.

"It's quite the coincidence, you and me ending up here, isn't it? Far away from home, after all this time?"

Theo nodded, wondering what was coming next.

"Superstitious people might say that fate has drawn us together for a reason. But not me. Communism has taught me to be rational and not starry-eyed. Chance is chance, however great the odds. I suggest you take the same approach, Theodore."

Alvah smiled and reached for his pipe. "That'll be all," he said. "Close the door behind you."

Theo walked back to the front line in a state of confusion. He felt like a man who had arrived at a destination he hadn't intended reaching without knowing how he got there. He'd taken a wrong turn somewhere along the way, and now it was too late to go back.

The last thing he wanted to do was to help Alvah, but he couldn't let Manny put a noose around his neck without trying to stop him. He'd heard enough about detention camps and disappearances to take Alvah's veiled threats seriously. His first instinct was to come clean and tell Manny what Alvah had said, but he quickly realized that this would just make Manny more defiant. To stand any chance of success, he had to persuade him that it would be in his own interest to stop his agitation, even if that meant effectively colluding with Alvah behind Manny's back. In this case, the end justified the means.

He did his best. He told Manny that his one-man quest for justice might be brave, but that it was never going to succeed, and he warned him that all he would achieve would be to add another name to the list of the dead. But all his arguments hit a brick wall.

"I've fought injustice all my life, wherever I've found it," Manny told him vehemently. "I've been beaten and kicked and jailed all the way from Brooklyn to Detroit and back again, and I never once gave up. You can't. You've got to get up, dust yourself off, and go back on the picket line until the bosses listen. *Organize!* That's what Joe Hill said, even if you get killed doing it, like he did. So, when I see injustice here in this battalion—rank injustice, worse than I've ever seen before anywhere back home—do you think I'm going to say 'Fine, go ahead, Mr. Copic, go ahead Mr. Katz, feel free to kill us and imprison us and tell us lies and treat us like animals. You're Communists, not capitalists, and so that makes it all right!'? Is that really what you want me to say? Because if it is, then you're not my friend, Theo, and I don't care if you saved my life in those fucking mountains!"

Theo didn't know how to respond. He remembered how he'd admired the pickets outside his father's factory who'd come back the second day after being beaten to the ground by Marty Meagle's Pinkerton goons on the first. Refusing to give up, just like Manny. If you were oppressed, you resisted. You stood up for what was right, in the same way that the beautiful girl in the evening gown had stood in the crowd at Olympia, waiting to be attacked by Mosley's thugs. What courage! Standing up was the basis on which he'd learned to live his life. It was why he'd volunteered for Spain. So how could he argue with Manny for doing just that? And yet he was sure no good would come of it. Alvah was ruthless. He'd deal with Manny if he had to. Martyr or no martyr. And Theo had lost too many friends already without losing another . . .

He stayed tongue-tied while Manny shook his head in disgust and went back to his half-finished bottle of wine, and to Theo's surprise—and Manny's too—it was Joseph who spoke up and carried on the argument:

"We came here to fight the Fascists, the last I heard," he said. "But you don't give them a mention, do you, Manny? It's the Communists you seem to be after."

"They're the ones oppressing us. They got half this battalion killed for no reason, and they don't want anyone to know about it. That's as good a reason to go after them as I can think of."

"Our comrades were killed attacking the enemy, which is what we came here to do. I agree that we didn't get the support we needed, but—"

"They lied about it. Through their teeth."

"You don't know that. Maybe Copic was promised tanks and planes and then the Russians changed their minds and wouldn't give them to him."

"Then he should've called off the attack."

"Maybe. I'm not saying he got it right, but his intention was to drive the Fascists off the hilltop, whereas you seem to think that we shouldn't try to attack them at all if they don't attack us, which makes me wonder what you think we're doing here in the first place. That's all."

"Fuck you, Joseph!" said Manny furiously, throwing his bottle over so hard that it smashed on the ground, spilling the last of the red wine out onto the dirt. "Copic knew we didn't stand a chance. Just like Katz did in the trench afterward when he was sending those poor bastards out. Half of us were untrained, for God's sake. Didn't even know how to fire our goddamn rifles. Remember that? But they didn't care. And it seems like you don't, either, the way you're making excuses for them. Why's that, Joseph, eh? Because you're a Communist, too, like them, doing their bidding? Is that it?"

Manny was half drunk and beside himself with rage. Theo hadn't seen the extent of it until Manny got on his feet, swaying from side to side. He thought Manny was going to attack Joseph, but instead he rushed over to Joseph's pack and began pulling his possessions out of the pockets. A photograph of a young Black couple taken in a turn-of-the-century studio somewhere, dressed up in their Sunday best, he standing, she sitting and looking earnestly into the camera—Joseph's parents, perhaps; a clothbound Bible much the worse for wear with a cross stamped on the front; letters in thin wrinkled envelopes; a comb missing several teeth . . .

It was an outrage, a violation of an unwritten rule. You didn't touch another man's pack. Because that was all the privacy the soldiers had in this wretched place. Theo couldn't understand why Joseph was just standing and watching, not doing anything to defend his property, but that didn't mean he was going to stand idly by and let Manny get away with it. He felt as angry as Manny, suddenly. Furious with him for not listening, for causing trouble when life was so hard already. Why did he think he was the only one with a conscience?

He rushed at Manny, grabbing his arm and forcing him to let go of the haversack. But it was too late. Manny had already found what he was looking for and was holding it above his head, out of Theo's reach, for everyone to see. A small card with a stamp and a number naming Joseph Freeman as a member of the Communist Party of the USA.

"See!" Manny shouted. "I knew it. You're one of them."

"So are most of us here," said Joseph quietly. "And proud of it too."

"Proud! You've got to be fucking kidding me. Ashamed—that's what you should be! You and Copic and Katz and the rest of you, worshipping at the feet of that bastard Stalin while he murders anyone who gets in his way. In Russia and here too."

He stared at Joseph, who steadily returned his gaze, saying nothing. Theo was impressed by Joseph's refusal to be provoked, and perhaps Manny was, too, because he lowered his arm and allowed Theo to take the membership card and replace it with Joseph's other possessions in the haversack, which he returned to its owner.

Manny sat down sullenly, and the silence continued for at least a minute before Joseph began to talk, lifting a curtain on a world that Theo had never known. "You're wrong if you think I worship anyone," he said. "I lost my faith when my father died, and I'm not fool enough to replace Christ Jesus with Stalin or anyone else. All men have feet of clay, as the good book tells us. But I do know that Stalin is the only one trying to help the Republic, while Britain and France and FDR sit on their hands and do nothing—or worse than nothing, letting Hitler and Mussolini wage war without lifting a finger to stop it. The

Soviet Union put rifles in our hands, tanks on the ground, planes in the sky. And whatever you want to say about them, these brigades were organized by the Comintern, and they've saved Madrid."

Theo nodded. What Manny had said about their own experience was true, but the fact remained that there was a wider picture that needed to be remembered too. The Communists were the only ones helping the Republic, and without them the war would probably already have been lost. That mattered, and Joseph was right to point it out.

And he hadn't finished. It was as if he'd listened to Manny's rage and bluster for long enough and was now determined to set the record straight. "You're a white man, Manny," he said, "and so it doesn't matter to you that the Communist Party is the only political organization in America that's trying to help my people. Why should it? Your unions that you fight for on those picket lines you're so proud of won't allow black members to join because they say we're stealing white men's jobs. Truth is, nobody wants us except the Communists. When landlords throw our furniture out on the street, they take it back up the stairs. When they turn off the gas and the electricity, the Communists turn it back on. When the white police arrest us for crimes we didn't commit, the party hires the best lawyers to defend us. It saved the Scottsboro Boys from the chair when no one else was going to, even though everyone in the state of Alabama knew those girls were lying. The party has made it so the whole country knows now that a Black man can't vote or sit on a jury in the Jim Crow South. And when the lynch mob comes for us in the middle of the night, they try to protect us. Gratitude—that's why I carry that card. Gratitude!"

"And I wouldn't be seen dead with it," said Manny, getting up and walking away.

It was springtime now. Carpets of crimson poppies covered the gray dirt, and fast-growing grapevines flowered on the trench parapets. The blasted olive trees in no-man's-land, which had seemed no better than deadwood in February, sprouted silvery leaves, and the soldiers had to go out with wire cutters at night to prune them back so that they wouldn't lose their view of the Fascist trenches. Once, they met a party of enemy soldiers who had been sent out for the same purpose, and the two groups scuttled away from each other in the darkness. There was no appetite for battle on either side and the front remained quiet, but the Lincolns continued to be denied leave and their discontent grew with every passing day.

It was fertile ground for Manny to sow the seeds of the mutiny that seemed to be his objective. Each petty frustration and irritation were grist to his mill. When letters didn't arrive, he told his comrades that they were being intercepted at Albacete by André Marty's censors, who were stealing the packs of Lucky Strike sent from home, leaving them to smoke the disgusting Spanish "pillowslips" that crumbled into flaky dust as soon as they were lit. Likewise, he suggested that their own letters were being kept at Albacete, too, to stop the truth about what had happened in the February battle from leaking out. Above all, he stoked their resentment against callous commanders who were living in the lap of luxury at brigade headquarters and taking off for the nightlife of Madrid and Albacete whenever the mood took them, while the Lincolns were left to rot in their trenches.

He continued to mock Alvah at every opportunity, glorying in the endless punishments that were inflicted upon him as a result, and the discontented soldiers rallied behind him and treated him like a hero. A week after their first conversation, Alvah called Theo aside to remonstrate, but he had to reluctantly accept that there was nothing Theo could do to restrain his friend.

The atmosphere had become so toxic that Alvah stopped holding political meetings, dealing only with Communist soldiers whose loyalty he could count on. One of these was Joseph, who had been promoted to sergeant at the same time that Oliver Law, the Black commander of the machine-gun section, had been made battalion commander.

"They're using you, you know that, Joe, don't you?" said Manny venomously after watching Joseph have his photograph taken with Law for the brigade newspaper.

"Sure, I do," said Joseph equably. "It makes the brigade look good back home to have Black men in command, but it's a red-letter day for us too. A first in our history. It shows what can happen if we're given the same chance as everyone else."

"It makes you an Uncle Tom. That's what it does," said Manny viciously and stepped back, exultant, when he saw that he had finally provoked Joseph into losing his temper.

"Hit me, Joe! I know you want to," Manny taunted, pointing to his chin, and Theo thought for a moment that Joseph was going to. His fists were clenched, but then he shook his head and Theo heard him say softly, as if to himself as he turned away, "Get thee behind me, Satan."

Joseph was right, Theo thought. It was as if Manny had become possessed by a demon. He'd changed unrecognizably from the free spirit brimming with curiosity and humor that Theo had met on the train in France. He never talked anymore about his Jewish grandmother or his life riding the rails from state to state. His focus had narrowed to the width of the Jarama trenches and his rage against those he held responsible for the massacre out in no-man's-land. The commanding officers and the Communist Party they represented had become the enemy, taking the place of the invisible Fascists at the top of the hill, and all he thought about was how to make them pay for their crimes. The fact that the criminals continued in command while selling the lie that the suicidal defeat had been a glorious victory filled him with an unbearable frustration that gnawed at his mind, driving him to the brink of madness. He used ever-increasing amounts of alcohol to dull the pain, starting his drinking when he woke up and not stopping until he finally collapsed into sleep in the early hours, but it served only to accelerate his mental disintegration and fuel his burgeoning paranoia. Anyone who wasn't with him was against him. He became suspicious and hostile whenever Theo renewed his efforts to persuade him to be less confrontational for his own good, and he treated Joseph as if he was Alvah Katz's mouthpiece.

It was as if he had a death wish, Theo thought. He was leaving Alvah with no choice but to move against him, regardless of the consequences, and within days that was exactly what happened.

Early in May, Alvah summoned the Lincolns to a meeting and told them that the government had suppressed a treasonous rebellion in Barcelona by Anarchists and Trotskyites belonging to the POUM—a dissident Marxist party opposed to Stalin. Hundreds had died in the fighting, but government troops had been rushed in from Valencia and were now in control of the streets.

"Yes, you should be angry," he said, looking around at the soldiers' shocked faces. "Here you are, risking your lives to defend the Republic while those you are trying to defend stab you in the back. They are in the pay of Franco. Now, more than ever, we must redouble our vigilance. These spies and saboteurs aren't just in Barcelona; they're here too. In this battalion. And we must root them out. Root them out, I say!"

Alvah paused, casting his eyes up and down the ranks as he allowed his words to sink in. Theo sensed a new steeliness and determination in his demeanor, as if he was executing the first steps of a carefully laid plan to reimpose his authority.

"It's not just physical sabotage that we must guard against, men," he went on. "These Trotskyites are trained to sow disunity and discontent. They make secret reports to the Fascists about our morale, and when they say it's dropped low enough, then Franco will know to attack. Remember, we are the Republic's front line of defense. Behind us is the road, and if the enemy captures that, then Madrid will fall. The stakes could not be higher. Watch! Listen! And if you find out anything suspicious, come and tell me and I will deal with it. There will be no half measures. I promise you that."

Later that day military policemen searched the trenches and shacks. Nothing was found, but word circulated that they were looking for a radio transmitter that was being used to send coded messages to the enemy.

"How are we supposed to send these messages? That's what I'd like to know," Manny said to Theo incredulously when the MPs had passed on, leaving the two of them alone in the section of the trench that it was their turn to guard that afternoon. "None of us speak the lingo, except you, and you're too honest to be a spy. Couldn't tell a lie to save your life, could you, old buddy?"

Theo shook his head. He wasn't paying much attention to what Manny was saying, because his thoughts were focused on Barcelona. Alvah had said hundreds were dead, and Theo was terrified that Maria might be one of them. He'd always thought he'd know, by some sixth sense, if something happened to her, but then he remembered her standing in the back of the flatbed truck as it sped past him up the Ramblas on the day of the army rebellion the previous summer, headed for the battle in the Plaça de Catalunya. She was fearless, and nothing would have stopped her fighting to save the revolution that she cared about so passionately. But that didn't mean she hadn't survived and gone back into hiding. So much was down to luck when bullets started flying. Some hit, some missed. He'd learned that from his own experience.

The not knowing was what was unbearable. He wanted to desert, to run back past the cookhouse and Morata and hitch rides down the highway until he got to Barcelona and could begin searching for Maria through the foul back alleys of Chinatown, just as he had before. Perhaps he would find her this time. Perhaps Primitivo and Carlos would be gone, and he and Maria could escape to start a new life together far away from war and revolution. But he knew all the time that he was building castles in the air. Maria would never leave, and he wouldn't either. He was gifted with unusual courage when it came to doing what he thought was right, but that also made it impossible for him to run away from what he'd signed up to.

He looked up and saw that Manny was watching him. "What?" he said, backing away from the scrutiny. He wanted to think about Maria, but he didn't want to talk about her. Not to Manny, not to anyone.

"Just that I reckon you and I are about the only ones in the battalion who are on the side of those Anarchists right now," said Manny quietly.

"What makes you say that?" asked Theo, more interested now. He'd picked up on the change in Manny's voice. Thoughtful and without the usual belligerence, as if Alvah's speech and the search for the radio might have sobered him up.

"You talked about them before the battle, when we were telling each other our memories. Remember?"

"I remember your grandmother's billowing breasts," said Theo, and they both laughed.

"And Uncle singing," said Manny. "I miss him. Which is crazy, I know, when he was only with us for such a short time. But he understood this place. He could see through Gal and Copic and Katz. He knew they were con artists, and he'd know what they're up to now, too, if he was here."

"What are you saying?"

"That they're taking us for a ride. Katz is using what's happened in Barcelona to get the men on his side when he knows full well that no one has got a radio transmitter or is sending any messages. He's manipulating them, just like the Communists have manipulated the Anarchists. They've provoked them into this so-called rebellion. I'd bet my bottom dollar on it."

"Why would they do that?"

"Because they're the ones who stand to gain from it being put down. Stalin's trying to take over the Republic from within, so the Anarchists are his enemy. He calls himself a revolutionary, but he hates revolution, just like he hates freedom. Power is what he wants. Always power. And no one can stop him getting it because he's the one supplying the arms. The Republic needs him to survive, and so they've done a deal with the Devil. And we all know what happens when you do that."

Theo nodded. Manny's analysis made sense. Maria had said exactly the same about the Communists in February, before there was any fighting in Barcelona. She'd told him they wanted power and intended to destroy the revolution, and now they were doing precisely that.

And behind the Communists was Stalin, sitting in his office in the Kremlin, reading reports and giving orders, manipulating people and events to suit his own ends. Puffing on his pipe, indifferent to the vast suffering he had caused. Millions of dead—shot, starved, frozen—lying in unmarked graves across Russia. Closing his eyes, Theo could see the dictator's larger-than-life face on the facade of the Colón and feel his hooded eyes that had seemed to follow him as he left the Plaça de Catalunya.

"He kills his own, too, of course. Like all devils do," Manny went on after a moment. "Because his suspicion knows no bounds, particularly when his flunkies have been in the West—exposed to corrupting influences. And since the massacre, I've taken comfort in the thought that Gal and Copic will get what's coming to them when they go back to Russia at the end of the war. A bullet in the back of the neck in the basement of the Lubyanka, if they're lucky. But Katz is American, and it drives me nuts to think he'll get away with what he's done. I won't let go of it, because I owe it to all those poor guys that died to try and get them some justice, and in the last few days, I'd really started to hope. Everyone had gotten so riled up with what they're doing to us here that I thought I might finally have a chance to bring him down. But then today he turns the tables on me in less than a minute"—Manny snapped his fingers—"and I'm a voice crying in the wilderness, while he's got the whole fucking battalion hanging on his every word. I underestimated him. I see that now."

Theo was thinking fast. It was the best conversation he'd had with Manny in months. Manny had talked seriously and lucidly instead of indulging in his usual shouting and hectoring, and he seemed to have finally realized that he wasn't going to be able to get the men to mutiny against Alvah. Maybe, Theo thought, he could now get him to back down for good, before it was too late.

Theo had sensed the change in Alvah at the meeting. He was going to move against Manny, but surely he could be persuaded to stay his hand if he thought that Manny was no longer a threat. That was what he'd been asking for before, so why wouldn't he agree to it now? Theo just needed Manny's agreement, and then he could get Alvah to back off and everything would be all right. There was still time. There had to be.

"You're right. Katz is clever. He's got the men on his side now, and I think he's going to come after you," Theo said, choosing his words carefully. "'Trotskyites sowing disunity and discontent'—that was aimed right in your direction. But it's not too late to stop that happening. If you promise to give up this vendetta you have against him, then I think I can get him to leave you alone."

"*You can get him*—how on earth would you do that?" asked Manny sharply.

"We know each other from before. I've told you that."

"Yes, and you've also told me he drove your father to suicide, which doesn't exactly make you and him best buddies, does it? So why is he going to start taking instruction from you all of a sudden? Tell me that."

Manny was staring at Theo, demanding an explanation, but Theo couldn't give him one without telling him about his conversation with Alvah. He cursed himself for not having told Manny about it at the time. Now, if it came out, it would look like he'd been colluding with Alvah all along.

"He's put you up to this, hasn't he?" Manny threw the accusation in Theo's face, and at the critical moment when he most needed to, Theo found he couldn't lie. Manny had got it right: he was too honest for his own good.

"It's not like that," he muttered, but his burning cheeks and averted eyes were tantamount to an admission of guilt.

"Yes, it is. It's exactly like that," said Manny, and Theo could hear the disgust in his voice. "You're worse than Joseph, you know that? At least he's honest about collaborating. And I thought you were my friend. What a putz I am!"

Theo sat slumped with his back to the wall of the trench. Manny had gone and he was alone. His rifle and pack were propped up beside him, and on the ground at his feet lay the normal detritus of their grimy lives—a filthy duckboard, several discarded tins, a broken bottle, someone's glove. Last night's candle had burned down to a waxy mess on the fire step opposite, surrounded by the butts of rolled-up cigarettes.

Above his head, a silver plane crossed the narrow strip of azure sky visible from the trench, glittering a moment in the sunlight before it was gone. Ours, theirs—it was too far away to know. In the distance, a heavy gun stuttered into life and then fell silent. Flies buzzed around Theo's head, and he threw up a futile hand to brush them away.

He closed his eyes and could hear shouts of command and running feet. The sound of ladders moving into place, rifle fire, someone nearby muttering a prayer . . . *Fix bayonets!* The ghosts of the dead were always waiting here in the trench, just behind his shoulder, at the edge of consciousness, ready to pull him back to where it all began. And ended too. Everything that had happened since the battle seemed now to Theo to be like the drawn-out echoes of that winter's day. Preordained, flowing to an inevitable conclusion that he could neither prevent nor modify. It was absurd to try.

He remembered Antonio walking back from the fortune teller's cottage. *"It's fate. You can't change what is written,"* he'd said, and six months later he was dead. Like so many in this cursed country. On battlefields like this, on roads strafed from the sky as they fled their towns and villages, hugging their meager belongings. Or lined up against the walls of graveyards, shot by their neighbors while others watched. In one place he'd read about, enterprising tradesmen had set up churro stands for the spectators; in another, an executioner had offered his handkerchief to a woman waiting her turn to face the firing squad because she'd sneezed. *"Gracias,"* she had said when she gave it back. *"Gracias!"*

*"They're obsessed with death,"* Andrew had told him. *"All of them, even if they don't want to admit it."* Andrew had known. Theo's hand went unconsciously to the pouch around his neck and the rosary inside it, as it always did when he thought of his stepfather. He missed him terribly, reading his letters—those that had made it past the censors—over and over again until they were falling apart at the seams in the bottom of his haversack.

As he often did at such moments, Theo pictured Andrew in the place he thought he would be—the library of the house in London. Deep in his leather chair with a book open on his knees, but lost in thought. He was thinking of Theo and Theo was thinking of him, and the imagined connection between them calmed Theo and pushed back the tide of despair that had been threatening to engulf him. He wasn't like Antonio. He refused to be ruled by destiny or whatever it was the old woman had seen in the palm of his hand. He hadn't betrayed Manny; he'd tried to save him from himself, and he was going to keep on trying for as long as he was able.

Someone was coming. A sentry to relieve him of duty, and Theo hurried back behind the line, looking for Manny. But no one had seen him except Joseph, whom he found cleaning his rifle outside one of the Hooverville shacks.

"It was weird. He came up behind me and tapped me on the shoulder and made me jump," said Joseph. "And then he said he was sorry and told me I was a good guy, which made me jump some more. It wasn't what I was expecting! Not after what has passed between us." Joseph laughed.

"Did he say anything else?"

"Yeah, one thing. He turned around after he'd gone a few steps and said: 'We saved Uncle, didn't we?' I thought it was funny, him putting it like a question when he knew we had, so I just said: 'Yeah, Manny, we did.' And he looked at me and said: 'That sure was something, wasn't it?' Those were his exact words. And then he took off."

"Where?"

"Back, toward the cookhouse," said Joseph, pointing. "Is something wrong?" he asked, noticing the worried look on Theo's face.

"I don't know. I hope not," said Theo, beginning to walk away.

"Do you want me to come with you?" Joseph called after him.

"No," said Theo. "Best not." He carried on walking for a few paces and then broke into a run.

It wasn't the cookhouse where Manny had been headed. Theo was sure of that. It was Alvah's office in battalion headquarters. He didn't know how long he'd stayed in the trench daydreaming after Manny had left, but he estimated that Manny had to have at least a twenty-minute start on him. He felt a growing fear gripping his chest and pushed himself to the limit to go faster.

He was out of condition, and beyond the cookhouse his lungs and legs hurt so much that each exhalation became a cry, but he refused to give in to the pain and kept going until he reached the HQ.

The place was empty, at least on the ground floor. There had to be something happening somewhere, which would mean that Alvah would be gone, too, and Manny would have missed him. It was going to be okay. Theo clutched at the straw of hope as he passed through the building and walked down the meandering path that led to Alvah's office at the back of the overgrown garden. He found to his surprise that the glass door was slightly ajar. He pulled it toward him and entered the room, and half tripped over the body of Easey Goldstein, which was lying stretched out across the flagstone floor.

He knew straightaway that Easey was dead because he'd felt his weight giving way lifelessly beneath him when he put out his hands to arrest his fall, and because Easey's eyes were empty like those of the corpses he'd helped carry to the fire after the battle. It was only the contorted expression on Easey's face that bore witness to the animal fury he'd been feeling at the moment of his death.

Beyond Easey was Manny, sitting in Alvah's chair behind the desk on the left side of the room. He was slumped to the side and his face was white with his mouth twisted like Easey's, but in pain, not rage, and Theo could see that he was conscious. There was blood on his tunic, and a pistol was lying on the desk in front of him.

"Theo. My guardian angel," he said, and his voice was soft, robbed of strength but not irony. "I should have guessed you'd show up. But you're too late this time, old buddy."

"No, it's going to be okay. I'll get help. You need to hold on . . ."

"No!" Manny had the pistol in his hands, pointing it at Theo. "You're going nowhere."

Theo took a step back. "You wouldn't," he said.

"Sure I would," said Manny. "I've got nothing to lose. Get over there where I can see you." He was gesturing with the gun toward a chair standing against the wall opposite the desk. It looked like the one Theo had sat in the last time he'd been in the room, talking to Alvah. Collaborating.

He wanted to run. He thought he was going to, but he sat instead. Perhaps because he had to. His legs were like jelly. From the running, from the shock, from having the pistol pointed at him. The craziness in the room made him feel that anything could happen—even that Manny could put a bullet in him for no reason.

"What happened?" he asked.

"I came for Katz, but I found this schmuck here instead. I hesitated, which was stupid, but it wasn't him I was after, and he rushed me when he saw I had the gun. We struggled—" Manny broke off as a wave of pain shook his body. "This wasn't what I wanted. I wanted . . . justice, I suppose. For everyone to take Katz down and for him to know they had. But I wasn't going to get justice. I saw that today. And so . . ." Manny waved at the room and then closed his eyes, exhausted from the effort of speech, but opened them again and raised the pistol as soon as he heard Theo moving in his chair.

"This is stupid," said Theo. "Alvah's not coming."

"How do you know?"

"There's no one in the building. He must have gone somewhere."

"Then he'll be back."

Theo realized he wasn't getting anywhere, so he tried another tack: "You don't know how badly you're hurt. You don't have to . . ."

"Die? Yes, I do. People know when it's their time. It's like letting go. You can or you can't. I could now. It'd be easy, but I won't."

He glanced toward the half-open door, and Theo could hear the noise too. Footfalls. Someone was approaching.

"No," he said, getting up. But there was a shadow on the window and the door was fully open and Alvah was there, framed in the light.

Theo was moving, but the sudden ear-shattering noise of the pistol shots stopped him in his tracks, so that he believed for a moment that he had been hit, too, until he looked down and saw Alvah lying across the threshold, covered in broken glass. He'd been hit in the head, and Theo knew instantly that he was dead.

Manny had fallen back in the chair, and the gun had slipped from his hands onto the floor. Theo kicked it away and bent over his friend, calling his name. There was no response, and he was sure Manny was gone, too, until he heard the faintest of whispers.

"Is he dead?"

"Yes."

"Good. Is there water?"

Theo nodded. There was the same decanter on the desk from which Alvah had poured him a glass of water when he had been here before. He did the same for Manny now and held the glass to his lips, but he shook his head.

"My hands," he said, and looking down, Theo could see that he had turned them over, palms up.

Theo poured a little of the water over them, and Manny lifted one to cover his eyes.

He was whispering again, and Theo held his ear to Manny's mouth to hear the six sacred words of the Jewish prayer as they came, faint as breath: *"Shema Yisrael: Adonai Eloheinu, Adonai Echad."*

Manny was silent. Motionless. Theo called his name once, twice, but there was no response. He folded his friend in his arms and he wept.

And when he looked up again, there were people in the room shouting, and Stalin was staring down at him from his framed photograph on the wall above the desk.

# 18

## ALBARES

Theo gave his account of events to the battalion adjutant in a small room off the main corridor of battalion headquarters, while a clerk wrote it down, and officers and orderlies passed backward and forward down the long corridor leading to the garden.

Halfway through the deposition, stretcher-bearers passed the open door, carrying loads covered in white sheets. Three of them, one after the other, with boots protruding at the bottom ends so that Theo knew them instantly apart— Alvah's polished, Easey's big and misshapen, and Manny's filthy and falling apart at the seams. He watched them go by, motionless and silent for a moment, and then returned to his narrative.

He felt that same numbness creeping over him that he'd experienced years before in New York after his father's suicide and the sudden collapse of his familiar boyhood world. He had no difficulty describing what had happened, but he had no emotional relationship to what he was saying. His voice was a monotone, unchanged even as he described Manny's death.

"You make it sound like everything you're telling me happened to somebody else," said the adjutant, leaning back in his chair and lighting a cigarette.

"Yes," said Theo. "It's exactly like that. I can't help it."

"I know you can't," said the adjutant sympathetically. "It's shock. It happens to everyone. You'll get over it."

But Theo didn't. At least not completely. Back in the trenches, he felt at first as if he was underwater, breathing through a tube. Voices were echoes;

what he was seeing was near and yet far away. Slowly sensation returned, but the numbness remained, and lying awake at night, he looked up at the stars and thought that something somewhere inside him was broken, perhaps beyond repair.

But on the surface everything remained the same. He ate, he slept, he stood on the trench fire step and watched the empty desolation of no-man's-land through a loophole, and he received no summons to battalion headquarters for further questioning. He'd felt sure that his association with Manny and his presence at Alvah's death would place him under suspicion, and that it would be only a matter of time before he'd find himself in the back of a truck headed down the road to Camp Lukács, the brutal prison outside Albacete, which the soldiers talked about in hushed, frightened whispers. But nothing happened. Spring turned to summer and that was all.

"I reckon the higher-ups think Manny did them a favor," said Joseph when Theo asked him what he thought. "Katz liked to throw his weight around and get everyone riled up when they just want to keep us quiet, holding the line, while they do whatever they're doing back there."

"Living the high life and drinking cocktails in Gal's swimming pool," said Theo, remembering Manny's colorful hearsay descriptions of life at brigade headquarters.

"Yeah, something like that," said Joseph, smiling.

But if that was the plan, it changed abruptly in the middle of June, when the Lincolns were finally withdrawn from the Jarama trenches and sent in trucks to Albares, a sleepy hilltop village thirty miles to the east of Madrid.

As the ragged, emaciated soldiers marched away down the slopes to Morata, they stopped at the cairn of limestone boulders covering the ashes of their dead comrades. They stopped and said nothing. Just stood there in the sunshine for a minute with their caps and helmets in their hands, and then went on, leaving the valley behind forever.

The trucks arrived in Albares in the late afternoon, depositing the soldiers in the main square, where the only two stone buildings in the village, the church and the town hall, faced each other at opposite ends of a cobblestoned rectangle.

Between them a low moss-covered fountain dripped water down into galvanized water troughs where the women washed clothes or filled clay jugs, carrying them away balanced on their heads, much to the soldiers' amazement.

So much immediately reminded Theo of Andalusia: the old men outside the café-bodega, drinking wine and playing cards and arguing incessantly about matters of no importance; the noise of flamenco coming from a loudspeaker on the wall above their heads, half drowned out by the barking of dogs and the shouting of barefoot children in dirty smocks as they jumped up to touch the soldiers' rifles and beg for chocolate; mules plodding by, pulling carts and snorting through their cavernous papery nostrils, like Ferdinand and Isabella, Antonio's faithful burros on whom he and Theo had ridden up into the hills all those years before.

Smells provided the most visceral connection of all—the acrid odor of rancid cooking oil and animal excrement mixed up with the aromatic scent of wood fires.

Spain was here, calling him back after all the months in the Jarama Valley when it had eluded him. Back to the country and the people that he'd fallen in love with and that he couldn't bear to let the Fascists destroy.

The soldiers were billeted in the church, from which all trace of its religious past had been removed. The raised chancel area at the back where the altar and sanctuary had once been had been converted to a kitchen, and the soldiers slept on straw mattresses in the nave. Lying awake at night among his snoring comrades, Theo remembered the emptiness of the church in Los Olivos on Maundy Thursday, after the cross had been removed and the statues covered up. That had been part of a cycle of rebirth that culminated in Christ's return in candlelit glory, carried back across the threshold on Easter Sunday. Here, Christ was gone forever, and Theo felt a momentary unexpected sense of desolation that he quickly got over by reminding himself that the change was testament to the courage of the Spanish people, who had finally thrown off the Church's centuries-old yoke of ignorance and oppression.

Someone had painted Este Es Nuestro País—This is our country—on the wall of the ayuntamiento in precise red letters, and the graffiti inspired him with the same excitement that he had felt on the day he arrived in Los Olivos and saw Viva La Anarquía daubed on the wall of the lower square. He remembered the braceros climbing the hill to vote in the election, braving the cacique and his men and daring to hope, and the workers flooding the streets of Barcelona five months later to stop the army taking their votes away. They had prevailed. The priests and the caciques were gone from Republican Spain, and in the evenings after work, the villagers sat in the ayuntamiento and learned to read and write. Theo looked at them through the window and thought that what he was seeing was worth fighting for. It was why he was here.

Early in the morning, while everyone was still asleep, he climbed the narrow wooden steps leading up into the church tower and sat under the black bell, looking out across the hills to Madrid as the rising sun bathed them in its orange glow. That city, too, had defied the Fascists. With the help of the International Brigades of which he was now a part.

At these moments, Theo was almost able to forget what had happened in the Jarama Valley and believe that he was in the right place at the right time. Touching history.

He felt such a deep bond connecting him to the people in their struggle to be free that it was as if he had become Spanish, too, and this separated him from his American comrades, who were fighting for an idea and not for a country about which they knew nothing. The soldiers and the villagers observed each other with incomprehension across insuperable barriers of language and culture. The peasants' wooden plows and handheld sickles made no sense to men who were used to combine harvesters working the fields of the Midwest. And the villagers, for their part, regarded the Americans as benevolent but alien beings who lived in skyscrapers in a faraway land where the streets were paved with gold. They were grateful to them for coming to fight, but backed away from them in dismay when the soldiers careered around the main square drunk and half naked, bawling out strange tuneless songs and trying to embrace their daughters, whose lives were governed by a complex set of rules and customs of which the soldiers were completely unaware. The Lincolns had arrived in the village with four months back pay in their pockets and had wasted no time in drinking the café dry, and on the third day, Oliver Law, the battalion commander, was forced to put a stop to their excesses by shutting the worst offenders up in a windowless granary, where they remained until they had come to their senses.

Theo had enjoyed the wonder of getting clean on the first day when a special water truck had arrived in the village with collapsible shower nozzles protruding from its central tank like the legs of a gigantic insect. But afterward he withdrew into himself, relishing the opportunity for privacy, which had been a nonexistent commodity in the trenches. Beyond morning and evening roll calls, the battalion officers seemed content to let the soldiers do as they liked, provided they didn't cause trouble.

Alone, Theo rode a roller coaster of emotion. The numbness he'd felt in the Jarama trenches had gone, usurped by a fever of reawakening. He walked up into the foothills in the shimmering afternoon light, when the air was thick with the singing of the cicadas, and watched gray-green lizards darting away into the undergrowth as he passed, and then when he grew tired, he lay down on a carpet of pine needles looking up at the dappled sky through the canopy of the tall trees, and thought of Antonio.

And in the square in the evening, he watched the girls circling hand in hand under the strings of colored bulbs hung from the pollarded plane trees and remembered Maria, whose presence permeated all his memories of Spain. Remembered and tried immediately to forget as he always did when he thought of her now, because he didn't know whether she was alive or dead and had no way of finding out.

He knew, of course, that forgetting was what he had promised Maria he wouldn't do, but he told himself that he was not breaking his vow, because he had no intention of permanently suppressing her from his mind. He loved her, and he couldn't have done that even if he'd wanted to. All he was doing now was trying to survive the pain of not knowing and of separation until he could leave the Lincolns behind and go in search of her.

One evening soon after their arrival, his introspection was interrupted when he heard someone calling his name. Looking up, he saw Joseph beckoning urgently to him from over by the fountain, where he was talking to two women who were reaching up to stroke his face and hair. It was comical how much taller he was than them, so that they had to stand on tiptoes to touch his head.

"What do they want?" Joseph asked. He was laughing, but it was a nervous laughter, as he clearly had no idea what he had done to merit this kind of attention.

"I don't think they've ever seen a Black man before," said Theo, laughing too.

But it was more than that. One of the women was crying and pulling on Joseph's arm and pointing to herself and to him and saying *"¡Esclavas, esclavos! ¡Y ahora somos libres!"* over and over again.

"She's saying you were both slaves," Theo said. "But now you both are free."

He had never seen Joseph so happy. His smile lit up his face, and there were tears on his cheeks as he bent down and hugged the women one after the other. "Yes, we are," he said. "She speaks the truth from her heart. Tell them this is the happiest day of my life," he told Theo, who translated and was met with volleys of quick-fire Spanish in response from the woman who had spoken before.

"She is inviting you to dinner. Tonight. At her house. She says it's not very big. Not like in America. But it would be an honor."

"Yes, yes," said Joseph enthusiastically, and then stopped short. "What about you?" he asked. "Are they inviting you?"

"No, I don't think so. You're the one they want."

"You have to ask her. You promised on the truck to Morata that you'd translate, remember?"

"Yeah, I guess I did," said Theo, smiling.

And in short order, his attendance was agreed upon and the time and place communicated, and the women departed with their daughters in tow, waving their hands and talking a mile a minute.

The house was at the end of a narrow street leading off the main square, built like its neighbors of sunbaked mud and straw with a thatched roof and a smoking chimney. There was very little furniture in the main room that they entered through a wide door from off the street. Just a few stools around a hearth at which an ancient woman—obviously the grandmother—was stirring a black cauldron hung over the fire. But everything was clean and neat, and the daughter that Theo recognized from the square was sweeping the floor with a birch-twig broom. She raised her head for a moment when Theo and Joseph entered and said *"Salud"* softly, and the flash of her beautiful dark-blue eyes reminded Theo painfully of Maria.

This wasn't enough for Joseph, who insisted on kissing the hands of not just the mother and daughter but the grandmother as well. She had a face as wrinkled as a prune, folded in on itself due to her lack of teeth, but she broke into a smile at the kiss and reached up and touched Joseph's cheek just as her daughter had done in the square. The smile transfigured her for a moment, and Theo could see that she, too, had been beautiful once.

"Don't ask her to tell your fortune!" said Theo only half jokingly, but Joseph didn't hear him amid the noise of everyone talking at once in a language of which he understood less than ten words. All he could do was laugh, and that made them laugh, too, so everyone was happy.

But then, all at once, they fell silent. The man of the house was coming through the door behind them. Under his straw hat, he was no taller than his wife, and his leathery, weather-beaten face was the tawny color of the stools by the fire. He greeted them with an elaborate courtesy, apologizing for being late and introducing himself by giving his full name—given name and father's and mother's surnames—Federico García Ruiz. He repeated Joseph's and Theo's first and last names several times, stumbling over the English pronunciation until he was satisfied that he had them right, and only then did he lead his tasseled donkey, which had been waiting patiently in the doorway behind him, over to a stabling area in the far corner of the room, where it buried its head in a manger before sinking down on its haunches to go to sleep.

The men ate on the stools, dipping spoons into the pan of rabbit stew and laying the meat on bread, while the women watched and the grandmother, who seemed to have taken a special shine to Joseph, made hand-to-mouth gestures to urge him to take more.

"Why aren't they eating too?" Joseph asked Theo.

"They will later," said Theo, even though he suspected that they had given up their share to their guests. He knew it would cause grave offense if he was to ask.

Federico plied them with wine and peppered Theo with questions about America. He sounded out the names of the cities and states where Theo and Joseph were from, pronouncing each syllable of Geor-gi-a and New York, and wanted to know the heights of the Statue of Liberty and the tallest skyscraper, insisting on Theo guessing when he said he didn't know.

Finally, he sat back and smiled. "I love America," he said, making it sound as if he were talking about a physical person. "She is the strongest and the richest and the tallest"—he pointed to Joseph—"and now that she is on our side, we will win. Nothing can stop us."

"But she isn't," said Theo. "We came ourselves. America didn't send us—and now they're trying to stop people coming."

His words had no effect. Nothing could puncture Federico's certainty of success. Theo and Joseph were American soldiers. They had come to fight the Fascists, and this meant that America was supporting the Republic—it was as simple as that. And after several halfhearted attempts, Theo gave up trying to explain.

"My son is fighting too. In Aragon," Federico said. "We have not heard from him in many weeks, and my wife says that we must pray for his safe return. I tell her there is no God to hear our prayers, but she does not believe me, so she prays anyway. Perhaps it will do some good." He shrugged his shoulders.

Joseph listened to Theo's translation and then told him to ask Federico if he had a photograph of his son.

Federico's wife got up and went to an opening in the wall and lifted the burlap sacking that served as a curtain to the bedroom. A minute later she returned with a cheaply framed photograph of a young man in his Sunday suit. He stood ramrod straight, and the thin growth of an incomplete mustache above his lip added to the impression of a boy who was trying to appear a man. He looked defiantly at the camera, as if daring it to do its worst.

There were tears in the mother's eyes as she handed the photograph of her son to Joseph.

"What is his name?" he asked.

"Marcos," she said.

Joseph looked hard at the young man's face and then up at the mother. "I think he will come home," he said.

The woman listened to Theo's translation and then took back the photograph and held it to her breast, crying unrestrainedly now. "Thank you," she said.

And after that everyone was happy, eating the Hershey chocolate bars that Theo and Joseph had brought as presents, until it was time to go. At the door, Federico vigorously shook their hands and bowed his head up and down like a marionette, and invited them to return for dinner on Saturday night so that they could talk more about America.

"Why did you tell her that?" Theo asked Joseph as they crossed the square in the moonlight on their way back to the church. "For all you know, her son's already dead and buried, which is why he hasn't been writing." He'd enjoyed the evening, but it irritated him that Joseph should have set himself up as an oracle.

"I told her because I believed it. And because that poor woman needs hope. More even than food," said Joseph, speaking with an unexpected vehemence. "Without hope, people wither and die. Like my father did when the Klan burnt down his church. He gave up."

"You mean he committed suicide?" asked Theo, surprised. He remembered Joseph saying that he'd lost his faith when his father died, but he'd never explained how that had happened.

"No, he couldn't have done that. Not without committing a mortal sin. But he lost his will to live, which amounts to the same thing. He turned his face to the wall."

"Why?"

"He'd seen boys that he'd known from when they were babies, that he'd baptized and taught in his Sunday school, falsely accused and lynched. No trial, no justice, just strung up from a tree until the life got sucked out of them, and they hung there above the baying crowd with their tongues out and their eyes bulging. Two Black men up above a sea of white faces. He preached against it because what else could he do, and the white men came and burnt down his church so that it was ashes on the ground. And after that he stopped believing in the possibility of deliverance. He lost his hope."

"I can understand that," said Theo sadly. "I think it's what happens when people believe and then they stop believing. They fall too far too fast. It happened to my father too. He believed in America, and then the Depression came and took it all away . . . He used a gun. There was nothing in his rulebook to stop him taking the easy way out."

Joseph stopped and took hold of Theo's arm. He could hear the bitterness in his voice. "I'm sorry, brother. I didn't know," he said, and he pulled Theo close into a hug. "It's hard to be left, isn't it? The anger's just a way of not feeling the hurt."

Theo and Joseph never got to go back to Federico's house, and there was not even time to say goodbye. The next morning, the battalion bugler sounded the "Assembly," summoning the Lincolns back from an intercompany baseball game, and within an hour they were climbing into a convoy of trucks that had driven up into the main square in a cloud of dust.

As if by alchemy, word traveled through the ranks that they were going into battle, but that it would be different this time. They were not alone but part of a vast army on the move. The Republic was taking the offensive for the first time in the war. The soldiers' motto would no longer be *"¡No pasarán!"* but *"¡Pasaremos!"* instead. They would drive the Fascists from the gates of Madrid and back as far as Toledo.

Theo was feverish with excitement. He believed with all the zeal of a convert that this battle would change the tide of the war and that everything he had told Maria in February was about to come true. With victory would come justice, and they could be together. Free in a new Spain.

The brigade marched by night and withdrew into the pine woods to sleep during the day on carpets of ferns. The Lincolns were at the rear, separated from the new George Washington Battalion by the British contingent, and at resting points the commissars were careful to keep the two American battalions apart, anxious to avoid the morale of the new troops being undermined by descriptions of the horrors of the Jarama battle in February.

But they need not have worried. The Lincolns were looking forward, not back. They sensed the planning and purpose behind the march, and the need for stealth to preserve the vital element of surprise added to their excitement. Fires were not permitted, and they had orders to keep the glow of their cigarettes concealed under their coats.

On the last night before the battle, they rested in the wooded grounds of a great estate that the soldiers christened the Pearly Gates after the ornamental iron posts they had passed between at the entrance to a long, overgrown drive. There was a swimming pool with water that had turned into a green slime in which a colony of frogs croaked in unison through the night, and glittering constellations spangled the cloudless sky so that it felt to the soldiers as if they were camped in an observatory on the top of the world.

It was an enchanted place. The air was fragrant with the scent of juniper and thyme and a stream babbled as it flowed down from the upper foothills of the sierras. In the moonlit darkness, Theo heard a rustling nearby and found himself looking into the eyes of a red stag with magnificent golden antlers and soft glowing eyes. It stood motionless for a moment, watching, before it turned back into the woods, leaving emptiness behind.

Out of sight somewhere, voices rose in song. It was a group of Welsh miners in the British Battalion whom Theo had heard singing in the Jarama Valley several times before, but now in the wooded nocturnal quiet, the effect was electrifying. The words were in Welsh, but the soldiers understood the songs because the music spoke to their hearts. Lying silent on the pine needles, wrapped in their blankets, they heard love and unity in adversity and hope for a new dawn, and belief, too, that it would come.

# Battle of Brunete – July 1937

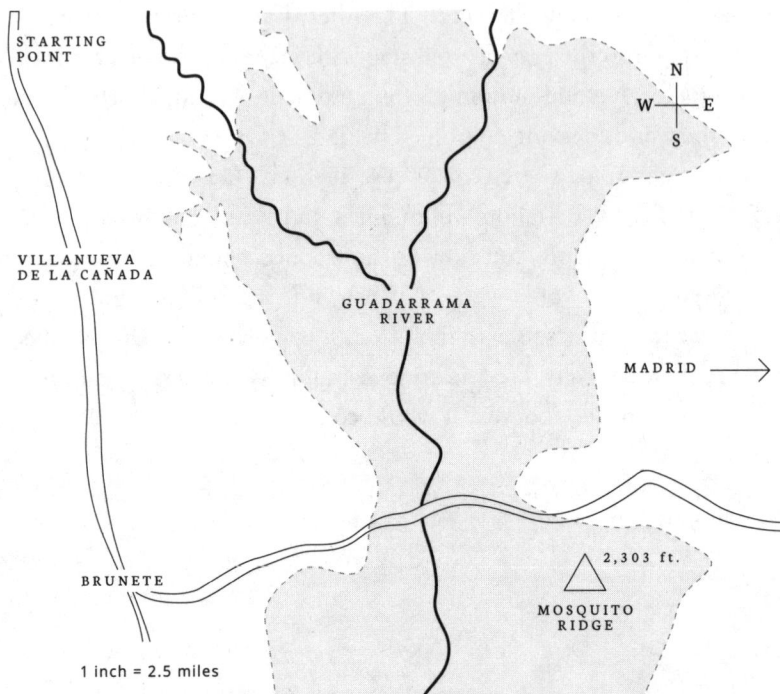

STARTING
POINT

N
W — E
S

VILLANUEVA
DE LA CAÑADA

GUADARRAMA
RIVER

MADRID ⟶

2,303 ft.

BRUNETE

MOSQUITO
RIDGE

1 inch = 2.5 miles

# 19

## BRUNETE

The battalion was underway again before dawn, headed downhill to the assembly points from where the attack was to take place, when all at once the Republican heavy guns opened up, smashing the silence and making the ground tremble beneath their feet. The soldiers hurried forward, anxious that they might miss the battle, just as the first gray light of day revealed the outlines of trees and rocks and the tense, wide-eyed faces of their companions.

They stopped on a knoll, looking down over the saucer-shaped plain of the Guadarrama Valley in the pale light of the early morning. The panoramic view was extraordinary, with every feature of the landscape laid out beneath them, as if on a topographic map.

Below where they were standing, a black macadam road ran straight as an arrow southward through the valley, passing at four-mile intervals through the towns of first Villanueva de la Cañada and then Brunete. Three miles to the east—the soldiers' left—the Guadarrama River appeared as a brown ribbon running parallel to the road, and beyond, on its other side, the ground rose in a series of hills and ravines to a high central ridge commanding the valley. Other small towns lay to the southwest and southeast, and columns of troops were fanning out toward them and down the road to Villanueva de la Cañada, supported by tanks and cavalry.

The artillery bombardment had continued ceaselessly since the Lincolns reached the ridge, and the shells passed over their heads with a noise like sheets being ripped, exploding in and around the towns, which were becoming shrouded in clouds of dust and smoke. They were being bombed from the air, too, by Republican airplanes, which seemed to have complete control of the skies. The bombs fell lackadaisically like rotating silver bottles, and the Lincolns let out a great cheer when a direct hit on a gasoline dump in the village of Quijorna in the southwest sent a vast column of flames and black smoke high into the sky.

Theo was a lowly infantryman awaiting orders, but for a moment, gazing down at the ocher-colored valley over which the summer sun was now shining, he imagined himself a general watching his tactical plans unfold. Like Napoleon at Austerlitz, moving his regiments around like chess pieces on a board, certain of his ability to outwit the enemy.

He felt a surge of optimism. This time, it would be different. This time, they had the planes and the tanks and the guns and the advantage of surprise—all the elements that had been missing in February. As the adrenaline coursed through his veins, he forgot the horrors of that terrible day and thought only of the chance to finally do battle with the hitherto-invisible Fascists and strike a blow for freedom. It was why he was here. It was what he had volunteered to do.

The Lincolns were being kept in reserve and were now the only troops left on the knoll, and Theo waited eagerly for the order to join the rest of the brigade in the advance down below.

Only the sight of Colonel Copic conferring with the battalion commander, Oliver Law, at the front of the knoll, gave Theo pause. Copic was dressed even more extravagantly than at Manny's court-martial. His high, polished boots, Sam Browne belt, and the big pistol on his hip shone in the sunlight, and leather cases for maps and binoculars dangled from his neck. He was using both, jabbing the map and then peering through the binoculars before going back to the map again while Law listened deferentially.

Theo remembered Copic rapping the table with the pistol at the court-martial when Manny had defied him, and he smiled as he recalled the crazy Russian general holding the colonel three feet in the air and shaking him, until Copic's eyes almost popped out of his head. But then he also remembered what Esmond had told him afterward about Copic's lack of military experience and what Uncle had said before the February battle about Copic's superior, General Gal, the strutting martinet with the full-length portrait of himself that had to be saluted by visitors to division headquarters: *"He's flying by the seat of his pants.*

*They all are. Gal, Copic, Katz, Merriman, the whole damned lot of them."* Alvah was dead and Captain Merriman was badly wounded, recovering somewhere behind the lines, but Gal and Copic were still in charge and the Lincolns' fate was in their hands.

Theo recalled Copic at Jarama shouting at Merriman down the field telephone: *"Attack now! . . . I will have you shot."* He was no Napoleon—he'd sent hundreds of good men to their deaths that day for no reason except his own willfulness. So what was he doing now?

Copic carefully folded his map and replaced it in its case, snapping the catch shut, and walked back under the trees, still talking to Law. Theo was able to hear a few sentences of what they were saying, because they passed within a few feet of where he was standing.

"Are you sure?" Law was asking. "The heights are the strongpoint. With them we control the valley and can push on."

"And we will," Copic replied impatiently. "But we must take Villanueva first. I've told you that. We can't leave the Fascists behind us. Any fool can see that. Plans change, Law. We underestimated their resistance, and now we must crush it. Send your men down and stop questioning my orders."

Copic had worked himself up into a temper by the time he finished the speech and everyone heard his final command, so that they didn't need to wait for it to be repeated by Oliver Law to fall into ranks and begin their descent.

The path was steep and winding, and the Lincolns had to frequently move aside to allow exhausted stretcher-bearers to clamber up past them on their way to the field hospital behind the ridge. The soldiers said nothing as they watched the blood of the wounded seeping through the stretcher canvas, but after each stop, they went a little slower.

As they descended, the noise of rifle and machine-gun fire grew louder. Theo heard it as the incessant patter of rain on a clay roof, perhaps because his brain had become fixated on the thought of water as the noonday sun beat down on his head. There were no trees to provide even a moment's shade, and he couldn't stop himself from drinking from his canteen, even though Joseph gripped his arm and told him to go easy, so that he had almost no water left by the time they reached the bottom of the hill.

All around him, soldiers were dropping their gas masks, blankets, food tins, even ammunition—anything to make their loads lighter as they struggled forward through knee-high wheat fields and up and down the hillocks and gullies that laced the valley floor that had looked so deceivingly flat from up above.

They could see Villanueva de la Cañada clearly now. The town was built compactly on the crest of a low hill, with the church tower rising high above the single-story houses just like in Los Olivos. The defenders had installed machine guns in the belfry and upper windows, and they were maintaining a sweeping fusillade down toward all five battalions that were encircling the town and returning fire as best they could. More machine guns in fortified emplacements around the outer rim of the town supported those in the tower.

A mile out, the Lincolns branched off the road to the right, passing the Washingtons and moving into a position about four hundred yards west of the town. Farther forward, the British were holding the road running south to the village of Brunete, where further intense fighting was in progress.

Now the Lincolns were in range of the Fascist guns, and there was little protection to be had on the barren plain. The wheat here had been harvested, and there was no more than dry stubble on the bone-dry ground. They tried to dig down into it, but the most they could achieve were pathetic mounds of dirt only a few inches high.

Theo felt as if time had slipped and he was back in no-man's-land at Jarama, lying exposed under the sun as bullets whined over his trembling body and wounded men all around cried out their pain, delirious with thirst. Only Joseph lying beside him anchored him to the present, and he tried to keep terror at bay by following his friend's example, concentrating his mind entirely on his rifle. Pulling and pushing the bolt, pressing down his elbows into the hard ground, and firing at the enemy gunners opposite. Over and over again until the rifle was too hot to handle and it fell from his hands.

He felt faint, exhausted from the long marches, weakened by hunger, and crazed by thirst. The dust and the glare had reduced his eyes to powdered slits. He turned his water bottle upside down, holding it to his lips, but nothing came out. Not even the scant comfort of moisture. The sun beat on his face and the sky tipped, and he felt Joseph shaking him and holding out his canteen.

"Tiny sips, like you're a tiny bird," said Joseph, and he was smiling, which Theo loved him for almost as much as for the water.

A hundred yards away, one of the Lincoln machine gunners was standing with his penis in his hand, trying and failing to urinate over the smoking cooling jacket of his gun barrel and shouting a string of extraordinarily inventive profanities that included reference to the dried-up teats of the Virgin Mary and the twenty-four testicles of the twelve apostles. It was surreal—perhaps the most bizarre moment Theo experienced in the entire war—and he was sure that an enemy bullet was going to cut the gunner off in midstream, but he remained miraculously unscathed throughout his invective, until he ducked down at the end, out of sight.

Slowly, the sun moved off the Lincolns' heads, sinking toward the western horizon behind them, and the intensity of the gunfire from the town slackened as the encircling battalions' own fire finally took effect. Orders were shouted down the line that they would attack in the morning, and Theo dropped his rifle and closed his eyes. It was over and he'd survived another day, and the heat was gone and he could sleep. *Sleep*: just thinking the word was enough to make it happen.

He awoke and everything was rattling. His brain in his head, his heart in his chest. Someone was shaking him and pulling him up. Joseph. He was shouting "Come on! Come on!" and Theo was on his feet, running, even though he felt like he was dreaming, too, and everyone all around was yelling. He half tripped on a rock but somehow kept going, focused on Joseph just in front, because without him everything would be chaos, with nothing to hold on to at all.

And then it was. Someone had thrown a grenade and he couldn't see, and when the dust cleared, he was alone. He veered toward the houses. They were close now. Two mattresses on a roof terrace were moving apart, and there was the snout of a gun and the legs of a tripod appearing, but he'd left them behind before they could hurt him, and he was sprinting toward the breastwork of sandbags down below. He leaped like a hurdler, not breaking stride, and landed in an empty trench, banging his knees. They hurt but not enough to stop him clambering up the other side into a street where people were running this way and that, some with their hands above their heads, shouting *";No dispares!"*—Don't shoot!—and he was running, too, because he was lost and scared, and he didn't know which way to go to get back to the Lincolns, where he belonged.

He stopped because there were no more houses. Just a wide black road that looked like the one they'd gone down in the morning. But this was the south end of town, not the north—it had to be, because he'd been running to the right when he'd entered Villanueva. There was a big group of people up ahead, walking away from the town. Women in bright dresses, children, an old man with a stick. They were huddled close together, shuffling, which made no sense. If they were escaping the town, why didn't they run? And then he saw why. There were Fascist soldiers concealed in the middle of the cluster, some with bayonets. They were using the defenseless townspeople as a human shield, just like Captain Darnell had done in Barcelona a year before.

And farther forward, in the ditches on either side of the road, there were other soldiers. From the British Battalion. Theo knew because he could hear their accents as they shouted at the refugees to get a fucking move on and get the hell out of the way. They obviously didn't yet know about the Fascists, and without thinking, Theo yelled "Watch out! They're behind them!" And he was still yelling, but his words were drowned out by an explosion of noise.

The Fascists were firing submachine guns and throwing grenades indiscriminately in all directions, and the British were shooting back, and some of the civilians were breaking away into the fields, but others were falling in the cross fire, and Theo backed away into the town to escape the bullets.

Now he was in a warren of climbing and descending streets that he couldn't tell apart in the twilight. It was as if he was going around in circles. Buildings were burning and the air was full of sulfur and smoke, and he tore off a piece of his tunic to hold over his nose to stop himself from choking. He could hear people shouting in Spanish and in English too. The British had entered the town enraged and were shooting anyone that they suspected of being a Fascist. From a doorway, he watched as two of them interrogated a barefoot man. One ripped the man's white shirt off his shoulder, looking for the telltale bruising from a rifle's recoil, and when he found it, the other soldier shot the man dead. Blew his brains out like it was nothing at all. Theo turned away and retched.

He fixed his eyes on the church tower at the center of the town and tried to keep moving toward it, forcing himself to walk instead of run, so that he could keep his panic at bay. The Lincolns had attacked the town from the side, and so this way seemed to offer the best chance of finding them. As he watched, flames spurted out through the high windows of the tower and a man jumped, disappearing from sight below the rooftops.

He couldn't reach the church. Two streets away, the heat and gunfire forced him back. Someone was shouting that there were snipers in the attics. He was in front of a café. He tried the door and found it locked, so he smashed out the glass with the butt of his rifle and went inside. There was water behind the counter and ham and bread and red sausage, and he ate and drank until he felt sick and then lay down on the floor between two tables, pulled his pack under his head for a pillow, and went to sleep.

He woke in the light, looking up at colored posters on the wall above his head, advertising long-gone bullfights, and thought for moment that he was in the café in Los Olivos and that Antonio's father would be coming through the door at any moment, limping on his wooden leg, until he remembered where he was and that Bernardo Alvarez was long dead.

*They cut off his head and put it on a pole and paraded it around the town.* Theo shivered, remembering Andrew's description of the café owner's fate, and wondered what horrors lay waiting for him outside in the ravaged town.

Through the shattered glass door, he could smell smoke but could see nothing except an empty street with no one passing by. The silence felt eerie and ominous after the end-of-the-world cacophony of the night before. As if it was the prelude to some new, more obscene violence.

He noticed for the first time a clock on the same wall as the bullfight posters, with a beatific image of Jesus staring out from the center and the hour hand almost at Christ's shoulder. Ten o'clock meant that he'd slept for nearly twelve hours, and he was afraid that he would be accused of desertion if he didn't find the Lincolns before they found him.

He filled his water bottle and hoisted his pack and rifle onto his shoulders but stopped at the door, looking back at the array of colored bottles lined up on the shelves behind the counter. He hesitated for a moment and then went back and poured himself a full glass of Caballero cognac and swallowed it whole. He felt the brandy burn his throat and stomach as it went down, but it gave him the Dutch courage he needed to leave his café sanctuary behind.

He wandered the streets, looking for soldiers in the hope that they could give him directions. Flames still flickered in some of the buildings, and here and there he passed women on their hands and knees, digging in the rubble, no doubt for lost personal possessions. A sewing machine or a cooking pot, perhaps. Relics of a life that had now been destroyed.

He encountered a boy, too, in torn, filthy clothes, almost colliding with him as he came around a street corner. Fifteen years old perhaps, maybe less—it was hard to tell when people were so emaciated. Theo thought he had never seen anyone look so scared. Scared of him. The boy backed away and then ran like a rabbit, darting from side to side in a desperate attempt to evade the expected bullet.

Theo remembered the cold-blooded murder he'd witnessed the night before and realized that it was his uniform that had had this effect on the boy. Was this what he intended when he put it on back in Albacete? To become an object of terror to teenage boys in small Spanish towns? Was this why he was here?

He was going down a hill and, all at once, he recognized where he was. The houses were ending and the road opened up before him, just like on the night before. Except that it was light now and there was no crowd of townspeople out in front, shuffling at bayonet point toward their doom. Instead, there were lines of figures in the fields on either side of the road, lying under blankets. They seemed so peaceful that he thought they were sleeping until he got closer and realized that they were dead. Every last one of them. Soldiers and civilians alike. Where a blanket had fallen to the side, he saw the hem of a woman's brightly colored dress, and swayed, alone with his guilt.

He'd shouted and the people had died. But he reasoned that the Fascists wouldn't have gotten past the British even if he hadn't called out. Not without being seen. There were too many of them, so that couldn't have been their intention. There was going to be a firefight whatever happened. By shouting, he had at least given the British the chance to defend themselves and the townspeople a moment to run before the Fascists had time to react. He'd saved lives. Surely, he had . . .

But the carefully constructed arguments he was making in his head had no effect on the guilt and desolation he felt in his heart. He was soiled by his experience. Changed, just as his stepfather had feared. And he thought at that moment that he would never be clean again.

At the end of the line of corpses, a party of French soldiers, stripped to the waist, were digging graves. When Theo asked for the Lincolns, they pointed him to a line of lemon trees a few hundred yards away across the fields.

It was an orchard full of soldiers with a windowless barn at the center in which their Fascist prisoners had been shut up. Theo peered in at them through a crack in the wooden walls, sitting huddled together with their hands around their knees in the semidarkness. He could smell their fear in the hot gloom.

"Not very impressive, are they?" said a familiar voice behind him.

"No, they're pathetic," said Theo sadly. He turned and put his arms around Joseph, holding on to him like he didn't want to let go. He felt an intense relief that his friend had survived, as if a prayer that he didn't know he'd been praying had been unexpectedly answered. Death was so ubiquitous, and he'd experienced such desolation since he'd left the café where he'd spent the night. In the ruined town, out on the road among the dead, seeing the wretched prisoners a moment before. But finding Joseph had meaning. It was something he could hold on to when everything else was slipping away.

And he sensed that Joseph felt the same. "I thought you'd gone to glory," his friend said, shaking his head in wonder.

"No," said Theo. "I just got lost. That's all. I'm here now."

# 20

## JOSEPH

They moved out an hour later, marching down the Brunete road with the Lincolns at the rear of the brigade, just like before. The news must have reached Fascist headquarters that Villanueva had changed hands, because their artillery had begun to bombard the town, battering the ruins.

"'How can a poor man stand such times and live?'" Joseph sang the old Blind Alfred Reed song in a melodic baritone, and Theo joined in with some of the words that he remembered from the times he'd listened to the poor protesters singing in Union Square when he was a boy. And closing his eyes, New York seemed suddenly so close that he could touch it with his outstretched hand. The trees in fall, the layers of leaves underfoot, the feel of the cool hard railings on the tips of his fingers as they walked out of the square into Fourteenth Street, leaving the quiet behind, with his father's hand on his shoulder. Leaning in—

"Left face!" came the order, and he was jolted back into a present that made less sense than his daydreams of the past. He was a soldier, which was the last thing he'd expected to be in life. He remembered how much he'd hated Barker and his ridiculous parade ground drills at Saint Gregory's, and now here he was, marching away with his comrades from a victory of sorts and following Barker-like commands without thinking. He marveled at the strangeness of his situation before the pressure of the hot sun overhead and the broken, uneven ground underfoot drove such abstract reflections from his mind.

The Lincolns had left the road and were crossing open country, southeast toward the river and beyond it, the high central ridge, flecked with trees, that

Theo had picked out from the surrounding landscape before they went into battle. He remembered how Captain Law, the battalion commander, had called the heights the strongpoint, and he saw now how they commanded the valley. What was waiting for them up there? Theo wondered, remembering how Law had wanted to march straight at them, but Copic had insisted they take Villanueva first. Was this another of Copic's mistakes? Had the delay lost them the advantage of surprise and allowed the Fascists time to regroup?

Certainly, there were more enemy planes. On the first day, the Republican Chato fighters and Tupolev bombers had dominated the skies, but now there were dogfights overhead as the two air forces fought for supremacy. The troops watched the aircraft looping and rolling over each other in desperate attempts to gain the advantage and cheered wildly, as if they were spectators at a championship football game, when a Fascist plane came down in flames.

But these victories were aberrations. Slowly, the Fascists were gaining the ascendancy as the untested Washington Battalion soon found, to their cost. They stayed in tight parade ground formation as they crossed the fields, which made them an easy target for a squadron of Italian Caproni bombers that swept down and killed twenty of them in a single run.

"Fat good all that training did them!" said the 2 Company lieutenant, shaking his head bitterly as the Lincolns passed by the huge bomb craters, turning their heads away from the sight of the dismembered American bodies lying at the edges, cooking in the hot sun.

"Can we bury them, sir?" Joseph asked the lieutenant, pointing up at a flock of wide-winged vultures slowly circling overhead. "Surely, they've got a right to that."

"No, they don't," the lieutenant shot back angrily. "They're dead! Can't you see that, Sergeant?"

Joseph took a step back, visibly shocked. Like Theo, he'd always got on well with the lieutenant, and he hadn't expected such a harsh response to what was obviously a reasonable request.

"I'm sorry. I don't like it any more than you do," said the lieutenant, seeing Joseph's reaction. "But our orders are not to stop. Not for anything."

But they already had stopped. For more than a day, to take Villanueva de la Cañada. The lieutenant's words added to Theo's growing fear that a fatal mistake had already been made by the same inept commanders who had sent the Lincolns to their deaths in February.

And the bombing of the Washingtons now compounded the delay. The disaster had taught them the danger of proximity, and they reacted by going to the opposite extreme, fanning out across the plain and losing contact with each other in the gullies and ravines. Chaos spread through the brigade, and by dusk they had still not reached the river.

In the dark, the temperature dropped quickly from hot to cold, and many of the soldiers shivered and rubbed their stomachs, bitterly regretting their earlier decision to throw away their food and blankets to lessen their loads in the heat. They muttered, too, about the delay, expressing aloud the anxiety that Theo had been experiencing all day. The euphoria they'd felt after capturing Villanueva had drained away, just like the water in their canteens.

Early the next morning, Russian tanks came up from the rear and led the soldiers down the steep sandy banks to the narrow trickling stream that was all that was left of the Guadarrama River after weeks of evaporation in the scorching summer heat. They splashed their faces and drank and gratefully filled their water bottles, and then followed the giant beetle-like tanks up through the dense canebrake on the other side, heading for the heights.

They were in the old hunting grounds of the Duke of Alba. Pheasants whirred in the undergrowth and rabbits scurried away, and hidden snipers waited to pick the soldiers off, trying to slow their advance.

Ahead, the ground rose steeply but unevenly to the final ridgeline from which the Fascists were pouring machine-gun fire down on the advancing troops, who were forced to stop and take cover behind isolated ilex trees and gorse bushes. The Lincolns were facing an impassable wall of shrapnel and lead just like the one they had encountered when they went over the top in February.

Only the tanks could have gotten through it, but they had turned tail after their leader had been blown apart by an anti-tank shell. One was all that had been required, and the Lincolns' hopes of success plummeted as they watched them go.

"Dig! Dig!" the officers were shouting, and the soldiers cursed them, protesting that they were digging their own graves, which many of them were. Now they all knew for certain what Theo had suspected since the day before: that they had arrived at the heights too late and that the iron door that might have been opened by surprise was locked and barred against them. And no one had a key.

Theo stared up through the bracken at the bare, precipitous approaches to the summit and saw the ridge as the same hard line that had defeated the Lincolns at Jarama. It was more than déjà vu. It was as if present and past had fused and the line was permanent in his mind, running through time. He knew it could never be reached, however hard the soldiers tried. It was where their dreams and hopes would always end. A visual representation of their despair.

The Lincolns called it Mosquito Ridge because the bombardment from above never ceased. Night and day the earth swayed and heaved and rocked and roared as the shells rained down on them. And bombs too. The Republican Chatos had disappeared from the sky, leaving the German Heinkels and Junkers free to empty their bomb bays wherever they chose, before flying back behind the ridge to reload. They shamelessly advertised their nationality with swastikas painted on their tail fins, and the cowering soldiers fired their rifles uselessly into the air and cursed their own countries for nonintervention—and cursed Gal and Copic, too, who had put them in this mess but kept sending up orders to attack. Captain Law was dead, killed by a stray shell before the Lincolns had even reached the final slope, but the adjutant who had taken over command of the battalion was no Merriman and ignored the instructions, knowing that they had no hope of success.

Theo felt the whistle and scream of every approaching shell or bomb in the small of his back, thinking that each one was aimed directly at his six-foot body. A few yards away from where he was lying, a soldier was chopped apart as if by a giant biscuit cutter that plunged into his back, skull, and buttocks, leaving gaping holes, and the flying shrapnel passed so close to Theo that it singed his neck red. But he remained unscathed. And Joseph too. Their bulging eyes and twisted mouths mirrors of each other's terror and pain.

Some lived and some died, and those that were badly wounded died, too, because there was no one to carry them back across the hot valley to the field hospital on the other side. The unburied corpses cooked in the hot sun, emanating a sickly-sweet smell that mixed with the rotten sulfurous stink of powder to poison the air. Each nauseous breath that Theo took was a struggle, a rasping search for oxygen that was being sucked out of the air by the suffocating July sun.

Every new hour seemed hotter than the last, and yet there was no water to drink and no food to eat. The Republicans had outrun their supply lines, and the soldiers looked back in despair as the Fascist planes bombed or strafed the supply trucks that were trying to cross the valley. Ration parties were reduced to running through the gullies in the moonlight with sacks of food and cans of water tied to their backs, and the watching soldiers laid macabre bets on whether or not they would get through.

Up above, by contrast, they could see the lights of trucks bringing up supplies to the Fascists on the top of the hill. The enemy had everything and they had nothing. Planes, guns, food, water, shelter from the sun . . . All that sustained the Lincolns in their extremity was a cussed determination to make their invisible tormentors pay if they ever came down from off their ridge.

On the third day, they did. As the Lincolns had hoped, the Fascists interpreted their silence as spelling the end of their resistance and sent tanks down the slope, followed by a platoon of infantry to wipe out the survivors. They must have been legionnaires, because Theo heard them shouting *"Viva la Muerte"* as they ran. The Lincolns waited patiently until the enemy was close and then opened up with a deadly fusillade of anti-tank and machine-gun and rifle fire. Three tanks were destroyed, and the few Fascists that were left alive fled back up the hill.

It was the first moment of success that the Lincolns had experienced since the Pyrrhic victory at Villanueva, and they erupted all around Theo into raucous cheering. But he was mute, crouched down over Joseph, who lay motionless on the ground. Their luck had run out. Joseph had been hit by a stray bullet.

Theo felt a hand on his arm and looked up at the company lieutenant. "Let me look at him," the lieutenant said, and Theo reluctantly got out of the way, watching intently as the lieutenant cut away Joseph's tunic and examined the wound.

"Help me lift him. Support his back," the lieutenant instructed, and Joseph groaned as he regained consciousness and then screamed out in agony as the lieutenant emptied a bottle of iodine over the wound and applied a field dressing. But Theo rejoiced at the noise. He'd thought his friend was dead.

"The bullet's gone clean through his shoulder, which is a good thing," said the lieutenant. "But I'm no doctor. I can't stop the bleeding inside or the infection if it comes, which it probably will. This is a bad place to be wounded. You know that as well as I do."

"There must be something you can do," said Theo desperately. He knew what the lieutenant was saying—he could hear the death sentence in his voice, and he felt as if the world was caving in. Joseph had been full of life a minute before, firing his rifle and shouting like the others. This couldn't be.

"I told you, I'm no doctor. Maybe, if we had one here, it would be different, but we don't. We're on our own," said the lieutenant, shrugging his shoulders as he got to his feet. Theo could hear the bitter resignation in his voice.

It was intolerable. Theo couldn't accept what he was being told. He wouldn't. Unthinking, he reached out his free hand from where he was kneeling beside Joseph on the ground and grabbed the lieutenant's leg.

The lieutenant looked down incredulously. "Let go!" he said. "That's an order."

But Theo didn't. He started talking instead, babbling almost. "Please. Let me take him back. Let me try. He matters . . ."

"*Matters!* What are you talking about?" asked the lieutenant, surprised by the unexpected word.

"He's good. Better than us. He makes it all make sense. Why we're here, what we're doing, who we are . . ."

The lieutenant stopped still, staring down at Theo kneeling like a beggar at his feet. Each of them frozen for a moment in their vertical relationship, as if posed in a painter's tableau or for a photograph.

Finally, unexpectedly, the lieutenant smiled. "First time I met you, Sterling, I thought you were crazy with all that Olympic talk, and it seems like I wasn't far wrong. You win. You can go. The field hospital is at Villanueva, the last I heard. I doubt you'll make it, but you can try. And here, take this. You can't carry him, and it might keep him walking at least for a bit."

It was a hip flask, just like Esmond's, filled with brandy. Theo put it to Joseph's lips and whispered in his ear: "A tiny sip, like you're a tiny bird." And Joseph smiled, swallowed, and got unsteadily to his feet.

At first they made reasonable progress. The brandy had revived Joseph, and he was able to walk almost unaided.

Near the bottom of the slope, they passed a new grave dug at the foot of a holm oak tree. A makeshift plaque nailed to the trunk read:

**OLIVER LAW, AGED 34, FIRST BLACK COMMANDER OF AN AMERICAN BATTALION. 07.09.37**

Above, a helmet, obviously Law's, hung from a low-hanging branch.

Joseph stood a moment, slightly swaying, with his right hand on his heart, and then turned to Theo and smiled. "The boys that buried him did right, putting that up," he said. "It was a wonder that he commanded us. Not something I'd thought to see in my lifetime."

They went on, stumbling through gullies and staggering up hills under the hot sun. Every few minutes Joseph's legs gave way and they stopped to rest. There was blood on his tunic, spreading out from his shoulder, and blood, too, around his mouth from where he had bitten through his lips as he fought the pain. He needed the brandy to give him the strength to carry on, but there was little left now in the hip flask.

Theo thought of nothing but the river. At first it had been a staging post in his mind—halfway to Villanueva de la Cañada—but now it had become the destination. He visualized the trickling stream. The taste of the water in the mouth and down the throat. The feel of it on the skin and in his hair. The water would save them, he told himself. Not because it was true, but because he had to believe in something that he could reach, and anything beyond the river was too far away.

But when they got there, it was dry. Three more days of summer heat had burned the trickling stream away, leaving only gray sand in the bed. Theo dug down, scooping frantically with his hands, but there was nothing. Not even moisture. He cried out on his knees, shaking his fists at the sun, while Joseph watched him from the bank, motionless.

"Not the Jordan," he whispered in a cracked voice when Theo came back, and Theo thought he could hear resignation in his friend's voice, but he wouldn't accept it. He hauled Joseph up, and they tottered forward. Through the riverbed and up the bank on the other side. Past a dead mule, covered in flies and inflated to double its size, and on into the wheat fields with vultures circling overhead.

Theo threw away his rifle. It was useless. The enemy was the sun, and you couldn't put a bullet in that. Everything was white. The sun, the sky, the wheat stalks—they shimmered and danced, and he thought he was hallucinating at first when he saw a bareheaded soldier in a ragged khaki uniform walking across the field toward the river. Theo stared, expecting the apparition to disappear like a desert mirage, but the soldier came on, looking neither to right nor left, and he didn't react when Theo shouted to him to stop. Just kept on walking, as if he hadn't heard.

Now that the soldier was closer, Theo could see that he had a bandage wound around his head, stained with blood, and a pack on his back. Maybe he had water. Theo knew that he couldn't let him pass. He lowered Joseph to the ground, told him he'd be back, and set off diagonally across the field to cut the soldier off. He hadn't the energy to run, and so he loped, still calling out and still getting no reaction, and the soldier stopped only when Theo was standing directly in front of him, and even then his eyes didn't seem to focus, looking beyond Theo into the distance, as if Theo was just an obstacle in his path to be gotten around and not a person at all.

"Where are you headed?" Theo asked. He thought he should say something friendly before asking for water. That he would stand a better chance of getting it that way.

"Home," the soldier said. His voice was monotone, without expression.

"Where's that?"

"Forty-Two East Twenty-Ninth Street, Brooklyn, New York." The man said the address exactly in the manner of a child who'd been taught to memorize it in case he got lost.

"Okay. Well, I think you're going the wrong way. The war's that way." Theo pointed back over his shoulder toward the river. "Home is behind you. You want to come with us? That's where we're headed."

The soldier said nothing. It was as if he hadn't heard and was just waiting for Theo to get out of the way so that he could resume his journey.

"Have you got any water?" Theo asked, standing his ground.

This time the soldier moved to go past, and Theo was about to try to stop him when he heard the noise of a plane. He looked up and saw a single black biplane coming directly toward them. He immediately knew it was German, recognizing it as one of the Heinkels that had bombed the Lincolns below Mosquito Ridge.

He dropped to the ground, pulling up his knees and pushing his hands up over his head. But the soldier paid the plane no attention, resuming his walk toward the river as if it wasn't there.

"Get down, you fool!" Theo shouted, but his voice was drowned out by the roar of the plane's engine and the screech of the bombs that it was dropping as it passed over. He felt their impact jar through his body as he pressed down against the hard earth, which was rising, pushing him away.

He could smell fire and smoke. The wheat was burning, and he had to get to Joseph. But the plane was coming back. Diving now to strafe. He could hear the whirr of the propeller and the machine-gun bullets whipping the ground near to where he was, and as the plane banked and roared away, he caught a glimpse of the pilot looking back and laughing like a beast.

It was hard to orient himself in the dust and smoke, but he set off toward where he thought he'd left Joseph, and almost immediately tripped over something on the ground, falling flat on his face.

He got to his feet, brushing the earth out of his eyes, and saw the soldier beside him lying face up in the wheat with a pool of seeping crimson blood where his throat had been. Theo pushed him onto his side, so that he wouldn't have to see that anymore, and searched the soldier's pack with trembling fingers. There was a full canteen of water, and food too. Untouched tins of Argentinian beef and biscuit.

He gathered it all in his hands and stumbled forward, calling Joseph's name over and over again, but receiving no reply. He didn't know now where he'd left him and everything looked the same. Wheat and rocks and, farther off, fire and black smoke where the bombs had dropped.

Had they hit Joseph? Was that why he was not answering? Why hadn't he marked the place where he'd left him? Why had he been such a fool?

He was looking for a needle in a haystack. He was Manny's mother crying out for her cat in Brooklyn and getting no reply. He was . . .

He stopped, alone in the wide valley, and took the rosary out of the pouch around his neck and prayed, holding it up to the blank blue sky. "Give me this. Please. Just this one thing," he beseeched the void.

Nothing. Silence, and then a rifle shot. It had to be Joseph. There was no one else it could be in this white desert.

And the noise had been behind Theo, not in front. He'd been walking away from his friend until he stopped to pray for his salvation.

He began retracing his steps, and a minute later he caught sight of Joseph sitting up in the wheat with the rifle he'd fired cradled in his arms.

He was upright, but his eyes weren't seeing and his ears weren't hearing until Theo poured the last of the brandy down his throat, followed by water, and he spluttered back into consciousness and was even able to join Theo in eating some of the beef.

"I was giving up, drifting away," he said, groping for words to describe an experience with which he was still trying to come to terms. "It was easy, just like going to sleep. A small thing. Not the be-all and end-all like you imagine it. And then the bombs and the gunfire changed that. It mattered that they missed, and I wanted to come back when I heard you calling, but I couldn't because you were going away, and then I saw your rifle. It was like you'd left it for a reason."

"I prayed for a sign," said Theo, struck with wonder. "And then I heard the shot."

Joseph stared at Theo, as if trying to decipher the meaning of what he'd said, and then raised his eyes, looking up at the sky. "Sometimes he's there. Just like when I was a child. The whole world in his hands. Other times, most times, I know better. Or worse . . ." He shook his head and smiled and lay back, closing his eyes.

Theo could hear the labor of his friend's breathing, and his blood-soaked tunic told its own story. He knew that Joseph's life was hanging by a thread, and all their luck with the rifle, the food, and the water would mean nothing if he couldn't get him to a doctor soon. He didn't think that Joseph would survive a night out in the cold, and they couldn't walk across open country in the dark. They had to keep going.

They set off again, following the sun as it dipped toward the west. A red ball of fire seen through a haze of ocher dust.

As he walked, Theo conjured up a vision in his mind's eye of the Pearly Gates up beyond the end of the valley. The stream washing over the white rocks, the croaking frogs and the invisible voices raised in song. The stag at the edge of the trees, watching. A refuge far away from this valley of dry bones.

He hadn't known when he came down off the knoll on that first day, ready for battle, that he was in truth descending a stairway into hell, with each step a photograph imprinted now on the scarred surface of his mind. The man executed in cold blood while he watched, somehow complicit, from the doorway in Villanueva; the man falling from the church tower as if in slow motion; the shell-shocked soldier whose water they'd drunk, who would never now be going home; the bloated, blackened bodies cooking in the sun below Mosquito Ridge.

The images stripped meaning from experience, pressing down on his mind and his soul. The pursuit of ideals became vain posturing under the pitiless, burning sun. All that mattered was the here and now. He and Joseph, putting one foot in front of the other, refusing to give up and die.

He remembered his friends—Antonio running and falling, Manny slipping away in Alvah's chair. He wouldn't let Joseph go. Nothing mattered now except that.

But it was hard. Joseph was leaning on him so heavily now that he was practically carrying him, and he hadn't the strength for that. Joseph's breath was a rasping rattle in his throat, and there was no more water.

Gravity told and they toppled to the ground, and Theo heard a voice cursing Joseph and a moment later realized it was his. But there was another noise too. Gone in a moment, but he'd heard enough to know what it was. An engine. Up ahead.

"We made it!" he shouted, bending down over Joseph and trying to pull him up. "The road's up there. Just a few more yards. Get up, damn you."

But Joseph didn't respond. He'd lost consciousness and Theo couldn't bring him back, however hard he tried.

He knelt, bending his mouth to Joseph's ear and whispered, "I've got to go up there and get help, but I'm coming back. Don't die on me, Joe. Don't you dare do that! You hear me?"

He got up and walked to the road and stood there on the tarmac, ready to wave down the next passing truck. He tried to stay focused, but there was nothing to focus on. Just the road and the fields and the shimmering light. He swayed a little and closed his eyes for a moment to rest, and straightaway, his legs gave way beneath him and he was lying as if in the bottom of a boat, gently rocking on a black sea. He slept.

And woke to the screech of brakes and the shriek of a Klaxon horn. A truck had braked to a juddering halt right behind him on the road, and the burly Spanish driver was getting out of his cab and approaching, gesticulating angrily with his hands and shouting.

But he was rendered speechless when Theo struggled to his feet, blundered toward him, and hugged him tight, calling him a savior, and pulled him by the arm down off the road to where Joseph was lying prostrate on the ground.

This time Theo was sure that Joseph was dead. He hadn't moved from where he'd left him, and a swarm of black flies was buzzing around his face. The driver brushed them aside and knelt, holding his cheek to Joseph's mouth, feeling for breath. Theo's heart stood still and then raced when the driver raised his thumb and hoisted Joseph up onto his back, as if he weighed nothing at all, and carried him to the truck with Theo following behind, gabbling his gratitude.

The field hospital had been set up in the same orchard outside Villanueva de la Cañada where the Lincolns had rested before they set out for the river on the second day. The barn where the Fascists had been imprisoned was now a combined ward and operating room, with its big doors open to the evening light, and Theo recognized the doctor as the same one who had helped Uncle at Jarama. It seemed lucky that it should be him, Theo thought. Uncle had survived.

"Where've you come from?" the doctor asked as he cut away Joseph's tunic, cleaned the wound, and set up a blood transfusion.

"Mosquito Ridge. We walked to the road, and then the truck brought us the rest of the way."

"You walked?" The doctor stopped what he was doing and looked at Theo, amazed.

"Yeah. I didn't want him to die."

"Well, maybe he won't because of you. You should be proud, son. You might just have saved his life."

Theo's hands shook and he began to cry. Great, heaving sobs that racked his body. He couldn't speak, even if he'd wanted to, and the doctor looked at him, concerned.

"You need to get something to eat and drink. There's a field kitchen out there with all you need, and then you should get some rest," he said kindly. "You can go back to your company in the morning. Everything will look better then."

"Go back?" Theo repeated, as if the words made no sense.

He walked over to the kitchen and ate a plate of hot stew washed down with wine, filled his water bottle, and helped himself to some tins of food to put in his pack, and then went back to the barn. Through the open door, he could see Joseph sleeping peacefully on a makeshift bed. It was only a few yards away from where he was standing, so he could make out the even rise and fall of his friend's chest. He nodded, satisfied by what he'd seen, and walked on out of the camp to the road, where he turned right, not left. Headed home, just like he'd told the shell-shocked soldier by the river whom he couldn't save.

The sun was sinking to the horizon, and the western sky was suffused in a wash of red and gold vermilion as he passed through Villanueva de la Cañada for the last time. It was a ghost town now, looking like the photographs he'd seen in books of ruined Belgian towns ravaged by the First World War. Broken buildings pockmarked by shrapnel; jagged, empty holes that had once been windows; rubble cascading across the sidewalks.

Somewhere out of sight, a wall collapsed. A noise of lurching and crashing and settling, followed by a cry, human perhaps, and then nothing except the sound of Theo's boots crunching through the grit and ash. He wouldn't stop. Not for anything.

He passed the smoke-blackened church in the main square, with its iron bell suspended motionless in the empty tower from where the machine guns had rotated their deadly fire on the first day, and went out through the north gate. Up ahead he could see the outline of the tree-covered hill at the end of the valley over which the evening star glittered in the twilight, drawing him on.

One foot in front of the other, retracing his steps down the straight black road and up the hill and through the trees—the blessed trees—until he heard water on stones and frogs croaking in the moonlight, and lay down on the thick pine needles with his pack for a pillow and closed his eyes and slept.

He woke in the early light, looking up the barrel of a rifle pointed straight down at his head. There were other rifles, too, and the men holding them were on horseback and the brown horses were pawing the ground close to where he was lying. He could feel their hot breath on his face.

They spoke French, calling him *déserteur*, and tied his hands with rope and set him off walking down the road with other AWOL soldiers whom they'd found hiding in the woods. Not too fast and with breaks for water. The horsemen were doing a job, and Theo was grateful that they seemed to have no desire to torment their prisoners. That, he imagined, would come later, when he and the other *déserteurs* reached wherever they were going.

The prisoners spoke ten different languages and struggled desperately to communicate with each other in a fantastic pidgin polyglot, apparently unaware that they were all saying the same things. That they had suffered terribly, been treated like animals, and should now be allowed to go home. Oh, and their captors were good-for-nothing apparatchiks who should be given a taste of what it was like at the front.

The prisoners' ceaseless litany of complaint rose up through the still air, disappearing unanswered into the canopies of the tall trees that grew on either side of the road. Either the horsemen didn't understand, or if they did, they didn't care, and Theo observed the whole strange scene detachedly, saying nothing, as if it was a comedy being played out on a stage in which he had no further role to play.

Or a tragedy. The lines from *Macbeth* that he'd learned in school floated into his mind:

> Life's but a walking shadow, a poor player,
> That struts and frets his hour upon the stage,
> And then is heard no more. It is a tale
> Told by an idiot, full of sound and fury,
> Signifying nothing.

Macbeth knew. About the way to dusty death. Just as Andrew did. He remembered his stepfather standing at the window, telling him about war. *"Dead trees, dead earth, dead water, dead men . . ."* He should have listened, but it was too late now.

He was emptied of feeling. He walked when he was told to walk, stopped when he was told to stop, and climbed compliantly into the back of the truck with the other prisoners when they got to the clearing in the woods where it was waiting to take them back to Albacete. Back down the same road that he and Joseph and Manny and the other volunteers had traveled in the opposite direction four months before, like latter-day Quixotes, eager for battle.

*"Breathing the free air."* Theo smiled, remembering what Joseph had said as they leaned out of the back of the truck on that winter afternoon, filling their lungs. Not so free anymore. They'd given everything they had, and now Manny was dead and Joseph was at death's door and he was a prisoner with his hands tied, on his way to an ugly future in a Communist jail.

# PART THREE

## BARCELONA

## SUMMER 1937

Power is not a means; it is an end. One does not establish a dictatorship in order to safeguard a revolution; one makes the revolution in order to establish the dictatorship. The object of persecution is persecution. The object of torture is torture. The object of power is power.

—*George Orwell, 1984*

# 21

## ESMOND

**CAMP LUKÁCS**. The sign—black on a white board—loomed up suddenly out of the bleak, dusty plain as the truck turned hard right and bounced up a rutted road to a metal gate in a tall barbed-wire fence that ran in an immense square around the camp buildings—a long whitewashed single-story house encircled by a cluster of ready-made clapboard huts with narrow slits for windows.

As the truck drove through the gate, Theo caught a glimpse of guards patrolling the perimeter with muzzled dogs and a soldier in sunglasses looking down at them from an observation tower. Nothing grew anywhere inside the compound. Not even weeds. It was worse even than he'd imagined.

The truck stopped and was at once surrounded by men in leather jackets with machine pistols at their belts, who pushed the prisoners into the main building and drove them down a corridor that opened out into a wide hall.

Two clerks took their fingerprints and asked them rapid-fire questions: name, nationality, battalion, date of birth, date of first arrival at Albacete—that last, Theo supposed, so they could cross-refer their records. Anyone who didn't answer quickly enough got smacked around the head by one of the goons. They were different from the horsemen in the woods. Not detached, but vibrant with malice, as if fed on the same raw meat as the attack dogs outside.

From the hall, the prisoners were herded across to the largest of the huts. A push in the back sent Theo tumbling to the dirt floor. Behind him, the metal door slammed shut and a key turned in the lock.

It was hot and humid in the semidarkness, and the prisoners took it in turns to beat on the door, but no one came. Some gave way to hysteria, crying and shouting in a babble of languages, while others like Theo withdrew into themselves, sitting against the walls with their knees drawn up in front of their faces and their arms tight across their chests as they tried in vain to shut themselves off from the misery all around them.

The prisoners were pressed in so close together that there was no room to stretch out even if they had wanted to, except in the far corner, where an overflowing toilet filled the hut with noxious fumes.

In the late afternoon they were taken outside and given a piece of stale bread and a bowl of watery soup containing a desiccated potato and some white beans—worse than anything that had come up in the galvanized washtubs from the cookhouse at Jarama. Then, after five minutes blinking in the light, they were pushed back inside the hut.

At night the prisoners clung to each other for comfort. Strangers holding on to strangers. No one beat on the door anymore, and they shrank back when it opened in the morning and the guards began taking them out for interrogation.

Theo was shocked when his name was called. He'd been thinking in the night about Carlos's description of his imprisonment in Asturias and remembered how Carlos had said that the prisoners there were tortured in alphabetical order, so he'd assumed wrongly that the same would happen here if torture was to be their fate. The wanton viciousness of the guards as they pushed and shoved Theo across the sunbaked ground to the main house made him tremble for what was coming next.

He was taken to a small room and strip-searched. The humiliation hurt Theo in a way that he hadn't yet experienced. It made him feel not just vulnerable but worthless. A body whose pretensions to individual significance were laughable.

One of the guards ripped the cotton pouch from Theo's neck and emptied the contents onto a table. The lock of Maria's brown hair fell gently to the floor, and Theo bent down without thinking to retrieve it, only to be stopped by a punch to the side of the head that sent him staggering back. His vision was a blur, and when he looked back, he couldn't see where the hair had gone.

He was braced for more violence, but none came. The guards were counting the money—pounds and pesetas—and Theo could see the cupidity in their eyes and their dirty, grasping fingers. They looked over at him, and Theo read the calculation going through their minds. Did he know how much there was? Would he tell their superior the amount? Who would the superior believe? In the end their fear won out over their greed, and they ordered him to put on his underclothes but nothing else, and one of them marched him down a corridor to a closed door at the end, marked with the name *Commandant Neumann*.

The guard knocked, and a loud, authoritative voice called out *"Venga!"* in response.

Inside, the commandant was seated behind a large desk, writing in a ledger book. Apart from his chair and two metal filing cabinets in the corner, it was the only piece of furniture in the room. He was wearing a tight-fitting khaki shirt open at the neck, with the sleeves rolled up past his elbows to the beginning of his muscular biceps. He was completely bald, and his shiny, shaven skull glowed in the sunlight that was pouring in through the wide window behind him. Beside his hand a large, silver-colored pistol lay on the desk, its barrel pointed at Theo where he stood waiting. The guard had retreated to the corner of the room after carefully placing the rosary, passport, and money beside the gun. There was a piece of paper there, too, which Theo recognized as the answers he'd given to the admitting clerk the day before.

The only sound in the room was the scratching of the pen. The commandant had stopped for a moment to glance over the paper but had then gone back to his work without looking up.

Theo had to urinate. The need came on him suddenly. Nothing one moment and then desperation the next. He asked to go to the toilet in Spanish and in English and in his schoolboy French, but the commandant ignored him. Soon he couldn't hold it anymore and he felt the sticky liquid running down his leg onto the floor, and he smelled it too. The shame was worse even than his earlier nakedness. The guard behind him guffawed and then choked back on his laughter when the commandant looked up.

Theo was not prepared for his eyes. They were deeply sunk beneath the overhang of his broad forehead, and they didn't seem to blink or twitch. It was as if the eyelids were paralyzed.

"Why did you desert?" the commandant demanded in English. He spoke fluently, although with a strong accent, and Theo guessed he was German.

"Because I couldn't fight anymore."

"Because you are a coward?"

"I couldn't go on. It wasn't a choice."

"Of course it was—a coward's choice!" said the commandant and nodded to the guard at the door, who came forward and slapped Theo. Enough to hurt but not enough to knock him down. Not yet.

The commandant picked up the money and counted it and whistled. "Who was paying you?" he demanded.

"Paying me?"

"For information. You must have told them a lot to earn this kind of money."

"I haven't told anyone anything. The money's mine. My stepfather gave it to me."

"Who is your stepfather?"

"Sir Andrew Campion-Bennett. He's British."

"Sir Andrew!" repeated the commandant, seizing on the name. "A British aristocrat—they're the people who are bankrolling Franco. And you, too, so it seems."

"No, it's not like that."

"Not like that? Why have you got this then?" the commandant asked, picking the rosary up off the desk between his thumb and forefinger, as if any closer contact might soil him.

"To keep me safe."

"It doesn't seem to be working too well, does it?" said the commandant, allowing himself a thin smile. "You're a Catholic spying for the Fascists. A traitor! That's what you are." After delivering his verdict, the commandant nodded again to the guard, who came forward and punched Theo hard on the side of the head in just the same place where he'd hit him before. This time Theo's legs gave way beneath him, and everything after that was a blur.

He was being kicked and dragged and kicked again, and he was curled up into a ball and someone was shouting "Don't! Please!" and that was him, and someone else who wasn't him was laughing, and a door was closing hard with a clang, and then there was just the pain as he lay doubled up, bleeding and soiled on a hard concrete floor. Alone.

Theo had no idea how long he lay where they'd left him. Perhaps he slept. Perhaps not. There was no way to measure time except by light or the absence of light coming in through the high, narrow window of the cell. Now, there was light, so it was still day.

Looking up, he could see that the whitewashed walls were covered in graffiti, just like in Figueres Castle. Names and dates and in one corner the name *Neumann* under a crudely drawn swastika. Under the window, someone had written in careful French: *Je me suis porté volontaire. J'ai le droit de rentrer chez moi.*—I volunteered. I have the right to go home. And below that: *J'ai combattu. Ils ne l'ont pas fait.*—I fought. They didn't. Theo wondered where the writer was now.

Sometimes there were footsteps outside; sometimes they stopped, and he was sure the guards had come for him. The phrase Carlos had used to describe the torture he'd been subjected to in Asturias kept reverberating in his head: *With rods, with water, with electricity . . .* Fear made him shake like a man suffering from palsy as he watched a disembodied eye gazing at him through the judas hole in the door, and he waited, not breathing, for the noise of the key turning in the lock, but instead the eye withdrew and the footsteps went away.

When the light faded, a tray was slid through a hatch in the door, containing the same food as the day before. He ate and he slept and when he awoke, it was dark and his head was hot with fever. He wanted them to come now. Anything would be better than the waiting and the isolation. Somewhere outside there was shouting, and a shot rang out, followed by silence. Theo wept.

Suddenly everything changed. There were loud voices outside and the door opened.

Theo took a step back. He thought Esmond was an apparition, just as he had at Jarama. He had been so convinced that the opening of the door would lead to a renewal of torment that he was completely unprepared for it to reveal that it would end.

But then, when Esmond stayed himself and didn't turn into the commandant, he staggered forward, gripping on to Esmond's arms.

"Christ, Theo, you look like you've gone ten rounds with Joe Louis," Esmond said, holding him up.

"I'm broken. I've got nothing left. Can you get me out of here? Please!" Theo's voice was a whisper. No louder than his breath.

"Sure I can," said Esmond, bending to hear. "That's why I'm here."

Esmond. His friend from long, long ago. Theo held on to him like a drowning man, but his legs were giving way beneath him, and he slipped down into a place where he knew no more.

The next hour was a blur of sensation, even after Theo had recovered consciousness. Cold water in his mouth and hot water on his head splashing down over hard, sticklike ribs that seemed to be pushing out through the skin of his emaciated body, curving around to the unyielding sternum. And after, a white towel—so unfamiliar in his hands—to make him dry, and new clothes to replace the ragged scarecrow uniform he'd worn for months. In a kitchen, a ham sandwich he had to think to chew, and when it was gone, Esmond and his driver—broad-shouldered and taciturn—supporting him outside to the beautiful black Hispano-Suiza motorcar with its huge silver headlamps and radiator grille shimmering like a mirage in the sun. Nothing standing in his way, nobody pulling him back. Just silence all around as he sank back into the rich leather upholstery and felt the engine purring into life.

As the car drew away, Theo glanced back over his shoulder at the sweatbox huts, feeling a fleeting, stabbing pity for his fellow deserters locked up inside with no hope of rescue, and then all at once the prison camp was gone and the highway stretched out in front—a gray ribbon running east like a river through the parched yellow land.

He slept and woke in another country from the one he'd left behind. The sea on his right, and on his left, lemon and orange groves, and above them, perched along the rising hills, honey-colored castles and churches flashing by as the powerful car ate up the miles.

Beside him, Esmond was reading a document typed in Cyrillic lettering. Russian, Theo supposed. He put it away when he saw that Theo was awake.

"Feeling better?" he asked.

"Yes," said Theo with a wan smile. "Thank you for saving my life."

"I'm glad I could. We got lucky. If Neumann had thought you were just a deserter, we wouldn't be sitting here now. He'd have carried on beating you black and blue, just like he does to everyone he gets his hands on in there, and no one would have been any the wiser. I doubt you'd have survived it for very long with the shape you're in. But instead he took one look at your money and that idiotic rosary you've been carrying around and jumped to the conclusion that you were a Fascist spy—a big catch that was going to cover him in glory. Once he'd decided that, he had to report it up the chain of command, which is how I got to hear about you, and as soon as I did, I jumped straight in the car and had Javier drive me halfway across Spain to rescue you. And here we are!"

"I thought you'd washed your hands of me. That's what you said you were going to do before."

"I didn't mean it. I thought you'd taken enough punishment after Jarama, and I was exasperated by your pigheadedness when you wouldn't let me take you out of there. That's all. I'm your friend, Theo. You should know that by now," said Esmond, patting Theo's knee reassuringly.

But Theo wasn't entirely reassured. He was convinced now that Manny had been right about the Communists. They were the enemy, just as much as the Fascists. They had destroyed the Lincolns and put him in Camp Lukács. Yes, Esmond had got him out, but that didn't change the fact that he was a Communist—and a powerful one, too, judging by his expensive car and driver and his ability to pull rank on Neumann.

"What are you doing here, Esmond?" he asked. "I thought you moved stuff around. That's what you told me in Oxford."

"People more than stuff these days," said Esmond airily. "I work to keep the Republic safe, just like you've been doing with the Internationals. What happens behind the lines can be just as important as what goes on at the front. I'm sure you know that."

"Safe from who?"

"From spies who want to betray her and revolutionaries who want to overthrow her. It's a full-time occupation, believe me."

"Who are the spies?"

"The POUM. They call themselves a workers' party and pretend they're Marxists, but it's all a front. The truth is they're Trotskyites working for Franco.

There's a highly organized fifth column in Barcelona, sending the Fascists vital information and getting ready to seize the town when they're given the signal, and we have to stamp it out while there's still time."

Theo remembered seeing the name POUM on some of the posters that had gone up around Barcelona in the heady days after the defeat of the army the previous summer. It was the same Trotskyite party that Alvah had blamed for the rebellion in Barcelona in May. Trotsky was Stalin's mortal enemy, exiled now in Mexico, and Theo felt sure that the Red Tsar would not tolerate the existence of any Communist party not loyal to him. *Stamp out*—the expression Esmond had used was uncharacteristically brutal, and Theo had picked up on the venom in his voice. It reminded him of that fanatical side of Esmond that used to peep out occasionally from behind his companionable exterior when they were at Saint Gregory's.

"If the POUM are the spies, then the Anarchists are the revolutionaries. Is that what you're saying?" Theo asked.

"Some of them are spies too. But yes, most of them are true believers. They're like stupid children who kick their parents out of the house and then let it go to rack and ruin because they haven't got a clue how to keep it going. Barcelona's the economic powerhouse of the Republic, and we can't win the war unless we mobilize its full potential. We need people running the factories who know what they're doing, not worker committees running them into the ground. And the Anarchists' Red Terror was a gift to the Fascists. Anyone can see that. France and England are never going to support the Republic if they think it's going to murder everyone in their beds and expropriate all their investments."

"They're not going to intervene," said Theo gloomily. "They know which side their bread's buttered."

"Maybe, maybe not. But we have to try to get them involved. It's the only way we're going to defeat Franco, with all the help he's getting from Hitler and Mussolini. The Fascists are the natural enemies of the democracies. If we can stay in the game and look reasonable, then things could change very quickly."

Theo nodded, remembering the German and Italian planes at Brunete. The Fascists had had too much power. Courage alone couldn't win against those odds. But he didn't have Esmond's faith in the future. How could he, after what he had seen? All the hope they'd felt on the march through the woods reduced to bitter despair amid the carnage of Mosquito Ridge. The memory of the battlefield set his hands trembling in his lap and he closed his eyes, trying desperately to clear his mind.

Esmond watched him with a look that melded curiosity and concern. "Don't look so miserable," he said encouragingly. "You're out of Camp Lukács and out of the army, and you can go back to your favorite city without the Anarchists putting you up against the nearest wall, as they most certainly would have done before they overplayed their hand in May. You should be dancing for joy instead of looking like you want to jump off a cliff."

"Is that where we're going? Barcelona?"

"Yes, you're going to help me for a few weeks before you go back to Oxford and resume your studies."

"Help you with what?"

"Interpreting. English to Spanish; Spanish to English. My Spanish is basic. Good enough for getting around, but not for anything more than that. And it's not just about translation; I need someone I can trust, and I can trust you, can't I, Theo? Now that I've saved your life."

Esmond asked the question in an offhand tone, but he watched Theo intently as he waited for his answer.

Theo nodded and even managed a smile. He knew he couldn't evade his promise to Esmond. Not now when his debt was so great. But Oxford was in the future, and today he was just excited to be returning to Barcelona. Esmond was right. He'd got lucky. No, more than lucky: his whole life had changed in a morning. He was headed not for the torture chamber but for the place he wanted to go. He needed to find Maria. He needed to know she was safe. Barcelona was where she'd hidden before, and he felt sure that that was where she would be hiding again. This time he would find her, and they could be together at last.

"That's more like it!" said Esmond, noticing Theo's smile. "We'll have fun. Just like in the old days but better. Barcelona's got a bit more to offer than Carborough! You know, you're my oldest friend, Theo. Maybe my only one. I'm a loner. Always have been. I don't make friends easily. I've missed you."

"I missed you too, Esmond," Theo replied, because that at least was true.

Theo was young, and a combination of good food and a comfortable bed enabled him to make a quick physical recovery from his ordeal at Brunete and in Camp Lukács, although the rest cure did nothing to address the mental scars that he had suffered in the six months since he first arrived in the Jarama Valley.

He carried within him that old feeling of numbness, coupled with a sense of something missing that was always tugging at his mind. The world appeared two-dimensional, as if the extra layer that gave it meaning and depth had been stripped away.

Memories of the trenches and the battlefields were more vivid to Theo than what was happening in the here and now, but he pushed them away like a man struggling to stay afloat, only for them to come back to haunt him in his dreams, from which he awoke sweating and crying out in the small hours. Just as his stepfather had feared, he had changed into something he was not. What remained uncertain was who this new Theo was going to be.

He refused to answer Esmond's questions about his life as a soldier, explaining that the memories were too painful. The only reference he made to Brunete was to ask Esmond to find out what had happened to Joseph Freeman. When Esmond came back with the news that Joseph had survived and was making a good recovery at the Villa Paz Hospital southeast of Madrid, Theo agreed to go out for the first time and have fun. Or at least try to.

They went to the Ritz because Esmond insisted and Theo had no basis to argue without referring to Maria, which he was determined not to do. Esmond had told him in the car coming back from Camp Lukács that his work for the Communists involved rounding up Anarchists whom he classed as enemies of the Republic, and Theo didn't want to set him on Maria's trail.

He couldn't believe his luck that he hadn't told Esmond about her when they'd talked in Oxford. Esmond had known back then that Theo had been chased out of Barcelona by the Anarchists, but the information he'd been given was that that was because of Theo's relationship to his stepfather, who was on the Anarchists' wanted list, and Theo had not felt the need to set him right and explain about Primitivo and Maria. Perhaps, too, he had realized even then that Esmond might be his oldest friend, but that that didn't mean he could be trusted.

Everything had changed since Theo went to the Ritz with Maria. It was as if the past was a figment of his disordered imagination. The **HOTEL GASTRONÓMICO**

**No. 1** sign no longer hung outside, the tables were no longer pushed together, and the poor were nowhere in sight. The waiters wore boiled shirts and bobbed their heads subserviently as they took orders for fine wine and food, and jewels glittered on the necks and wrists of the women in evening dress.

It was the same all over Barcelona. The bourgeoisie had come out of hiding. They wore ties and hats and smart summer suits, no longer feeling the need to disguise themselves in their servants' clothing or in the blue mono uniform of the Anarchists that had disappeared from the streets, along with the red-and-black flags and the CNT posters, ripped down from off the walls.

*"Now do you believe?"* Maria had asked him that night as they sat side by side, wedged between the militiaman and the old lady. *"I'm beginning to,"* he'd replied. Fools that they'd been. Chasing chimeras. The revolution was gone, as if it had never been, and the loss of the past filled Theo with that same tinseled melancholy he'd been prey to all his life ever since he'd first felt it on Coney Island when he was a boy.

"What's wrong?" asked Esmond with a hint of annoyance. "We agreed to have a good time. Remember?"

"I'm sorry. It's just strange being back here. That's all," Theo said, realizing he had to provide some explanation for his low spirits. "Everything was so heady a year ago. We were drunk on victory, I guess, and we didn't know how it was all going to turn out."

"So that's it. Mooning over those damned Anarchists again. I don't know what's wrong with you, Theo. Really, I don't. They wanted to kill you and yet you act like they're your best friends!"

"I think it's because I wanted what they wanted. Not the violence, but freedom and the right for the people to take control of their own lives. It's what I was fighting for with the Lincolns, or at least I thought so."

"And we want that too," said Esmond. "But only when we've won the war. Until then we've got to do whatever's necessary to win it. It's common sense, but the Anarchists haven't got any of that. They just want to tend their garden and ignore the elephant on the other side of the hedge who's coming to trample it. It beats me that you can't see what idiots they are."

"I see both sides. Yes, you need to win, but the people have to have something to fight for, too, and I don't think they've got that now, at least not in this town."

"You don't like the Communists. That's what you're saying, isn't it?"

"I think that they're after power for its own sake. Following orders coming from somewhere else. So I don't trust what they say about the future. No."

"Which means you don't trust me. Is that right?"

Theo shrugged his shoulders, and to his great surprise, Esmond laughed.

"I've forgotten how contrary you are, Theo. Do you remember how it used to make me so mad at school? I'd go off and sulk for weeks because you wouldn't agree with me. But now I realize it's one of your best traits. It's who you are. Always asking questions, always having doubts, never giving in to anyone. But then when there's a challenge that anyone else would run away from, you jump in without even thinking about the danger. Into Olympia, into the brigades, into the next battle. You're one of a kind, Theo Sterling. You really are."

Esmond raised his glass of champagne to Theo, who blushed, touched not only by the compliments Esmond had paid him but also by their complete unexpectedness. They chased his blues away at least temporarily, and he laughed as much as Esmond when they stopped at a shooting gallery in Plaça de Catalunya to play Anti-Fascist Bang Bang. Crude iron representations of Franco, Mola, and several other Fascist generals had replaced the usual ducks and bobbed slowly across the firing line on a revolving mechanical track.

Esmond missed with every single shot, but Theo's experience with the Lincolns had made him a fair marksman, and taking down all five generals with his five bullets won him a goldfish that he liberated in the fountain, and he smiled when Esmond suggested that the shooting gallery should add an Anarchist leader or two to the track to give amateurs like him a chance.

But his happiness evaporated when he glanced back toward the Hotel Colón—the Communists' headquarters—and met the hooded eyes of Stalin staring down from the facade. *"They take everything. Even you."* He heard Maria's voice again like a whisper in his inner ear, and he had no answer to her accusation.

Esmond made no secret of the fact that he was working for the Republic's intelligence service, the Servicio de Información Militar, or SIM. Theo never found out the title of his job, but it was clear that it was high up, at the level where those running the service interacted with the Soviet intelligence officers stationed in Barcelona. Sometimes Esmond would talk to them on the phone in Russian or meet them at the Colón for consultations.

On these occasions Theo waited for him in the lobby. There was no sign of Alfonso or any of the old staff, who had been replaced by cold-eyed apparatchiks with revolvers on their hips. Theo plucked up his courage and asked them if they knew where he could find the concierge who had worked there before the war, but they shrugged their shoulders and said they knew nothing. Alfonso belonged to an era that had vanished into history, and it saddened Theo to know that he would never see his friend again.

Officially, the SIM was a branch of the Spanish government, but it was an open secret that it was controlled by the Communists. They had jails all over Barcelona that everyone, including Esmond, referred to openly as *checas*—a word derived from the *Cheka*, the Soviet secret police—and Esmond sometimes visited them with Theo to carry out interrogations at which Theo acted as the interpreter.

The SIM's main center of operations, however, was in Montjuïc Castle, the centuries-old fortress on the high summit of Montjuïc Hill southwest of the city. Theo remembered how Antonio had pointed the castle out to him the previous summer and described its evil reputation. The Madrid government had constructed it in the eighteenth century to dominate Barcelona, and its cannons had bombarded the city on a number of occasions. The Anarchists hated the castle because their fighters had been tortured and executed there after rebellions that had been brutally suppressed in 1896 and 1909.

Esmond could have stayed at the castle if he wished. There was accommodation available above his office, but he always left when his work was done at the end of the day and took Theo with him in the Hispano to the Güell Palace off the Ramblas. Always with his driver, Javier, in silent attendance.

Theo recognized the palace from the previous summer, when he had run past its long, classical facade to bring the news of the Anarchists' victory on the Paral·lel to Durruti. Now, the Catalan government had requisitioned it for war use and given it over to the secret police.

Esmond loved the palace, and a look of delight lit up his face whenever the Hispano passed through the wrought iron entrance archway and entered the cavernous lamplit vestibule. Theo thought he understood why. It was as if they had gone through the portal to a magic kingdom, utterly unrelated to the busy, run-down world outside. The sudden change was extraordinary. Sound was muffled by the pinewood paving and the monumental walls of polished blue-gray stone glowed on either side of the two carriage lanes that ran like underground streets through to the coach house behind. Between them, a wide carpeted staircase ascended up into the interior of the palace like the beginning of a story from the *Arabian Nights*. Looking up, Theo felt the same thrill as when he'd gazed spellbound at Arthur Rackham's pictures in the books that his stepfather had given him when he was a boy.

He experienced the magic that the architect, Antoni Gaudí, had intended when he designed and built the palace for his fabulously rich patron, the Catholic industrialist Eusebi Güell, fifty years before. What surprised him was that Esmond felt it too. It was not what he would have expected from a Marxist materialist for whom Güell should have been the archetypal class enemy.

He thought perhaps that it was the palace's inverted watchfulness that drew Esmond. It was unlike any other house that Theo had ever known because it looked in and not out. The rooms on each floor were arranged around the magnificent great hall that rose through three stories to a circular white eye in a tessellated ceiling of translucent rose-pink limestone. Inside the hall, a small chapel decorated in sumptuous gold leaf was the womb of the building, the holy of holies at its central core.

Sometimes Theo found Esmond running his hands over the surfaces, feeling the textures of the different cladding materials—ebony and rosewood and walnut; brass and stone and wrought iron. "I feel it's alive. Breathing. The walls are its skin," he told Theo, and took him down a ramp of river pebbles to the basement stables, where the roof was supported on a forest of mushroom-shaped columns made of brick. "They're growing. That's what Gaudí meant us to feel. I'm sure of it," he said, peering into the cavernous shadows as if he thought that the ghost of the architect might be waiting there, ready to answer.

There were cells down in the basement, too, where high-value prisoners were sometimes brought for interrogation, but Esmond rarely worked in the palace. He used it instead as a place of relaxation and spent most of his time in the Room of Lost Steps, which occupied a vital position on the main floor overlooking the street. The room acted as the vestibule and light source for the great hall, and Gaudí had spared no expense on sumptuous and lavish decoration to symbolize the wealth and power of the owner. An elaborately coffered oak ceiling was decorated with wrought iron ornaments, while three groups of elaborately designed marble columns separated a narrow gallery overlooking the street from the rest of the space.

Esmond loved the room and its mysterious name, explaining to Theo that it was an architectural term for an antechamber to a throne room or hall of justice. A room where supplicants waited, walking up and down, thinking of what lay ahead. Lost steps trod on the threshold of success or despair.

He kept a locked kneehole desk in the room that had once belonged to Eusebi Güell, but he rarely worked at it, using it instead as a surface on which to play chess with Theo late into the night, the pieces glowing in the light of the double lamps whose bulbous white globes were fixed at the ends of long, intricately designed brass holders climbing up the sides of the marble entrance archways.

He played with apparent insouciance, drinking Eusebi Güell's wine and singing along to the same old jazz records that Theo remembered from Saint Gregory's, which he played on a wind-up box gramophone that he kept in the corner of the room, but he never made mistakes and wore Theo down with his slowly building attacks, so that Theo almost never won.

And then, when the first hint of dawn crept through the windows, he would take a flashlight and lead Theo up the dark stairways to the roof terrace and wander among the forest of brightly colored chimneys with a final glass of wine in his hand. The ceramic and porcelain tiles interspersed with fragments of white marble glimmered in the first rays of the sun rising over the Mediterranean, and Esmond raised his glass and drank to Antoni Gaudí, the greatest man who'd ever lived.

"Greater than Marx?" Theo asked, laughing.

"Definitely."

"Greater than Stalin?"

"Without a doubt!" Esmond shouted and threw his glass Russian-style against the thickly glazed sandstone of the spire and burst out laughing too.

Esmond did not keep Theo a prisoner. On days when he had no need of him, he was happy to let him go out into the city. He knew there was no chance of

Theo escaping because he'd got his money and passport under lock and key. He'd seized them back from Commandant Neumann on the day he rescued Theo from Camp Lukács and had told Theo, once they got to Barcelona, that he was keeping them safe for him until they were needed for his return to England.

In place of the passport, he provided Theo with a paper document identifying him as a police interpreter and periodically handed him small amounts of pesetas as pocket money. But Theo did not complain. He had no wish to run. His mind was set on finding Maria.

He searched for her on the Paral·lel and in Chinatown, just as he had a year before, but with the same lack of success. No one had heard of her. And when he asked about Carlos, linking the name with the Moulin Rouge, they looked frightened and hurried away, assuming he was from the Communist police, which was of course ironically true.

The heart had gone out of the people. Their sullen, hungry expressions reminded Theo of the downtrodden unemployed in New York in the Depression. There were the same broken-down men combing the sidewalks for cigarette ends and the same bread queues stretching down streets and around corners. When the food ran out, Assault Guards on horseback dispersed the protesting women with their rifle butts.

Theo remembered Maria telling him in February about the athenaeum where she'd worked in the evening. He wished he'd asked her where it was, but he knew that it would be gone. *"Women can choose what to do with their lives,"* she'd told him joyfully. No longer. Brothels were back in business, and hope for a better future had been blown away on the polluted wind. The sense of loss felt personal, filling him with a gray sadness that he could not shake off.

On the Paral·lel, sirens blew, and Theo thought for a moment that they were calling the workers out to fight until he realized that they were warning of an air raid. He stayed where he was, watching people running down into the metro and coming up again minutes later when the all-clear sounded. Not this time, but soon. The threat of coming destruction hung in the air, and he knew he had to find Maria before it was too late.

# 22

## THE GÜELL PALACE

It didn't take Theo long to understand what Esmond was doing. In every interrogation, he tried to trick the prisoner he was questioning into a confession that he or she was a member of the proscribed POUM party. If he succeeded, then he needed to do no more to establish guilt, because it was now official government policy that anyone who was a member of the POUM was also a fifth columnist working to destroy the Republic from within.

This was a victory for Communist propaganda. All over Barcelona, the walls were covered in dramatic posters showing POUM masks being ripped off heads to reveal demonic Fascist faces hiding behind. ¡**FUERA LA CARETA!**—Off with the mask!—they demanded in foot-high lettering. Esmond acted like he was simply answering the popular call.

But Theo thought the whole idea was ludicrous and told Esmond so, taking advantage of his friend's apparent new willingness to discuss anything without getting upset.

"Why would people join a Marxist party and then spend their time trying to help the Fascists win the war? Explain that to me," he challenged Esmond.

"Because they're not real Marxists. They're Trotskyites," said Esmond. "Their leader, Andrés Nin, was Trotsky's secretary. Maybe you didn't know that."

"And Trotsky's a Fascist? Is that what you're saying? The last I heard, he was Lenin's right-hand man."

"He's a traitor. He wants to destroy Communism, and he'll do anything in his power to achieve that." Esmond sounded like he was reciting an article of faith.

"Destroy Stalin, maybe, but not Communism," Theo countered. "I don't know as much as you about Marxism, but one thing I'm damned sure of is that Marxists aren't Fascists."

"These ones are. We've uncovered a conspiracy involving thousands. It's more sophisticated than you can imagine."

"Show me the evidence!" Theo demanded.

"You know I can't do that. You'll just have to take my word for it."

"How can I when it makes no sense? You're the cleverest person I know, Esmond, and I don't think you believe this nonsense any more than I do. You're just saying there's a conspiracy because it justifies what you're doing, and then you try to drag as many poor fools into it as you can—Anarchists, POUM, anyone who'll make a confession. Because the bigger you can make the plot out to be, the more power and resources you can say you need to fight it. The Communists are using these lies about the POUM to take over the Republic. That's what you're doing, isn't it?"

Esmond shook his head, smiling. He'd changed since Saint Gregory's. Criticism had no effect on him anymore. It just seemed to amuse him. His imperviousness infuriated Theo.

"The truth doesn't matter to you, does it?" Theo told him, raising his voice in frustration. "You're just like Alvah. If Stalin tells you that one and one is three, then that's a fact as far as you're concerned. Father Laurence was right. You've sold yourself to the Devil!"

"The Devil, as you call him, is the only one helping the Republic," said Esmond dryly. "And that's what I'm trying to do too."

Once, in this same city, Theo had leaped at the chance to be an interpreter. Now he hated the work. It made him a collaborator.

He felt a soldier's solidarity with the prisoners Esmond was interrogating, many of whom had been fighting on the Aragon front west of Barcelona. Back home for a week's well-deserved leave, only to be picked up by the Communist secret police and thrown into one of their foul *checas*. Theo remembered the laconic sentence inscribed on the cell wall at Camp Lukács: *J'ai combattu. Ils ne l'ont pas fait.* I fought. They didn't. Esmond hadn't fought. He'd stayed in grand hotels and palaces behind the lines while others gave their lives for the Republic. Moving stuff around. What gave him the right to accuse these brave men of helping the enemy?

Esmond's victims were the poor and the dispossessed. Ragged, filthy, half starved, in their smocks and alpargatas. They were the people Theo had come to Spain to fight for, and now here he was, assisting in their destruction!

It was unbearable. He had to do something. At interrogations, he began to add a rapid instruction to the prisoners when he translated Esmond's questions, telling them to say that they had nothing to do with the POUM. He was confident that Esmond didn't know enough Spanish to understand. Javier was more of a risk, but he stayed over by the door and was unlikely to hear, provided Theo kept his message quick and his voice low.

But as the days passed, he grew careless. Perhaps it was the driver's taciturnity and permanent look of detached indifference that deceived Theo, but he began to assume that Javier wasn't listening, until one afternoon when he suddenly felt a strong hand on his arm, pulling him to his feet in the middle of an interrogation. He hadn't heard Javier come up behind him and so was taken completely by surprise.

He struggled to resist but stopped when he looked over at Esmond and saw from the look on his face that Javier was acting under his direction. Esmond must have suspected him before and brought Javier closer to confirm his suspicions.

"There's something I need to show you," said Esmond. He didn't shout or look angry, but there was an unfamiliar steeliness in his voice that frightened Theo.

He let Javier take him out. He had no choice—the driver's meaty hand was like a vise around his wrist. Esmond followed behind with the prisoner whom Theo had failed to save. He had a gun in his hand.

The interrogation room was halfway down a vaulted corridor open on one side to the castle's parade ground. Theo had always approached it from the left, but now they turned right and began to descend a staircase, leaving the daylight behind. He could hear the low moaning before he got to the bottom. Persistent and unchanging. He recognized it from Camp Lukács. The sound of hell.

They came to a line of dark, damp dungeons. Esmond took a key from his pocket to open one of the doors and pushed his prisoner inside to join a group of other hopeless men in rags who backed away trembling into the corners of the cell. Theo could see the whites of their eyes and feel their terror as they broke out into a chorus of desperate pleading—*"Por favor, por favor . . ."*—cut off when the door was shut. Clearly, whatever lay outside the cells was far more horrifying to them than the misery they were experiencing inside.

Theo, Esmond, and Javier resumed their descent, going down a few more concrete steps and around a corner into a farther area of more modern cells in which the floors sloped this way and that, built with bricks set on edge. Dazzling lights flashed on and off and here, the half-naked, disoriented inmates were curled up fetus-like, trying to shield their eyes. Beyond, at the end of the corridor, they came to a door with a worn sign on the front: **PROHIBIDA LA ENTRADA**. Javier pushed it open with his free hand and pulled Theo inside.

There was no one in the room. Just a big chair facing the door. It was mounted on a concrete base and might have seemed like a throne if it hadn't been made out of such cheap wood. Electrical wires ran along its arms and then back across the concrete floor like tentacles to an outlet in the far wall. Theo immediately tried to back away, as if from a live beast, but Javier held him in place, and so Theo twisted his head around instead, focusing on a table in the corner behind him, which was the only other piece of furniture in the room. On top, an empty wine bottle and an apple lay beside a piece of black rubber piping.

The obscene casualness of the display appalled Theo. The hopelessness of it, the lack of recourse. It made him think of the Goya painting Maria had once described to him—the facelessness of the executioners, the terror of the condemned. And the pain, the terrible pain . . .

A naked bulb dangling down from the cracked plaster ceiling illuminated a mess of congealed blood and hair lying on the ground near where Theo was standing. Instinctively, he pulled back again, and this time Javier let go of his wrist. Without Javier's hand holding him upright, he lost his balance and had to grip the edge of the table to keep from falling over. But he let it go straightaway, as if it, too, was electrically charged. The table was part of the horror.

"Do you see?" said a voice behind him. Esmond's. Calm, not threatening at all.

"Yes." The word came out as a whisper; Theo could hardly speak.

"This is what was going to happen. This is what I saved you from."

Theo's hands trembled uncontrollably as memories of Camp Lukács came flooding back into his mind, and he needed not just Javier's support but Esmond's, too, to get back up the stairs into the light. How could he have forgotten the terror he'd felt in that dreadful place before Esmond came to his rescue? Terror of what he'd now been made to see. Nightmares made real.

"I had to show you. You gave me no choice," Esmond told him, and Theo could hear the regret in his voice. It even sounded sincere. "You need to understand that I can't protect you if you try to sabotage another interrogation. You'll be arrested as a deserter and taken back to Albacete, and now you know what they'll do to you. What's in that room and worse. They don't just think you're a deserter; they think you're a spy."

"You know that's not true," said Theo desperately. "I'm no more a spy than those people you've got downstairs. What's happened to you, Esmond? What have you become?"

"I'm what I always was. A faithful member of the Communist Party."

"I thought you were my friend."

"I am. I saved you, didn't I? There's nothing I won't do for you, Theo, but not if you try to disrupt my work. I need your promise that you won't do it again."

Theo nodded. He had no choice.

"Good," said Esmond, looking pleased as he sat back down behind his desk and stretched out his legs. "Now let's put all that behind us. Why don't you take a walk to clear your head, and then we'll go out to dinner? I have a few calls to make, but I'll be ready in half an hour."

"A walk?" repeated Theo. It was the last thing he'd expected Esmond to suggest.

"Sure. Anywhere you like. I trust you, and even if I'm wrong, there's nowhere for you to hide. Look, we've got your photograph." Esmond pulled a file out of a stack on the side of his desk and turned it around so Theo could see his photograph paper-clipped to the front.

There he was. The Theo of six months before, staring into the camera with an awkward smile, about to embark on his great adventure with the Lincoln Battalion. He remembered the excitement he'd felt when he saw the Stars and Stripes on the clerk's table at Albacete. All that hope, all that belief that he could make a difference in the world, reduced to dust in six short months. Destroyed by incompetent, power-hungry Communists who took no responsibility for their actions. Lies, lies, and more lies leading him to this accursed place where he was now helping them to take over the country that he had come to fight for.

He went up on the battlements of the castle, thinking that he might throw himself off. But he'd never intended it. He was not like his father. The physical urge to live was too strong within him, and the seagulls circling overhead screeched their contempt of his vain posturing.

He walked to the northeast end of the parapet and gazed down at the great city spread out below. A chaos of church spires and factory chimneys, palaces, and hovels glowing in the early-evening sunlight. Down there somewhere was Maria. She was why he was here. He had to find her.

They ate at an Italian restaurant in the old city—the Barri Gòtic—while Javier sat in the car outside. Through the window, Theo could see him eating an apple and wondered whether he'd picked it up from the table in the torture room. It was probably his apple anyway, Theo thought, remembering the air of casual ownership with which Javier had pushed open the door, ignoring the **No Admittance** sign. And if Javier was the torturer, then Esmond would be the one giving the instructions. "More electricity, less electricity, more . . ." The two of them were inseparable. Brain and brawn.

Theo looked at his friend calmly eating on the other side of the table and thought he didn't know him at all. He remembered the tousle-haired boy making him tea in his book-lined room at Saint Gregory's, while the gramophone played "Brother, Can You Spare a Dime?" The boy who'd taught him his moral compass. How could he have become this monster?

From the restaurant, Javier drove them down the Ramblas to the Güell Palace. There were no other cars parked in the coach house behind the vestibule and the palace seemed deserted, apart from the porter sitting in his lodge at the front of the building. But the silence of the thick stone walls was unnerving, and Theo felt he was being watched by unseen eyes as he followed Esmond up the marble stairs and through empty, echoing halls until they came to the Room of Lost Steps.

Esmond poured vintage wine from a decanter into two of Eusebi Güell's crystal glasses and opened the mahogany box containing the ebony and ivory chessmen, which he set up on the board between them, positioning each piece carefully in the center of its square. Then he sat back in his chair and sighed with contentment, waiting for Theo to make the first move. He seemed oblivious to all that had happened earlier at the castle, acting as if nothing had changed between them.

But Theo couldn't shake off his anxiety. All the time, he kept expecting Javier to come up behind him again. The driver was not in the room, but he knew he was somewhere nearby, waiting in the shadows. Theo held his right wrist in his left hand, turning it slowly from side to side as he struggled with the memory of Javier's strong fingers pressing down into his skin, forcing him to bend to his will.

He lost one game and then another in quick succession, making schoolboy mistakes. His hand trembled as he moved his pieces, and when he looked up, he saw that Esmond was watching him.

"I'm sorry," Theo said, stumbling over his words. "I'm finding it hard to concentrate. I think there's something wrong with me . . ."

His eyes filled with tears and he couldn't talk anymore. He gripped the arms of his chair, fighting for self-control, but it was a losing battle. His breath when he exhaled was a sob racking his body, and everything around him swirled. The room was alive. The metal ornaments hanging from the multilayered wooden ceiling above his head were like upturned plants reaching down toward him, and the twisting wrought iron lamp holders had become snakes with flickering tongues.

He felt an arm around his shoulder. Gentle and comforting, reminding him of long ago at Saint Gregory's when he'd told Esmond about his father. "It's okay," Esmond said. He was squatting down beside Theo just like he did then. "There's nothing wrong with you that we can't fix. It just takes time. That's all."

The telephone on the desk rang and Esmond got up to answer it. He listened and spoke in Russian and listened some more, and when he put the receiver down, he was excited and full of energy, calling Javier into the room. He appeared to have forgotten Theo's distress.

"There are three prisoners coming," he told Javier. "They were captured tonight in Chinatown. One of them is important. On our most-wanted list. His name's Carlos. I want to question him first. Bring him up when they get here."

"I'm going to need your help," he said, turning to Theo as soon as Javier had left the room. "Are you ready?"

Theo nodded, but Esmond looked into his eyes for verification. The sympathy he'd been showing minutes before had disappeared, replaced by distrust and suspicion.

"Good," he said, apparently satisfied with what he'd seen. "This is your opportunity for redemption, Theo. Make sure you take it."

The prisoners arrived half an hour later. Theo was standing by the window, looking down into the twilit street when he saw a speeding car brake and turn into the palace with a screech of tires. Behind him, Esmond was writing at the desk from which the chess pieces and wineglasses had been packed away.

Theo was alert and expectant. Esmond's announcement of the prisoner's name had snapped him out of his emotional collapse. *Carlos* was a common name, of course, but the ex-president of the Anarchist Tribunal would certainly qualify to be on the Communists' most-wanted list, and Chinatown was where Theo would have expected him to hide. He had an intuition that Carlos was going to turn out to be the Carlos he knew. And if anyone knew where Maria was, it would be him. Theo had absolutely no idea how he could extract that information from a prisoner who hated him during an interrogation in which he was himself being closely watched, but that didn't dent his excitement. The belief that he would find Maria had kept Theo going through the long days and nights since he'd returned to Barcelona, and this new development felt like it might be the first step along the path toward achieving his goal.

So he wasn't surprised when the Carlos he knew appeared in the doorway, closely followed by Javier, who had a gun in his hand. Emaciation had made Carlos's face narrower and more pointed than before, as if it was now a pastiche rather than an imitation of an El Greco painting, but his eyes were the same burning coals, and the rope ties on his wrists and ankles, which forced him to waddle, had no effect on the charismatic power that Theo felt again as soon as he entered the room.

None of this surprised Theo. What took him aback was Carlos's apparent failure to recognize him. He looked through him rather than at him as he shuffled past and was pushed by Javier down into the chair where Theo had been sitting before, facing Esmond across the desk.

He refused to answer questions, even when Javier began to hit his head with the back of his hand. He just took the blows, keeping his eyes fixed on Esmond with a look of amused contempt. Carlos had been in this position before, Theo remembered. He'd survived rounds of torture in Asturias.

Esmond became exasperated. He picked up the phone and began dialing a number, and then stopped.

"Do you speak Russian?" he asked, speaking in Spanish.

"No," said Carlos, choosing to answer for the first time.

"I don't believe you," said Esmond, getting up from his chair. "I need to make another call. Watch him; watch both of them. I won't be long," he instructed Javier as he went out.

While Esmond was away, Carlos leaned forward and spoke in a rapid whisper, not looking at Theo and hardly seeming to move his mouth. "She's downstairs. They'll kill her if you don't do something."

It had taken only a couple of seconds, and now Carlos was still as a statue. Javier clearly hadn't heard, because he'd stayed by the door.

Thoughts raced through Theo's mind. He needed to go to Maria, but he couldn't. He knew Javier wouldn't let him out of the room. He was going to have to wait until Esmond came back to get his permission. To do what? To go to the toilet. He racked his brain, but he couldn't think of a better excuse.

He got up and asked as soon as Esmond came back. Esmond looked irritated but nodded.

"I won't be long," Theo said.

He ran down the stairs and back through the vestibule to the coach house. The car he'd seen from above was parked beside Esmond's Hispano. There was no one inside.

He went down the ramp to the stables, forcing himself to walk now, so as not to attract attention. At the bottom, a burly guard was eating. He had a pistol on his hip, and there were keys lying on the table beside his food. Bigger than you'd use for a car, which made sense. There would've needed to be a guard and a driver to escort the prisoners. The driver had to be somewhere else in the palace. Gossiping with the porter, perhaps, in his lodge at the front of the building.

"I'm the interpreter," Theo said. "I've come for the girl. Esmond wants her upstairs."

"Esmond?"

Simon Tolkien

"The man in charge. The interrogator."

"Oh, the Russian. Okay."

The guard got up with a sigh, picking up the keys and pulling his suspenders up over his shoulders. He'd taken the gun from out of its holster and had it in his hand.

Theo's mind worked in overdrive. He had to take the guard out down here. He might not get the chance when they got upstairs and the risk of noise would be greater. But what could he use? He couldn't get the gun.

He looked down, inventorying the objects on the table. A loaf of bread, a slab of cheese with a clasp knife lying nearby, a half-full bottle of wine and a glass. He rejected the knife and picked up the bottle instead, following the guard as he walked behind the nearest mushroom-shaped column.

"Just the girl?" asked the guard, talking back over his shoulder. "There's two of them."

"Yeah. Just her."

"She's nice looking. I wouldn't mind a bit of her myself."

Theo gripped the bottle hard, holding it behind his back. The man's crudity helped steel him for what he was going to have to do.

They reached the cell. Through the metal bars, he could see Maria and Primitivo with their wrists and ankles tied, just like Carlos, upstairs. He ignored Primitivo, hardly even aware that he was there. His eyes were fastened on Maria. He'd found her at last, just as he'd always believed he would. There was blood on her cheek and dirt in her hair. She was starved and wild looking. Not like he'd ever seen her before, but she was Maria. His Maria. The girl he loved.

"Stand back," the guard ordered and opened the door, and Theo brought the bottle down hard on the back of his head.

The guard slumped to the ground. Wine was everywhere, and blood too. The guard wasn't moving, and Theo prayed that he wasn't dead, filled now with a sudden remorse for what he'd done. The burst of energy that had propelled him down the stairs had dissipated, and he swayed uncertainly where he stood.

He felt an elbow in his side as Primitivo pushed past him, diving for the gun where it had fallen from the guard's hand onto the floor. A moment later he was holding it in his tied hands, aiming it at the man's head.

"No," Maria said in a loud whisper. "They'll hear."

346

Primitivo hesitated and then turned the gun on Theo. "Where's Carlos?" he demanded.

"Upstairs."

"How many with him?"

"Two."

Primitivo bent down and hit the guard on the head three times with the butt of the pistol. It was as if he was hammering a nail into a wall. The casual brutality made Theo wince and he thought he was going to be sick, but Primitivo was pointing the gun at him again. "Cut her ties," he ordered, gesturing toward the clasp knife on the table. "And don't you come anywhere near me with that thing."

Maria held out her wrists, and Theo's hands shook as he tried to cut through the rope. He looked up into her eyes for a moment and caught the briefest of smiles, and that steadied him as he finally got her hands free.

He knelt down but Primitivo stopped him before he could begin freeing Maria's ankles. "Stay exactly where you are," Primitivo told him and then got Maria to do the work herself and cut his ties too. And when she was finished, he took the knife from her and put it in his pocket.

"Now show us where they are," he ordered Theo, gesturing with his gun toward the ramp. "And keep your fucking mouth shut."

Theo was furious with himself. He knew he should have waited to wield the bottle until the guard had got Maria out of the cell and relocked the door, but instead he'd allowed Primitivo to get out too. How could he have been so stupid?

*Three prisoners.* He should have known whom the third would be, but the thought of Primitivo hadn't even entered his mind. Getting Maria out and escaping with her had been all he'd been thinking about as he ran down the stairs, and then he'd nerved himself to strike the blow as he followed the guard across the basement, and he hadn't been able to pull back when he saw Primitivo in the cell with Maria.

There was still no one in the coach house, and they passed through the open oak doors into the lamplit vestibule. Up ahead, he could see the back of the porter's head through the frosted glass of the lodge door. The street was only a few yards away through the open archways on either side. Beckoning to him like freedom.

"Can't we just go?" he whispered, taking hold of Maria's hand and pointing. "Please?"

But she shook her head. "We can't leave Carlos," she said, whispering too.

"Too right we can't, you damn coward!" hissed Primitivo furiously, pushing the cold, hard muzzle of the gun into Theo's temple before pointing it up the stairs. "Go!"

Theo climbed. He had no choice. But he was frightened for Esmond now, not just Maria. He'd forgotten the torture room. Esmond was his friend, who had saved him. His oldest friend, whom he loved.

He felt that the two halves of his life were rushing toward each other and that the force of the collision would break them both, but he could do nothing to stop it from happening.

He walked through the silent mezzanine and started up the second staircase. He could hear a voice to his left. Esmond. He was going to call out a warning, but it was too late. Primitivo had run on ahead, and there was the sound of gunfire reverberating off the walls. Three, maybe four shots, all mixed up together. Brutally loud so that his ears exploded and he staggered back, catching hold of Maria.

He forced himself forward into the room, holding her hand, and almost fell over Primitivo, who was lying on the floor, just across the threshold. There was a sound of moaning and it was coming from him, or perhaps from Javier, who was over to his left, writhing on the ground. Theo looked up and saw Esmond sitting in his chair at the desk and knew straightaway that he was dead from the way his head had fallen to the side.

"No!" He could hear the word but did not know it was his own voice crying it out as he stumbled across the floor to his friend and took him in his arms and wept. Esmond's body was warm and soft, but his eyes were empty. The person who'd lived inside had gone.

Another gunshot threw him backward toward the arcade of columns in front of the windows. The pain in his ears was terrible. He thought they were going to burst, and the room was reeling. Iron and marble and wood, mixed up as if in a kaleidoscope. Carlos was inside it, turning, too, and Theo had no idea where he had come from. He closed his eyes and swallowed hard, and when he opened them again, his vision was still blurred, but at least everything was the right side up. He could see that Carlos was holding a pistol in his hands, which were tied together at the wrists. And he'd shot Javier with it. That was what the gunshot must have been, because Javier wasn't moving anymore.

But Carlos was. Over to Primitivo. He pointed the gun down and Primitivo put his hand up, as if to ward off a blow and cried out, "No. I saved you."

Carlos replied quietly, as if he was participating in a normal conversation: "Yes, you did. And now I'm saving you. You know what they'll do to you if they find you."

Theo put his hands over his ears just before Carlos fired, pulling his head down. His whole body was trembling and he was sure he would be next. He waited for the shot, but nothing happened.

He looked back up and Maria was going through Primitivo's pockets. She extracted the guard's clasp knife and cut Carlos's ties. Then she stooped down and picked up Primitivo's pistol. She showed no interest in his body, and Theo thought she must be happy he was dead.

Carlos stretched out his hands to get the blood moving through them, and Theo caught a glimpse of the raw red lesions on the palms that he'd seen in Los Olivos years before. He understood now that he wasn't going to be shot, but he had no emotional reaction to the information. He just absorbed it as a fact.

Nothing mattered except that Maria was here with him. Here at the end of it all. After all the vain searching that had almost driven hope from his heart, he had found her. Against all the odds. Found her and saved her. From Esmond, whom he had betrayed. He'd paid the price in blood, so surely now what he'd longed for would be. Primitivo was dead; the Anarchist dream was over; this time the story would have a different ending, and he and Maria could be together, at last. Love would have its day.

He walked toward her with his hands outstretched. Her name was on his lips. He met her eye. And stopped, understanding in an instant everything.

He knew that she could not come with him. Not now, not ever. If she did, she would leave herself behind, and he could not ask her to do that. He'd been a fool to think it possible.

She was like his mother. Wedded to her faith. The certainty of her belief was what had made his mother glow so bright, and it was the same with Maria. It made her beautiful but apart, separated from him by a gulf he could not cross. She belonged to a Spain he could not reach. Before he had thought he might, but not now. Not after all he had seen and done. He needed to stop fighting and heal himself, or otherwise he would die. He needed to go home. If that was still possible.

Carlos gazed around the room, taking in the coffered ceiling, the marble columns, the wrought iron lamps. "Gaudí!" He spat out the name, as if it was an obscenity. "This place is an abomination. We should have bombed it when we had the chance."

He turned to Theo. "We need a car," he said. "Who has the keys?"

*We*—Carlos knew Maria was coming with him, just as he knew that Theo was not. *"You're not one of us"*—Theo remembered the judgment Carlos had passed on him years before. It had been true then and it was true now.

"He should," Theo said, pointing to Javier. "I don't know where the other driver is."

"Hiding, I expect," said Carlos with a sneer, watching while Maria went through Javier's pockets. "I'd thank you for saving my life, except that you didn't. You'd have run with her if you could, but she was never going to go with you. I knew that."

"I saved her, though," said Theo. "That means something."

Carlos didn't reply. He just walked out of the room and looked back at Maria, expecting her to follow. He shrugged his shoulders when she didn't move and stood waiting for her at the top of the stairs.

Theo went toward her, and she stepped forward too. He took her in his arms and kissed her. She was looking into his eyes, and hers were so beautiful. Sapphire, like the color of the evening. Or the sea. He could drown in them, cease to be.

"I love you," he said, because it was all he could think to say.

"I know," she said sadly. "I love you too. But it's not enough, is it?"

She ran her finger over his face softly from forehead to chin, just like she had once before. And then turned and walked away.

# 23

## LAWRENCE FERNSWORTH

Theo stood rooted to the spot. Gazing after Maria, gazing back at Esmond. Downstairs, he heard a car start, and crossing to the windows, he watched the Hispano turn out into the street, driving away fast toward the Paral·lel.

*"You will save your friend, and you will betray your friend."* Now he knew what the old woman had meant. What her hooded eyes had seen as they stared down into his palm, tracing the lines with her bony fingers.

*"It's fate. You can't change what is written."* He heard Antonio's voice. Whispers of the dead. Esmond in his chair, Primitivo on the floor, Javier . . . the silence in the room was extraordinary after the earsplitting noise of the gunshots. It was alive, pregnant with intention. The Communist secret police would come—probably they had already been summoned by the porter or the other driver—and when they found him, he would be held responsible: *"You know what they'll do to you if they find you."*

He had to get out of Barcelona. But how? He had no money, no papers, except the useless interpreter document Esmond had given him, and the Communists had his photograph. He'd be picked up in hours, unless he could find someone to help him.

Who? He was alone, friendless.

Theo's mind raced. There was one person he knew in Barcelona, although *knew* was an exaggeration—he'd met him only once. The reporter, Lawrence Fernsworth, whom Booker had introduced him to in the hotel bar on the night before Primitivo came after him. The last time he'd had to flee the city.

Fernsworth had given him his card. God knows where that was now! But he'd said it didn't matter if he lost it because the telephone number was easy to remember. *The first five prime numbers in sequence.* But Theo had forgotten what prime numbers were. He racked his brain, going back to old mathematics lessons at Saint Gregory's when he was preparing for the school certificate. There'd been a silly rhyme to remember them by. All the teachers had loved mnemonics. *Two, three, five, and seven / Then will be eleven.* That was it! 235711.

He rushed over to the desk and pulled the telephone to the side to avoid having to lean over Esmond's slumped body, but then he had to ball his hand into a fist for a moment to stop it shaking so that he could dial the numbers.

The call connected, but there was no answer. Just the ringtone, going on and on. *"I'm often away with my work,"* Fernsworth had said. Maybe he didn't even live in Barcelona anymore. But then, just as Theo was about to replace the handset, a familiar voice answered and he pulled it back to his ear.

"This is Theo Sterling, Mr. Fernsworth. You probably won't remember me. We met last summer. We were talking with Charles Booker in the bar of his hotel and you said I could call—"

"The Europa. Yes, I remember."

"You do?"

"Yes. Remembering detail is an essential part of my job description. How are you, Theo?"

"I'm . . ." Theo stopped, unable to think of a word to adequately describe how he felt. "Scared," he said. "I'm in a lot of trouble, and I don't know what to do. Will you help me? I know it sounds crazy, you don't know me from Adam. But I've got no one else to ask. You're my only hope . . ."

Theo was babbling, his words tumbling over each other, as he tried to keep his panic at bay.

"Where are you?" Fernsworth cut in.

"The Güell Palace. There are three men dead in here. One of them, Esmond—he was my friend. A Communist. High up. They're going to blame me. I let the prisoners go and they did this. It wasn't what I wanted. I—"

Theo was jabbering again, and this time he stopped it on his own, cursing himself for his inability to talk coherently. But perhaps Fernsworth's work as a war reporter had made him an expert in dealing with hysterical eyewitnesses on the telephone, because with a few short, well-directed questions he soon managed to get a fairly accurate picture of Theo's situation.

"You need to get out of Spain tonight," he said. "Have you any papers?"

"No, Esmond took my passport. The Communists, I mean. Wait!"

Theo reached down with his free hand past Esmond's arm to the drawer in the middle of the desk and pulled. It was open, but Esmond's body meant that he could get it back only a little way, so he put down the handset and shoved the chair back. The force of the movement pushed the top half of Esmond's body to the side, so that his arm and head now dangled over the floor. Drops of blood dripped down like leakage from a tap.

Theo's gorge rose, and he swallowed a mouthful of bile and moaned.

"Are you okay?" Fernsworth's concerned voice came up out of the handset. "What's happening?"

"Yes, I'm all right," said Theo, picking it up for a moment. "I'm just looking . . ."

He rummaged through the drawer with both hands, spilling the contents. Pens, keys, typed papers—some in Cyrillic, a photograph of twelve young men in suits standing in a line with Esmond in the middle. Behind them, the towers of the Kremlin.

The passports were at the back of the drawer. All different colors. One burgundy. His. There was a roll of money there, too, tied up with a rubber band. And beside it, beads and a tiny cross: Andrew's rosary. It had saved him before. Would it save him again?

"I've got the passport," Theo said triumphantly, picking up the handset. "Money too."

"Good," said Fernsworth. "Now you need to leave. Go to the Ramblas and cross over to the other side. There's a square with a fountain and an arcade leading up to it where you can stay out of sight. Try not to attract attention to yourself. I'll be there in ten minutes."

The line went dead and Theo replaced the handset. He looked at Esmond, appalled by the mess of his body. Like Marat in his bath. But there was nothing he could do. He had to go. He picked up the rosary and put it in his pocket with the passport and the money, and backed away to the door.

It was hard to leave the room. He felt as if some power—Esmond's ghost, perhaps—was holding him there until the Communists arrived to punish him for his betrayal.

He shook the thought from his head. It was stupid. Esmond had no power. He was dead. Theo turned and almost tripped over Primitivo's corpse and had to hold on to a marble column for a moment to regain his balance and gather his strength before he went down the staircase. He strained to listen, sure that someone was going to come at him out of the shadows, but the only sound he could hear was the noise of his footfalls on the steps.

Down below, the porter's head was no longer visible behind the frosted glass of the lodge door. Perhaps he had fled with the driver of the car that had brought Maria, or maybe he was waiting in a recess, ready to spring out with a gun. Theo stood in the wrought iron archway at the front of the building, cautiously putting out his head to look both ways, but the road was empty, and after a moment he plucked up his courage and walked quickly away toward the Ramblas, following the same route he'd run down a year before to bring the news of the victory on the Paral·lel to Durruti.

Theo remembered Durruti's tight embrace, the oxlike strength of his body, and the utter certainty in his voice—*"We're going to be free, Theodore."* But he'd been wrong. No one was free. People were subjected to power or enthralled by power. For now, and as it ever shall be. Theo had learned that much.

He stayed in the shadows as Fernsworth had instructed him to do, passing the rosary beads through his fingers, just as he'd done at Jarama and Brunete. Why had Esmond kept it? But he already knew the answer. It was evidence of guilt, like the money. To be used if necessary. Because anything was justified to safeguard the cause. *"I had to show you. You gave me no choice."* He could hear Esmond's voice in his head, just as if he was still alive, and his own, answering back: "I had no choice too. I had to let her out. I'm sorry, Esmond. I'm sorry I betrayed you."

Silence. It was almost dark now, but over by the fountain something was moving, coming closer. A cat. It stopped, yellow eyes watching him intently, and then stalked away. Hunting.

Minutes passed, and he began to doubt that Fernsworth would come. Why should he? They'd met only once. They weren't friends. Panic gripped him. He couldn't stay where he was.

He'd just stepped out of the arcade into the Ramblas when a car came up out of nowhere and screeched to a halt beside him. A man in a gray summer suit and a trilby hat got out and called his name.

Lawrence Fernsworth was exactly as Theo remembered him. Immaculately dressed, urbane, and unflustered. Just as before, in his chest pocket he sported a pocket square handkerchief that matched his tie. Green this time instead of pale blue. It also matched the color of the Model Y Ford he was driving, although Theo assumed that that was a coincidence.

Once they were on their way, Fernsworth exuded calm, asking Theo questions about his experiences as a soldier and an interpreter and listening carefully to his answers. But his apparent composure was completely at odds with the aggressive way in which he drove, turning corners on squealing tires and pushing the little two-door car to the limits of its capacity as it tore through the dark city streets. The disconnect was like a skit from a silent movie that Theo would have applauded in the cinema, but inside the car it increased his alarm and apprehension. He knew that Fernsworth wouldn't be driving like a maniac if he didn't think he had to.

"How far is it to the border?" he asked nervously.

"A hundred miles. We should be there by midnight with any luck."

"Could the border guards know by then? About me?"

"Yes. The police can telegraph. Whether they will, I don't know. I suppose it depends on how soon they find your friend, and whether they know you were there."

"And if they do telegraph?"

"They'll take you back for questioning. Me, I don't know. I can plead ignorance, I suppose. And my press pass usually helps. The government doesn't like to make enemies of the foreign newspapers."

"Why are you doing this for me?"

"Because I don't like what the Communists are doing. They brought good people like you here to fight, threw them into battles they couldn't win, and now they persecute them when they want to go home. And what they're doing to the POUM and the Anarchists is even worse. They're working to take over the Republic from the inside and turn it into Stalin's plaything."

"Will they succeed?"

"Maybe, but it doesn't matter. The Republic can't win the war. Not unless the democracies intervene, and they won't. They haven't the stomach to take on Germany and Italy. One day, perhaps, but not here. And with Hitler's and Mussolini's help, Franco is too strong. You've seen it yourself on the battlefield. It'll take time, but that's what Franco wants. A slow advance gives him the chance to eradicate his enemies. Anarchists and Communists are all the same to him. Not human beings but vermin that needs to be wiped out. *Limpieza*, he calls it—the great cleaning. It appalls me."

"Why do you stay if there's no hope?"

"To tell the truth. I believe in that."

They were on the coast road now, driving in the moonlight between the blue-black sea and the mountains. It wound and turned precipitately, and Fernsworth had to slow his speed. Theo looked up toward the snowcapped peaks and marveled that he had crossed them. Risking all to reach the blood-soaked land on the other side, from which he was now fleeing for the second time.

"I've been a fool. I thought I could make the world a better place. I should have known it doesn't work that way," Theo said bitterly, feeling the cold night air on his face like an awakening to a bleak reality that had always been there but to which he had been blind up until now.

"It was noble to try," said Fernsworth. "There's nobody whom I admire more in this world than those who fight for justice even though they're doomed to fail. Men like you, Theo. You're my inspiration, which is why I didn't need to think twice when I got your call."

Theo flushed. The compliment was a flash of gold in the dark night of his despair. A strange and unexpected gift.

They were descending now past scrub oaks and black rock toward a small bay, and up ahead the border crossing loomed into view. Fernsworth stopped and a guard came out of a small stone house and approached the car. He had a pistol in a holster on his hip and a flashlight in his hand. Fernsworth handed him their documents, and he glanced at them. Theo held his breath, willing the guard to give them back and wave them through, but instead he told them to wait and went back inside.

A minute passed and then another. Theo looked at Fernsworth, who shook his head. He stared at the moonlit road up ahead, measuring the distance if he ran. But he knew it wouldn't work. The French would stop him and send him back once they heard gunshots, even if he got that far.

The door of the customhouse opened and the guard came out. His pistol was still in its holster, and the documents were in his hand. He passed them through the window and wished them *buen viaje*—safe travels—as he waved them on into the night.

Fernsworth rented rooms at a hotel in Perpignan. Sleep and food restored at least some of Theo's strength, and he ran his hands over his limbs, grateful for his survival. He hadn't expected it, he realized now. Death had stroked him with its icy fingers in the Güell Palace, and he remembered its touch.

He felt an intense gratitude to Fernsworth that he couldn't put properly into words when they parted at the station.

"You saved me," he said. "I don't know how to repay you."

"You can buy me dinner at Delmonico's in New York when the war is over. We'll bring Charlie Booker and make a night of it."

"Agreed," said Theo warmly, thinking that he'd invite Frank Vogel too. Lost friends from another lifetime to whom he could now miraculously return.

He shook Fernsworth's hand and then pulled him close and hugged him, because it was the only way he could think to tell him how he felt.

When he released him, Fernsworth looked flustered for the first time as he straightened out his clothes. He reacted as if it was the first time he'd ever been hugged, but he seemed pleased with the experience, and Theo was happy that he had followed his instincts.

As the train moved out, Theo looked back at the goods yard where poor, frightened Henri in the yellow jersey had counted the volunteers on that winter morning six months earlier. Most of them were probably dead now. Like Manny. Theo remembered how Manny had called out the stations that they passed— Béziers, Narbonne, Perpignan. Now he saw them go by in reverse. He was returning the way he'd come, empty-handed and alone. Sadder, older, wiser perhaps. He remembered the old woman's prophecy: *"You run forward faster, faster, but you will go back to where you began."* She'd known. He had come full circle, and now he would have to begin again.

He passed through Paris as if in a dream, and reached the coast. He stood on the deck of the boat, watching another sea glittering in the sunshine, and then rode another train through familiar green countryside. Sleepy stations adorned with hanging baskets of flowering geraniums, pubs with painted signs on village greens, and ancient silver-gray churches surrounded by gravestones sinking into mossy ground. England, insular and unchanged. Indifferent to faraway Spain and its incomprehensible troubles.

In London, he took a taxi to Grosvenor Square and walked up the steps of his stepfather's house and pressed the bell.

Waiting for the door to open, he took the rosary out of his pocket and gazed at it in wonder, as if he was seeing it for the first time. So fragile and yet so strong. Andrew had taken it to war and now he had too. And each time it had survived, and they had, too, coming back to this same house. It bound them together. They and those that came before them too.

A maid whom he recognized answered the door and called out his name, and he could hear quick steps on the stairs. He stood where he was, swaying slightly from side to side, and a moment later felt familiar arms encircling him, pulling him close, and heard a familiar voice in his ear:

"Theo, my son. I knew you'd come home."

✝✝✝

# AUTHOR'S NOTE ON CHARACTERS

Some of the characters in this book are based on real people.

Buenaventura Durruti and Francisco Ascaso were leaders of the Anarchist movement in Barcelona in 1936. Their deaths are as described in the novel.

André Marty was the Political Commissar and chief organizer of the International Brigades from 1936 to 1938. He operated from the brigade headquarters and training base in Albacete and gained a notorious reputation for persecuting volunteers whom he accused of spying for the Fascists. He was elected to the French National Assembly as a Communist deputy at the end of the Second World War, and died of cancer in 1956.

Captain Robert Merriman commanded the Lincoln Battalion at the Battle of Jarama in February 1937. He was seriously wounded in the failed attack on the twenty-seventh and so was not present at the Battle of Brunete in July of the same year. He returned to frontline service later that year and died in unknown circumstances after he was captured by Franco's troops in April 1938.

Colonel Vladimir Copic commanded the Fifteenth International Brigade at Jarama and Brunete. He retained his position until 1938, when he was recalled to the Soviet Union and shot on Stalin's orders. His superior, General Gal, suffered the same fate.

Lawrence Fernsworth was an American journalist who reported on the Spanish Civil War for *The Times* of London and *The New York Times*. He had a well-deserved reputation for seeking out the truth, regardless of his own personal viewpoint. He died in New Hampshire in 1977.

One other real person who does not speak in the novel but makes a lasting impression on Theo Sterling as a man of courage is Antonio Escobar, who commanded the Civil Guard in Barcelona in July 1936 and evacuated rebel soldiers from the Hotel Colón on the nineteenth and from the Carmelite monastery on the twentieth. He is the subject of the wonderful book *General Escobar's War* by José Luis Olaizola, which I warmly recommend to my readers.

Eric Blair (George Orwell) fought in Spain in the same time period as Theo and had some similar experiences that he vividly described in his memoir, *Homage to Catalonia*, but he does not appear as a character in this novel. His life and writing have, however, been an essential source of inspiration for me. No one, in my opinion, told the sad Thirties story of utopian belief and bitter disillusionment better than him—a story that is as relevant today as it was then.

נוּ נוּ

# ACKNOWLEDGMENTS

I am deeply grateful to all those at Amazon Publishing who have helped guide the two Theo Sterling novels through to publication. Many people have made important contributions to this process, but I would like in particular to thank Danielle Marshall, who has been Theo's strongest advocate and supporter, and Chantelle Aimée Osman, who has been a wonderful supervising editor. James Gallagher, Jen Bentham, Robin O'Dell, and Sarah Engel did excellent work, copyediting and proofreading the manuscript and leaving no stone unturned, and Rachel Gul has orchestrated an excellent publicity campaign. I also appreciate the help given to me by Carmen Johnson and Vernon Sanders.

I also wish to thank Nan Talese and David Brawn for believing in my writing; Chris Smith, Verlyn Flieger, and Tracy and Nicholas Tolkien for their reading of the manuscript and helpful suggestions; Beena Kamlani and David Downing for their excellent and complementary editing work, which has hugely improved both novels; and my agent, Marly Rusoff, for sticking with me through thick and thin.

Catherine Howley drew the excellent maps that appear in *The Room of Lost Steps* and provided me with invaluable historical assistance in relation to events in Barcelona in 1936 and 1937, and Nick Lloyd gave me a hugely helpful tour of the city and shared with me his wonderful walking museum. I also wish to thank Andy Phipps for his help with my website.

I have been engaged with Theo Sterling's story for more than eight years, and the support of my family—my wife, Tracy; my children, Nicholas and Anna; and my late aunt, Prisca—and my friends Tom Johnson, Brett Simon, and

Robert Cutter has helped to keep me going through what has been a very long and arduous journey. I thank them all from the bottom of my heart.

And last but not least, I am grateful to my two pugs, Sadie and Roxanne, who have kept me company throughout, staying up with me through many, many long watches of the night. Dogs are truly a man's best friend.

# ABOUT THE AUTHOR

*Photo © 2024 Nicholas Tolkien*

Simon Tolkien is the author of *No Man's Land, Orders from Berlin, The King of Diamonds, The Inheritance*, and *Final Witness*. He studied modern history at Trinity College, Oxford, and went on to become a London barrister specializing in criminal defense. Simon is the grandson of J.R.R. Tolkien and is a director of the Tolkien Estate. In 2022 he was named as series consultant to the Amazon TV series *The Rings of Power*. He lives with his wife, vintage fashion author Tracy Tolkien, and their two children, Nicholas and Anna, in Southern California. For more information, visit www.simontolkien.com.